Montana Wolves

The Complete Collection

Chloe Cole

Montana Wolves: Books 1-4
Chloe Cole
First Edition
Copyright © 2015 – Frog Prints Publishing
All rights reserved.

Cover design: Roderick Bell
Formatting: Polgarus Studio

CONTENTS

Prey 1

Awakening 71

Redemption 173

Opposition 297

Prey

Montana Wolves Book One

Chloe Cole

Introduction

When a gorgeous stranger rescues her from a vicious wolf attack, nature photographer Amalie Baptista can't seem to fight the attraction to her savior. What she doesn't know is that giving in to him could mean giving up life as she knows it…

Alpha male Liam Albrecht is breaking every rule for the curvy, captivating Amalie, risking his place within the pack and his own life to protect her. As discord among the clans reaches a fever pitch, he must find a way to save her from the monsters among them.

Chapter One

October 1st
Pray, Montana

Amalie cursed under her breath and shot the GPS suctioned to the windshield the evil eye. Right before the finish line, twenty-four hours into her twenty-five hour journey, the thing was on the fritz.

She'd hated it from the second she'd turned it on. The smug recorded voice calling out instructions—a bewildering ten seconds too late—really rubbed her the wrong way. She'd dubbed the unit "Carole" after her sister, who rubbed her the exact same way. Carole—the GPS—had clearly decided the distaste was mutual, and was giving her the electronic equivalent of the middle finger by conking out in the middle of nowhere.

With a snort of disgust, Amalie pulled off to the side of the narrow road to use her blessedly silent map to try and figure out where the hell she was. She popped the SUV into park and stepped out of the car, the crisp air hitting her like a slap. As she turned to open the back door, a trickle of unrest skittered up her spine. She brushed off the sensation, chalking it up to her intense dislike of being lost.

She reached into the back seat and rifled through her well-worn pack to find the map and a yellow highlighter. After grabbing her thermos of coffee, she tramped over to a birch tree a dozen yards from the road and sank down to spread out her map. She'd just honed in on her location when the shrubs behind her rustled. She turned her head quickly toward the sound but saw nothing. Probably just a rabbit or a deer. No point in being paranoid.

Up close, some might consider the forest intimidating, the hulking trees, the encroaching darkness, but to her it represented freedom in the purest sense. Freedom from the phone, the smell of exhaust, the sounds of horns blaring, and most of all, people. The woods were awe-inspiring, sure, and maybe a little creepy as dusk began to settle. Nevertheless, once she found her way to the entrance point, she would be hiking every inch of it for the better part of the next week, and she couldn't wait to get started. What better way to call attention to the plight of wolves in the area than to photograph them in their environment? The fact that she'd convinced her boss at the magazine to foot the bill was icing on the cake.

As she looked up and took in the beauty of the Montana sky, which somehow seemed bigger and bluer than any other sky, some of her tension drained away. This was supposed to be a working vacation, and she'd promised herself she would enjoy it.

She reluctantly tore her gaze from the glorious view and turned her focus to getting back on the road. She pored over the map, relieved to find where she'd missed a turn. Carole had only cost her about fifteen minutes or so, and it was a relief not to have to backtrack very far.

She pulled the top off the marker with her teeth, snapped it onto the back and carefully highlighted her route so she could see it easily while driving. Satisfied, she leaned back against the tree and sipped her coffee, soothed by the warmth and the scent of Irish cream wafting from the thermos.

Just as her lids began to drift closed for a minute of rest and meditation, she saw a flash of brown out of the corner of her eye. She turned her head sharply, her pulse kicking up a notch. City life was clearly making her soft. She was going to be photographing all sorts of wildlife over the next week and jumping at every little thing wasn't going to cut it. She needed to get a grip.

As she stood to gather her belongings, she froze as another sound came from behind her. This time, there was no chance it was her imagination.

Her heart tripped and her mouth grew dry at the low, menacing growl. She didn't dare move as her body trembled from the strain of remaining still, despite every instinct urging her to flee. The growl continued, accompanied by the sound of slow, deliberate movement and the crunching of leaves, growing louder by the second.

Staying still was no longer an option. Whatever was behind that sound was almost upon her and she refused to cower like a child. Straightening slowly and turning to face the beast, her blood ran cold. A large brown wolf crouched low, moving steadily closer, already less than fifteen yards away.

Wolves don't attack humans, especially not a lone wolf, she reminded herself. This particular individual had obviously not gotten the memo, though, because its amber gaze locked on her, ears flattening against its skull as it padded closer.

She gripped the highlighter tightly and cursed her bad luck that it wasn't a pen or sharpened pencil that she might've used as a weapon. Now, the best she could hope for would be to strike the wolf in the eye with the open highlighter when it attacked. The worst? She'd die but at least the rest of the pack would know this particular wolf was important. A bubble of hysterical laughter rose to her lips and she smothered it with a hand. She was one second from flipping out, and that wouldn't do at all. She needed to stay calm.

As the wolf slunk closer, she ran through her options. She could make a run for the car. It wasn't far, and she might not be exactly svelte, but she was pretty fast. But even if she managed to get there, the time it took to open the door and get in would surely seal her doom. She had the thermos of coffee. While the liquid wasn't hot enough to damage the thickly furred creature, the thermos itself was heavy and could be used as a bludgeon of sorts. Though the wolf seemed large, she might be able to wind up a good swing and disorient it enough to dash to the car.

Either way, she was out of time—the wolf was closing in. She reached down slowly to grab the thermos, afraid that any quick movement would escalate the situation. She realized her mistake instantly. Her bent form was at its smallest and off balance when the beast leapt upon her a second later. She slammed into the ground and the air whooshed from her lungs. The highlighter flew from her grasp, but she held on to the thermos. Doing her best to cover her neck and face with her free hand, she struggled for air. The wolf's jaws closed around her side, puncturing her clothes and sinking into her flesh.

She let out an ear-piercing scream as she swung the thermos into the animal's head. The wolf released her for a moment and glared at her malevolently. She raised her arm to deliver a second blow, but another low growl—this one behind her—stayed her hand.

A second wolf.

With mounting horror she realized that any slim hope she'd had of escaping this nightmare alive had just evaporated. Holding off one of the enormous creatures had been a pipe dream, but fighting off a whole pack? Impossible.

Her thoughts derailed as she realized her initial attacker had ceased moving as well. It peeled back its lips, let out an answering growl, and slowly stepped off of her, moving toward the sound behind her.

Everything seemed to slow as Amalie rolled to her uninjured side. She barely made it to her knees when the excruciating pain of the bite finally registered through her haze of shock. She fell back onto her side with a cry and turned her head to see the brown wolf approaching the second, much larger animal. *A timber wolf, male.*

Try as she might to formulate a plan, or move, or do...*something*, she could not take her eyes off the creature. He was magnificent. The largest wolf she'd ever seen, his coat a burnished bronze. He was so compelling that for a brief, surreal moment she cursed herself for not grabbing her camera when she got out of the car.

The timber wolf stopped growling and, as if he felt her watching him, moved his gaze to hers. She gasped. His eyes were a molten gold flecked with green, and exuded the warmest, most intelligent light. In her peripheral vision, she saw the smaller brown wolf move to take advantage of the timber's distraction.

She screamed as it lunged, and the timber wolf feinted to the right. Amalie cringed as the smaller wolf closed its jaws onto his powerful neck muscles. He'd moved just in time, and was spared a killing bite to the jugular. He snarled in fury as he shook off his attacker and they began to fight in earnest, pawing and snapping at one another. The clack of teeth and their guttural snarls echoed through the trees.

Amalie shook her head to clear it and fought the darkness threatening to pull her under. She had to make a move. Struggling to her hands and knees, she tried to inch her way toward the car, all the while watching the battle. A scant few feet from the car, her vision began to blur. She looked down at her side where a trail of thick, bright red blood flowed steadily from the wound. A wave of nausea rolled over her and dots of light exploded behind her eyes. She stopped, the frosty breath puffing from her lips as she pressed a hand over her side to stem the bleeding. Just a little further. She turned her head to see if the battling wolves had noticed her progress, but they seemed oblivious.

Right as she was about to resume her painful crusade, the smaller wolf let out a high-pitched yelp. It seemed to finally recognize it was outmatched, breaking into a run toward the thickly-treed forest. She waited, breathless, hoping the massive timber wolf would pursue his foe. Instead, he turned his magnificent head in her direction and, panting from exertion, loped toward her. Heart pounding wildly in her chest, she tried to scuttle the last few feet to the car, but the last of her strength seeped away, leaving her on empty.

She lay on her stomach and closed her eyes, desperately praying that the blood loss would kill her before the timber wolf's teeth tore into her flesh. Ironic that the very animals she had come here to save would kill her. As least she wouldn't be around to hear Carole's "I told you so."

Warm breath caressed her cheek and she peeked through her lids one last time to look into the most beautiful eyes she had ever seen. This time, however, they belonged to the face of a man.

Her head swam, the world went topsy-turvy and then, she knew no more.

Chapter Two

Liam Albrecht was in a foul mood. And when Liam suffered, he made sure they all suffered right along with him. He prowled the large study in circles like a shark hunting its prey. All of the pent up frustration, anger, and worry of the past two days had filled him with nervous energy and a violent sense of anxiety. He could cheerfully strangle someone right now.

The woman would live; he was certain of it. And while he was inexplicably relieved and comforted by that knowledge, it was also going to cause problems. *Major* problems.

His contemplation was interrupted by distant footsteps coming from the far end of the hallway. He could tell by the quick, purposeful stride and the faint scent of lemon it was Maggie. When the knock on the door came a minute later, he was seated behind his enormous walnut desk with his hands folded in front of him, awaiting her arrival.

She didn't wait to be invited in, but swept through the door like a storm before stalking over to the desk and hissing, "What have you done, Liam? What the *hell* have you done?"

Narrowing his eyes, he stared at her hard for a long moment before she let out a shaky sigh and looked away.

He hated to pull rank, but she knew better than to challenge him. "Let's pretend that didn't just happen and start over again, shall we?"

She nodded and took a deep breath before she spoke again. "I apologize. Yes, let's start again. Please tell me what happened out there. Rumors are running rampant and I'm... We're *all* very concerned."

"I understand your concerns, but I'm not in the habit of explaining myself. I would never do anything to jeopardize this family." The, "and surely you're not suggesting otherwise," was left unspoken, but she got the message loud and clear and had the good grace to blush.

"Of course not. I have the utmost faith in you, Liam. I just-"

"Let the rest of the pack know I've called a meeting with the area alphas for tomorrow night," he cut in sharply. "I would rather control the situation and have the discussion on our turf than wait for them to contact me. Hopefully, the opportunity to speak and obtain answers will appease them for now. I have to work. Shut the door behind you." He picked up the file on his desk and spun his chair around to face the fireplace.

Silence reigned for a taut moment, but finally Maggie's heels sounded on the floor and the door closed with a defiant snap.

Liam let out a long, pent up breath and scrubbed a weary hand over his face. He hated coming down on her, but if he didn't nip this nonsense in the bud, she'd be the first of many at his door questioning him. Hell, he'd never let them know it, but at this point, he wasn't even sure he was doing the right thing.

He glanced down at the open file folder in front of him and stared into the face of the woman at the root of all his troubles.

Amalie Baptista.

He took in her stubborn little chin, the rounded cheeks, and the lips that were just a touch too full. But it was her eyes, those damn eyes, that had done him in. A brown so rich they were almost black, almond shaped, and tilted up at the corner. They laughed up at him from the photograph, almost mockingly.

He groaned and sat back in his chair, pinching the bridge of his nose between his thumb and forefinger as Maggie's question rang through his mind like a warning bell.

What have you done, Liam? What the hell have you done?

***

The pain came before she even opened her eyes. Damn, it felt like someone had tried to rip her guts out. Amalie moved to sit up but regretted it immediately as the ache in her side went from throbbing to excruciating. What the hell had happened to her?

As if she'd beckoned them, memories crashed through the last of the grogginess and flitted through her brain like an old movie reel. Fur and teeth and blood…

Holy shit. Someone—no, some*thing*—*had* tried to rip her guts out. She'd been attacked by wolves. *No, not wolves*, she mentally corrected herself, *wolf*. She squeezed her eyes closed again and tried to hone in on details. She remembered the smaller wolf running off and the dark-haired stranger rescuing her, but then it was a total blank, no matter how hard she thought. After another minute, she gave up as her head began to pound from the effort.

She crabbed backward, sitting up gingerly until she could survey her surroundings in the dim light. The room was opulent and the size of her entire apartment back home. Not a hospital, and definitely not something she could afford in the way of a hotel room. Had the man who'd helped her carried her to his house? She was no lightweight, and her cheeks burned at the thought.

Embarrassment was eclipsed by fear and confusion and she quickly swung her legs over the side of the bed. A chill swept over as she realized she had nothing on but a t-shirt, so long that it stopped only a few inches short of her knees. Someone had changed her clothing as well.

Footsteps sounded outside the doorway and she scuttled back under the blankets, covering herself from chin to toes. Probably a silly reaction. Her visitor was likely the man who had saved her from bleeding to death. Odds were he wasn't going to molest her. Then again, maybe he was some creeper who'd helped her just so he could starve her and then Buffalo Bill her later.

A soft knock sounded.

"May I come in?" a deep, oddly familiar voice called through the door.

"Yes." After all, if he planned on making a dress out of her skin, would he really have knocked?

As the knob turned, a tingle ran through her. Not one born of fear, but one of anticipation, which made no sense. The door swung open, and she recognized him immediately: the stranger who'd helped her. A bit of the tension seeped out of her. She was glad he hadn't been a figment of her imagination. Stepping into the room, he closed the door behind him. Her breath came out in a gasp as she met his gaze in the dim light.

"Hello," he said after a long moment.

She remained mute and continued to stare at him. The man was…well, beautiful. Over six feet tall with dark hair, he was muscular without being bulky. His face was carved from stone. The severity of his straight nose and sharp cheekbones was undercut by the raw sensuality of his sculpted mouth. And while she took in those details with a quick glance, she was drawn again and again to those eyes. So familiar, a mix of gold and green she'd seen only once before, they burned into hers with an intensity that made her shiver. What was happening to her?

***

Liam drank in the sight of the striking woman lying in his bed and fought a surge of possessiveness. From the second he'd laid eyes on her, he'd suffered a fierce and puzzling need to claim her. She was lovely, to be sure. A little softer, more rounded than the women he was used to, but in a way he found compelling, and he couldn't stop thinking about what it would be grip her full hips in his hand and-

He shoved the thought away and tried to keep his voice calm and his presence as non-threatening as possible. Not an easy feat when he wanted to lace his fingers into her sweet smelling hair and kiss her senseless. "How are you feeling?" he asked as he walked toward her.

"I'm okay. I mean, my side hurts and I have a terrible headache, but I'm okay." She backed up on the bed, her eyes wide.

She looked like she was about to run screaming from the room, so he went to the fireplace under the pretense of adding wood in order to give her some space. The last thing he needed was for her to get spooked and take off. Then he'd have to chase her down, and that certainly wouldn't earn her trust, which he desperately needed if he was going to get them out of this mess.

"Who are you?" she asked softly. "What were you doing out there? And how did you manage to get us away from the wolves?"

He paused a moment, trying to think of how to answer each question without scaring her, but knowing there was little time for coddling. Tomorrow night he had to meet with the other packs armed and ready with both a good explanation for his behavior and a resolution to the problem. Anything less would spell disaster.

He opted to give her bite-sized bits of information for now. Once she'd rested and they'd gotten her pain under control, he'd delve into the heavier, hard to swallow stuff.

"My name is Liam Albrecht. You're in my home just outside of Pray, Montana, a few miles from where you were attacked. I was out hiking when I heard the commotion." Jesus, when he'd see her, bloodied and on her back, he'd nearly lost his mind.

He shoved the thought away and offered her what he hoped was a comforting smile. "Now that I've introduced myself, it only seems fair that I admit I also know who you are. When I brought you back, I looked through your belongings to identify you. Amalie Baptista, nature photographer, yes?"

She nodded wordlessly, eyes still glassy with something close to shock. He'd given her the basics, and before he said anything else, he needed to get her into a more stable frame of mind.

"I'm going to get you some food and something to drink. There's some aspirin on your nightstand along with a bottle of water. I'll be back soon. Try to rest while I'm gone. I'll answer all of your questions when I get back. Don't be afraid, Amalie. You're safe here." He turned to go, but her shrill call stopped him.

"Wait! Please, don't go. Something…strange happened out there. I can't remember, but I know something isn't…" she trailed off, confusion clouding her dark eyes.

He hated leaving her like this, but she needed sustenance and time to rest. If she didn't regain some of her strength before he told her the truth, the shock could send her into a tailspin.

"One hour. I promise." He left, shutting the door behind him with a snap.

Yep. One hour before he had to tell beautiful, strong, amazing Amalie Baptista that her life would never be the same.

Chapter Three

True to his word, sixty minutes later Liam made his way back to Amalie's room—his room, rather, not that he planned on sharing it with her—with a dinner tray. He knocked, but received no answer. He let himself in, shutting the door behind him, and looked toward the bed. She was sprawled out, dressed in only his t-shirt, the blankets kicked to the floor during what appeared to be a fitful sleep. He set the tray on a table next to the bed with every intention of leaving, but his mouth went dry as he stood over her. Man, was she gorgeous. Long, shapely legs and that plump ass… He pushed away the carnal thoughts.

She muttered softly in her sleep and he strained to understand what she was saying, but all he could make out was the word "hot." Unfortunately, that was enough. He'd hoped for another half a day, maybe more, to work up to an explanation before she began to show any symptoms. Now, however, it seemed he'd be lucky if he had a few hours before she sensed something amiss within her. The time for coddling was over.

He laid his hand gently on her back and spoke her name to wake her. She was indeed hot, the heat of her skin burning through the t-shirt and heating the skin of his hand.

Amalie's body instantly pressed back toward his touch. She moaned, and he swore under his breath as he tried to remain detached. He needed to help her deal with the changes she was going through, not take advantage of her weakness. As he moved to pull his hand away, she protested, rolling onto her back. Eyes still closed, she sat up and tugged the t-shirt over her head. She sank back onto the bed, naked but for the bandage on her side, and he wanted to throw his head back and howl. Her breasts were magnificent, golden and full, and blood rushed to his groin at the sight. The need to cover her…to make her his…to slide his cock in and out until she screamed his name, was almost overwhelming.

She took his hand again, and pressed it to her shoulder, moving it down her arm, then back up and over to the other arm. The whole time, she made sleepy, sexy humming sounds in the back of her throat.

He groaned out loud, trying desperately to steel himself against her silken skin and erotic murmurs. She wasn't herself. The hunger was upon her, and she was caught in the throes. He needed to put a stop to this, but he simply couldn't muster the will to pull away.

Her eyes flickered open and she peered at him through a thick fringe of black lashes. Her face was flushed, her brown eyes glassy, her breathing coming in short, choppy gasps. "I feel…funny. Hot," she murmured. "But no pain at all. What did you give me? Surely aspirin wouldn't have helped that much. Everything seems so crisp and clear. And something is strange. I should be mortified right now. But I'm entirely unconcerned about being naked in front of you."

In fact, as her gaze raked over his body, she seemed rather put out that he wasn't naked as well. Taking the hand she still held, she cradled her cheek with his palm. Then, with slow but infinite purpose, she dragged his fingertips down her neck and across her breast. She arched into his grasp until he cupped her, whimpering as her nipple pebbled beneath his touch. Another blade of lust sliced through him and he pulled his hand back as if burned. The second he escaped her grasp, she trapped him again, this time, winding her arms around his neck. He tugged at her wrists, but her mouth was on his, open and hot. She licked at him gently, pressing for entry and he couldn't refuse her.

Helplessly, almost of its own volition, his hand moved back to cover her breast, kneading first one then the other. So soft. So lush. He growled and she growled back, biting and sucking at his bottom lip.

Insanity. It was pure insanity, and he could no more stop it than he could the moon from rising.

She used her weight to draw him down, slowly, inexorably toward the bed next to her. Once he was seated, she wasted no time, climbing onto his lap and straddling him. She pressed her sweet heat against his denim-encased erection and pushed his mouth to her breast. Thoughts of refusing her sizzled away again at the sight of her naked flesh offered so willingly. He latched onto her nipple and sucked hard, his body temperature skyrocketing as she rhythmically ground her softness against his throbbing cock.

He was strong—the fucking alpha—and she was laying him low with her uninhibited responses. He needed to push her away, to focus on the things he needed to tell her, but she was making it damned near impossible. The scent of her want hung thick in the air, and it was driving him a little more insane with every indrawn breath. If he didn't stop now, there would be no stopping.

Calling on the last shred of his rapidly waning willpower, he tore his mouth from her breast.

"Amalie, we can't. You're going to hurt yourself. There are things we need to discuss. Dammit!" he ground out as she continued to flex her hips against him. He grabbed her hands and pinned them behind her. Unfortunately, that only succeeded in thrusting her gorgeous breasts an inch from his face. He closed his eyes, but the sight of her ripe body was burned into his brain forever.

She pushed wriggled beneath him and he opened his eyes. Desperation shone in her gaze. "Please. I'm begging you. Don't stop."

He bit back a curse as the truth of his situation became painfully clear. The hunger was rampant in her now. She would not, *could* not listen to what he had to say in her current state. He needed her relaxed, and there was only one way to get her there.

Liam took a deep, steadying breath and lifted her away from his body. Unfortunately her delectable scent filled his head—pears and womanhood. *Okay, no more nose breathing.* Amalie struggled as he pressed her down onto the mattress, anchoring her in place with his weight. He skimmed his hands over her curvy form, stroking her heated flesh as she arched and gasped.

She tried to caress him in return, but he froze in place. "If you touch me again I'll stop." He was a hair's breadth from snapping and it she put her hands on him, he was done for.

She stilled instantly and he plucked at her nipple before slipping one hand between her legs. He could feel the heat of her pussy before he even touched her and his stomach clenched with need. Steeling himself for the onslaught, he dipped one finger into her. The molten folds closed over him hungrily and he wasted no time. She was beyond ready and making her wait was unnecessary torture. He thrust in deep, with long, firm strokes.

"Oh my god, yes!" Her hips pulsed frantically, pushing him to increase the relentless rhythm he'd set, as her head tossed back and forth.

Liam bit his lip hard enough to draw blood as he tried to control his every instinct screaming at him take her. To bury himself to the hilt. She was soft. So tight. He was losing his mind from the effort of holding back.

He looked down at her face, and regretted instantly because it only made it worse. Her mouth was open, her breath coming in short pants, all while her own rapt gaze was glued to his fingers sliding in and out of her pussy.

"Fuck," he ground out, and then bent low to suck her nipple as he plunged a second finger deep into her. She tensed for a moment, then let out a low, long groan and began to ride his hand in earnest. Her hips arched as he drove his fingers into her again and again, suckling her nipple and humming his encouragement. If he didn't finish her soon, the last of his resolve would melt away and he'd be doing the unthinkable.

He pressed a thumb against her clit and suddenly her she was crying out his name. The blood pounded in his ears as his cock throbbed, desperate for release.

"That's it baby, let me feel you," he ground out.

Her flesh pulsed around his fingers as she let out a long, low scream. His cock twitched and jerked in perfect rhythm with her clenching pussy as she came hard, her wetness raining down his fingers.

She was still trembling a long moment later when he finally had the strength to pull away. He thrust himself away from her as quickly as he could and stood at the foot of the bed.

"What… Why are you going? Did I do something wrong?" she asked, cheeks flushing.

"Amalie," he said, his voice low and strained, "we need to talk and we had to get that out of the way before you could listen, but I won't take advantage of you more than the situation demands." He looked away from her and took a deep, shuddering breath. "Please cover yourself." Christ, she was making this hard on him.

She quickly pulled the sheets up to her neck and squeezed her eyes closed, turning her face away. "I'm sorry. I don't know what came over me."

He wanted to comfort her. To tell her it wasn't her fault, but he was on the razor's edge and he needed to get the fuck away from her before he did something they'd both regret. "We'll talk about that in a few minutes." He rifled through his dresser and threw a clean T-shirt and a pair of boxer shorts in her general direction. "Get dressed and hop back into bed. Start to work on that tray of food. The liquids will do you good and you need to eat to keep up your strength because of the injury. I'll be back shortly and hopefully by that time we'll both be in a better frame of mind to have this discussion."

He retreated to the open door of the bathroom without looking back, in desperate need of some distance from her scent, her eyes, her face.

Once in his bathroom, he closed the door behind him, pausing to bang his forehead against the cool wood once, then a second time. This situation, already dire, was getting worse by the second. His wolf wanted her bad and if he didn't get a handle on things or it could mean disaster for them all. Especially Amalie.

God, she was amazing. Those legs, that mouth, those eyes… His cock throbbed insistently. There was no way he could go back out there like this. He would take a quick, cold shower and get his shit together before facing her again.

He turned the shower on warm to lessen the shock of getting in and took off his clothes, his erection springing out in relief as he stripped off his jeans. He stepped under the spray and tried to think of anything but Amalie, inching the nozzle toward cold. But visions of her sprawled across his bed, those firm, perfect breasts on display, assailed him.

He gritted his teeth and made it colder.

He'd never felt anything sexier than his fingers moving inside her tight, wet warmth as she came.

He cranked the nozzle to full on frigid and the water steamed off his overheated body, but still he throbbed.

Fuck it.

He turned the water back to warm and took his aching cock in his fist, squeezing firmly, and let out a low groan. Pumping his hand up and down, he let the memory of her wash over him…her scent, the sound of her breath catching in her throat as he touched her, the silk of her skin.

He worked himself faster, his breath coming in pants as he pictured her stretched under him, her hips jerking and twisting, his fingers sliding in and out of her.

With a shaking hand planted firmly against the tile, he held himself up as the pressure built low in his stomach. He squeezed his cock tighter, imagining it was Amalie's hand stroking him. Heat pooled in his belly as his movements grew more urgent. Reality morphed to fantasy and he saw Amalie on all fours, taking his cock from behind as he closed his teeth over her shoulder. Amalie on her knees, sucking his shaft deep and then pulling back to lap at the broad head. Amalie astride him, head tossed back, rounded hips working like pistons as she took her pleasure.

"Fu-uck!"

He came in a rush of sensation, groaning her name over and over as hot cum spurted from his swollen cock. His body shuddered with relief as the pressure that had his balls in a vice let up some. Closing his eyes, he let the warm water sluice over his face as he tried to catch his breath. Better. That was better. He should at least be able to manage a conversation with Amalie now.

The second he thought of her, everything she was crowded his senses again and his cock went hard as a stone.

He was in trouble. Big trouble.

Chapter Four

As soon as Liam left the room, Amalie fought back her mortification, threw off the covers and dove into the clothes he'd given her. The boxer shorts clung to her bottom and hugged her stomach, but at least the shirt was big. These were *his* clothes. She was in *his* room. She'd taken advantage of a stranger who had risked his life to save her own. Hell, he'd even given her his bedroom and she'd refused to take no for an answer. What had come over her?

But just as quickly as the embarrassment had come, it was gone, leaving a gnawing hunger like she'd never felt before it its wake. Her stomach growled fiercely as she surveyed the tray of food. Cold roasted chicken, coleslaw, a roll, and iced tea. She'd just put the first forkful in her mouth when she heard the sound of the shower being turned on. Liam was right in the next room. Naked. Her pulse pounded and her nipples grew taut again.

Jesus, why was it so fucking hot in this house?

Willing herself not to think about him, or what she'd just done, she took a deep drink of her cold tea. She settled in to the meal, almost on autopilot, and was just finishing the last bite when she heard what sounded like a low groan from the bathroom. Frozen, she listened intently. Another groan.

Her cheeks burned as realization set in. Liam hadn't left because he didn't want her. He'd left because he did. *Too* much maybe? A sizzle of heat went through her and she resisted the urge to knock on the door and see if she could join him.

The door opened a few minutes later and Liam came out fully dressed in a pair of gym pants slung low on his hips and a t-shirt that clung to his broad chest. She couldn't meet his gaze as he dragged a chair next to the bed and lowered himself into it.

"Sorry. I realize now that I wasn't as quiet as I might have been, and I can tell by the way you're fastidiously avoiding my gaze that you heard me. I hope I didn't embarrass or disgust you, but trust me, it was a necessary evil." He flashed her a rueful smile.

She forgot to breathe for a moment as she took his full measure. The smile, combined with his disarming honesty and damn sexy body, stole her wits. She'd been far from disgusted by his activities, and was only disappointed she didn't get to watch. Not that she was going to tell him that.

All of a sudden, she was really hot again.

"Something is seriously wrong with me," she croaked. "Maybe the wolf bite is infected." Amalie lowered her hand to the bandaged wound on her side and was surprised to feel no pain at all when she touched it gingerly. She pressed harder, still nothing.

She looked questioningly at Liam and reached down to remove the bandage. Her jaw dropped when her flesh was revealed. Aside from being a little pink like a newly healed scrape, it looked fine. No stitches, no wound, and no scar.

"What is this?" she whispered, her skin prickling with a sense of impending doom.

He met her gaze and spoke quietly, "I'm going to explain everything, but I need to ask you to be quiet until I'm done. I know you have questions but we don't have a lot of time and we need to get through this as quickly as possible. Can you do that?" he asked.

She nodded dumbly, somehow knowing that what he said over the next few minutes was going to change her life in some profound way.

"There no easy way to say this, so I'm just going to let it rip." He pursed his lips and crossed his muscular arms over his chest. "I'm a werewolf. And now, so are you."

Amalie's head began to spin as she struggled to drag air into her suddenly tight lungs. *Holy crap*. She'd almost had sex with a guy who was bat-shit crazy. She was in his bed right now with no weapon, no phone, and no hope of overtaking him. Frantic, she searched the room for an escape route.

"Stop," he barked. "Look at me."

She did as he commanded.

"Come off the bed and stand before me."

Again, to her own confusion, she complied. It was like her body wasn't her own. She was inclined…*compelled* to follow his demands despite her conscious mind urging her to fight or take flight. He was crazy, and she was serving herself up to him like a Christmas goose.

She tried to fight the pull as he urged her, wordlessly now, to meet his golden gaze. Panic lapped at her as she willed herself to look away, but couldn't.

"I'm the alpha male of this pack," he said. "Your instincts, though not fully developed, will not allow you to easily disobey me. My mind is going to touch yours again. Don't be afraid, Amalie."

She gasped as visions rushed her consciousness, almost like forgotten memories. Wolves, a dozen or more, running together. She envied their camaraderie as she watched them in her mind's eye, moving almost as one. A flash and the wolves became people. They gathered and talked and laughed, like a large, boisterous family. Another flash, and she saw a tiny brown wolf pup nuzzled by a large white wolf, clearly its mother. Then, an image of the wolf pup alone, howling for his mother's return.

The final vision caused her to cry out. The white wolf, her beautiful fur matted with blood and gore, bullet holes riddling her body, dead at the feet of a man with a gun. Amalie's heart broke, not only for the white she-wolf and her pup, but also for herself. She felt like she'd just lost a loved one. Tears streamed down her face and she turned away in embarrassment.

Jesus, what was happening to her?

Chapter Five

Liam watched Amalie and waited, guilt weighing heavily upon him. Barging into her thoughts had been a necessary evil, but that didn't make it any more palatable. The last thing he wanted was to hurt this woman, which scared the hell out of him. He barely knew her, and he shouldn't care one way or another about her. The family came first, before anyone or anything. But for some reason, she'd felt like a part of him from the very first. And when she looked at him, it was as if he'd found something he didn't know he'd been looking for.

He wished there had been a kinder, gentler way to explain things, but time was of the essence. He could tell by her dazed expression and the slump of her shoulders that she accepted what he said as the truth. She just needed time to process it.

"So now what?" she asked wearily when her tears finally dried. "When the moon is full I turn into a wolf and start killing people? I don't mean to seem ungrateful. I appreciate you saving me, but I'd rather be dead."

Her eyes were dull with shock, the plump apples of her cheeks still flushed from the insidious changes taking place inside of her.

"No, Amalie. It doesn't have to be that way. That's not how we are. You have a choice. But we can talk more about that later. Here is what you need to know now.

"Your body is changing. And yes, the moon does play a role this first time. Lucky for you the next full moon will be in a few days, so this intermittent period that is causing you discomfort will be short. Turning is uncomfortable at first, mostly because you can't control what is happening, not due to any pain. The physical aspects of transforming are mild, but it can be scary. I'll be with you every step of the way. After the initial change, you'll have the ability to change at will. It takes practice, but within a few months you'll be able to transition without much effort at all."

"Will I know I'm human when I'm a wolf? Will I feel and think like myself? What if I hurt someone the way that wolf hurt me?" she asked, the last of the color draining from her face.

"You'll still have conscious thought, but you'll need to hunt and eat meat. Doesn't have to be people." He nearly smiled at the look of relief in her eyes. "The upside of all this is that you'll be stronger, faster, and heal more quickly. We're not immortal, but we're damn hard to kill, and werewolves live exceptionally long lives. Two hundred years, sometimes more, barring an unnatural death."

Liam paused for a moment to see if she was absorbing all of the information, or if she had tuned him out. Her clear, focused gaze met his, urging him on, so he continued, "All of your senses will be amplified. Your appetite for all things will increase and have a keener edge. Although we're not 'better' than humans, we're physically superior, and keeping our super-engines running optimally takes more of everything."

"More of everything?" she asked, sounding wary again.

"Yes, which is why you needed that orgasm. Even so, I want to apologize. I needed to talk to you, and because of your body's newfound hunger, you couldn't hear me." His smile felt tight. "Then again, maybe I'm just rationalizing my behavior because I wanted to touch you so badly, but I truly didn't see any alternative at the time. I won't let it happen again."

"So, you're saying that I only want you like this because I'm changing? And I would've behaved that way with anyone who'd walked into the room?" Amalie asked, her voice shrill. "Am I just going to walk around grinding myself on every guy I see?"

A stab of male satisfaction speared through him as she spoke of wanting him in the present tense, followed swiftly by a bolt of white hot fury at the thought of her rubbing her sweet, soft body against another man. Tamping down his emotions as best he could, he tried to be reasonable in his answer.

"I'm not certain. I've never seen anyone go through the first change. I'd like to believe it's just because I'm so damn irresistible, but I'm not that arrogant." Except, he was. There was no way she would've been that responsive, that sensual, with just anyone. That, he couldn't swallow. "But there are deeper issues at play here. Amalie, all of the wolves in our pack were born, not turned. Turning a human into a werewolf is not only against the law within the wolf pack of Pray, it's a violation of the Supreme Laws of Wolves."

"So the wolf who bit me…he's part of your pack? Will he be arrested or?"

"His name is Mikhail. He's a member of another pack, and shouldn't have been in our territory at all. He won't be arrested. There are no 'were-police'. If he'd been trying to turn you, his pack's alpha would've punished him. But Mikhail wasn't trying to turn you. He was trying to kill you. Unfortunately, hunting humans is not against our laws. Many pack leaders forbid the practice, but …" Liam had to look away from the horror on Amalie's face before he could continue. "Some don't. They say that hunting a human is no worse than a human hunting a deer for food. So, in the eyes of his alpha, the only law he broke was trespassing on our territory to hunt."

Amalie's eyes hardened. "Well, in the real world we call that attempted murder."

He ignored her sarcasm and dove to the heart of the problem. "Before turning was outlawed, werewolves would 'gift' a beloved human friend or lover with the bite, in order to bestow long life and superior health. In many cases, the human didn't ask for it and turned against their wolf companion, resulting in accusations and witch hunts. In other cases, turned werewolves abused their newfound power." Liam took Amalie's hand and tried to ignore the electricity that arced between them. "I have a very real problem in that you've been bitten by a werewolf and are alive to tell the tale. Someone had to be held accountable for your turning. And, since I'm the one who interfered and stopped Mikhail from killing you, that person is me."

"So you're telling me that you'll be punished for saving my life?" Amalie asked, her nostrils flaring. "That's absurd. What kind of man would you be if you ignored someone getting mauled?"

"That's the thing. I'm not a man, Amalie. I'm the alpha male of a wolf pack. I'm half animal. Things are not so black and white in my—*our* world."

She swallowed visibly, her neck muscles tensing. "So what now?"

"The area packs will meet, a trial of sorts will be held, and a course of action will be voted on. There are a lot of gray areas here since it wasn't my intention to turn you. But in the eyes of some of the elders, it won't matter. They'll believe that I should have let nature take its course."

He didn't want to tell her the rest, but most of his apprehension wasn't for himself. What would keep the other packs from deciding to rectify his wrongdoing by eliminating the problem altogether? And from their viewpoint, Amalie was the problem. As crazy as it was, he'd felt an almost primal attraction the second he'd laid eyes on her and he seethed at the idea of someone hurting her.

She lifted her chin, steely determination lighting her eyes. "I'm coming with you. I'll explain what happened and everything will be okay. Well, as okay as things could be, considering. I can't let you be punished for protecting me."

A surge of pride coursed through him. He'd known instinctively she would be a loyal friend and a fierce enemy. Her offer to stand by him as they faced their accusers only served to strengthen his resolve to protect her. He nodded. "They'll want to see you anyway. And when they do, maybe they'll understand why I had no choice."

She tipped her head to the side, her gaze questioning.

"You have no real sense of how special you are, do you?" He longed to tell her why she was extraordinary, but he'd given her so much life-changing information. She needed time to process everything. "Enough for now. I've given you a lot to think about, and your body needs to rest for the changes to come."

He got up from the chair and walked toward the door. Feeling her gaze on his back, he stopped at the doorway and turned to face her. His heart lurched at the need etched plainly on her face.

He gripped the doorknob, lust racing through him. "Fair warning: you need to stop looking at me like that. Tonight I was as much of a gentleman as a wolf like me can possibly be. But, if you're smart, you'll keep your distance. I can't promise I'll be able to manage my desire a second time."

She met his gaze in the dim light and replied steadily, "I'll make you a deal, Chief. If you stop looking at me like you want to bend me over something, I'll stop looking back like I want you to." And with that she rolled to her side, and closed her eyes.

As he walked out, Liam shook his head, his mouth twisting into a wry smile. She was amazing. He'd known it the second he'd seen her fighting off Mikhail with her thermos. Add to that her incredible beauty, strength and loyalty. And passion…he couldn't forget the passion. She'd be a prize for any man and a credit to their pack. Now he just had to determine if she wanted him for real, or if her desire was due to her transformation.

Only time would tell.

Chapter Six

Amalie awoke the next morning before daybreak but glad that she'd slept at all. After Liam had left the night before, she'd tossed and turned, trying to let everything sink in. Eventually though, the need for sleep had overpowered her and silenced her churning mind.

She looked at the clock next to the bed. 6:00 a.m. She was starving. And hot. What else was new?

Not sure whether she should leave the room, she tiptoed to the door and peered into the corridor. The house was quiet, so she padded lightly down the hall to a set of stairs before cautiously descending to the kitchen. She stopped short when she saw Liam sitting at the table alone with a steaming cup of coffee before him.

He raked her with a lengthy, appreciative perusal, from her almost bare legs to her near transparent t-shirt. "Good morning," he drawled.

Her nipples tightened under his hot stare, and she turned away quickly, plucking at her shirt ineffectually.

"Stop looking at me like that." Her voice sounded husky, much to her annoyance. "I can't help—" she broke off as a male voice behind her boomed.

"Well, hello there! I'm Billy. And you must be Amalie."

She turned to face a large blond man with emerald green eyes. Gorgeous. He wiggled his eyebrows and bowed gallantly.

Amalie blushed to the roots of her hair. Stammering a quick hello, she turned to Liam and blurted, "I'm hungry but I don't have any clothes, so I'm just going to leave now." And with that, she ran back up the stairs to his room.

She shut the door behind her, threw herself on the bed, and covered her face. What was wrong with her? Every time she got near Liam she wanted to jump his bones, and now his friend had seen her half naked.

She cringed as the door opened and closed.

"I brought you some fruit for now. Once I find you better clothes, I'll come back and take you downstairs for something more substantial."

"Go away," she said, her voice muffled by the pillow.

"Amalie, none of this is your fault. Your physical reactions right now are no reflection on you as a person. Billy is quite a specimen, and I'd be surprised if you weren't attracted to him, given your current state of transition. In a few days you'll be back in control and this will be a distant memory."

She raised her head and gave him a narrowed-eyed stare as his words sank in. "What are you talking about? I don't even know him. Some *stranger* just saw my boobs along with half my ass, and witnessed us about to jump each other in the kitchen. I'm marinating in my shame. That's a purely *human* reaction, I assure you." She flopped face down back onto the pillow and covered her head with the blanket.

He reached down and lifted the blanket off of her, uncovering her backside and legs. "So you're saying you don't want Billy then?"

Amalie struggled to wrestle the blanket from him but stopped abruptly when he pressed his hand to her shoulder and slowly slid it down her back and over the curve of her ass, stopping to rest on her hip. He squeezed the fullness there sharply, and she let out a strangled squeak as need swamped her. What was it about this man?

"Of-of course not."

He remained silent for a moment, slipping his hand over backside.

"Liam," she muttered into the pillow. "Do not mess with me right now. I'm in a fragile state and I can't take it."

"Oh, Amalie, I'm not messing with you. Tell me to stop and I will. But tell me now."

He slid his hand under the waistband of her boxer shorts and squeezed her bare flesh. She writhed against him but couldn't bring herself to say the words. Because she didn't want him to stop. As shameful as it might be, she wanted him to keep going and going.

He gripped the shorts in his hand and pulled them roughly down her legs, stopping at the back of her knees to caress her lightly there before moving back up her body.

"This needs to come off," he growled, as he grabbed the neck of her t-shirt with both hands. It tore easily in his powerful grip and a moment later lay in tattered halves around her. He wrapped a fist in her long dark hair and pulled, turning her head sharply to one side. The tension between her legs built to near pain at the rawness of it all and she urged him on with a moan.

Licking and biting at her neck, gently at first then harder, he parted her legs with his hand. He slid one finger down the cleft between her cheeks then slipped into her moist heat as he reached her core. She whimpered and pressed back against his hand.

He worked her with his finger as he trailed his tongue from her neck to her back and down to her bottom. He bit one cheek, and then lapped delicately at the tender spot with his tongue. Grasping her hips, he tossed her onto her back. He closed his teeth over the flesh on her hip then her thigh, kissing and touching all around, but avoiding the sweet spot. She began to squirm, desperate to feel his mouth on her.

"What is it, love? Tell me what you want," he whispered darkly.

"Please."

"Please what?"

"Please put your mouth on me, Liam."

"Where? Show me." His eyes went dark as night as he watched her hand slide between her thighs, and down into her slit. "Damn, you're sexy."

He took her hand and thrust one of her fingers into her pussy, pressing deep. At the same time, he bent and covered her with his tongue, lapping then sucking. She cried out and moved against his mouth. He quickened the pace, licking and suckling harder and faster until waves of ecstasy threatened to pull her under. She yanked her hand from his grasp and grabbed his hair, tugging sharply.

"Not this time," she hissed, and pulled him up until he covered her.

She reached between them, clasped his cock through his gym pants and squeezed, reveling in the heavy weight of it in her hand. She wanted him inside her so badly, she could taste it. Luckily, she didn't have long to wait. With a vicious tug, he pulled her boxers the rest of the way off before stripping his pants and shirt off and tossing them aside.

She lifted a hand to his chest, stilling him. "Stop."

Everything between them had been so one-sided. The need to make him as crazy as he was making her consumed her.

***

Dear God, she wanted to stop. Liam closed his eyes and put a hand to the bed, steeling himself to get up and try to walk away. It was understandable that she was confused and having second thoughts. He would just have to console himself with the knowledge that it wasn't the change causing her to respond to him. She hadn't given Billy a second look. That was something, at least. If she needed more time to get used to the idea of being with him, he'd give it to her. A few more cold showers wouldn't kill him, and once she realized that this was—

A puff of warm breath on his stomach was the only warning he had before Amalie's lips closed over his cock. He froze, exerting every ounce of control not to thrust himself deep into her hungry mouth as the rest of the blood in his body drained south. He looked down to where her dark, shiny hair caressed his hips as her head bobbed over him. Thank god, she hadn't wanted him to stop. She just wanted a chance to touch him.

A surge of satisfaction poured through him. "Deeper," he groaned, his thighs flexing as she complied. His hips moved of their own accord as she sucked him off, harder each time, until the sensitive head of his cock bumped the soft flesh at the back of her throat. He gripped her hair and held her there for a long moment as the need to come battered at him. With a gasp, he pulled her away. The drag of her lips and tongue as she expelled him almost sent him over the edge.

He looked down again and she gave him a siren's smile before sliding up his body and pressing her wet, swollen lips to his.

He nipped her sharply, and she moaned.

"No more teasing," he rasped.

He moved over her, positioning himself between her legs. She paused and gave him a questioning glance. "No need for protection. We don't get sick like that, and pups...well, that's a whole other discussion."

One she clearly didn't feel compelled to have right then, because she pulled him close so they were chest to chest, and rubbed her breasts over his torso and her soft stomach against his. His breathing grew labored as she guided him to her hot pussy. She surged upward, seeking his cock.

Liam pinned her hips with his hands. She couldn't take all of him so quickly. Slowly, he slid into her, inch by inch. Halfway, he pulled out and began the steady slide back in. She struggled against him, begging with her body for more. He gritted his teeth, fighting to maintain control. Amalie growled, then reached back and gripped his ass with both hands, thrusting him into her until he was seated to the hilt. He sank into her molten heat and gasped as she stretched to accommodate him..

His body screamed for release. He wanted to pump in and out of her until she begged him to let her come. But she lay so quiet, the tiny part of his brain that was still functioning was afraid he'd injured her. To his immense relief, a moment later, she began to bounce her hips against his. He started to say a silent prayer of thanks but was cut short as her slick inner walls squeezed him. He matched her rhythm with long, slow, deep strokes. They moved faster, and he bent his head to lick and suck her nipple as he plunged into her again and again.

Her body tensed, tightening around him, and a low, vibrating moan started deep in her throat. He swelled to the point of pain and thrust further into her. His stomach grew tight and a tingling sensation spread to his loins. She called his name, her nails digging into his back.

"I'm here," he murmured as she convulsed. He tried to wait so she could come again and again, but she gripped him so tightly, her pussy milking him like a fist. As she pressed her luscious lips to his, all conscious thought fled as his body flexed one last time. He thrust deep, groaning her name as his body exploded, and he emptied himself into her.

Home.

Chapter Seven

Amalie awoke to find herself cocooned in Liam's strong arms as he slept. She peaked at the clock and burrowed deeper into the covers. They had hours until the meeting of the wolf packs, and, at that moment, she felt fabulous. She knew it would be short-lived. The real world would come crashing in and this small sense of peace and belonging for once in her life would be shattered. For the moment though?

She pressed her head to Liam's shoulder and kissed him on the neck. He stirred and drew her closer.

"Good morning again, love."

Unfamiliar warmth spread through her at the endearment. Probably an offhand term of endearment, but it struck a chord deep inside her.

"Good morning again to you, too."

He stroked his fingers along her bare spine. "We have the whole day before the trial, and I'd like to spend it with you."

"I'd like that," she responded, careful to keep her tone light. It wouldn't do to let him know how close she felt to him already, as if they'd been lovers for years instead of hours. Or how the promise of spending the day with him was as thrilling as the bike

Santa had brought that one Christmas morning. But at the same time, she wasn't going to turn away the opportunity to spend time with him. Especially since their time could be so short. After the trial, it could all be over.

What if she never saw him again? Amalie swallowed the lump suddenly lodged in her throat. Choosing not to examine that too closely, she asked the question that had been in the back of her mind since the night before.

"Liam, the image of the white wolf...the memory you shared with me? She's been haunting me. Would you tell me about her?"

His smile disappeared and her stomach churned as his eyes lost focus. "Sara was a member of our pack. Her mate is...was Jax. They have a son, Ryan. We'd taken him on a hunt...his first," he said softly, with a shake of his head. "Jax was away on business, but Ryan had begged to come along and Sara agreed, but wanted to start him with something small. The two of them strayed from where the rest of the pack was hunting larger game so she could teach him to track rabbits." He smiled then and her heart tripped. "Little Ryan was off the wall with excitement, hoping to call his dad that night and tell him about his first kill."

Liam's eyes turned glassy and his jaw tensed. She held him tightly as she tried to control her own emotions that seemed so tied to his.

"Sara was careful to stay in the most remote part of the forest as Ryan still hadn't mastered changing yet. Sometimes he shifted back and forth when trying to maintain wolf form, and she wouldn't risk any wandering hikers or hunters seeing him shift.

I was with the rest of the pack. We'd just taken down an elk when we heard the shots."

Liam paused, his voice breaking as he took a breath. Tears stung her own eyes as she waited for him to continue.

"We all immediately reached for Sara's mind to see if they were okay, but she was gone so quickly. We ran as fast as we could, but by the time we got there, Ryan was circling her bloodied body, whimpering. We were too late." He scrubbed a hand over his face and shook his head as if trying to erase the memory. "I went to Ryan, pulled him away while the others attempted to revive her. I tapped into his consciousness, but he was in shock. It was almost like he didn't even know what had happened himself. All I could gather was that a large man had come out of nowhere and fired at him. Sara dove in front of him and took the bullet.

"One shot would have felled a regular wolf, but a werewolf like Sara would have healed from that in minutes. The bastard...he kept firing and firing, as if he knew..." Liam's muscles bunched tightly beneath Amalie's hands. She wanted to ease his pain, but she was helpless.

"Sara told Ryan to run and he did, but not far. When the shots finally ceased, he returned to his mother and we arrived moments later. She'd taken eighteen bullets, some at near point blank range. There was too much damage inflicted too quickly for her body to heal.

"I wanted to find him and kill him. I could smell him in the area, probably still out looking for Ryan, but as much as we wanted revenge, we had to get the cub to safety first. We brought him back to the house and left the women to care for him while we retrieved Sara's body and went to find her killer."

The flesh around Liam's mouth paled, and Amalie knew with a sinking heart what he was going to say next.

"She was gone." He swallowed hard and shrugged helplessly. "Some of the pack members see that as proof that he was just another hunter, looking for a pelt. And others think maybe he was taking out his hatred on her because some wolf had killed one of his chickens or something. But I know in my soul that's not the case. Her murderer was no ordinary hunter, and I don't think we've seen the last of him."

She stroked his back, drawing calming circles over his smooth flesh with her fingertips. "For some reason, I suspect your instincts are rarely wrong."

"In the past few months I've tried to work with Ryan to get him to remember the man's face so that we can see him and find him. But he can't, or won't, remember. And I don't blame him. It was the worst day of my life. I can't imagine how awful it was for the boy."

Nor could she, but she could feel it. All of it. Maybe that same wolf-bond with her new brethren was what had her feeling so close to Liam already. Even now, the thought of walking away and never seeing him again made her feel empty inside.

They were both quiet for a long, tense moment until her he rolled away and stood, a strained smile stretching his lips. "How about I get us some food?"

He clearly needed a minute to get himself together, so she nodded right as her stomach growled. Liam's low, genuine chuckle chipped away at the icy chill that had settled over her heart.

"I'm like a mind reader, I guess. Be back in a few."

He went down to the kitchen, leaving her alone with her swirling, chaotic thoughts. By the time he came back a few minutes later, she'd given up trying to make sense of it all. The task was just giving her a headache. She had to accept that things were going to be in flux for the foreseeable future and she'd be plagued with more questions than answers. Hopefully, after tonight, she'd get past this first hurdle and everyday things would get a little clearer. For now, though, she was determined to enjoy this oasis of time with Liam.

He smiled from the doorway, arms laden with a heaping tray of food and her heart skittered.

"Grab that blanket."

She did, and laid in on the floor, where they set up an impromptu picnic. "So, Amalie Baptista," he said between bites of roast beef. "What was it about our neck of the woods that drew you out the big, bad forest all alone? Didn't Little Red Riding Hood teach you anything?" he asked with a twinkle in his eye.

She sent him a grin. "I love the outdoors. And Little Red Riding Hood *did* teach me something. In fact, the whole reason I came to Pray was to kick off my campaign to reinstate laws to protect the wolf population. I want the public to see how precious are."

"I didn't realize you were so passionate about the subject."

Amalie nodded, warming to her topic. "I'm sure you know that the government's position is horrific. As soon as area residents started bitching about the growing wolf population, Fish, Wildlife, and Parks was more than eager to issue hunting licenses. Never mind the wolves are a bad winter or minor epidemic away from the endangered list. I'll never understand how a person could kill such beautiful creatures."

Liam had stopped eating and was staring at her with something akin to wonder.

"What?" she asked.

"You. You're the beautiful creature."

Her face was hot from her passionate diatribe, as well as from his praise. "Stop distracting me from my point. It isn't fair that wolves were almost wiped from existence. And for what?" she demanded. "Because they hunted elk that people wanted to hunt for themselves? This earth belongs to all creatures, not just man."

Liam leaned in and kissed her hard on the mouth then grinned. "You're wonderful. And gorgeous to boot. All fired up over something most people couldn't care less about. You really are special, Amalie, and I'm going to do everything in my power to make sure everyone knows it tonight."

Her heart began to pound and her body temperature spiked as Liam kissed her again, this time with lascivious intent. Pushing the food aside, Liam did as she'd hoped and bent her over on all fours. He entered her quickly, almost violently.

All of her apprehension melted away as he rode her hard from behind, driving his cock in and out at a punishing pace, branding her…owning her.

Without a slow, purposeful build, her climax struck like a freight train, blurring her vision. She cried out, her legs quivering as she planted her ass flush against his hips, holding him deep while her muscles clutched his throbbing cock.

Liam leaned forward, draping his frame across her back to clamp his teeth on her shoulder. She rotated her hips once, grinding against him. His body tensed as he came, shudders wracking his body as he curled over her, his groans ringing in her ear.

When her heart stopped racing, Amalie lowered herself to the floor and pressed her face to the plush carpet. Liam followed, sprawling his body over hers, taking the brunt of his weight on his knees. He was so clearly enthralled with her body that the self-consciousness she usually felt with a lover was nowhere to be found. It was so freeing, she wanted to weep. He pressed a soft kiss to her nape, and stroked her side rhythmically as they caught their breath.

They spent the rest of the day in bed, trying to distract each other from thinking about what was to come. By the time the sun set and the room grew dark as the sun, she was deliciously sore, satisfied, and, for once, blessedly cool. The beast growing within her had been sated, at least temporarily.

"There's nothing I'd rather do than stay here with you, but we have a meeting to attend," he said gently.

Everything came rushing back and Amalie sat up, filled with determination. She'd found complete and total bliss for the first time in her life with Liam. If he wanted her, she would stay in Pray. There was no way she was going to let someone take it away before they had a chance to see if a relationship between them could work. She had acquaintances from work that she'd gotten drinks with in the past, but beyond that, what else did she have to go back for? She and her sister were never close, and her parents had been dead for years. The concept that she might have stumbled into a family...into a life where she felt cared for and supported entirely by accident was enough to get her up and moving. Time to find out what tomorrow would bring.

She took his hand and squeezed his fingers. "Let's go."

Chapter Eight

An hour later, Amalie tried to quell her nervousness as they approached the great room of the house where members of the area packs were waiting for them to arrive. She and Liam had risen and dressed quickly, Amalie donning her ripped but now clean jeans and one of Liam's shirts.

They were late. They'd tried to leave earlier, but Amalie had been assailed by a particularly brutal hot flash. Her fear and nervousness were wreaking havoc on her already chaotic body chemistry. Liam had convinced her to lie down for a few minutes while he pressed a cool, damp cloth to her face and forced her to drink two glasses of ice water.

Now, as they prepared to enter the room, she said a silent prayer for Liam's safety. He gave her hand a reassuring squeeze and released it to open the door. He walked in first and she followed behind, keeping her attention on his back.

She heard murmurs and whispers from the dozens of attendees already present, but tried to shut them out as he led her past rows of occupied chairs to the center of the room. Her skin felt too tight for her body, and she was beginning to overheat again as her earlier sense of well-being evaporated.

Liam stopped next to a long, mahogany table at the front of the group. He gestured for Amalie to sit and followed suit. Three men sat at a second table beside them. They all looked completely different, but each radiated confidence and power. Clearly, the other pack leaders.

The room quieted as Liam cleared his throat and began to speak. "We are here to discuss the events that took place on Pray lands three evenings past."

Amalie started at his cool, authoritative tone. Something within her stirred... a sense of pride in him and a bone-deep respect. She understood in a flash that it was the wolf in her recognizing him as the alpha male of her pack. It should've irked her, that concept of a male leader, but in this instance, it felt right because as much as she respected him, he respected her. From what she'd seen when he'd shared his memories with her, each member had their place within the pack, as would she—assuming they let her stay.

Her gaze was drawn to her alpha, to his powerful body pulsing with vitality. In fact, she realized the entire room was focused only on him. She let go of the last of her reservations and embraced the feeling of being a part of something, a part of Liam.

"Thank you all for coming. I would have come to you, but given the circumstances, I thought it best to keep Amalie here until after the change. She has been through quite a lot." Liam spoke respectfully, making eye contact first with the alphas, and then the rest of the audience.

She flicked a glance around the room at large for the first time, trying to gauge the mood, but froze as her gaze connected with a pair of amber eyes that seemed familiar and as cold and empty as a child's doll.

Mikhail.

Her stomach clenched as he gave her a wolf's grin, looking so pleased with himself. Like he knew something she didn't and, whatever it was, it wasn't good.

Icy fear chilled her heated body, almost paralyzing her. She could almost feel the malice pouring off him in waves and the agony of his teeth ripping into her side.

Then, a comforting presence enveloped her, like a warm hug, filled with compassion and support. She looked up and saw Billy watching her, and she knew, as clearly as if he'd spoken the words to her, that he accepted her into the pack and under his protection. Tears of gratitude sprung to her eyes.

Tentatively, she reached out further with her mind but could only feel Liam and Billy. That was okay. She was not alone; she was part of something, a pack of three at least, for as long as she was allowed to stay in Pray. Strengthened, she pulled her gaze away from Billy's and defiantly met Mikhail's malevolent stare. She broke away when Liam's consciousness pulled at her. Her alpha wanted her to pay attention and she snapped to it.

Liam had stopped talking and a middle-aged ginger-haired man, one of the alphas, stood to face her.

"I am Joseph, Big Sky Canyon Wolf Pack. To my left is Alexander of the Kotke Wolf Pack," he said, gesturing to a wiry, sandy-haired man with a cold gleam in his eyes. "And to my right is Niles of the Stone Creek Wolf Pack." He pointed to a very large, almost bear-like man with black, bushy hair and a serious expression before facing the room at large.

"I have been chosen by the pack alphas to mediate this inquiry. I've spoken to many of you over the past two days and have heard from all parties that Amalie was being hunted by Mikhail and that you, Liam, intervened to prevent the kill. Does anyone dispute this?" he asked, looking specifically to Liam.

Amalie's heart sank as she recognized instantly which way this wind was blowing. Liam had made it seem like they had a chance here, but if Joseph's tone was any indication, his mind was already made up.

And she'd lost her new family before she'd even gotten to know them.

***

Bastards. This was going to be a fucking bloodbath if they thought they were going to come into his house and roll over him. So far, there had been no mention of Mikhail hunting on Pray lands, or the fact that Mikhail had broken Liam's law that prohibited the hunting of humans in his territory. Interesting and very telling omissions.

Joseph stared at him expectantly, waiting for a response, and Liam bit back a sharp retort. "What you say is true. But why isn't Mikhail up here as well? And why doesn't your narrative include his trespassing?"

Joseph nodded stiffly. "It's true we did not expect to deal with his crime of trespass this evening. He was only a few miles outside of his territory, and frankly, his transgression pales in comparison to the events that followed. It's imperative we focus on the more immediate problem. We have not dealt with a turning in a very long time."

Liam flexed his hands to keep them from fisting. This wasn't going well. Joseph was one of the three pack leaders present, but he wasn't Mikhail's pack leader. And that meant that Mikhail had the support of not only his own pack, but the Big Sky Canyon Pack as well. If he already had two of the other three packs aligned with his cause…well, he and Amalie were fighting against even worse odds than he'd anticipated.

He'd take that fight, though—he didn't have another choice. "I ask to put that decision to a vote. Mikhail's trespassing was the catalyst for all of the events that followed. I don't see how he can be absolved of guilt. He was on my land when he attacked Amalie. None of this would have happened if he hadn't been hunting humans on *my land*."

Murmurs of disapproval came from the back of the room. Liam cursed himself for his poor choice of words. To Mikhail's brethren, the Kotke Wolf Pack, calling the hunt an "attack" was offensive. An attack was vicious and insinuated cruel intentions. While some of the Kotke werewolves held a certain disdain for humans, most did not hate them any more than a man might hate a cow or a turkey. He'd let his own fury and outrage on Amalie's behalf get in the way of the diplomacy that was required of someone in his position and he vowed not to let it happen again. "I don't want to downplay the events that followed, but the events are tied together and should be dealt with together. All those in favor of Mikhail joining us at the inquiry table, lift your hands."

As Liam's eyes scanned the room, it was clear the majority agreed with him. He let out a pent-up breath. It wasn't much, but it was a start.

Mikhail stood and walked over to the table. He passed close enough to Amalie's chair that his body brushed her shoulders and she flinched. Hot rage poured through Liam and he longed to kill the bastard where he stood. Mikhail sat down next to him with a mocking grin.

Joseph cleared his throat. "As I was saying, there is no dispute with regard to the events that took place. But right now we have come together for answers to questions and solutions to problems. Prior to your arrival we took a vote about the girl. It was decided, almost unanimously, that she should not be at this meeting. She is a human until the full moon and has no business attending these proceedings. There is nothing she can offer to the discussion and, moreover, we cannot allow her presence to sway us from doing what we know to be right for our race. She has no understanding of our ways and allowing her further insight when she is not yet one of us seems foolhardy to the point of recklessness."

Joseph motioned to a dark-haired woman from the Big Sky Canyon Pack whom Liam considered a friend. "Chandra, please escort the young lady into the sitting room next door."

As she walked toward the table, Chandra refused to meet Liam's eyes. He understood her fear…all of their fears. They were scared of the unknown, afraid of reliving the horrors their ancestors had suffered. Having their homes burned and being hunted as demons. And the loss of Sara was so fresh in their minds.

He just wanted them to have the chance to know Amalie, because once they did, they would realize she could be trusted. He felt her wild-eyed gaze on him and tried to calm her with his mind.

"Liam, please, I need to stay," she whispered as she was led away. "What if they hurt you?"

"Don't worry, sweetie," Mikhail whispered silkily, just loud enough for the three of them to hear. "If they kill Liam or send him packing, you and I can finish where we left off."

Chapter Nine

Amalie gasped as Liam growled low in his throat and leapt to his feet. He grabbed the ends of the heavy, ornate table and flipped it like it was nothing more than a pile of twigs. Mikhail stood and moved, swinging wildly at Liam, landing a glancing blow to his side. Liam's huge fist went flying and connected solidly with Mikhail's jaw, a loud crack sounding through the room.

Amalie grabbed Liam's arm and held tight. He looked down at her, eyes blazing with fury, and she realized he was not himself. He had begun to change, shoulder muscles bunching, the shape of his face altering just slightly. She gaped and pulled her hand back.

A moment later, the other alphas latched onto Liam and Mikhail, dragging them apart. Mikhail also seemed to be struggling against the change, but was having less success than Liam. He was almost completely wolf when the woman called Chandra tugged Amalie's arm.

"Come now. It's dangerous for you to be here." She pulled Amalie toward the door.

Amalie looked back at Liam and as their eyes met, the fiery rage in his gaze died out. He touched her mind, reassuring her that he was okay, that everything would be okay. She allowed herself to be led away, knowing she had no alternative. Hadn't she caused him enough grief already? If her presence was going to add fuel to the tension between him and Mikhail, maybe he was better off if she was out of the way.

She stared at him as long as she could, pressing into his mind over and over how special their short time together had been to her. She only hoped she'd get the chance to tell him to his face.

***

Liam struggled against the hands grabbing at him and stilled as he watched Chandra guide Amalie from the great room. His heart tripped as he realized with gut-wrenching certainty that they wanted to kill her. Joseph's demand that she leave the room wasn't because she didn't belong. It was because they didn't want her to know they'd already decided her fate. That it was too dangerous…no…they were too fearful to allow her to live. And while some probably believed that as a lesser being she didn't deserve such consideration, the majority would have found it cruel to speak of the sentence in front of her.

Liam closed his eyes and tried to quell the nausea that overcame him as Amalie's emotions crowded his brain. He blocked her quickly, sickened he couldn't respond, but knowing if he opened himself to her she would feel his fear for her.

The loss of Sara still weighed so heavily upon him. The knowledge that he'd failed her so completely had almost crippled him. He had been her alpha and he hadn't protected her. Losing Amalie too…failing her too?

It would break him.

Determined, he turned to the alphas still trying to calm Mikhail. Liam tried to lift a hand, but realized with a start that his arms were still pinned to his side. He looked up to see Billy's face.

"You okay, Boss? Under control?" He loosened his grip and, at Liam's reassurance, released him completely. He tugged Liam away from the rest and spoke in low tones. "It's bad, man. I tried to tell them before you guys got here. I tried to argue, but they're hell-bent. Even some of our pack… They're just afraid, you know? What happened to Sara is still fresh in their minds. Most humans can't be trusted." Billy's gaze met his with frank honesty. "I told them that any discussion should wait until you arrived, but the Kotke pressed their advantage. It was like they were trying to incite a mob. They're willing to forgive your crime if you demonstrate remorse. But to do so would be to admit saving her was a mistake and one you wouldn't repeat. They want Amalie destroyed. I'm willing to stand by you, and by Amalie, but you need to convince the rest of them."

Liam nodded once, bile rising in his throat. Desperation clawed at him as he reached out to Billy's consciousness. He allowed Billy to feel the churning in his gut, to see Amalie through his eyes, to feel his terror for her, his rage at the idea of her being hurt. He closed the connection after just a few moments, but it was enough. Amalie, right or wrong, was his chosen mate.

Billy's face morphed into a mask of determination. "If you can't sway everyone, then at least show our pack what you showed me. Screw the rest of them. We need to unite on this if we have any hope of saving her."

Around them, the commotion had quieted. The table was righted by one of the alphas and Joseph asked everyone to be seated once again. He sat himself between Liam and Mikhail.

"Let us continue," he said sharply.

Werewolves' tempers were sometimes short, and quick bursts of violence between packs were not uncommon. In fact, given the circumstances, the lack of an altercation would have been surprising, but Joseph wasted no time using the scuffle to his advantage.

"Already this *human's* presence has caused tension and violence between our packs. We may not always agree, but in order for our survival we must stick together. We cannot allow this mistake to cost us our existence, and I fear that is what is at stake." He shook his head grimly, as if his next words pained him to utter. "All those in favor of removing the risk, in the most humane way possible, lift your hands."

It took every ounce of discipline he had not to tear the motherfucker's head off. When no one immediately stirred, though, the anger died and a tiny kernel of hope formed in his chest. Maybe he was wrong. Maybe they still had a chance.

Then a hand shot up, followed by a second. Soon, half the people in the room had their hands in the air, but most wouldn't meet his eyes.

Liam stood and said a silent prayer. "Brothers and sisters, lower your hands until I've said my piece. I'm willing to accept any punishment you see fit for my interference. But I can't accept that you would condone pre-meditated murder." Several hands wavered and whispers rolled across the room. "You can try to pretty it up, and tell yourselves you voted to 'correct a mistake' or 'remove a risk'. But if you're fooling yourselves. You can paint a cow chip yellow and call it gold, but at the end of the day, it's still a piece of shit. And planning to kill an innocent woman is still straight up murder. Is this what we have become?"

As he gazed around the room, many squirmed in their seats. Even for the Kotke pack, a hunt was one thing, but cold-blooded murder was something else.

Alexander, Mikhail's alpha, stood and slow-clapped in Liam's direction. "Bravo! That was a rousing speech. However, the fact remains that you interfered with the circle of life. When you watch the Discovery Channel and you see the little baby elephant about to be overtaken by the lions, don't you think the cameraman could do something about it? Except he doesn't. Because that is nature, Liam. That is *life*. It is sometimes cruel and difficult. Survival of the fittest." Some of the audience nodded, but others still looked dubious. Unfortunately, however, he wasn't finished.

"And what's your plan if she lives, Liam? She stays and becomes part of your pack? What will happen when this woman's loved ones come looking for her? Attention!" He slapped the table with his open palms. "We end up under a microscope. Her family will ask questions. Are we a cult that convinced her to leave her life behind? Why does she seem so different? You're bringing destruction to our doorstep, and for what? Because you're a sucker for a pretty face?" Alexander sneered in disdain.

"We've already lost one wolf this year to humans." The other alphas grunted in agreement. "Are you willing to risk us all? Or maybe you think that once she changes she'll go back to her city life and pretend that nothing happened? It's cruel to let her think that. She'll need to move to be near the woods, probably have to quit her job. She'll suffer depression from not being with a pack, and eventually she *will* tell someone, if only to share her pain. And then what? This cannot end well, Liam."

Alexander's voice rang with sincerity, but Liam saw the crafty look in his cruel eyes. Mixing the truth with lies made for a stronger case and apparently, it was working. When Liam looked into the faces of his pack, he realized he'd lost them.

Billy looked at him imploringly. *Show them*, he urged.

Alexander's voice boomed again. "All have had their chance to speak. Let us have a final vote. All those in favor of eliminating the woman, hands up."

Liam watched helplessly as the hands rose around him. He looked across the room to see Jax's hand rise, then Maggie's, and then two more from his pack.

Billy was right. He had no other choice.

He pressed his consciousness outward as forcefully as he dared, putting everything out there. They would see, through his eyes, Amalie's tears for Sara and her outrage on behalf of the wolves. They would feel his pain and fear, and most of all; they would know how he felt about her. As he poured out his heart, he prayed.

Jax's gaze snapped to meet his. Maggie's hand wavered in the air, only half-raised.

"The woman is my true mate," Liam growled, the rightness of his words lending him strength. "She will stay here with us and become part of our pack. She has only one sister for family, and she will not look for her. You, my pack, have trusted me to safeguard you and make good decisions these past thirty years. I trust and believe in Amalie. If you have faith in me as your alpha, you will accept my decision and put your hands down now."

He took a deep breath, and tried to keep his voice steady. "If not, you have two options. You can leave the pack, or, if the majority of you feel I'm wrong, Amalie and I will leave together and you can select a new alpha." It would break his heart if it came to that, no question, but he couldn't have Amalie's blood on his hands. He scanned the room, eyeing the wolves from the other packs. "For the rest of you, know this: vote or no, brother or not, the first to touch my mate will have to come through me first."

Liam held his breath as the world seemed to move in slow motion. Hands began to lower, and soon his entire pack sat, arms at their sides, necks exposed to him in respectful supplication. He would have followed through on his threat if he'd had to, but losing a member of his pack would have been like losing a limb. The relief that they would stand with him was almost too much to bear.

He waited to see what the other packs would do. To see if he'd led his brothers and sisters into a war with his ultimatum. The Kotkes still had their hands high in the air, as did the majority of the Big Sky Canyon crew. He was glad to see that

Niles and all of Stone Creek were with him. At least they had one ally.

Joseph glared at him. "This is not how we do things. A vote must be ca—"

Liam cut him short. "As I said Joseph, a vote is pointless. Regardless of the results, you cannot have her."

Joseph and Alexander both stood and called to their respective packs. Joseph, in his ignorance, wanted to cling to the old, rigid ways. He could not accept that Liam was bucking the system, and as the elder, the slight would not be easily forgiven.

As for Alexander, Liam wondered if he had given him too much credit all these years. He sensed a cruelty in him that he had not seen before, and if Mikhail was any indication, some of his pack had a similar nature. Werewolves were just like people in that sense. There were good and bad. He'd maintained ties with the Kotke because he'd believed they needed to stick together. But at what cost? It wasn't worth compromising his morals or beliefs.

They had nothing in common with the wolves of Kotke and had just needed a catalyst to break away from them altogether. And Joseph and the Big Sky wolves needed to be more adaptable. Perhaps someday they could mend fences, but for now Liam felt free and right for the first time in a long while.

Alexander moved toward the door, then turned and met Liam's gaze. "You've not heard the last of this," he promised. "You've made a dangerous enemy in the Kotke. Watch your back." He marched out, his pack following close behind him.

Joseph stood by the door and called to Chandra, who was still in the sitting room with Amalie. The door burst open and

Amalie bounded across the room into Liam's arms, with Chandra trailing slowly behind her.

He held Amalie tight. "Will you stay with me? With us?" he murmured into her sweet-smelling hair.

"Yes. Yes, of course I will." Her voice broke as she pulled back to look up at him. "Thank God you aren't hurt!" She kissed his face repeatedly. "What happened? Tell me what happened. I was so worried." As he held her body close to his, he touched her mind so she could see what had transpired.

"Chandra, let's go. We leave this place now," Joseph barked. He turned, assuming she would follow.

Everyone's attention turned to Chandra, who shook her head slowly. "In order for a pack to work, wolves must feel their alpha is the best choice to lead them. After what I witnessed tonight and after spending time, albeit short, with Amalie, I'm no longer convinced you're the one I would follow." She turned to face Liam. "I would like to stay with the wolf pack of Pray, if you will have me."

Liam reached for his wolves, mentally posing the question. Their responses came quickly. It was unanimous; and just like that, they were twelve.

Joseph gave Chandra a steely glare and stormed out of the room.

Niles moved toward the door. He stopped and grasped Liam's hand, his round face wrinkling into a huge grin. "Well, you sure stirred the shit didn't you, boy-o? That's all right. I never liked them anyway. It was time, Liam. And whatever the ramifications, we'll deal with them together." He gestured to his group and they filed out the door.

Finally, it was just Liam and his pack, both old and new. He turned to them. "Thank you. I'm humbled by your trust and I promise I won't disappoint you."

They all came in close and, one by one, hugged him and Amalie. Jax was last in line, and Liam felt his pain as if it were his own.

Amalie held her hand out to him, and, reluctantly, he took it. "I know it was hard for you to put your trust in a human. I promise I will strive to deserve it every day of my life."

"I didn't do it for you. I did it for Liam, and for myself." He swallowed hard, and shook his head. "I can barely get through the day now, but I manage for Ryan's sake. If I allowed Liam to suffer that same pain, what would that make me? I would not willingly put anyone through such grief. For now, I'm withholding judgment on you. It may take me a while, Amalie." With that, he turned and headed upstairs to check on his sleeping son.

"So is it time to eat or what?" Billy asked hopefully, and they all headed into the kitchen, leaving only Liam and Amalie behind.

"You hungry?" Liam asked.

"Nope," she replied, and they both laughed as her stomach growled. "Well, yes then. But we can eat after." She leaned up and nipped at his chin.

"You don't have to tell me twice, woman." He scooped her into his arms and jogged lightly up the stairs to their bedroom where he closed the door and locked it behind them.

Epilogue

October 31ˢᵗ
Pray, Montana

The air was cold and crisp in Pray, Montana on Halloween night. Under a moon so full it appeared as if it might burst, the forest pulsed with life. A large, male timber wolf padded forward into a clearing. A sable female of uncommon grace and beauty followed close behind him, her nose brushing his flank. They stood bathed in moonbeams and waited as the rest of their pack moved into the light. The male wolf let out a long, soulful howl and all but the sable wolf joined him in song. Their chorus rose and swelled until she, too, was swept up. She tested her voice, letting out a wobbly howl. The wolves nipped and nudged her playfully as she did, both teasing and encouraging. The timber wolf then turned and loped off, picking up speed as the rest followed. Soon they were running. Separate beings moving as one, in perfect harmony with one another and their land

Just a few miles away in a little cabin, seated in front of a cozy fire sat a man. He poured over maps, jotted coordinates, and absently stroked the good luck charm strapped to his belt. A pristine white wolf's foot.

He laughed to himself as he thought about the past few months. After years of searching he'd finally caught a break. He'd botched it some because he hadn't known how they functioned. But now he did, and soon he would be avenged. Soon everyone who had mocked him would be a believer. Soon he would have living proof.

Proof that monsters existed, and they lived in Pray, Montana.

Awakening

Montana Wolves Book Two

Chloe Cole

Introduction

Jax Mulaney's beloved mate is dead and her killer's trail has gone cold. Eaten up by grief and guilt, it's an effort just to get through the day. Now, after a year in mourning, his animal instincts have reawakened. As he struggles to control the need clawing at him, his pack-mate Chandra's sexy body and snappy wit put his self-discipline to the test.

Chandra is heartsick watching Jax struggle, and wants nothing more than to comfort him. If she takes his offer of passion without strings, she knows she's in for a world of hurt. But if she refuses, she might blow her one chance to convince him that she can rock his world and fill the empty space in his heart.

Will Jax let love in, only to risk having it taken away again?

Chapter One

Pray, Montana
March 10th

Chandra woke to the sound of footsteps stumbling up the stairs, then down the hallway past her bedroom door. She peered at the clock next to her bed and groaned. *3:00 a.m.*

It was clearly time to ask Liam if she could move quarters to the next wing over. She'd still be close enough if little Ryan needed to stop by at night to talk, but far enough away that she could avoid having to hear the grand, late-night entrances his father, Jax, had gotten into the habit of making this past month. It was too painful being this close, watching him come apart at the seams a little more each day.

A feminine peal of laughter interrupted her thoughts. She closed her eyes as her heart squeezed painfully in her chest. *Oh, no way.* Jax had been lucky so far that Ryan had slept through his drunken entrances over the past weeks, but there was no way he could sleep through that. How could he do this to them? *To Ryan*, she amended quickly.

The laugh, nasal and high-pitched, sounded again, and Chandra rolled off her bed onto her feet. The sympathy she'd felt moments before evaporated instantly under the white heat of fury.

Clearly, the two lovebirds were so entranced with one another they were entirely unconcerned about the feelings of the sweet little boy sleeping a few doors down. If they were making this much noise before they even made it to the bedroom, Chandra cringed to think of the kind of racket they would make once they were inside.

She was halfway out the door to give them a piece of her mind before she realized she was buck naked. Stalking quickly to her dresser, she grabbed a nightgown, jamming it over her head as she headed to Jax's bedroom.

She reached his door and gave it two sharp raps. Giggles erupted from the room, and the voices within modulated to the overly exaggerated whispers only drunkards could manage.

Stumbling footsteps moved closer and then paused. The door swung open to reveal a disheveled Jax. His short, honey curls were tousled, and his shirt was opened to the waist, revealing his hard stomach and bare chest. The verbal lashing she had mentally rehearsed on the way down the hall died at the sight of him. Blood roared in her ears as desire hit her hard, momentarily eclipsing her anger.

"See anything you like?" he asked in that drunken whisper as he weaved in place, leaning heavily on the doorjamb.

Chandra tore her gaze away from his body and met his bleary eyes, mentally cursing herself for being distracted by his physique when she was so mad at him she could scream.

She rallied quickly, working up a fair imitation of an incredulous snort. "Uh, yeah, if I'm ever in the market for a drunken dumb-ass I will definitely look you up. But for now, I'm all set. I wanted to come by and tell you that you and your obnoxious friend are loud enough to wake the dead and, unless you want your son to come and witness this, you might want to shut it down for the night, Champ."

A petite but buxom blonde with improbably large breasts encased in an impossibly small shirt stumbled up behind him, wrapping her arms around his midsection possessively. The cloying scent of liberally applied Chanel perfume was so overwhelming to Chandra's sensitive nose, she almost gagged.

Still, as angry as she was, relief coursed through her as it finally registered that the blonde woman was exactly that: a woman, of the regular human variety. She wasn't a werewolf like herself and Jax, so there was no way the relationship was heading anywhere serious. But that didn't explain what the hell she was doing in the house.

Blondie pouted over Jax's shoulder and whined, "Jax, who is this woman? And why is she talking about me that way?"

"That's a great question. Who *do* you think you are, Chandra?" His eyes seemed to have cleared a bit, and his tone was challenging.

Not willing to back down, Chandra met his gaze with a cool glare. "Do the right thing here. Give her some cab fare and send her on her way. And next time, go to her place. Don't you think Ryan's been through enough?"

Jax's eyes grew icy. He shrugged the blonde off his shoulders and said softly, "Amber, why don't you go ahead and make us a drink. I'll be back in one minute."

He grasped Chandra's wrists, pulled her down the hallway back into her own room and then shut the door behind them.

"Let me go," she bit out, wrenching her wrists from his grasp, heart pounding wildly at both his touch and the anger-fueled adrenaline coursing through her veins.

"You've overstepped your bounds, Chandra. I appreciate all your help with Ryan these past few months and value our friendship. But no one knows or understands what my son is going through more than me. Apparently you forgot that he's having a sleepover at Niles' place tonight with his son, Spencer. He. Is. Not. Here."

As he spoke, his eyes blazed with anger and something else…hurt?

"I would never, ever bring home some one-night stand if he were. And it kinda pisses me off that you think I would."

Chandra's stomach lurched as she realized what Jax said was true. Ryan had told her about it earlier in the week. He was even excited about it, in his own subdued way. How had she forgotten? As she thought about it, she realized she hadn't seen him in the family room after dinner, but she figured he was out with Jax. It had totally slipped her mind.

Embarrassment refueled her anger. "Well, maybe I would have thought of that if you hadn't woken me up with your cavorting at three in the morning. Even if it wasn't for the woman, this has got to stop. The drinking. The late nights." She threw her head back and glared at him. "You're acting like a college kid."

"And *you're* acting like a jealous mate."

***

Shit. What had made him say that?

Probably the bourbon, asshole.

The words hung heavy between them for a moment before Chandra's pale cheeks bloomed with furious color. Jax couldn't say why, but even when he felt bad about baiting her, nothing in his current life gave him greater satisfaction than seeing her riled up like this. With her unruly mane of auburn curls and her green eyes flashing fire, she looked like an avenging angel.

If he wasn't so pissed off, he would have grinned at her, just to rile her up even more. But he *was* pissed. Who was she to judge him? She couldn't possibly understand what it had been like for him to lose Sara.

His stomach clenched painfully at the thought of his deceased mate. He tried to picture her pretty face. It took a while these days, longer than it should have, and he hated himself for it. It was like a cruel joke.

For the first few months after her death, he'd wanted to forget her. The way she'd smelled, her soft laugh and forgiving nature. He *tried* to forget, because thinking of her hurt too much. But she was part of everything around him. When he dressed in the morning, he would find her pink fluffy socks mixed in with his. Outside his bedroom window, her rose garden had continued to bloom. Christ, when he went to the bathroom, her fucking soap was on the side of the tub. He couldn't turn around without her presence right there, slamming him in the gut.

But now? Nine months later, he wanted—*needed*—to remember her, or else it was going to be like she'd never been there at all. What could Chandra know of that pain?

Almost as bad as losing Sara, though, was the knowledge that he had failed her. And now, it seemed like he was failing his son as well.

Chandra had apparently recovered from her initial shock at his comment and took advantage of his silence to let loose on him. "Jealous mate? *Jealous mate*? I wouldn't be your mate if you and Scooby Doo were the last two canines on the planet."

He didn't respond, caught up in his own painful revelation. The fire in her eyes died as she looked at him, and the anger seemed to drain away.

"Damn it, Jax, how about caring friend? That's what I'm trying to be here."

He turned away and scrubbed a hand over his face as he slumped down in the chair at the foot of her bed. The pleasant buzz he'd spent all night cultivating faded and now it all just felt a little sad.

"You're right," he muttered. "I don't know what the hell I'm doing. I do the best I can with Ryan. I try to help him through this. But it hurts so much. It's almost like when my pain and his combine, I can't take it. The first few months after Sara died, I was in shock. I didn't even really think about tomorrow or the fact that I would never see her face or hear her voice again, you know?"

She nodded, her expression mirroring the pain he felt in his chest.

"But then watching Liam and Amalie together. And Thanksgiving. And Christmas. It's moving so fast. When I go out after he's asleep, it's in hopes that a few drinks will take the edge off. Because it's real now. The world just keeps on turning, and she's never coming back." His throat tightened. "I'm…starting to forget her face, Chan, and that kills me."

She walked to him, arms open, and cradled his head to her stomach, rocking slowly, murmuring words meant to comfort. He wrapped his arms around her hips and held on tight as she swayed, letting her warmth soothe his battered soul.

They stayed that way until a shrill voice from down the hall called out, "Jaxy, where are yoo-oo? Come out, come out wherever you are! I'm gonna get lost in this house again trying to find you."

Jax stiffened and pulled his head back. How to handle his would-be paramour's grating entreaties when he wanted nothing more than to stay here and let Chandra hold him for a little longer?

"Holy mother of God, is that a seal barking?" he deadpanned, hoping to lighten things a bit before he left her.

She let out a guffaw and covered her mouth to stifle it. "Now, now, Jaxy, that's a terrible thing to say about your new girlfriend. You'd better get back in there before she wakes up the whole house with that honking."

There was little chance of that. The house was huge and he, Ryan, and Chandra were the only ones with rooms in the east wing, but she was right. He had to figure out what to do with

Amber. Especially now that he realized he didn't want her after all.

"Yeah, I guess." He stood and shifted from one foot to the other, trying to figure out what to say next. "Listen, thanks for caring. I really do appreciate everything you've done for me and Ryan these past few months. You've been a great friend to me, and he's crazy about you." He hugged her tight against his chest.

As he squeezed her close, he realized with a start that she was wearing only a thin nightgown that barely covered her bottom. A surge of lust rocked through him, the kind he'd neglected to feel with the woman in the next room, and he nearly groaned. Had she always smelled so good? Like clean sheets and sunshine. He fought the urge to bury his face in her hair and gave her one last squeeze before he let her go.

She turned and started for the door to let him out as he followed a short distance behind. He tried not to stare, but damn if the cheeks of her behind weren't peeking out from the hem of her too-short nightgown. It took all of his strength not to reach out and palm one of those cheeks to see if it felt as silky and plump as it looked. Something primal he thought had died with Sara was stirring within him more and more every time he was around Chandra, and it was distracting as hell.

Need.

Not your standard biological function variety that manifested itself in morning wood, wet dreams, or the ability to bump uglies with some stranger. No, this had nothing to do with basic biology. This was raw, uncut chemistry.

Sex had been the last thing on his mind for the better part of a year. But he was an animal, a wolf at heart, and werewolves had hungers that humans couldn't understand. Over the past few months, it had been a struggle. The instinct to mate, especially for a powerful, virile male, was strong. It was an internal, grinding need that had to be addressed. In the absence of it, he'd become irritable.

Chandra was probably aware of some of that, hell, he'd hardly been a treat to deal with lately, but what she didn't know was that the iron control he'd been exercising to this point was starting to slip. He sometimes found himself having to focus just to stay in one form or another. When he got stressed, his body temperature rose, urging him to change. He had to get that under wraps, or it could be dangerous for both him *and* his pack. If he changed at the wrong time, in the wrong place? Disaster. They might be monsters, but there was *nothing* more monstrous than a group of fearful humans. One only had to look to the "witches" of Salem to see that.

None of that knowledge had quelled the need, though, and once Chandra had joined the pack this past fall, it had gotten almost unbearable. She was so vital and unconsciously sexy. Even the way she walked—hips twitching, shoulders back—made him want to roll up behind her, wrap his hand in her hair and pull her against him so he could feel that ass grinding against his swollen cock.

It was exactly thoughts like those that had made him start going out to the bars a few nights a week, at first hoping he could get drunk enough to dull the ache gnawing at him and get some sleep. He quickly realized that wasn't going to work, and over the past week or so had come to terms with the fact that he needed to find a fuck buddy who could get his mind off his packmate. Fast.

Good sex, no messy strings that would interfere with his day to day life.

Then, Amber had walked in. She wasn't really his type, but she'd been persistent. And that was good. He didn't want to burn for her anyway. He figured he'd take her out, show her a good time and, if all went well, have mutually satisfying sex. With Ryan out and his libido at a critical point, he was going to bite the bullet and get it done come hell or high water.

Until Chandra had banged on his door.

And as she walked in front of him, hips swaying, the need that had been clawing at him for the past few months once again narrowed to a pinprick of pulsing energy with a clear target.

Chandra.

Chapter Two

When Chandra awoke, her eyes were scratchy, and she was feeling out of sorts. As she rolled onto her back and stretched, thoughts of Jax and the night before rushed in.

It hadn't exactly gone well.

Even now she found herself blinking back tears, calling herself all kinds of a fool for thinking that something had shifted between them when she was holding him. He had been quick to remind her she was a great friend, a buddy. That was all. She'd better get used to the fact that there were going to be women for him. If not Amber, then someone else.

There was nothing wrong with that. He wasn't a eunuch, for crying out loud. He had the right to a private life, and the right to move on. She knew from her own experience how hard it was to be without a partner, especially for a were. Her old pack had slim pickings in the worthy males department, and she'd gone it solo for a very long time. It was an unnatural state for their kind, and loneliness took its toll. As long as Ryan wasn't home, she should have no beef with Jax trying to feel a little less lonely. He'd suffered enough already.

She'd realized that last night, and right when he'd been about to go back into his room, she'd bit the bullet and had choked out an apology. He turned to meet her gaze, warm chocolate eyes burning into hers. Then he'd leaned in close, his breath tickling her mouth. Her stomach had done a flip, but at the last moment he veered and kissed her cheek lightly before pulling back a scant inch and whispering, "See you in the morning."

With that, he opened the door and walked into his bedroom, closing the door behind him.

She yanked the sheet over her head and groaned.

What the hell was that about? Just when she thought she'd had him figured. She was used to his teasing, but this had been different. He had looked…intense. She shivered as she recalled his hot gaze. A gaze that had haunted her all night, joining forces with her jealous thoughts to slowly drive her insane.

What was he doing? Was Amber still there?

From 4:00 a.m. until the last time she had looked at the clock at 5:47, she had laid perfectly still, ears straining to hear his door opening and Amber on her way out. The sound never came. She'd been hoping that after their heart-to-heart Jax might send the little tart packing. Furious with herself for even caring what—or who—he did, she tried to focus on something else.

She thought back to the first time she had noticed him, *really* noticed him. It had been a brisk night in October of the previous year. She and her pack, the wolves of Big Sky Canyon, had come to Pray for a meeting with all the area wolves. After a rift had driven a wedge between their two packs, Chandra, never one to follow along blindly, had chosen to stay with the wolf pack of Pray.

She closed her eyes as she recalled how hard it had been to leave. Following their alpha's misguided example, her pack had been doing things that had not sat right with her for a long time. Hunting humans, encroaching on farmlands that resulted in the killing of timber wolves in the area. The Big Sky clan was getting more and more bloodthirsty and less and less careful.

When her alpha had voted to murder a woman in cold blood, it had been the catalyst she needed to break away from them. Her former packmates had been forbidden from contacting her since she left, and she missed some of them, but worse was the tension that night had created between the area packs. Alliances were made, gauntlets thrown…there was a storm brewing and, in spite of a quiet winter, it was only a matter of time before things imploded in the were community in a big, bloody way.

And still? She was happier than she'd ever been. She felt at home with her new pack in a way that she never had with the old. And, even in the short time they had been together, the friendships she'd made with all her new packmates, especially Amalie—the very woman her former pack had voted to kill—Maggie, and Billy, had progressed to the point that they felt like family. Not to mention that her relationship with their alpha, Liam, was one of mutual respect and harmony. He was strong but approachable, firm but fair. Everything one could want in a leader.

Then there was Jax.

She thought again about that fateful night, when everything had changed for her. She'd walked into the beautiful great room of the Pray house with her pack, tuning out the low buzz of conversation around her as she scanned the room. She stopped as her gaze was drawn to a man she didn't recognize. That had seemed strange because, despite being in different packs, everybody knew everybody to one degree or another. He looked haunted, his dark eyes staring into hers but not really seeing her.

Then she knew: Jax. Before Sara had died, his power had been almost palpable. She had seen them all together two summers before at a gathering by the lake. They were a beautiful family. Sara had been blessed with a cascade of corn silk hair and eyes the color of pansies in the springtime. Her temperament was as sweet as her face, and Chandra had looked on as they played by the water with Ryan. She remembered thinking how lucky they were and made a secret promise to herself she would not settle for less than that when she finally chose a mate and had a family of her own.

Less than a year later, Sara was dead. Shot to death by a man who some of the area werewolves claimed was just a regular Montana hunter who had gotten lucky. Chandra doubted that. It took a little more than luck to kill a full-grown werewolf. And a game hunter would've assumed that a single, well-placed bullet would have killed a regular wolf Sara's size. Maybe two. By the time the pack reached her, she'd been shot eighteen times. To Chandra's mind, the only reason he would have kept reloading and shooting, ruining the prized, lily-white pelt in the process, was if he knew one bullet wasn't going to cut it.

No, Chandra, along with most of the wolves of Pray, felt like this man knew what he was doing. That he had somehow figured out, or at least had a hunch, that Sara was a werewolf.

While this terrible, life-changing tragedy played out, Jax had been out of town. He had known instantly due to his bond with his mate that she was no longer alive and had rushed back. Ryan had been there with Sara and, at his mother's desperate urgings, had managed to get away when the shooting began. But in the end, Jax's wife was dead, and she still hadn't been avenged.

"I failed my mate," he'd said to Chandra earlier.

She shook her head briskly to ward off the ghosts of the past, focusing once again on the present.

And *presently,* Jax was probably still tangled beneath the sheets with that woman.

Chandra swung her legs over the side of the bed and hoisted her still weary body up. She brushed her teeth and took a few angry swipes at her hair with a comb before pulling it into a loose knot on top of her head. Maybe a run would clear her head. She quickly changed into workout gear and headed for the stairs, but a woman's tinny voice sounded from behind her, assaulting her eardrums and stalling her in her tracks.

"Hey there, Red, whatcha doing?"

Chandra sucked in a breath and bit her lip hard. She so didn't need this shit right now.

"Hello there," she said, pasting a smile on before turning to face a disheveled Amber. "Aren't you looking lovely this morning?" She attempted to cut their interaction short by turning back toward the stairs.

"Thanks." Amber didn't cooperate and stepped back into view. "Jax just buzzed my cab through the gates so I'm heading out." She slid her arms into the coat that she'd been holding and hoisted her purse back onto her shoulder. "He was exhausted so he went back to bed."

Fan-fucking-tastic.

"Nice place you have here," she drawled, glancing around at the art decorating the hallway walls with an appreciative nod. "Kinda weird all of you living together though. I mean, the house is big enough and all, and I know Jax said the bunch of you are partners and run the business out of the house and whatnot, but still…kinda weird having seven roommates, isn't it?" Amber's gaze stayed on Chandra's face longer than was comfortable.

Spidey senses tingling, she manufactured a laugh and replied, "Yeah, more than a little weird. But our boss, Liam, is what you might call eccentric. He feels like the partners that play together will stay together. And—," she lowered her voice to a conspiratorial whisper, glancing around as if to make sure no one was listening, "—he's a slave driver to boot. He loves to call meetings on a Saturday afternoon or some nonsense just to make sure we're all eating, sleeping and breathing real estate, you know?"

A horn blared, and Chandra said a little prayer of thanks to the cab company for their impeccable timing.

"Well, it was nice talking to you." With that and a breezy wave, she turned on the balls of her feet and jogged lightly down the stairs, replaying their conversation over in her head. She hoped she'd added enough detail to make their odd living arrangement plausible, but not too much that it had sounded forced. Amber didn't exactly seem like the brightest star in the sky, but she might be ambitious and that could be just as dangerous.

Once Chandra was alone in the kitchen, she made for the window and watched Amber get into the taxi with a sigh of relief.

This was why they didn't bring humans home to play with. It wasn't expressly forbidden, but it was definitely discouraged. Her pack did business with humans every day, and many of them had human friends or acquaintances. But they didn't let them get too close, or they invariably started asking tough questions like Amber had done.

If he had no plans to hook up with her again, and everyone was asleep anyway, maybe he hadn't seen the harm in bringing her over. They all knew better than to change indoors. Wolves were insanely destructive and they all liked a nice house, so it wasn't like she would've seen anything she shouldn't have.

Still, since she'd been with this pack, she couldn't recall a single time any of them had brought a human home. Billy kept a room in town where he entertained lady friends, and if Maggie had a boyfriend, Chandra sure didn't know about it. The rest of the pack followed suit, spending most of their time with one another or the other area wolves.

She might not have a right to be jealous, but Jax was Liam's second, and his right hand in all things. He was also the brains behind their business ventures. The others looked up to him and respected him. He needed to lead by example, and, as his friend, it was up to her to remind him of that.

She went to the cabinet and took out her favorite mug, one that Jax had given her for Christmas. It had a picture of Little Red Riding Hood on it and read *Anyone who confuses a wolf with their grandmother DESERVES to get eaten.*

She filled it with the steaming coffee from the pot on the counter and sniffed appreciatively before taking a deep swallow. It scalded her tongue, which healed almost instantly, but it was worth it as she felt the glorious jolt of caffeine skim through her veins, clearing out the cobwebs in her brain. She drained her cup and refilled before heading back up the stairs to take the proverbial bull by the horns.

She knocked lightly on Jax's door but didn't wait for a response to let herself in. The room was dark, all the shades drawn tight, and she could just make out the shape of him in his bed.

"Go away," he grumbled, covering his head beneath a pillow. "Wait!" He stirred again and poked his head out. "Do I smell coffee?"

Chandra sighed and brought her cup over, setting it into his outstretched hand. She sat down on the foot of the bed as he struggled into a half-seated position and began to drink her coffee.

"Headache?" she asked dryly.

"Nah, not too bad. Strong constitution, you know. What time is it?"

"About nine o'clock."

He smothered a yawn. "Tired, though. Long night, I hardly slept."

Chandra resisted the urge to jab him in the solar plexus and tried not to imagine he and Amber rolling around on the bed together. She reached out and touched a half-melted candle on the dresser with her forefinger before picking up a book of matches and reading the words emblazoned on it. "What's The Naughty Kitty?"

"The name of the club where Amber dances."

Dances.

He clearly wasn't talking the Viennese waltz, and she bit back a growl.

"Whatever." She dropped the matchbook and stood, determined to say her piece in spite of the ache just being in the room was causing her. "It's really none of my concern what time you and your friend finally went to sleep last night. I'm here to talk to you and I want to get it out of the way so I can go for a run. You really shouldn't be bringing women to the house." She held up a hand as he opened his mouth to speak. "I know your personal life is none of my business, but she was asking me a lot of questions this morning."

Plus, I'm crazy about you, and seeing you with someone else breaks my heart.

Jesus, she had to get those feelings on lock. Sure, he was sexy. And gorgeous. And smart. And, aside from his recent late night jaunts, he was a great dad as well as a good person. But she couldn't allow herself to be in love with him. That would be nuts, to hand her heart over to someone who was still in love with someone else, whether that someone else was still of this world or not. It was an exercise in futility and a recipe for pain.

So why did she suddenly have the urge to be a masochist?

AWAKENING

***

Jax was still feeling a little bleary, but he couldn't help noticing the sudden change in Chandra. She'd been the same way last night. One minute she was furious at him; the next she was comforting him in her arms.

He recalled the way she'd felt and shifted restlessly under his sheets, hoping to hide his immediate and evident reaction to her. Even now, hair up and in her running clothes, she looked superhot. Her hoodie was unzipped, and a sliver of sleek stomach was visible. Her creamy breasts, high and firm, pressed subtly against her sports tank. They were perfectly proportioned to her sturdy, toned frame. She couldn't be more different from the more flamboyantly built Amber.

Then he thought of Sara's willowy frame, her almost ethereal loveliness, and he realized why he had chosen Amber as a candidate to help him ease back into real life. She was the polar opposite of Sara. Maybe, deep down, he wanted to make sure he couldn't mix them up in his mind; that he didn't sully Sara's memory somehow by trying to replace her with a replica. It had been an error on his part. If he truly thought about what Sara would have wanted for him, he would have found someone who gave him some peace and some happiness.

He might not be ready to move on completely, but if he was going to do this—and he was; abstaining was no longer an option—he wanted to do it right, in a way that would add something positive to his life. Drunken grappling with a stranger wasn't going to cut it.

Fun, sexy times with a friend. Shared satisfaction. Someone who got him, understood his emotional limitations and who would still want to be friends after.

What he needed was Chandra.

Chapter Three

Chandra shifted under the weight of Jax's stare and cleared her throat as she turned away. He'd been quiet for so long, it was starting to freak her out.

"Well, if you don't feel like talking, I'm going to go get some exercise." As she moved toward the door, he halted her with a hand on her wrist.

He put the coffee down on his bedside table in a slow, deliberate manner. "Why don't you wait a minute and I'll come with you?"

She swallowed hard, pulse pounding, wondering at her reaction to such an innocuous question. "Sure," she said, trying to keep her voice light. "But hurry up, because I'm going now."

"Not a problem," he replied with a wicked grin.

He released her, slid to the opposite side of the bed and jumped to his feet, totally nude. He walked over to a hamper, then grabbed a pair of sweatpants off the top of the pile. His back to her, he bent low and slid the pants on, sans underwear, mercifully covering his distractingly naked bottom. Her heart banged against her ribs and she resisted the urge to reach for him…to yank those pants back down and get a look at him from the front.

He glanced over his shoulder. "Well? What are you waiting for?" he asked, brows raised, before jogging out the door.

Chandra stood rooted to the floor for a moment, unsure of how to react. She had never seen him totally naked, and was still completely flustered by his nonchalance. God, his back was gorgeous though. Tan, lean muscles trailing down to a firm ass that begged to be squeezed…

Whatever. If it didn't bother him, it didn't bother her, and she wasn't going to give him the satisfaction of mentioning it.

She bounded down the steps to catch up to him and they met in the foyer.

"You going to get sneakers?" she asked, glancing at his bare feet.

"Nah," he replied. "If we're going to run, let's run."

So they would run as wolves. *No wonder he had put on those ratty old sweats*, she thought. Made the lack of underwear seem a lot more sensible now. She looked regretfully down at her cute little Nike workout clothes and gave them a mental kiss goodbye. Wouldn't be the first, or the last, outfit she had ruined.

He took off out the door in a sprint, heading straight for the trees. She followed close behind. The air was crisp, and near freezing, but were-blood ran hot and it felt good on her too-warm cheeks.

Surrounding the house was a square mile of thick woods. It was private property that belonged to the pack and was fenced around the perimeter. With a state-of-the-art security system complete with cameras at all entrances and exits of the property—they didn't record within the compound, having their activities committed to film would be too dangerous—it was one of the few places they were basically free to roam without fear of being seen. Werewolves typically marked fifty miles or more for hunting territory, so it was useless in that regard, but they were able to take advantage of the relatively large grounds for exercise and training.

Once she and Jax hit the woods, he wasted no time, leaping high in the air and exploding into wolf form. His sweats practically disintegrated around him, leaving behind a glorious tawny colored wolf, so large and powerful, she couldn't help but marvel at his beauty.

"Showoff!" she shouted.

Despite her teasing, her blood sang as she looked on. She loved to watch him shift. He did it like that every time, with absolute abandon, as if he couldn't wait to get out of his skin. It was one of the rare times she saw a glimmer of the old Jax, crackling with life and power as he had before Sara died.

Chandra ran to join him, full speed, and threw off her hoodie. She could feel her muscles lengthen and her bones shift into place as she leaped. She landed gracefully on the ground as a wolf and, without missing a step, tore after him.

They ran together, chasing one another, nipping and playing, for the better part of an hour. By the time they stopped at the icy stream for a drink of water, they were both breathless and panting, but her heart was so full, she felt like she could burst.

Why couldn't she feel this exact way about someone else? Someone who wanted her. Someone who wasn't so tortured by the past that they couldn't see to the future.

She took another long drink, letting the cold water run down her parched throat. It was going to be fine. She'd get over this feeling soon enough, and maybe someday, she'd find a mate who loved her the way Jax had loved Sara.

Almost as if she'd called to him, Jax's mind touched hers, asking if she was ready to change back now. She barked out a mental chuckle for his benefit. As a general rule, they always stayed in wolf form until they returned to the homestead. There was a barn out back they'd fitted with hot showers and clean clothes so that, in the event a hunt got bloody, they'd be able to clean up before heading inside. It also allowed them some measure of modesty, rather than everyone strolling around naked as they moved between human and wolf form.

He was obviously yanking her chain, suggesting she shift back with him standing right there. Talk about awkward.

She sent him a mental eye roll paired with an "as if" snort and turned, loping back toward the house, his mocking laughter ringing in her head. He lagged behind and she beat him to the barn, pressing the button that opened the door with her nose. It swung wide, and she padded across the room, stepping into one of the shower stalls. Jax chose the stall directly next to hers.

Doing her best to ignore him, she let her limbs go loose and willed herself to let the human in her take center stage. A moment later, the change was complete and she stood, naked in the narrow space.

The wall between them came only to shoulder height, and she peeked out of the corner of her eye to see how much, or how little, of Jax was visible from her angle. Broad shoulders only, fortunately. The last thing she needed was more temptation. Already her hands itched with the need to touch him.

Like Amber had last night...

She barely managed to swallow the instinctive growl rising in her throat. "You must be exhausted now after all the late night activity, and then running around on almost no sleep there, Loverboy."

Her cheeks burned as she realized what a prig she sounded like. To his credit, Jax only laughed. She refused to meet his gaze as she turned on the hot spray with a jerk, and he followed suit.

"Actually, I'm not tired at all," he said, after leaning in to wet his hair. "In fact, I feel totally refreshed. That run was exactly what I needed to clear my head."

She let the water run over her face, over her tired eyes and down her cheeks, her emotions growing more riotous by the second. The fact that he felt totally refreshed and she felt like she was going to burst with pent up frustration and confusion was too much to bear. The scales finally tipped as the need to know edged out her need to avoid further humiliation.

She swiped the water from her eyes and faced him head on, pulse hammering.

"Why her, Jax? What does she have that-" She broke off and shoved a lock of hair from her face with a trembling hand. "Why bring her to the house? Help me understand."

He met her gaze and she searched his for answers in his fathomless brown eyes.

"Why her?" He shrugged and let out a bitter laugh. "Honestly? Because I thought I needed somebody I could never actually care about. And why bring her home? I don't know. Maybe so someone would try to stop me—"

"I tried!" she cut in vehemently. No frigging way was he laying this on her. "You would not be stopped."

"I didn't do it, Chan." He blew out a sigh and shook his head. "I couldn't do it. I went back to the room and was going to send her home, but it was late, and she asked if she could stay. She was almost passed out, it was the middle of the night, and I felt like a heel for leading her on anyway, so I said okay. But I slept on the sofa. I called her a cab this morning and then got in my bed when she left. The end. I don't plan on seeing her ever again."

She almost passed out with relief. He wasn't hers, but at least he wasn't anyone else's either. She could live with that. A little more time and she would get over him. She was just glad she didn't have to do it while he paraded another woman around the house.

The steam rose around them as he moved closer to the shared wall of the shower. "Now that we have that out of the way, I wanted to talk to you about something." His face was as serious as a heart attack. "Something important."

"Oh?" The relief she'd felt a moment before curdled in her belly and she steeled herself for an emotional blow.

"See, Chan, I have a problem," he continued, his voice husky. "I haven't been with anyone since Sara died."

He paused, as if to let that sit, and she tried to wrap her mind around it. A year was a long time for a man and would have felt seven times longer than that for a wolf. Not acting out sexually for that length of time must have been agonizing for him.

"I can't go on like this. Hell, I can't even function. But I'm not the type of guy to go around having sex with random women." The gaze he'd locked on her went hot and her stomach bottomed out. "So I've been thinking. We're both werewolves and in need of companionship. I know you haven't been with anyone since you came to Pray. That's a long enough dry spell that it can't be comfortable. I don't know how you feel about me, but I care about you a lot, and I also think you're drop-dead sexy. If you're game, I'd like to see if we can't…help each other out a little."

She opened her mouth to reply, a thousand emotions crowding in at once, fighting for supremacy, but he held up a hand.

"Wait. Let me finish. If we aren't happy with the situation and either of us wants to back out or stop, or if you find one you want as your mate, then it ends and we remain friends."

Her pulse pounded as she stared at his beautiful, solemn face. He was dead fucking serious.

Her world tilted on its axis.

"Before you answer, I want you to know one thing." He looked at her hard, his eyes burning with need. "If you give me the chance, I swear I'll make it good for you. What do you say?"

Chandra swallowed hard and actually began to shake. He was right about one thing: it had been a long time for her. He didn't even know how long. His words alone had her body ready.

She didn't mull it over or even give herself a chance to come up with the dozens of good reasons not to do it. Her instincts were telling her to take him however she could get him for however long he would have her, and a smart wolf never ignored her instincts.

She reached her hand out and slowly turned the shower off.

Chapter Four

Jax's gut clenched as Chandra turned the water off in total silence.

Shit.

She was so offended, she wasn't even going to dignify his question with an answer. He'd really screwed that up. Things would be weird between them now, and he felt strangely bereft at the thought.

Her stall door closed with a click and he bent his head under the hot spray, forcing himself not to embarrass her further by watching her walk away. A second later, his own door opened and he started in surprise.

As he pulled his head from under the spray and wiped at his face, Chandra stepped in and shut the door behind her.

"I thought…"

His voice trailed off as she leaned up on her tiptoes to nip lightly at his chin. She moved her lips down the line of his jaw, then to the pulse that was pounding in his neck. She bit down hard and touched his mind with hers. He gasped as carnal images, her fantasies, assailed him.

Chandra, on her knees before him, holding him captive with her hand, sucking and licking him. Chandra on her back, legs wrapped around his waist and him sliding in and out of her pussy. Chandra straddling him, rocking on top of him, her wild hair flying.

His blood thrummed, and he groaned. "Oh, this is going to be so good, Chan. So damn good."

He gently pushed her away from him, then grasped both her wrists in his hand and held them above her head. He leaned into her, moving her hard against the shower wall, and pressed his hips and chest to hers. She moaned and arched her back, straining to get closer to him as he rotated his hips and ground against her. What a beauty. A red wolf with moss green eyes, she was strong and quick and as fine a wolf as she was a woman.

She began to pant, rocking against him, begging him, "Come on, Jax."

He continued, sliding his wet hand down her neck, over her straining breasts but skimming past her nipples. Down her belly and between her thighs. He cupped her pussy and gave a firm squeeze, and she writhed against his hand.

She struggled harder against his wrist and whispered, "I want to touch you."

He shook his head. Not to be denied, she looked at him and struggled in earnest now, pushing herself and him away from the wall with a mighty shove of her hips. He relished her strength as she made it difficult to hold her. He removed his hand from between her legs, reached around her back, and gave her a light slap on the ass. She stilled as he squeezed there and anchored her more fully against him once more.

"Again. Harder," she demanded. He growled low in his throat and again slapped her firmly. She gasped and arched her hips, tilting them forward and back against his surging cock.

He closed his eyes for a moment and shook his head to clear it, then bent and sucked her raspberry nipple into his mouth. As he flicked it with his tongue and bit down gently, he felt her whole body tighten.

Jesus, she was going to come just like this.

They hadn't even kissed yet and already he couldn't figure out how he was going to stop himself from joining her. In that moment he didn't care. He wanted to watch her as she peaked for him.

Chandra's body stiffened like it was being held up by a wire that was about to snap. All of Jax's senses shimmered as he focused on the heat of the spray, the feel of her hard nipple against his tongue, and his swollen cock pulsing against her. He delivered another stinging slap to her ass and sucked hard, grinding against her, as the pleasure-pain sent her over the edge.

She gasped, then chanted in a low voice, "Yeah, yeah, yeah."

Jax pulled away so he could watch her at the end. Her head tossed back, eyes closed, she bit her lip hard, water sluicing down her face, neck, and breasts. He'd never seen anything so hot in his life. She was his equal in every sense. He didn't need to check himself or be afraid of hurting or scaring her with his strength. She was a warrior like him, and this was a dance, a tease, and a battle of wills as much as it was lovemaking. It was a new experience for him, and he relished the freedom.

As she began to quiet in his arms, he lifted her easily by the hips. She followed his lead, wrapping her long, muscular legs around his waist, pressing her moist, hot core directly over his rock-hard erection.

"Are we safe?" he choked out, praying she said yes. They weren't susceptible to diseases, and female weres only came into their fertile time once every three months, so odds were good they were in the clear, but when she nodded, he wanted to pass out from the relief.

She looked him straight in the eyes as she reached between them, took him firmly in her hand, and guided his swollen tip into her tight heat. His breathing grew shallow, and he strained to keep from thrusting too hard too soon. Then she reached out and grabbed his hair in her fist, pulling his mouth to hers in a hot, open mouth kiss. She pulled back slightly and traced his lips with her tongue before sucking his lower lip into her mouth.

Unable to hold back any longer, he squeezed her hips tight and slid himself further into her, inch by agonizing inch until he filled her. The sultry steam that enveloped them felt almost cool compared to the molten heat of her. He began to move in long, deep strokes, thinking each one would be the last as his body demanded release.

Urged on by the sounds of pleasure pouring from her mouth into his, he thrust harder, faster. Her consciousness brushed his as her body tensed, and she climaxed again. Liquid desire, hers and his, poured through him, a sensual elixir. He flexed deep, seating himself to the hilt as her inner muscles pulsed around him squeezing like an unseen fist.

"Damn it, Chan, you're killing me."

The heat and pressure coiled low in his loins and then it was over. He was coming hard, his cock jerking deep inside her as he groaned.

His breathing slowed, and he released her hips, sliding out of her. She let out a soft gasp and it took all of his concentration not to slide back into her and start all over again.

He set her feet on the floor and met her gaze. She wore a lazy, satisfied smile, and he was glad she didn't seem to have any second thoughts.

He pressed his forehead against hers and said, "That wasn't too bad, now was it?"

She laughed. "No, I guess it was okay for a first time. Clearly we'll need some practice though. There's always room for improvement."

"If we improve on that, I'm pretty sure it'll kill me," he said solemnly. "Seriously, Chan, that was amazing. I feel so much lighter, like a dark cloud and all the tension was lifted away. Thank you."

Regret filled him as he realized what time it was. The last thing he wanted to do was leave her now, but he had to go. He kissed her lightly on the mouth. "I hate to do this, but I'm scheduled to pick Ryan up from Niles' house in a half hour."

"No problem," she replied with a quick smile. "I'll see you later on." She walked out of the shower stall, head held high, and grabbed a towel from the rack beside her, seemingly unconcerned about her nakedness, which had him hard as steel all over again.

He watched, tongue stuck to the roof of his mouth as she dried off quickly and threw on some jeans and a sweater.

"Will you be home for dinner?" he asked, before he could think better of it. That was a question a mate would ask, not a friend, and he wondered if she'd call him on it.

"As far as I know," she said slowly, meeting his gaze. "Why?"

Why, indeed?

"The chef is making lamb tonight. I know you like it, so I was just wondering." He tried to sound nonchalant, but wanted to kick himself for making things awkward between them already. He was going to have to work on his post-sex banter if he had any hope of making this a regular thing. And, damn, did he want this to be a regular thing.

Chandra chewed her bottom lip and shuffled from foot to foot in silence for a moment before answering. "Lamb sounds good. I'll…uh, see you then." Pink-cheeked, she waved in his general direction and then spun around and rushed out of the barn like someone was chasing her.

He was still cursing himself when he climbed into his car a few minutes later. The key to this whole kingdom was going to be making sure their friendship didn't suffer. The second that started to happen, they'd need to re-evaluate, and frankly, he didn't want to re-evaluate.

He wanted it all.

His cake while he ate it. Searingly hot sex with Chandra whenever they chose, and their fun, teasing closeness the rest of the time. He'd considered asking her to go with him to get Ryan, wanting to prolong their time together, but what he really needed was some space from her. Away from her scent, and her voice, and those eyes that sucked him in.

Things between them had been even hotter than he'd expected. They'd fit together like a hand in a glove, and now thoughts were plaguing him that shouldn't be. This was sex, flat out. A release of tension. Some good times between friends. He wasn't ready for a relationship, that was for damned sure.

So then why did he miss her already?

Chapter Five

As Chandra left the barn, she did her level best to keep her shit together. The fact that Jax hadn't asked her to go along to pick up Ryan with him had stung a little, but it was what she'd expected from him. He obviously wanted to make a point that this was going to be exactly what he'd said. Friends with benefits.

It was his behavior afterwards that had been flat out confounding. He'd seemed so eager to find out if she'd be around later that evening, and so focused in on her. Kind of like a high school boy with a crush, which was ridiculous.

She smothered down the hope that burned in her heart and tried to keep her feet flat on the ground as she headed back toward the homestead. Jax had been totally up-front from the beginning. She wasn't his mate or even his girlfriend. They were friends, and she needed to make sure she didn't let the bonus stuff go to her head or she was going to be in deep trouble.

It wasn't easy to do, though, as little tremors still rocked her. Every detail played like a movie in her head. The line of his jaw, the feel of his skin, the way he filled her so perfectly. She'd felt so good wrapped in his arms, face buried in his neck. Even now, she felt boneless, fluid, like mercury.

Big deal; great sex. Get over it, you sap.

Wrapped in her own world, she was halfway to the house before she noted the strong scent of Chanel lingering in the air. Puzzled, she inhaled deeply, and again the overpowering perfume crowded her senses. Amber had left almost two hours ago. Out here in the open air, with this breeze, the scent should have been almost imperceptible by now. Especially since Amber had only gone from the door to her taxi.

Or had she…

Chandra's hackles rose, and she picked up her pace to a jog. By the time she got through front door, the scent had all but dissipated, but her discomfort had not. Something wasn't right. She knew it in her bones.

"Hey, how's it going?" Amalie stood in the foyer, her pretty, round face split into a smile. She was armed with her camera, as usual, and seemed to be on her way out.

"Pretty good. Just came back in from a run with Jax, you?" Chandra tried to keep her tone light. No point in worrying the alpha's mate over what might be nothing.

"Fine, thanks. Everything okay with you? You look a little…spooked." Her perceptive gaze searched Chandra's face.

Spooked was the perfect word for how she felt. Filled with a vague but overwhelming sense of unrest. Maybe it was lack of sleep combined with nerves over what had happened with Jax.

And maybe that scent had triggered some residual—albeit, irrational—jealousy and you're being a paranoid fool.

It was true, she realized with a start. Despite Jax's assurances that nothing had happened between them, she still couldn't shake her irritation over seeing that woman with her hands on him. And that was before he'd been hers.

Not that he was hers now.

"Nope, all good." She smiled at Amalie so hard that her flaming cheeks hurt, but she could feel herself cracking under the other woman's intense scrutiny. Did she look as freshly sexed as she felt?

"I don't think so. Something weird is...holy shit!" Amalee squealed, setting her camera down on the side table in the foyer before grabbing Chandra's hands. "You guys did it, didn't you?" She scrunched her pert nose. "Don't lie. I can smell him on you."

Damn that woman and her eerily keen nose. She'd only been a werewolf for four months, but she was already in tune with her newly-hyperaware senses in a way that never ceased to astonish Chandra. She'd been sure the fact that she and Jax had made love under the spray of the shower would mask his scent enough to pass it off as incidental contact, not worth mentioning.

Guess not.

"Oh, I can't wait to tell Liam. I told him weeks ago this was going to happen. The way you two look at each other." Amalie fanned herself and pretended to faint before giving her a smug grin. "Totally called it. So is this public news yet or do I have to keep hush hush?"

"Um...it's not...we're not..." She and Jax hadn't discussed whether they were going to try to keep their little arrangement a secret. Better to play it safe. "If you can keep it quiet for a while, I'd appreciate it."

Amalie lifted her hands to her lips and mimicked locking them shut. "You have my word."

Which was good enough for Chandra. The alpha's new mate had proven to be a fantastic addition to the pack and already Chandra trusted her more than she had most of her old pack, who she'd grown up with. It was a testament to Liam that he'd found a woman as morally grounded as he was and had molded his pack to be. If she made a promise, she'd do her damnedest to keep it.

Chandra let out a breath and tipped her head in thanks. "Great. If something changes, I'll let you know. I've got to run out and do some errands, though." And hopefully catch a rat while she was at it. *Speaking of which...* "Hey, is Liam around?"

The security cameras and recordings were kept in the alpha's office, and she was dying to get a look and see if Amber had truly left when that taxi had arrived. At the same time, she didn't want to call attention to Jax's overnight indiscretion. If something was truly wrong, she'd have no choice, but there was no point in putting him on Liam's bad side yet. Jax was overrun with guilt as it was, and the last thing she wanted was to add to his burden. No, she'd check it out herself and if she sensed a bigger issue, she'd go to Jax directly.

Luckily, of all the scenarios Chandra had run through, the most likely seemed that Amber was feeling put off by Jax's rejection. Maybe she couldn't fathom why she'd been sent packing, unfulfilled, and had decided to spy on Jax a little to figure it out.

Did that make the woman a little nutty? Yes. But was she dangerous? Probably not.

"He's working in his office. There's an investment opportunity on Jade Lake and he's obsessed with getting a boat now." Amalie winked at her conspiratorially. "You know our boys and their toys, right?"

Chandra forced a laugh, but her stomach churned. Was that going to be the thing, now? Couples jokes? Maybe she should've explained about the friends with benefits thing after all. She didn't want Amalie getting her hopes up that it could be something more.

Like you are?

She pushed the subconscious thought aside abruptly and said a quick goodbye to Amalie before scurrying down the hall like her ass was on fire, hoping to avoid contact with the rest of her pack.

If Jax had meant what he said, and wanted to keep it strictly sex, there was no point in letting anyone else in on their arrangement. Things got around, and the last thing she wanted was for poor Ryan to be affected by this. It would be terrible for him to get ideas about her becoming his stepmom, but it would be just as bad if he wasn't ready to face the idea of his father moving on.

Someday she'd have a family of her own, and, if she was lucky, a son like Ryan. One whose laugh would warm her from the inside out. And a mate who made her feel safe and special, and loved.

A tingle spread from her chest as she recalled her time with Jax. Whatever happened, even if it ended tomorrow, she'd never forget it.

She was halfway up the stairs when she caught it again…Amber's stale but lingering perfume. Chandra's instincts went white hot, another stark warning that something was amiss. She wasn't here anymore, that much was for certain. Chandra would smell her now that she'd tuned her senses to the other woman's scent, but this couldn't be ignored for even another second.

She headed to her bedroom, on a mission to solve this mystery before she did anything else for the day. Snatching up her cell phone, she tapped out a quick Google search.

The Naughty Kitty wasn't far, maybe twenty miles away. She tapped her finger lightly on the case of her phone, mulling over her options. She hated to admit it, but Amber was too pretty to be relegated to the strip club's afternoon shift. She had the face and body for prime time, so odds were, if Chandra went there during the day time, Amber wouldn't be there. She could use the opportunity to ask around, see if there was anything strange about her, or if maybe she was a notorious weirdo stalker at least. Then again, if she waited until tonight, she could try to talk to the rat face to face.

Decisions, decisions.

She couldn't get into Liam's office right now, and the need to be doing *something* to get to the bottom of things won out. She washed up a second time, using a fair dose of mandarin orange body lotion to mask Jax's scent, before changing and jogging back down the stairs and straight out the door.

When she arrived at The Naughty Kitty less than an hour later, she was stunned to find the parking lot half full. Granted, it was the weekend, but the concept that there were at least thirty grown men so impatient to see some naked tail that they figured noon was a good time to get out to the club was surprising to say the least.

Note to self: If in need of fast cash, consider stripping.

She shoved open her car door and stepped out, taking a deep breath of the crisp air. It was all going to be fine. Maybe she was being paranoid, but that was okay. Her pack was her family, and family was all she had. Better to be paranoid than caught off guard.

She strode toward the door, smirking when she saw the sign hanging above it featuring a female cartoon cat with a Jessica Rabbit body encased in a bustier. Naughty Kitty, indeed.

She stepped through the doors, conscious of her carriage. Time to look confident and comfortable. The fact that she was a woman alone would definitely cause some speculation, but she'd thought ahead.

"Can I help you?"

An attractive and well-dressed woman in her early thirties stood behind a podium in front of the door, smiling inquisitively.

"Um, yes." She perused the space with interest, surprised for the second time by this establishment. The lounge area was actually really nice. What she'd assumed would be a tawdry dump with a lot of red velvet and gaudily made up chippies walking around with their boobs out was actually quite the opposite. It was dim, but very clean and glamorous in an old

Hollywood sense. Wide, curve-backed couches, low slung tables, and a gorgeous, gleaming walnut bar gave it a ritzy feel that she was digging.

The room was empty, save for her and a couple members of the staff, but she could hear slow, grooving music oozing through the curtains to the right.

She faced the brunette, admiring her classic red lipstick and fifties-style dress before replying. "I was hoping to fill out an application."

To her credit, the hostess didn't even flinch. "Server or dancer?"

Chandra glanced down and almost laughed. Her b-on-a-good-day cups weren't exactly the kind men threw money at, but she was oddly flattered. "Server."

"I will go grab you a form, and you can have a seat at the bar. Trudy will get you a drink while you wait."

She sat down at the bar and a redhead in a tasteful but sexy corset top came over. "Hi there, I'm Trudy. You looking to bartend or cocktail waitress?"

She hadn't thought that far ahead and shrugged. "I'm easy. Either or."

"Adaptable. I like it." Trudy gestured behind her to the array of bottles. "So what'll it be?"

Thinking it would encourage girl talk, Chandra ordered a glass of Merlot, making sure to give Trudy a large tip.

"This place is so nice, I've never been inside," she said, before taking a sip of her wine.

Trudy's grin didn't waver and she nodded enthusiastically. "It's a good place to work, all things considered. Not what I imagined I'd be doing at thirty, but my student loans aren't going to pay themselves," she said with a good-natured chuckle.

Her warmth made Chandra feel like a heel, but she'd come here for a reason, and it wasn't to make friends.

"I hear you there. Hey, I have a friend who works here, actually. Maybe you know her. Amber. Petite, long blond hair?"

Trudy instantly shut down, and looked away, her face going pale. "Shit, I knew something was wrong. She's been so strapped for cash lately, and all this drama with losing her house. I won't lie, it's been affecting her big time." She paused and wrapped one arm around her stomach, eyes going wide. "God, she's not dead, is she?"

Chandra set down her glass, her pulse racing out of control. Jesus, what had she stumbled onto? "No, no, nothing like that. At least, not when I saw her this morning. What would make you ask that?"

Trudy's shoulders slumped a little in relief, but she stiffened and backed away a moment later, hands held up in front of her defensively.

"I don't want any trouble. She...she was here with a weird-looking guy. Older. In his fifties. I overheard them talking money. I don't know what he was into, but he looked...off. Not right in the head. I told her when he left that she should watch her ass. I've seen those types before and they can get some strange ideas in their heads. I don't know if she kept the money or her date with him, but it definitely got me worrying about her."

Chandra chewed on that information, considering her next move. Amber's extracurricular activities had nothing to do with her or Jax, now that he wasn't planning to see her again, but that didn't make her any more comfortable about the situation.

If Amber really hadn't left when she'd pretended to, maybe jealousy wasn't her motivation after all. Maybe she was so desperate for money that she'd seen the lux accommodations and decided to case the joint? If she planned to rob them, she was in for a rough go of it. Wolves were territorial by nature and her pack wouldn't take kindly to a human trying to steal from them.

She opened her mouth to ask another question, but Trudy's chin was raised and she looked like she was done talking. In fact, she was already moving away, suddenly eager to polish the glasses on the other end of the bar.

Chandra plucked another ten dollar bill and a business card from her pocket and left them on the bar before sliding off the stool and standing.

"I appreciate it more than you know, Trudy. If you think she's in trouble or want to tell me anything, call me. I promise she'll never know that we talked."

By the time she got back to the house, the anger she'd felt that morning had softened, mixing with confusion and something else she didn't want to feel toward Amber.

Sympathy.

She couldn't afford to feel sorry for someone who might be a threat to her pack, no matter what the circumstance. Later that night, once everyone had gone to bed, she'd see if the security tapes shed any light on things. Hopefully, they'd show nothing out of the ordinary and she could forget all about Amber Jansen.

If not? Well, she'd handle it.

And then Amber Jansen would truly be in need of some sympathy.

Chapter Six

As Jax entered the house with Ryan following behind, he still had a bounce in his step from his morning activities. His time with Chandra had been amazing, and he was seriously hoping they would be able to go for round two later that night.

He tried to remember the last time he'd felt so good. Before Sara had died, for sure. His heart clenched in his chest at the thought, but it was quickly replaced by a bittersweet warmth as he turned and looked at their son. Ryan resembled his mother so much. Had her gentle way and soft, kind eyes.

As he gazed at his boy, something inside Jax clicked with enough force that his knees nearly buckled. He'd been so caught up in his own pain and guilt that he'd missed something vital. It didn't matter if he had to look at Sara's picture to remember exactly what she looked like because the best part of her would be with him forever. It was right in front of him all along.

His throat burned and he cleared it with a gruff cough.

"Whatcha looking at?" Ryan asked, his cherubic face squeezed into a frown.

"Just you, Buddy. You look so much like your mom sometimes."

Ryan regarded his father warily through blue eyes. "I thought you didn't want to talk about her?"

His gut churned at those words, but he pushed forward. It was a new day, and there was no point in dwelling on his past mistakes. All he could do was make today better than yesterday, for both him and his son.

"Yeah, well, that's going to have to change. See, it was hard for me to talk about your mom after she died because it hurt so much. But I'm thinking maybe it's time we start. What do you think about that?"

Ryan looked thoughtful for a moment. "Yeah. Yeah, I think it's a real good idea, because I don't want to forget her, you know?" At the end, his voice clogged with tears, and Jax knelt before him and hugged him close, ruffling his mop of blonde curls.

"We won't forget her. We'll never forget her. I'm sorry that I haven't wanted to talk about her, and I am so sorry that my own sadness kept me from seeing how much you needed to. But I promise to do better, okay?"

Ryan nodded earnestly and wiped his tears away with a fist. "Okay."

"Now, come on, let's go get some hot chocolate and take it upstairs. We'll get a bunch of pictures from the attic and spread them out on the bed and talk about all those great years we got to spend with your mom. Did you know that, when you were a baby, you were so small we used to give you baths in the sink?"

The boy's laughter skimmed over him like a song as they talked. And for the first time in almost a year, he felt truly, honestly happy.

A few hours later, Ryan had gotten his fill of dad time and bolted off to the family room to play video games with Billy. Jax made some business calls, but after only a few, found his thoughts returning again and again to his shower partner. She was never far from his thoughts lately, now more than ever.

He set his cell down and went in search of her. Why deny himself the pleasure of her company just because they made an agreement to keep things easy? Hanging out for a while before dinner didn't have to be complicated. Hell, they'd done it plenty of times before they'd ever spent time together naked.

"Have you seen Chandra?"

Amalie sat on the great room floor, dozens of nature shots splayed out before her. "Hi to you too," she said with a grin. "I saw her earlier, but I was out most of the day. Did you check her bedroom?"

The question was innocent enough, but the gleam in her eyes when she said it had him stopping in his tracks. "Not yet. If she's behind closed doors, she's probably busy."

Like the rest of the pack, Chandra held a position within their real estate development corporation. She was on the business side of things with he and Liam, and spent at least a few hours every day both online and on the phone getting information about zoning and permits. She also worked closely with Billy and Maggie and the rest of the crew on getting construction timelines together. All in all, she was great at her job, and an integral part of making things run smoothly, so he hated to interrupt her if she was working, but it was the weekend.

And you're already making excuses to be with her more than normal. Down boy.

He focused his attention back on Amalie, who was still watching him with a bemused smile. He opened his mouth and then let it snap shut again. If she did know something, even if he asked, she wasn't going to tell him. Girl code and all that. And if she didn't know something, he'd be telling her something just by asking. He played it safe and backed out of the room with a tip of his head. "Catch up with you later."

Amalie called after him as he took the stairs two at a time. "No hurry. Dinner won't be for another hour or so."

He approached Chandra's door and knocked twice in rapid succession. A friendly, uncomplicated knock if he'd ever heard one.

"Come in."

He stepped into her room to find her on all fours, folded into an upside down, contorted V-shape. "Jesus, are you okay?"

She scowled up at him. "Of course I'm okay. It's yoga. Down dog. I'm feeling tense and I thought it might help me relax."

He considered telling her he knew a better way to help her relax, but managed to keep it to himself. If he wanted to spend time with her again, he had to make sure he kept their agreement in mind and break up the intensity of their sexual encounters with something lighter. Mellow, easy times, like friends did.

At least, until later that night, when he hoped he could invoke the benefits part of their verbal contract for a second time.

She'd changed again, and was rocking a pair of form-fitting yoga pants that did astonishing things for her already spectacular ass. His cock nudged the zipper of his jeans as she rolled gracefully to her feet.

"Want to hang out?"

She seemed to hesitate, but then nodded slowly. "Okay. And do what?"

"We have an hour until dinner," he said, repeating what Amalie had told him. Carnal thoughts of the things they could do to one another in an hour rose to his mind and he pushed them away. "We could play cards, maybe? Or chess?"

She turned and eyed him quizzically. "What about pool?"

He laughed out loud then. Chandra was a notorious pool shark and never passed up an opportunity to trounce one of them when she got the chance. That was fine with him, he could take it. And if he got to ogle that ass a little when she bent to make her shots, well, that wouldn't hurt his feelings one bit.

He led the way down the stairs, happy to note that whatever had been occupying her thoughts seemed to fade into the background as she talked shit to him.

"Watch and learn, pal. School is officially in session," she announced, gesturing to the long, felt-covered table with a flourish as they stepped into the game room. "Should we keep it short and sweet, or should I give you a fighting chance?"

He loved to see her like this. Confident, in her element. It made his blood go hot.

Then again, he also liked to see her frazzled. Undone. A little nervous. "Short and sweet isn't really my bag. I like to take my time, and we already rushed through one thing today."

Her eyes went wide and she went silent for a full ten seconds before recovering. "Ha. Good one." Her voice sounded tinny as she strode around to the back of the table and pulled out the rack. "Best of three, loser does the dishes tonight."

They had a dishwasher, so that wouldn't be much of a hardship, but he had better stakes in mind.

"How about best of three, winner chooses the prize?" He hadn't intended for his voice to go husky, or for his legs to carry him close enough that their bodies almost brushed.

She took a step back and gave him the deer in the headlights look again, throat working as she swallowed hard.

"Is it going to be like this?" she asked, finally, running a hand through her hair. "Like, are you going to flirt with me all the time now, or just in private? I'm not trying to complicate things already, but I need to know."

If he'd wanted her flustered, he'd succeeded, and it was almost enough to make him feel guilty.

Almost.

He closed the gap between them again, and she craned her neck to look up at him.

"Amalie already figured it out just by sniffing me." She was breathless, and he could see the pulse in her neck beating wildly. "And it's not going to be long before the others know too, if we're not careful."

He backed away until he was out of range of the scent of her skin and picked up a pool cue, pretending to test it for weight while his thoughts raced.

So he'd been reading Amalie right. She knew. He expected to feel stressed by the knowledge, but as he poked around for some negative feelings on the subject, he found himself shrugging.

"Fuck it. I don't really care what they know. We're grown." Not to mention, with libidos as high as they were for weres, it was common to have sexual partners without there necessarily being a relationship present.

"And Ryan?" She eyed him warily and he set down the cue.

Her concerns on that front were valid and he nodded. "Okay, so we act like business as usual around the others, being extra careful around Ryan unless..." He trailed off, realizing what he'd been about to say and knowing he shouldn't say it.

Unless we take this to the next level.

Saying it would only muddy the waters. He'd made strides with getting past the devastation of losing Sara, but sharing his life with another woman? Having a true relationship? That was something he still couldn't wrap his head around yet, even with Chandra.

"Got it. Business as usual, especially around Ryan." She held his gaze for a tense moment before snatching up a pool cue. "Let's get this party started, shall we?"

***

"Can someone pass me the pumpernickel?"

Business as usual, her ass.

Chandra picked up the basket piled high with different types of breads and handed it to Liam across the table with a stiff smile.

AWAKENING

Dinner was interminable. Every minute felt like twenty as their friends teased and joked and ate. Course after course of thick, hot clam chowder, ham and mashed potatoes, roasted lamb and orange-glazed duck. The procession of food seemed endless. She usually loved it—werewolves were a hungry bunch and thrived on the fellowship and camaraderie of sharing a meal—but tonight? Tonight, all she wanted to do was find out what punishment Jax planned on meting out.

He reached out to grab a buttered roll and his shoulder brushed her breast.

"Excuse me," he murmured. But as he retracted his hand, he brushed by her again, this time grazing her sensitive nipple.

She gasped as heat suffused her from head to toe. With a quick glance around, she confirmed that no one had noticed. They were busy chattering away about their day, the food and pack business. In fact, if it hadn't been for the tension pouring off Jax in waves, she might have thought it was an accident.

It was exactly that sexual energy that had thrown her pool game right into the shitter. Every time she'd tried to make a shot, she could feel his hot gaze on her and she could barely think straight, never mind shoot straight. He'd beat her handily, two games in a row. Now she was in gambler's debt without any clue exactly what she owed him.

A vision of the two of them in the deep tub in Jax's bathroom burrowed its way into her mind. Him behind her, propped up against the white porcelain, her lying back against him, gripping the edges of the tub as he cupped her breasts, toying with her nipples.

She shoveled a fork-load of potatoes into her mouth to keep from groaning. He'd been using their wolfy connection to send mini-porno flicks starring the two of them to her mind for the past twenty minutes, and they were fucking with her head big time. She pushed back, sending him a vision of her dumping an entire roasted duck into his lap and a bowl of corn onto his head.

He let out a crack of laughter and everyone paused mid-conversation and looked his way.

"What's so funny?" Liam asked, brows raised quizzically.

Jax's grin didn't waiver. "Chandra just told me a joke." He went on to share some random anecdote with the pack, giving her a much-needed moment to get a grip.

If this was how friends with benefits went, where every interaction they had was laced with sexual tension making it impossible to be in a room together and behave normally, she was in for some trouble. If she hadn't been in love with him before, their soul-searing connection that morning had all but sealed the deal for her, and every moment they spent together with him treating her the way a lover would only set the hook deeper.

She hadn't wanted to tell him how she really felt, knowing it could very well scare him away altogether, but she was realizing more and more that she wasn't cut out for this. If he was sure he didn't have the capacity to ever love again, she needed to step back and reconsider this decision no matter how much it killed her.

She vowed to talk to him about that ASAP—she shifted restlessly in her seat—or after they had sex one more time, at least. Although, if he kept up these antics, they'd both be done before they even got through dinner.

For another half hour, they played their parts, but every time she got too comfortable, Jax was there, using his dirty thoughts to throw her off balance. By the time the dessert dishes were cleared, she was a hot, trembling mess.

He walked by her, arms loaded with dishes, and dipped his head low to whisper in her ear. "Amalie and Liam are taking all the cubs to get ice cream and to the drive in. We have two hours, minimum. Meet me in my room. I'd like to collect my prize."

He nipped her earlobe, and walked away, leaving her standing there, nodding wordlessly despite the doubts crowding in. One more time, to take it all in, commit every kiss, every touch, every stroke to memory, before she pulled away from him in a last ditch effort at self-preservation.

She said a quick goodbye to the moviegoers and ran up the stairs, giving herself a stern talking to the whole way. Booty call or not, she still had to make sure she got into Liam's office at some point tonight to put her Amber fears to rest, one way or another. She'd spend an hour with Jax and then do what needed to be done.

She stopped off at her room first to brush her teeth before walking what felt like the Green Mile to Jax's room. It had been so much less nerve-jangling when it had been spontaneous. At least she could blame her lack of self-discipline on the fact that she hadn't had the time to think it through.

Now, though, there was no such comfort. She knew exactly what she was doing, and was doing it anyway, turning a blind eye to the consequences. Like eating an entire box of Valentine's chocolates. Only Jax was better than chocolates.

He opened the door before she'd even had a chance to knock.

"What took you so long?" He pulled her in and closed the door behind them.

She braced herself, ready and waiting for him to pounce. The pressure between her thighs had been building all through dinner and, nerves or no, she couldn't wait to tear his clothes off. To have him rocking deep inside her again until they both exploded.

"Don't go anywhere. I'm going to start the bath," he said softly, tracing her bottom lip with his forefinger before padding to the bathroom.

She stared after him, stunned. "Are you serious right now? Can't we do that another time? I really-"

"Nope," he called out over the sound of running water. "I've been thinking about this all night long and I'm calling in my marker."

She shifted from foot to foot, and crossed her arms over her chest, debating whether to test him. Surely, if she just walked up and grabbed his man-kit and took the reins, he wouldn't stop her. They could take a bath afterword.

"Not going to work," he said, stepping back into sight.

Her breath caught as she took in the view. He was barechested already, his wide shoulders looking like they needed her nails digging into them. The thick, ropey muscles of his abs looking like they needed her fingers dragging across them. The narrow trail of hair disappearing beneath his low-slung jeans looking like it needed her tongue to follow.

"You're beautiful." She hadn't realized she'd spoken aloud and her cheeks warmed.

He prowled toward her, the intensity of his gaze making her skin prickle with goose bumps. "I'm glad you think so, Chan."

He paused a few feet away and let his hands drift to the button on his jeans. She reached for him then, intent on helping him with his zipper because, Jesus, he was taking his sweet time about it.

"I won't be rushed. Not this time," he murmured.

He hooked a finger under her shirt collar and yanked, his unbridled power splitting it down the center.

"I liked that shirt," she murmured, only half-aware of what she was saying. The expression on his face was like that of a starving man, and was distracting as hell.

"So I'll buy you a new one," he promised, before tipping his head to her neck and pressing his mouth to her collarbone. She shivered, the soft, tentative touch adding another log to the already stoked fire. But she needed more than that. So much more.

He continued his journey downward, trailing his mouth over the modest swell of her breasts before his busy fingers worked the catch on her bra effortlessly. He tugged it over her arms and tossed it aside with her tattered shirt.

"That's what I've been thinking about all day. You, bare-breasted, eyes shining, short of breath, waiting for me."

He pulled her into the circle of his arms and slanted his mouth over hers. She needed no coaxing, and kissed him with everything she had. Their tongues wound together in an intimate dance, and his thick arousal pressed insistently against her belly.

She pulled back and gasped, "Please, Jax. Bath later." She nipped his mouth sharply and he groaned before stepping back.

"You tempt me, woman, but I'm going to get my way this time." He worked her stretchy pants over her hips with exquisite slowness, watching with hot eyes as more of her was bared to him. "I can't unsee it. I'd imagined what you looked like naked before, but now that I know, it's burned in my brain and I can't get it out of my mind."

His voice was low and gritty with need, the sound of it sending a bolt of electricity through her. He might not love her, but he wanted her, and at that moment, it was enough.

He dropped to his knees and slid her pants and underwear down the rest of the way in one motion. Clutching his broad shoulders, she stepped out of them quickly and kicked them aside. He didn't stand right away and she fought the urge to cover herself.

"You're so beautiful here." His warm breath washed over her core and she gripped his shoulders tighter. "So soft, and pretty and sweet."

When he lapped at her, long and slow, she let out a moan.

"That feels..." she trailed off as words failed her, but he didn't wait for her to continue. Instead, he settled in closer, gripping her hips in his hands before diving in again. His mouth was glorious, hot and clever. His agile tongue finding her clit and rubbing it with single-minded intent. Gently at first, a teasing flick, and then harder, a deep massage.

She was writhing within thirty seconds, aching for him to finish it.

"Please, don't stop," she whimpered, hips fluttering helplessly, so close to the edge she could almost taste it.

His fingers tightened, anchoring her closer as he pulled her relentlessly toward a mind-blowing climax.

She felt the pressure building, higher and faster. He released one hip and forced her thighs apart before sliding two fingers deep inside her. The instant fullness combined with the drag of his skin against hers was the final straw. He thrust again and worked the nub of nerves with his tongue and she screamed. The orgasm was like a battering ram, destroying everything in its path as it crashed into her. She didn't know her name or where she was, but she knew him and his mouth and those fingers.

Jax.

"God, that's so fucking hot," he grunted, fingers still seated deep inside her as he pulled back to look up at her. "Now, get into the bathtub, because I'm not even close to done with you." He slid his hand from her and stood, taking her arm to steady her.

She didn't even realize she was still shaking like a leaf. She wet her lips and nodded dimly, trying to find her way back to reality. He seemed to realize she was still dazed and scooped her up without another word. When he set her on the cool tile floor, she realized he still had half his clothes on. That wouldn't do at all.

She undressed him much the same way he'd done to her. Peppering his skin with kisses, caressing his lean stomach, whispering words of praise. When he was as naked as she was, she stood back and admired her handiwork.

His cock was stiff, jutting out from between his muscular legs, and it was all she could do not to drop to her knees and take him into her mouth.

"Stop looking at me like that. It's killing me," he uttered through gritted teeth. "There will be time for that later."

He gestured toward the massive, now-filled bathtub and she climbed in, hissing as the hot water enveloped her. She'd seen the vision he'd sent her, so she knew exactly how he'd pictured it. Shimmying forward, she made room for him behind her.

He climbed in, and pulled her back against him until their bodies were flush. His erection pushed against her lower back and she squirmed, aching to get closer. In spite of the monumental orgasm, she was still ravenous for him and aching.

"This is how I wanted it," he rasped, the puff of air from his lips tickling her ear. "So I could reach every part of you. See every inch of you. See my hands on your silky skin."

He brought his arms around her and cupped both of her breasts on a sigh.

"So good."

He tugged at her already spiked nipples, sending a shot of heat pulsing between her thighs, building the ache up faster than a wildfire. She whispered his name and let her head fall to the side. She couldn't reach any part of him, so there was no point in fighting it. She'd let him take control.

For now.

He worked her body into a frenzy, all the while whispering words of encouragement. When he pressed her forward so he could stand, she moved to rise with him, but he pressed her back.

"I'll only be a second." His eyes were filled with promise as he gazed down at her and reached for the shower head.

Her already galloping heart went into overdrive as he reclaimed his place behind her. She settled back against him, letting her thighs fall open, desperate for what she knew he could give her. She was almost mindless with need when he slid the showerhead between her thighs and pressed the button.

"Oh, God!" She arched her back as the water rushed out, pounded against her clit in a mind-melting, sensual assault. "Holy shit," she groaned, tossing her head against his chest as he worked the showerhead in circles against her aching flesh. Slow at first, then more quickly. He pushed another button and the steady stream turned to a low, vibrating pulse that made her toes curl.

He pushed her forward, his grunt low in her ear as he bit out a command. "Up on your knees, Chan. Now."

She did as he said, straddling him backward, wild with need, quaking with desire. He kept the pressure of the showerhead firmly against her and the tub squeaked as he positioned himself beneath her. A breathless second later, he was driving her hips downward, impaling her on his giant, swollen cock.

She moaned wordlessly, letting her eyes drift shut as he continued, wedging himself deep inside her until he could go no further. He didn't have to move an inch. Filled with his thick cock, water battering at her sensitized clit, she came in a hard rush, crying out his name as she rocked over him.

"Take it, that's it babe, take what you need," he urged, flexing against her, using one hand to help her grind against him.

She sucked in a breath, trying to make sense of his words over the rush of blood in her ears. He held her that way, pinned to him, until she stilled a long moment later. Her body twitched over him when she realized he was still hard as stone.

Perfect.

She swallowed hard and rose on shaky legs until their bodies separated. "You had your way. Now I'll have mine."

He lunged for her, and protested, but this time, she wouldn't be denied. She turned off the water and plucked the showerhead from his unresisting hand and set it aside. Then she sank to her knees again, this time facing him.

His face was a mask of agony and desire as she cupped him gently, marveling at his size. She'd felt it, and seen it in passing, but close up, he was a marvel. His cock was long and thick, and so hard, if felt like bone. When she squeezed, it jerked in her hand.

"Fuck," he growled, spearing his fingers into her hair. "Your hands are-"

He broke off with a groan as she dipped her head and swallowed him whole, without preamble, sucking him deep into her throat with a hum of satisfaction.

His hands tightened in her hair and he arched his hips forward, anchoring her there for a second before releasing her. She used his thighs to steady herself and satisfaction flowed through her as she felt his quads quaking. That was good. She was shaking too. He'd taken her to heaven and back, more than once, and she was going to make damned sure he followed.

"If you keep it up, it's going to be game over," he muttered, his voice low and tight.

She responded by sucking harder, hollowing out her cheeks, stroking the swollen head of his cock with her tongue with each pass.

"Jesus Christ."

He tried to pull away, but she pushed him back and held him in place by his hips, desperate to feel him explode in her mouth. Needing to wreck him the way he'd wrecked her.

"Chan- Oh, shit."

She knew the second the tide had turned. Instead of pulling back, he was arching forward, hips pumping him a little further into her mouth each time. His cock grew impossibly large and she did her best to take every inch of him, opening her throat, letting his thick heat fill her.

"Ahh, fuck!"

He cupped her head then, pinning her against him as he exploded, bursts of hot liquid spurting against the back of her throat. His legs were flexed so tight, they could have been made of steel and she clung to them, a soul deep satisfaction coursing through her.

She'd made it good for him, she knew she had, and if this was their last time together, at least he would remember it.

He pulled away gently, his breath still coming in harsh gasps. "That was amazing." He pulled her back against him again and wrapped his arms around her. "Totally amazing."

Her heart gave a squeeze, his words adding one more dash of sweet to the bitter. She'd just have to hope it would be enough to last her a lifetime.

They stayed wrapped together until the water grew cool, and when she stepped out, he was waiting with a giant, fluffy towel. She tried to take it from him, but he resisted, using it himself to dry her from head to toe. The gesture made her throat ache with unshed tears and she stepped back, pasting on a smile that she hoped would hold long enough for her to get out of the room.

"I've got a couple things to do," she said softly. "And Ryan will be back soon."

A frown creased his forehead and his gaze searched her face. "Everything okay?"

"Yeah, everything's great."

She wasn't going to have a conversation with him about wanting to end their arrangement right after they'd had sex. Especially not with him standing there, still naked. She'd be far too easily swayed, even if he wasn't trying. Tomorrow was soon enough, when they were both dressed and there was a little more distance from the last time he'd been inside her.

"Seriously, all good. I just don't want to get caught sneaking out of your room. I'll see you in the morning, all right?"

He eyed her dubiously but then nodded. "Yeah, okay."

She donned her clothes quickly with her back to him and then rushed out the door before she could change her mind. Guilt pricked at her hard, but she pushed it aside.

At least she hadn't lied about everything. She did have a couple things to do before the night was over. Number one on her list?

Getting a quick look at those security tapes before Liam got back and deal with Amber Jansen.

Chapter Seven

As she stepped into her little Victorian home, Amber made straight for the light switch and checked every corner of the room. She couldn't shake the eerie feeling she was being followed. Interacting again with the angry woman at Jax's that morning had been uncomfortable enough, but what she'd thought she'd seen after that?

Freaked her right the fuck out.

She set her bag down on the table and made a cup of oolong to soothe her jangling nerves. While she waited for the kettle to boil, she went upstairs, scrubbed off the makeup from that night's show, and changed into jeans.

Back in the kitchen, she sat and sipped her tea, glancing at her watch. He'd said he'd be there by eleven, but it was going on quarter after now, and with every tick of the clock, she was regretting her decision more and more.

When Tobias Wheeler had first approached her at The Naughty Kitty a couple of weeks before, she'd been skeptical. But once he'd produced half the money up-front—five thousand dollars cash—she'd put aside her reservations and tried to listen with an open mind. The burlesque business was booming, but she was in a jam and five grand would go a long way to getting her out of it.

Wheeler had explained that he was a private investigator hired by a coalition of victims in a string of large-scale burglaries over the past year. Millions of dollars in paintings, antiques, and jewelry had been stolen, and he had finally found the culprits. Unfortunately, there was no concrete evidence. He needed someone on the inside to get some information, get a look at the property, maybe snap a few pictures to start building a case to present to police.

He'd given her a picture of Jax, told her where he liked to hang out, and said that her job would be to get to know him and wrangle an invitation to his house. If he didn't take the bait and wasn't interested in her, as long as she'd given her best effort, she could keep the five thousand. If she got in, managed to get a look around and some basic information, maybe a few pictures, he would follow up with another five.

At the time, she'd ignored all the risks. All she'd seen was a light at the end of a long, dark tunnel. With the creditors and tax collectors breathing down her neck, threatening to take the house her beloved Nana had left her, it was a no-brainer. Besides, he'd assured her no one would get hurt. In fact, she was doing her civic duty.

But as she waited for Wheeler, she was second-guessing herself, big time. First off, Jax had been really sweet to her. Even though they hadn't slept together—the original plan had been for her to feign passing out, but his chivalry had made that unnecessary—he'd still offered her his bed, given her cab fare, and treated her with respect, despite her playing the blonde bimbo routine to the hilt. Usually guys took that to mean it was okay to treat a woman like trash.

But not Jax.

Humiliation burned the guilt away as she recalled the look of disdain on the redhead's face. *Chandra.* The other woman wasn't a fan, so clearly Amber's act had been convincing, but for some reason that didn't make her feel any better.

She gave a snort of self-disgust. What did she care if some cat burglar thought she was stupid anyway? Just because Jax had been charming and seemed genuine, that didn't mean he was innocent. He could have been as insincere as she had been.

Then there was Chandra's behavior when Amber had asked her a few, simple questions. She had gotten jumpy at the mere mention of their living arrangement and business interests. That, combined with the staggering amount of expensive art and furniture in that house, did make Wheeler's story seem plausible.

Even as she reviewed the evidence over and over in her head, she couldn't quell that niggling feeling in her gut. The one that had her wondering why, if the items had indeed been stolen, they would be stupid enough to leave them out like that for anyone to see. Sheer arrogance that they wouldn't be caught? Then again, who knew what people were capable of? She only had to turn on the news to be reminded of that.

She pushed down her doubts and rifled through the stack of pictures and notes she'd compiled that morning. Not for the first time, she found herself particularly drawn to the images she had taken of the interior of the barn.

Why would anyone have a dozen outdoor showers? Maybe to wash off any evidence, change their clothes, and burn anything related to their crimes?

Again she gave herself a mental shake. None of it mattered to her one bit. Her job was complete. All she had to do now was hand the information over, collect her money and move on. No point in dwelling after the deed was done. She shoved the pictures into the bag in front of her and zipped it closed.

If only she could keep herself from dwelling on what else she had thought she'd seen…something way stranger than some outdoor showers.

She pushed the disturbing thought from her mind. Lack of sleep and a few drinks the night before had made her disoriented. That was all.

Before her goose bumps had subsided, a noise by the door caught her attention. She looked up with a start as the kitchen door swung open, heart careening out of control as her eyes lighted on a familiar but unexpected face.

Shit.

***

Chandra walked into Amber's house as if she had every right to be there. As she crossed the threshold, though, she wondered again if she should call Jax or one of her other packmates. Not that she'd need the backup to deal with one, miniature-sized human, but she might need them to keep her from murdering her.

Amber started visibly when she saw Chandra, and her freshly-scrubbed cheeks went pale.

She was afraid. That was good. Hopefully this little Q & A would go quickly.

Chandra grabbed a fussy little teak chair across from Amber, flipped it around and plopped down, straddling it backward. "Hey, there, toots. Mind telling me what the hell is going on?"

"Wh-what do you mean? And what are you doing here?"

"Look at me." Her voice echoed like a whip crack in the tiny kitchen.

Amber met her gaze and tried to look brave, but Chandra could smell her fear.

"I am going to give you one chance. One. Chance." She held up her index finger, irritated to note that it was shaking. She only hoped Amber realized that it wasn't trembling from fear, but from barely suppressed rage. "If I don't like your answer, I swear to you, you're going to wish you were never born."

Chandra indulged in a feral smile as Amber's throat worked furiously.

"Let me tell you what I know so far, that way you don't waste your one chance on a lie. I know you didn't really leave in the cab this morning. We have cameras that run the perimeter of the property. Imagine my surprise when I looked at the security footage from today and saw you walking out of the driveway and getting into a different taxi parked on the street. That was more than an hour after the first cab had left, supposedly with you in it. Strange, isn't it?"

She tipped her head and shrugged.

"Needless to say, I was curious...thinking maybe you'd left and then come back for something you had forgotten. But when I rewound the video further, I was surprised to see that the car I watched you get into was empty when it pulled onto the street, save for the driver. So you pretended to leave this morning, got out of the cab and basically trespassed on our property without informing anyone of your presence. That seems like highly suspicious behavior. Now, I'm going to ask you once again-" She stopped short as a faint scent tickled her nose. She began to rise as Amber cut in.

"Listen, I'm sorry. I didn't..." Her voice trailed off as her gaze flicked to something over Chandra's shoulder. "Wait, no!" Amber called out, but before Chandra could turn, a sharp pain registered in her neck, and her world went black.

Chapter Eight

Amber stared incredulously into the face of the man who had hired her, chilled to the bone. "What did you do to her?" she asked in a strangled whisper.

"She's fine," he said as he walked across the room, a dart gun in his hand. "It was just a sedative."

He crouched in front of Chandra, who was slumped over in her chair. He stared at her for a long moment, then turned to face Amber, his eyes burning with an almost feverish light.

"She followed you. I had hoped, but I couldn't be sure… Oh, what a specimen." Sweat had broken out on his upper lip despite the cold, and he stroked Chandra's hair. "She's perfect," he whispered.

Amber's body began to shake uncontrollably. "No, no, you can't do that to someone," she muttered through chattering teeth as she tried to make sense of it all. "I'm calling the police." Like she should have done when he'd first come to her with his crazy offer.

She reached into her purse for her cell phone but froze when she saw the expression on Tobias Wheeler's face as he straightened, pointing the gun in her direction.

"Go ahead and call the police the second I leave. Make sure you tell them about how you trespassed on their property, took pictures, and spied on them. But she and I will be long gone by the time they get here, and you'll be the one in the cell. You're knee-deep in this." He screwed his flushed face into a twisted smile. If it was meant to reassure her, it failed miserably. "Or you could just let it go, forget we ever met, and everything can go back to normal for you. I know it doesn't seem like it right now, but I'm the good guy. You don't know what you're dealing with. Don't you see? I'm not the monster here."

He stood, gun still trained in her direction, and grabbed the tote bag from the table. As he rifled through it, she took the time to look around the kitchen in search of a weapon. He stood directly between her and the wooden block that held all the knives, but if she moved quickly enough, she might be able to grab the cast iron skillet on the stove.

Her heart hammered wildly in her chest, and she was on number two in her mental countdown to three when he faced her again.

"You did a good job with the pictures," he said with an approving smile, "So I hate to have to do this, but it seems like we're at an impasse." He opened his briefcase and extracted a length of rope and a piece of cloth.

The window of opportunity had closed, and panic made her stomach pitch. He leaned toward her, making short work of tying her to the chair. The sour stench of his sweat filled her nostrils and bile rose to her throat.

"Please, don't do this," she begged, terror coursing through her in icy waves.

He continued binding her as if she hadn't spoken, even whistling as he worked. He tested the ropes a few moments later and finished by tying a length of cloth around her mouth.

As he stood back to survey his handiwork, Chandra began to stir from across the table. Wheeler moved fast, extracting something from his pocket as he approached her. Amber screamed from behind her gag as he jabbed the barely conscious woman in the neck with an obscenely large syringe.

Surely a needle that size would kill her.

Sick with guilt and dread, Amber watched helplessly as the madman half-lifted, half-dragged Chandra to the door. She struggled against her restraints as the door closed behind them, only one thought in her terror-filled mind.

This woman could die, and it was all her fault.

***

"Sounds like we're all on the same page," Liam announced, slapping his hands on his knees before rising. "I'm about ready for bed, though."

Jax stood with him and stretched. "I'm right behind you."

Too bad he'd be sleeping alone. Chandra had left his bedroom only a couple hours before, but he found himself every bit as hungry for her as he'd been before. He briefly entertained the idea of stopping by her room and asking her if she was interested in a sleepover, but then reality set in. Friends with benefits didn't do sleepovers.

So maybe you want something more with her, asshole.

He pinched his eyes closed, fighting off the headache that had been plaguing him for the past twenty minutes. It had been an eventful day, packed full of revelations and introspection. He'd made great strides with his son, and had his first—and second—sexual encounter with a woman since Sara died. Maybe it was better to let it all marinate for a day before making life decisions.

"I'll call the lumber place and make sure they have what we need to get started ASAP," Billy said from his perch on the back of the couch, derailing Jax's wayward thoughts.

The three of them had been discussing a lucrative real estate deal that they'd locked up that evening, adding to the sense of wellbeing Jax had been feeling. All in all, things were right and tight and he was looking forward to waking up the next morning, a feeling he'd been missing for a long time.

As he crossed the room to the stairs, the low-level throb in his temples turned into a blinding flash of pain and a vision flickered in his mind, stopping him in his tracks. It was so very faint he could hardly make it out. He tried to bring the vision into focus, shutting out the conversation behind him, but it was blurred, fading in and out.

Strange. It looked like Amber. Tied to a chair. Again the image dimmed and he grappled mentally, struggling to grab hold of the link, but it was no use. His heart was pounding so hard he thought it might explode. He could only see what one of his brethren was seeing when they linked with him, which meant one of his pack members was in a room with Amber and they were trying to tell him that something was very wrong.

Chandra.

He felt her then, her essence trying to touch his mind. Her fear and confusion rippled through him, but it was unfocused, disoriented. For a single moment, he sensed a male presence, heard a low, muffled voice. The image flickered once more, like the tail of a firefly, and then she was gone.

"Hey, man, you okay? You look a little pale," Billy asked, putting a hand on his shoulder.

All-encompassing rage rocked him to the core and he could feel himself shifting, barely riding the line between man and beast. He moved like lightning, heading to the door, letting out a roar so loud it shook the rafters.

"Someone took her," he growled. "Someone took Chandra."

***

Chandra opened her eyes and groaned. The room was spinning. Even the dim light of the bulb swinging overhead intensified the throbbing in her head. *What had happened?*

She tried to focus, taking in her surroundings. Nothing looked familiar. She tried to sit up straight but couldn't. Despair momentarily paralyzed her as the realization hit: she was chained. The animal in her throbbed, the bone-deep hatred of being trapped stirring up a dangerous concoction of fury and fear.

She gathered every ounce of self-control she possessed and clamped down hard to control her panic and stave off the impending change.

Taking a deep breath, she assessed what had happened. The last thing she remembered was talking to Amber. She had scented a human male nearby but before she could turn around, she was shot by something in the neck. Judging by the way she was feeling, she must have been tranquilized with an elephant gun or something. How long had she been out? She twisted to glance at the watch on her wrist. Quarter after midnight. So just under an hour.

Chandra tested the thick chains at her wrists, then her ankles. They didn't budge.

Titanium.

Even in her weakened condition, she was pretty strong by human standards, but not that strong.

She briefly contemplated unleashing her beast, then dismissed it outright. While the change would increase her strength and agility to some degree, she had no idea if she would be strong enough, even as a wolf, to break the shackles. She could end up in worse shape than she was right now, with her large paws mangled by the too-tight shackles in the wrong position.

Even if she was willing to take that risk, her assailant could be watching her right now. To change form in front of a human was a violation of Supreme Law. The penalty for such a crime could range from a serious physical punishment to exile or even death. Worse, allowing humans to know of their existence could potentially put all of her brethren in mortal danger.

She considered mentally reaching out to Jax again, but first she had to focus and piece together some clues, figure out what was going on and where she was. Leading her pack into a trap was not an option.

She closed her eyes and breathed in deeply, her sensitive nose capturing a medley of aromas. The scent of evergreens, ponderosa pines, and dripping sap coalesced to form an oh-so familiar bouquet.

She was in the deep woods.

The revelation comforted her to some small degree. If she could get out of the shackles, there would be no stopping her. She could change without fear of being seen and then she'd be home free. There wasn't a man alive who could catch her in the woods if she didn't want to be caught.

She opened her eyes and surveyed the room again more closely. Although it was dim, she could see it was very sparsely furnished. Small with unfinished oak walls, it was clearly one room of a rustic cabin. She'd run through probably a hundred miles of woods in the Pray area and seen as many cabins that would fit the bill.

Frustrated, she again closed her eyes and this time listened, allowing the sounds to permeate her consciousness. A myriad of forest creatures created a cacophony, but nothing stood out that would be helpful in narrowing down her possible location.

She was about to give up when she heard it: the babble of nearby moving water.

All right, so she was in the forest, in a small cabin surrounded by evergreens and pines, and within twenty-five yards or so of a brook or stream. She must have been transported by car and, even if they'd traveled quickly, her assailant would have spent a considerable amount of time getting her into and out of the vehicle. Not to mention the time it took to chain her up.

Even if she'd been unconscious for an hour, she would still have to be within fifteen miles or so of Amber's house considering all of the factors that would have slowed her kidnapper down.

It wasn't much, but it was something. Now at least she could give her packmates a couple of clues to work with.

She focused her mind and, casting her energy outward, once again tried to reach for Jax.

Chapter Nine

By the time Amber's door burst open more than an hour later, her throat was raw from screaming. Three giant men barreled into her kitchen, Jax in the lead. When she looked into his wild, furious eyes, she should have been afraid for her life. Instead, all she felt was relief.

He swore under his breath and quickly went around, untying the cloth that gagged her.

Before he said anything, words tumbled from her in a rush. "You have to get her. Jesus, Jax, he took Chandra. I am so sorry. I'll do anything, anything to help you. He's crazy. Burglars or not, what he did to her… I didn't know, I swear, I didn't know—" Her babbling confession stopped as the lump in her throat choked off any further words. Her chest heaved as she began to sob.

Jax bent low to face her, his voice tight. "You need to calm the fuck down and talk to me, Amber. Who? Who took her?" he demanded.

She tried to speak, but all that came out were more wracking sobs. How could she have done this? If Chandra died, the woman's blood was on her hands. And with as insane as Tobias had looked? Death wasn't even the most terrifying fate possible. She hung her head in despair, the shock of it all finally setting in.

"Stop it. Stop crying and fucking talk to me," Jax growled, voice shaking with unchecked fury.

A tall, dark man with golden eyes stepped in. "That's not going to help Chandra. You need to calm down, Jax." He took his friend's arm and pulled him upright, his calm control a welcomed presence in a room filled with chaotic emotion. "Come with me, let's search the house and grounds for clues and let Billy speak to Amber."

Jax's jaw went tense and it seemed like he would argue but instead he gave a clipped nod and the two moved toward the hallway, speaking in low, urgent voices as they began their search.

The one they'd referred to as Billy walked over to her. He reached toward her and she flinched involuntarily.

"I'm just going to untie you now, all right?"

He didn't wait for an answer but bent behind her and, with one, swift jerk, snapped the ropes that bound her. He slipped one of his thickly muscled arms around her shoulders and the other behind her knees and lifted her easily from the chair.

The warmth of his body seeped into her, and she instinctively curled closer to him. The chills that had wracked her began to subside as she allowed the false sense of security to take the edge off her shock and terror. She needed to get it together if she was going to help them save their friend.

He carried her to the living room and sat her in an oversized recliner. Why was he being so damn nice? She'd made an awful, terrible mistake that could cost Chandra her life and he was treating her like she was the victim.

Fresh, guilty tears sprang to her eyes, and she bit her lip hard to keep them from spilling out.

Billy laid a blanket over her and sat on the floor next to her, rubbing her arm, giving her a chance to compose herself.

She took a deep, shuddering breath. "He told me you were burglars. He told me I was helping."

"Burglars?"

Her stomach bottomed out as the baffled expression on his face told her what she'd already begun to suspect. Tobias Wheeler was not only a psychopath, he was also a liar.

"Start from the beginning, Amber," he encouraged.

She told him about her initial meeting with Wheeler, how they'd come to their agreement, and what she had done. "We need to call the police. He said I shouldn't because I'll be in trouble too, but I don't care. We need to call them right now. I don't know what he's going to do with her."

"We can't call the police. It's…complicated."

"What do you mean? Your friend has been *kidnapped*."

So maybe they weren't thieves, but clearly they'd been doing something illegal. Why else would he be so against contacting the authorities?

"Look, whatever you're into and whatever trouble it may cause you to have that revealed, we still need to call the cops. What if he kills her? Or worse." Her insides cramped as she again contemplated all the horrors Chandra might face.

"We're no criminals, Amber. I don't have time to get into it with you, but at the very least you need to trust that. This man…Wheeler…he's the villain here. And my friends and I need to find him. Give us twenty-four hours to save her. If we fail, you can call in the police and tell them everything. Please." His voice grew soft. "Her life might depend on it."

His deep green eyes shined with sincerity and something else—something a little dangerous.

Then she thought of Wheeler and, in that instant, she made her decision. Billy and his friends might be a little shady, but Tobias Wheeler was insane. If she had to make a deal with the devil to get Chandra away from him, she would.

Because if Chandra died, it would haunt her for the rest of her life.

"Okay. How can I help?"

"What can you tell me about him? What does he look like? Did he ever give you any indication of where he lived or why he took Chandra?"

She filled him in on every detail she could think of, but when he was about to go, she stopped him.

"Something else weird. He said that I did a good job. That he figured I would get some interesting photos but deep down had hoped one of you would follow me back here." She wrung her hands in her lap and tried again to block out what she'd seen at that house. "Then he…" She paused and swallowed hard. "He said that she was an amazing specimen. Probably the ranting of a lunatic but-"

"*Shit.*" Billy's faced turned bone white as his eyes narrowed into slits.

If she had doubted that he was dangerous before, she doubted no more.

***

Jax and Liam had gone through the house quickly and finished walking the perimeter, having found only some footprints and tire tracks for their troubles. But they'd caught Chandra's scent as well as that of the human male, so they couldn't have been gone long, an hour or so at most.

He tried not to think about what could be happening to her, tried to focus on it as if it was a job—finding something that was lost.

Something that meant everything to him.

They moved purposefully back toward the house, but Jax stopped short when his head started to hum.

"Chan?" he breathed, his heart knocking painfully against his ribs. She was reaching out to him. He pressed back, strengthening their link. *Are you okay?*

I'm okay, but I'm chained and can't get free. Something real bad is going down.

Do you know where you are?

Deep woods, near a brook. Amber...she might be hurt. I don't know what her role was in this, but I don't think she's dangerous. I was at her house. He came there for me. I'm within twenty miles of there, I think.

A vision of a cramped, dimly lit room permeated his thoughts, and he knew that Chandra was showing him her prison. He could see her wrists and ankles bound by thick chains. His gut twisted with rage. His vision blurred, and his bones began to shift, but he fought it, dragging in a deep lungful of air.

Amber's fine. We need to focus on you. More information. I need more. Come on, think! He pushed, letting his desperation get the better of him.

I don't have any more.

The sharp edge of her panic-laced fear sliced through him. He pulled back a bit and tried to calm her.

Okay, it's okay. We're going to find you. Me, Liam, and Billy are going to come get you. Hold tight, I'll stay with you as long as I can. Who is he, Chan? Have you seen him before?

Oh my God, he's coming. Jax, he's coming.

The link wavered as her concentration faltered. All he could feel was her icy terror.

Stay with me, damn it! Let me see him.

The link was fuzzy, like the grainy footage of an old movie, but he saw the door to the dingy room open and a man step through holding a gun. He was tall, in his late forties, wearing jeans, a flannel shirt, and a satisfied grin.

He looked so normal, lean build, thinning brown hair, plain face. Then Jax noticed something white hooked to his belt buckle. Too large to be a rabbit's foot, it was—

Agony ripped through him as he bent at the waist, the urge to vomit overwhelming.

Sara.

Her lovely white paw on a chain around his belt loop. The vision shuddered and was gone.

"No!" he shouted. He felt a hand on his shoulder, shaking him.

Liam stared, but Jax could not speak. They linked briefly and, as Liam saw what Jax had seen, his face crumpled in grief. Billy walked out of the house a moment later, his cheeks ashen.

"It's him," he said, voice stark with pain. "It's the same guy."

Jax lifted his head and met Liam's eyes with his own. "I won't let him take her from me, too. Do you hear me? I won't." He'd failed Sara, but he wouldn't fail Chandra. Not when he'd led this trouble to their door.

His alpha gave him a grim nod. "Let's go."

They moved, almost as one, toward the woods surrounding Amber's house.

A selfless soul, even from the beyond, Sara had unwittingly given them a clue to Chandra's whereabouts. She'd been killed about ten miles from where they stood. They had combed those woods many times since her death and knew the dozen or so cabins in that area. In all likelihood, Chandra was in one of those cabins. If they could get there quickly, they could still catch her scent and have a chance of finding her.

Unable to contain himself another moment, Jax began to run full speed. He leaped high in the air and burst into wolf form, still in flight, Liam and Billy a few steps behind.

Somebody was going to die tonight, and it wouldn't be a member of his pack.

Not this time.

***

Chandra fought hysteria as she stared at the paw. She only hoped she'd broken the link between her and Jax before he saw it too. Seeing his mate's paw like that, being treated as a trophy, would rip his heart out.

This was the monster that had killed Sara.

"Hey, there, missy. Awake now, finally? I gave you enough juice to kill a rhino, and it only kept you down for an hour. I'm very impressed. That's a good thing." His tone was upbeat and excited, which chilled Chandra to the bone. "The more you impress me, the more incentive I'll have to keep you around," he continued. "We're going to be doing a lot of tests over the coming weeks to see what exactly you are capable of. We can do it the hard way, or we can do it the easy way. Your choice."

"I have no idea what you're talking about, you sick bastard. What did you do with Amber?" Chandra asked, relieved that her voice didn't reveal her shock and fear. Jax had said the other woman was all right, but who knew if he was just trying to placate her and keep her calm.

Her captor had the nerve to look affronted. "She's fine. I tied her up and left her there. She's no threat to me. She doesn't even know my real name. Besides, I wouldn't hurt a woman. What do you take me for, some kind of animal?"

"What the hell do you call this?" she asked incredulously, gesturing at her shackles with a nod of her head.

"You can't fool me." His voice dropped to a whisper as he moved into the room, never lowering the gun. "See, I know what you *really* are. I always knew you existed, but I could never prove it. Then, I saw it with my own eyes." He smacked his lips in satisfaction. "A little one. I watched them hunt for a while through my binoculars, him and the white wolf. And the damnedest thing happened. He changed! *Changed.* Into a human, for just a second."

Chandra's hands started to shake as the pieces of the puzzle clicked into place.

"I was all set to take him and started to move in close for the shot, but the white one came out of nowhere. I had no choice. It was her or me. Once I got her back here I did some tests, tried to salvage some proof, but by that point she was nothing more than a dead wolf."

He paced, warming to the topic. "I knew then that I needed a live one. So I watched and waited and did my research. Saw the men from your place searching the woods around the spot where I killed her. Could've been a coincidence, but when I looked into your living arrangements and began to watch the strange comings and goings, I was pretty sure. Your security setup made it difficult to find proof, but I got my little spy. After that, it was child's play." He pulled out her shredded sports bra from his pants pocket. "This and some pictures of the barn, and I knew I had the right folks. Amber made the perfect bait."

He absently rubbed the paw at his hip, sighed with regret, then shook off his reverie, giving her a broad smile. "Shame. But no matter, though. I have you, and soon enough everyone will know the truth. I'll finally get the credit I deserve and all those people who laughed at me will bow at my feet."

Chandra tried to think of anything but Sara's fate and her sweet, now-motherless child Ryan.

"You need to see a doctor." She forced the words past her numb lips, managing to affect a pitying tone despite her growing fury. "Clearly, I'm nothing more than a normal woman. Surely you can see that?" she implored. "I don't know anything about a wolf being killed. Hunting isn't a crime, but kidnapping is, and it's taken very seriously by the police. If you let me go now, we can forget this ever happened."

She forced tears to well in her eyes, hoping she looked pitiful while she bit back her anger. Maybe if he could see her as a human being, like him…

His hand shook slightly, and his voice took on an edge of hysteria as he spoke. "I wish people would stop saying that to me. I don't need a doctor. I *am* a doctor. And you are a monster. A clever one, I'll give you that, but a monster nonetheless. Now, you and I are going to get to know each other a little better. I'd hoped you would cooperate, hoped maybe you would even want me to try to cure you, but if you won't be nice…"

He walked toward her, pulling a wicked looking needle from his pocket.

She no choice. She had to risk changing as she could not—*would not*—allow him to drug her and perform God knows what grisly experiments on her.

Hoping to buy herself a moment or two with shock value, she burst into wolf form in an instant, steeling herself for the pain in her wrists and ankles.

Three of the four shackles gave way. The fourth was still on her right hind leg, stuck tight, above the joint. She rolled to her side desperate to get out of the submissive position she was in and stood on the bed using her three good legs. A low growl worked its way from deep in her throat.

The doctor had stopped mid-stride and stared in awe. "Amazing. I knew it. I *knew* it!" He lowered the needle, putting it back into his pocket, and instead aimed the gun at her. "I was going to give you something mild this time, but I can see that isn't going to work." He closed one eye and fixed her in his sights.

She would not allow him to render her helpless again. Chandra steeled herself and wrenched her body hard to the side just as she heard the gun go off. The bone in her hind leg snapped, and she howled in pain. Fighting through the agony, she pulled her limp, malleable leg from the chain.

She looked up to see him struggling to get another cartridge into the gun and set up for a second shot, but she wasted no time. His wild eyes met hers, and she leaped from the bed, snarling as her jaws closed over his gun-wielding arm like a steel trap. He screamed, and the gun clattered to the floor.

A sharp sting in her side registered through the fury, and she looked down in despair to see the doctor's needle protruding from between her ribs.

She'd gambled and failed. Not only was she helpless, she'd also exposed her pack to a madman. She should have let him kill her.

As her vision grew blurry, she reached for Jax one last time before slipping into oblivion.

Run. Pack everyone up and get out of Pray. He's coming.
I'm so sorry.

Chapter Ten

Jax held his nose firmly to the ground as he moved through the forest. The pack had spread out over a three-mile area around where Sara had been killed and were in constant mental contact with one another. No one had caught Chandra's scent yet, and they were preparing to move to another section of woods when a sound caught his attention

He pricked his ears, listening intently, opening his thoughts, and pressing outward for Chandra. Again, nothing. He had been trying to reconnect with her since they left Amber's house, and he was terrified because he had received no response. He held onto the hope that she was sedated again or somehow distracted.

He wouldn't allow himself to think of the alternative.

A sound came then, and this time it was clear. Chandra, barking and snarling. His heart leaped. He turned to the noise and broke into a run, sending out the call to his packmates.

They had found her.

So sorry.

Chandra's weakened thoughts blasted into his consciousness only to fade away an instant later. Jax let out a long, mournful howl as pain lanced his heart. Could fate be so cruel as to take her from him when they were so close?

He covered the last few yards to the old, rickety door and launched himself into it, smashing it to pieces as he entered the cabin. He followed her scent to the bedroom and charged inside.

Chandra lay motionless on the floor, her face covered in blood. Heart in his throat, he ran to her side, sniffing and licking her face tenderly. Not her blood. She was breathing, he realized with relief. He scanned her body quickly for injuries and noted her leg twisted at an awkward angle. Painful but not life threatening.

The rest of the pack entered the room and surrounded her, snuffling and licking her gently. His overwhelming relief was eclipsed by ice-cold fury as he scented the human male. Jax met Liam's eyes.

Get her home. I'll be there shortly.

The alpha's response rang in his head. *We go together.*

Fuck that.

I appreciate the concern, but I'm doing this alone. If I need you, I'll call.

Without waiting for a reply, he padded forward, intent on the hunt, the beat of his animal heart the only sound he could hear. As the scent of blood grew stronger, so did his rage. It pulsed through him like a giant, seething beast, all consuming. This monster of a man would pay for hurting Chandra, and Sara's death would finally be avenged. Then maybe he could forgive himself for not being there when she'd needed him most. And, just maybe, he would be deserving of happiness again.

A subtle movement caught his attention. Narrowing keen eyes, he spotted him.

Crouched low behind a bush was the man who had killed Sara, the man who had hurt Chandra, the focus of every shred of anger and pain in his battered heart. His vision blurred into a haze of red. All conscious thought fled as he allowed the wolf to dominate, eclipsing every last bit of humanity in him.

Letting loose a feral snarl, he launched into the air, clearing the twenty feet that separated him from his prey, and a terrible scream echoed through the darkening forest.

***

Chandra awoke to a warm sponge being dragged across her skin. It was lovely. She sighed contentedly as gentle hands pulled a freshly laundered t-shirt over her head.

She gasped and came awake with a start, sitting up quickly. She was rewarded with a pounding in her head that took her breath away as everything came rushing back to her.

"Jax?"

"I'm here, Chan, I'm right here," he said, reaching out to grab her hand.

"You found me," she croaked, looking into his warm, brown eyes. "And you saved me."

"I found you, babe, but *you* saved you. The bastard had taken off bleeding like a stuck pig by the time I got there. You were great." There was a note of pride in his voice that warmed her from the inside out.

"Is he…?"

"He won't ever hurt anyone ever again," he said with a grim smile.

Relief flashed through her, but it was tempered with grief. "Thank you. Jax, about Sara, I'm so very sorry. What he did to her…" Her eyes filled with tears.

"I'm the one who's sorry. I put you at risk…all of you. And if something happened to you-" He broke off, leaned close and pressed a light kiss to her forehead. "Get some rest. We can talk in the morning."

She flexed her right leg and was relieved to feel it was almost healed and only caused her a twinge of discomfort.

She lay back onto the pillow, still exhausted and drained from the combination of drugs, adrenaline, and the effort it took to heal. Still, she fought sleep. "And Amber? Is Amber okay?"

"Yeah, she's fine. She's here at the house for tonight. I think she's still in shock. Billy is watching her. We have some decisions to make there. She saw some things she shouldn't have, and you know how some of the other packs deal with shit like that. If they find out-" He broke off and shook his head. "You know what? That's for another day. For now, everything is good. Great, even. You're alive and home, and I don't give a flying fuck about anything else."

"Home. Yes," she mumbled, her eyelids fluttering one last time before the lure of sleep grew too strong and pulled her slowly under.

When she awoke again, hours later, for a moment she didn't know where she was, and fear gripped her. Taking a slow, deep breath, she calmed herself. Everything was okay. She was home, in her bed.

And Jax was still with her.

His strong arms tightened around her waist. She turned to face him, returning his embrace.

"Hey, there," he said, his voice husky from sleep.

"Hey, yourself."

"Feeling better?"

"Yup." She tested her leg again and nodded. "Almost like new."

She began to pull away, suddenly conscious of the fact that she was treating him like her mate. He hadn't signed on for that, and she wasn't going to embarrass herself by being the needy woman smothering him just because he'd saved her.

Jax held her fast. "Where are you going?" he asked, sweeping his hand down to her hip, anchoring her close.

"Mmm," she sighed and fought the urge to rub against him.

"You're asking for trouble making noises like that."

Her pulse spiked at the thought of such trouble, and she gave into her urge, arching toward him. After all they'd been through, she wanted…no, needed to feel alive. To feel the joy and freedom that being with Jax would bring. Maybe one more time wouldn't hurt.

Hell, who was she kidding? Giving him up was going to kill her no matter when she did it. She might take this moment and use it to wipe away the memories of the night before and replace them with something beautiful.

She groaned as his hard length rode her hip and she leaned forward, inhaling his delicious, musky scent.

"Chan, are you sure you're okay for this?"

"Yes. Oh yes."

She let her eyes drift closed as he leaned in to kiss her. His mouth met hers, hot and hungry, as she let her hand drift down his back, kneading his taut muscles.

"You feel so good," she murmured into his mouth. She pushed him away then, pressing him back into the mattress. She slung her leg over his hips and straddled him, slowly lowering herself until she could feel his thickening erection through the thin cloth the separated them.

Reaching down, she grasped the hem of her T-shirt and pulled it over her head in one swift motion, baring herself to his hungry gaze.

"Oh, Chan," he groaned, reaching up and cupping her breasts in his hands.

Chandra arched her back, whimpering as he caressed her hardening nipples. Her hips began to rock against his as he pinched and teased.

He looked down at her and said through gritted teeth, "You probably want to stop doing that."

He pulled her down toward him and flicked her nipple with his tongue, then drew it into his hot mouth. Her hips pulsed faster against his, almost of their own accord.

Jax turned his attention to her other breast as his hand snaked slowly down her side, tripping lightly over her hip. The other hand slid between her thighs and, splaying his open palm over the cloth of her panties, he squeezed. Heat rushed to her core as she trembled above him.

With the flick of his wrist, her panties were gone, replaced by his warm, hard hand. He covered her moist heat and slid a finger deep inside. Her body tensing as he flexed rhythmically.

She pulled away, determined to have him all. Reaching between them, she cupped his swollen cock in her hand, lifting him to press against her. He probed, his thick length finding its mark. Flexing his hips, he pushed into her until he was seated fully. She tried to make it last, to savor the sensation, but she was overwhelmed. Her body clenched around him over and over as he worked his hips relentlessly. First long and slow, then faster, until she began to cry out.

Shuddering over him, her body exploded, gripping his cock tight as the waves crashed over her. He stiffened beneath her, holding her hips tight in his hands as he surged forward one last time, his cock pulsing and jerking inside her as he came.

His face was still buried in her neck, his breathing heavy, when he mumbled something.

"What?" she gasped, still trying to catch her breath as she pulled away.

He stared up into her face and pulled her close again, brushing his lips against her cheek. "I said I think I love you, Chan."

Her heart stuttered in her chest. He cared for her, sure, she knew that, especially after last night. But love? An ember of hope flickered to life within her. She shook her head, refusing to give into it until she was sure. She didn't think she could take the pain if it was nothing more than pillow talk. "I thought you-"

He held up a hand and cut her off. "I know what I said before," he admitted, "but after we made love yesterday, I felt so happy, so complete. I wanted to talk to you once I got my head together, but you were gone. Then, when I thought I lost you—" He broke off, closing his eyes. "I'm lying. I don't think I love you. I know I do. We can take it slow. Work Ryan into the idea bit by bit. But now that I have you, I never want to let you go. Tell me you'll at least think about it. When we've had some distance from this shit storm."

Tears streamed down her cheeks as she cupped his face in her hands. "I don't need to think about it. I'm pretty sure I loved you the moment I walked through the door."

He let out a low growl of satisfaction, and squeezed her against him. "I was so blinded by guilt and sadness, I couldn't see it. Even when I started falling for you, I fought it because it felt like a betrayal. But now I know that there is nothing in the world Sara would have wanted more than for me to have found you. She would've loved you and she would be so grateful for what you've done for me and Ryan. We have a second chance at happiness."

Chandra buried her face in his neck and cried, but this time, her tears were ones of joy. She'd left her pack in search of a place to belong. She'd never imagined she'd find a little family all her own, here in the wolf pack of Pray.

Redemption

Montana Wolves Book Three

Chloe Cole

Introduction

Amber Jansen is losing her mind. After a near tragic run-in with a psychopath, she's trying to go back to life as she knew it, but she can't seem to shake the feeling that something is still terribly wrong. Plagued with nightmares and panic attacks, she wonders if she's buried some important piece of information in the depths of her mind. Information so disturbing that remembering it could destroy her…

Wolf-shifter Billy MacKenzie has lived by one rule and one rule only: The pack comes first. Always. But when Amber Jansen accidentally sees something she shouldn't have, he feels an unprecedented desire to protect her from the powers that be, who would rather silence her forever than risk being exposed.

If he breaks the laws of his kind to shield her, he'll leave himself vulnerable to the one woman he wants but can never have.

Prologue

Amber Jansen stared at her reflection and wondered dully if she was going to lose her job.

She wouldn't be surprised. She'd taken a two-week leave of absence already, telling her boss she'd pulled a muscle. But even now, the vitality was missing from her face, and her hair was as lackluster as her skin.

The black bustier she wore was looser than it should have been since she'd lost ten pounds she couldn't spare, and she was totally exhausted. If she wanted to keep dancing—and by extension, paying the bills—something was going to have to give. Three weeks had passed since she'd been tied to a chair while a woman was attacked and kidnapped by Tobias Wheeler right in front of her, and she was no closer to moving past it than she had been the day it happened.

She stripped off her costume hastily, and then stepped into the dressing room shower. Turning the water on full blast, she leaned her back against the cool tiles and pressed her balled fists over her eyes, determined to halt the instant replay that was her now-constant companion.

She began to hum. Then, desperate to shut out the insistent images, she began to sing the lullaby her grandmother used to sing when Amber was small.

She could almost hear that clear soprano; could almost feel the soft hand stroking her hair as they rocked in the chair. How she wished she was still alive to sing to her and comfort her. She had never needed it more.

God dammit, get a hold of yourself, woman. There's no such thing as werewolves.

Her voice broke as she began to sob.

Chapter One

One week later, Pray, Montana

"We should never have let her go like that," Billy said as he leaned forward in the wide, leather chair by the fireplace. Try as he might, weeks after the incident, he still hadn't been able to get Amber Jansen out of his head.

The expression on her face when she'd realized that she almost cost Chandra her life.

Or the one after that, when she'd seen him shift into a werewolf from afar.

His stomach clenched at the recollection. Fuck, he'd hated that he'd scared her.

"You all keep saying that, but what was the alternative?" Liam asked, scrubbing his hand over his face. The alpha stood in the center of the great room, eyeing each member of his pack questioningly. "Anyone?"

Billy shifted in his seat, pissed off and primed to argue, but with nothing that even remotely qualified as a solution to add to the conversation. He'd been losing sleep for the past month trying to solve this particular problem and kept coming up empty.

"I don't know what the right thing to do was," Amalie said, finally breaking the silence. "I just know that sending her back home like nothing happened was wrong. She never believed the whole 'delusion triggered by stress' nonsense we tried to feed her. I've heard of PTSD, but who the hell goes through a traumatic event and imagines they saw a werewolf? Of course she's going to be asking questions, and causing problems. Maybe we should tell her the truth. Keep her here for a while until we can gauge how she's taking it."

She shook her head slowly and then shrugged, a bleak expression on her pretty but strained face as she looked at Liam. "And, if she decides to blow the lid off of it, we run."

"Telling her the truth isn't an option."

The alpha's tone was sharper with his mate than Billy had ever heard it before and he winced on her behalf.

"We barely avoided an all-out clan battle when I told you we were shifters," Liam continued, "And you'd already been bitten and on your way to becoming a werewolf. Amber is totally human. At minimum, telling her would result in repercussions from the other packs when they found out. Tensions are still high and alliances are fragile. Another straw on that camel's back and…"

He trailed off, but there was no need to elaborate.

He was talking about war.

Billy clenched his jaw, the feeling of helplessness weighing on him so heavily, it made his gut ache. There was no perfect answer here, and in lieu of that, the pack was almost always going to pick what was least destructive to the pack as a whole. Several of them were already nodding their agreement, murmuring softly amongst themselves, but Liam held up a hand to silence them.

"And yes, worst case scenario is that she blows the lid off. But if humans know about us, believe me when I tell you, we can't run far enough. We've seen it too many times. People are dangerous when faced with the unknown. Our kind was almost wiped out more than once due to crazed mobs. At the end of the day, no matter how strong we are, we're still outnumbered more than ten million to one. I'm not willing to risk it for a woman we hardly know. Especially if her life isn't in imminent danger." Liam looked questioningly at his second in command. "Jax?"

"I'm sorry, but I just don't have a lot of sympathy." He slid a muscled arm around his mate and held her close. "She's the one who put Chandra in danger to start. To my mind, her thinking she's got some screws loose is getting off easy. I would have cheerfully cut her throat at the time."

A snarl rose in Billy's throat but he choked it back. If he'd been in Jax's position, he might feel the same way. But more than that, the level of attachment he felt to Amber after only knowing her a short time was out of line. Probably just some twisted savior complex because he'd been the one to take care of her the night everything had gone down.

He stayed silent as his packmate continued.

"That said, I know Chan feels differently, and I respect that. She's a more forgiving soul than I am. I'm definitely concerned about Amber prying and the research she's been doing, though.

And it makes me think that some steps need to be taken to help her make peace with what she saw. Or forget it altogether." Jax shrugged and shook his head slowly. "If there was some way we could alter her memory, that would be the best option."

Billy's hackles rose again, and he couldn't stay quiet any longer. "Hey, yeah, that's a great idea. Why don't you call the Men in Black and ask them if we could use their flashy thing to wipe her memory?" he asked, laying on the sarcasm, thick. "I wish I thought of that."

He could feel the weight of Jax's stare and turned to face his friend. Clearly, not happy. He had nothing but love for the guy, but Jax had a chip on his shoulder a mile wide about humans since Tobias Wheeler had kidnapped his mate.

Wheeler was a flat-out psycho obsessed with proving they were werewolves, and he'd enlisted an unwitting Amber to help him. He'd told her he was a private investigator hired by victims of a recent rash of burglaries, and that he had found the culprits. If she would infiltrate the compound and gather some concrete evidence for the police, he would give her the reward money, not to mention that she would be doing her civic duty.

It wasn't until she'd inadvertently lured Chandra into Wheeler's clutches that she had realized her mistake.

Billy, like all of his packmates, had been furious with her at first. But when he'd scooped her trembling little body into his arms, his anger had melted away. She'd been terrified, completely vulnerable, and the fierce and sudden need to protect had welled up inside him, unbidden.

Even more surprising than that? He had wanted to run out of that house with her in his arms; to shield her from the fury of his pack … his *family*.

What the hell was *that* about?

Jax still held his gaze, and for a moment, the atmosphere grew even more strained until Billy blew out a sigh, willing some of the tension from his body. It wasn't Jax's fault this had happened. Taking it out on him wasn't going to help.

And his friend wasn't wrong. Amber was in this mess because she'd made a serious error in judgment. She had trusted the wrong person and had eventually led a psychopath into their midst. That naïveté had almost proven deadly.

Too bad the events of that day had robbed her of that naïveté. It would have been really helpful now. If only she'd believed their story, they could've all just moved on like nothing had happened.

But he'd seen her face after the fact. She was already fragile and devastated by the consequences of her actions, wracked with guilt. Seeing something that couldn't be explained by anything that made sense to her had been the final straw.

Her mind was slowly coming unraveled.

As they took turns randomly checking up on her and watching from afar, it was becoming more and more clear that she was spiraling out of control. At first it seemed like depression, she was near catatonic, unable to make her shifts at work. But lately, she was almost manic. At the library, furiously pawing through books on folklore and scouring ancient microfiche.

He tried not to think of how fragile she'd looked the last time he saw her. And he tried even harder not to think about why the hell he cared so much. For some reason, though, he couldn't get her out of his head. Call him crazy, but the thought of that one terrible mistake ruining her whole life sickened him.

He refused to let that happen.

"As much as memory wiping would be helpful right now, we don't have that ability," he said, keeping his tone even in spite of the riot going on inside him. "We need to focus on something real and actionable. Something that will give us an idea on where her head is at so we can attempt to do some immediate damage control before the other packs get wind of this."

He pushed himself to his feet and crossed his arms over his chest, making sure that, even though he was being nice, they all knew he was ready to go toe-to-toe with anyone who wanted to get in his face about it.

"I can tail her," Maggie chimed in, raising a hand. "She's never even seen me before so it seems like an easy solution."

Bad idea. Maggie already had a biased against humans. She'd only see the worst in Amber and everything she saw would be tainted by that. "Which is why I should do it," Billy said, hoping his alpha would see the logic in that. "We've done as much as we can with long range recon. Time to get in closer. Make a move to talk to her face to face. And since it was me she saw changing into wolf form, it should be me who fixes it. If she keeps pressing the issue and her research efforts catch the attention of the Kotke or the Big Sky Canyon packs, we could all be in as much physical danger as we would be if we just told her the truth."

And that included Amber.

Liam eyed him for a long moment before tipping his head in a curt nod. "You did spend time with her that night, and she seemed to trust you to some degree. Use that to find out what she'd doing and who she's been talking to about that night. Maybe tell her you wanted to see if she's coping okay with everything. Depending on what you find out, we can also use this as an opportunity to place a listening device in her purse. If she's truly onto us and flapping her gums about it to other people, we need to hear about it sooner than later."

The thought of hiding a bug on her grated on him, but he'd cross that bridge later. He'd won the battle. There was no point in fighting the war when he wasn't even sure if there needed to be one.

He shook off his discomfort and focused on their alpha as he called the meeting to an end.

"Okay, so we're all in agreement with that, then. We'll reconvene in a week and reassess the situation to see if something more drastic needs to be done. Once you've determined her state of mind, try again to convince her that what she saw was just a hallucination. Really work all the angles. Tell her the volatile combination of lack of sleep, shock, and the ranting of a madman had worked on her brain until it had a brief hiccup before getting back on track again," Liam said, offering a clipped nod to the group as a whole. "See you all at dinnertime."

The room began to clear as everyone went about their business, but Billy stayed behind, still deep in thought. This plan wasn't much better than no plan at all, but he couldn't bring himself to tell that to his alpha. He hadn't just been given permission to see Amber again. He'd been given a direct order.

Whether or not he was able to convince her that what she saw was her imagination, he was going to get to spend time with her and make sure she was all right.

And, for the moment, that was enough.

Chapter Two

Amber sat on the floor of her living room, surrounded by books. She'd spent three hours at the library that morning and she was no better off than she'd been before. So far, after a week of research and visiting three different libraries, she had zip. *Nada* about the existence of werewolves in Montana.

A blonde curl flopped in front of one eye and she blew it away on an exasperated sigh, eyeing the stack of books with disgust. Almost at the end of the pile, and it was looking like she was going to have to bite the bullet and face her second biggest fear, right behind werewolves. The internet.

Raised by her grandmother from the time she was ten, she was useless with computers. Nana had said it would be beneath the dignity of her charming old Victorian home to harbor something so modern within her elegantly papered walls and Amber never had the will to fight her on it. In fact, she'd only just bought a Keurig to replace the old coffee percolator after her grandmother's death, and even that felt like a tiny betrayal.

In spite of the lack of modern amenities, Amber had always loved this home. Loved to pretend that the ornate glass doorknobs were diamonds and that the dumbwaiter was a secret passageway. The place had magic in it.

And speaking of magic...

She had work to do. A quick stretch and then back to it. She stood and bent low at the waist, pressing her palms flat to the floor, and letting out a groan as her muscles lengthened.

She'd made the conscious choice to start taking care of herself again after hitting rock-bottom the week before. It had gotten so bad, she'd contemplated checking into a mental institution that night. By the time she'd calmed enough to leave her dressing room and drive home, it was two in the morning. When she'd gotten there, she'd fallen into an exhausted sleep, and dreamt of Billy.

There he'd stood in her living room, just like in real life the night of the kidnapping, mussed mop of golden curls, concern shining in his amazing, emerald green eyes.

"Where is Chandra?" he'd asked. She opened her mouth, but her dream-self couldn't speak. Billy shook his head. Disappointed in her? Then he'd turned and walked out the door.

She moved to the window to watch his departure, but he didn't head for the car. Instead, he went to the side of her yard where he met up with his friends. Then, together, fueled by some sudden sense of urgency, they ran to the edge of the woods.

She'd turned away, but out of the corner of her eye, she saw Billy leap high into the air. And when he landed, he was a man no more.

In his place was a giant, tawny wolf. It loped the last few steps into the forest, and was gone.

She'd awoken from the dream in a cold sweat, heart pounding. While it wasn't entirely accurate, the reality of it had been pretty close to what she remembered.

In the weeks after the incident, she'd tried to swallow the excuses she'd been fed; shadows in the night, shock, fear, lack of sleep. All pretty convincing. Almost costing a woman her life and being tied up by a lunatic had been a lot for her mind to handle. But she was strong, had lived through some pretty bad stuff in the past, and werewolf hallucination was a first.

She'd tried to let it go and move on, but as she replayed the dream in her mind, she noted the details that had been stored away by her memory. She wasn't crazy, *something* had happened, and she was going to prove it. Action was power, and she had a plan.

She sat back on the floor with renewed resolve and opened the next book in the pile. Then, she began to read.

***

Billy spent the thirty-mile drive to Bozeman deep in thought. How he was going to pull this whole thing off without ruining a woman's life in the process, he didn't know, but he was damn sure going to try.

He walked into The Naughty Kitty with grim determination despite being apprehensive about the job ahead. Amber affected him in ways he couldn't explain or curtail, and he had a mission;

clean up the mess he'd made, and get the hell out. Losing sight of that could be dangerous for them all.

He made his way into the club and headed straight for the hostess' station.

"Here for dinner or just the show?" the pretty brunette manning the desk asked with a smile.

Her wholesome good looks and relatively conservative clothes surprised him. As he looked around, he realized the whole place was different than he'd imagined it. Clean and elegant in an old-world way, with lots of red velvet and gold accents. He'd figured he'd walk in to a dingy shit-hole to find girls sporting tassels and G-strings left and right.

Bemused, he shook his head and returned the hostess expectant smile. "Just the show."

She led him through an archway into a separate room and gestured to a table near the front of the stage.

"This one work?"

He nodded his thanks, slipped her a twenty, and then sat, keeping his eyes peeled for any sign of Amber.

Luckily, he didn't have long to wait.

"Welcome to The Naughty Kitty. What can I get you to drin—" Amber stood next to his table, staring down at him as the smile slid from her pretty face. "Billy?"

She flicked a glance around the room like she was looking for somewhere to run, but then finally met his gaze head-on. "What are you doing here?"

His pulse rocketed the way it did every time he saw her and he willed himself to calm the fuck down. He was there to help his pack while still making sure he was able to find a way to keep Amber safe. Now wasn't the time for distractions.

"I came here to see you, actually. To see how you were holding up," he replied, giving her a furtive onceover.

She looked better than when he'd seen her last, looking on from afar. Less pale and thin. Still painfully beautiful. Could be that all his concern had been for nothing and she'd decided to let it go and move on. Half of him was relieved. Best case scenario was that she was happy and healthy.

But the other half? The half that was drawn to her in a way that had him tied in knots even now as he looked at her? Regretted that he didn't have an excuse to spend more time in her presence, no matter how short-sighted and stupid it was.

Humans and wolves didn't mix.

She straightened her shoulders and seemed to collect herself as she dragged a hand through her long, blonde hair. "I appreciate the concern. Funny, I'd been wanting to get in touch with you, too, but didn't have your number and didn't want to make waves by coming out to the house. I was hoping we could talk."

Okay, so maybe she wasn't ready to let it go after all.

"Sure. When?"

"If you plan on sticking around for the show, we can do it tonight. I'm on early rotation so I've only got one performance and then I'm done."

He nodded as his groin tightened. This wasn't the seedy strip club he'd been expecting, but it wasn't called The Naughty Kitty for nothing. Now he was going to have to stand by and watch Amber do…whatever it was she did on that stage.

And something told him it was going to be heaven and hell in equal measure.

Low background music began to play, and she gave him a finger wiggle. "I've got to go. That's the cue for the dancers to head backstage."

He couldn't help but watch her go. The fitted black skirt she wore was longer, coming to mid-calf, and the shirt wrapped around her like an embrace, but neither was over-the-top sexy.

Until she started walking.

Her full hips swung like a pendulum, hypnotizing him. That ass was enough to make a grown man weep and he had to close his eyes to stop the rising tide of lust building in his groin before he had a huge problem on his hands.

"Drink?"

His eyes snapped open and he found another waitress, this one a redhead, smiling down at him. "Sure, I'll take a beer. Whatever's on tap and ice cold."

Just as she returned a few minutes later with his pint, the lights flickered and began to dim.

"Ooh, show's going to start. This is a great number, you're going to love it," she whispered, before flitting off to the next table.

The background music slowed to a stop before strains of another song flowed from the speakers. The tune was sassy and sexy, and familiar enough that it had him tapping his toe.

When the red curtain opened and a lone figure stepped onto the stage, the toe-tapping stopped as his whole world shifted. A woman, her profile in silhouette, posed, shrouded in shadow, but he would recognize that body anywhere.

Amber.

Billy knew it as surely as he knew his own name. She was tiny, maybe 5'2", but she was built like a brick house. Tiny waist, curvy hips, and breasts so voluptuous for someone so petite, you'd think they would have to be fake.

But, nope.

He'd held her in his arms for a brief moment and his heightened sense of touch had confirmed that she was 100% natural.

His throat went bone-dry and he took a long slug from his glass, gaze never leaving the stage. The spotlight flicked on, and Amber turned to face the audience.

The skirt was gone, and in its place was its far shorter cousin, leaving her gorgeous legs bare, all the way from thigh to tiny, black stiletto.

The blood rushed from his head to his cock, leaving him momentarily disoriented. He strained forward, his chest flush against the table as he waited for her next move.

And move she did. The next five minutes had him ready to climb the walls. She bumped, she grinded, she twitched and she turned. With each shimmy, another piece of clothing went flying, and the need clawing at him grew.

As the song wound down, she slunk to center stage in what remained of her clothing—a black, lace bra and a matching pair of panties—to give the hooting crowd a smile. Her gaze connected with his, and the smile faltered.

Had she felt it, all the way from there? The weight of his want? The pull of his need? He hadn't wanted her to know. Hadn't wanted her to see…

But that wasn't even the worst part. The worst part was what he'd seen on her face in return.

She wanted him too.

She might not even know it consciously yet, but it was there. A recognition…an acknowledgement of his attraction and a physical response she couldn't hide. Not from him. The delicate flare of her nostrils, the way her eyes went wide and dark, the slow drag of her tongue against that full bottom lip.

By the time the music ended and she bustled off stage, the breath was sawing in and out of his lungs and his vision was hazed in red, a sure sign that his wolf was just as aware of Amber as he was, and it wanted out. The catcalls of the men around him only made the situation worse as a jealousy unlike anything he'd ever felt pulsed through him, making his blood run hot.

He pushed back the plush leather chair and stood, dropping a ten on the table before heading down the aisle toward the sign marked "Restrooms."

It didn't take much to figure out which way she'd gone. One sniff of the air, and he caught the citrusy warmth that was her scent. He followed it down the long corridor to an unmarked door and stepped through. It led to a second hallway lined with doors.

He bypassed the first two and slowed to a stop in front of the third. A fading gold star marked the gleaming wood and he rapped on it sharply.

"Amber?"

The door across from him opened and a black-haired woman dressed like a Vegas showgirl stepped out.

"Can I help you?" she asked, her gaze drifting slowly from his face downward to rest on his man-kit for a long moment before returning to meet his.

He had no plan beyond getting close to Amber again, and rocked back on his heels, unsure of what to say. "I was actually hoping to see Amber," he said, working up what he hoped was a genial smile and shoving his hands in his pockets.

"Right." She chuckled and cocked her head to one side. "The question is, does Amber want to see you?"

The door behind him opened and he turned to see the lady in question staring up at him. "Hey, come on in," she said, stepping back to make room for him.

"You good, girl?" the woman in the Vegas gear called from across the way.

"Yeah, thanks, Mila," Amber said, ushering him in before waving to her friend. "He's good people."

She closed the door behind her and seemed to take a deep breath before turning to face him again.

"I could've just met you out there…"

She sure could've. What the fuck was he supposed to say to that? He couldn't wait that long? That he'd lost all control and couldn't fight the grinding need to be near her again?

"Yeah, we hadn't hammered out the details, so I wasn't sure."

She nodded, accepting his excuse without question even as he exercised every last shred of self-discipline to keep from yanking her into his arms and kissing her senseless.

She'd changed out of her clothes already and was wearing a pair of yoga pants and a hoody that made her look like she'd just stepped off a college campus, going from steamy sexpot to adorable in three minutes flat.

He resisted the urge to scoop her up and carry her out of the place as the silence stretched between them, thick as taffy on a summer day, until finally, he broke it. "Can we go somewhere private to talk?"

She glanced around the little room like she didn't know where she was for a moment and then nodded. "Yeah. I've just got to get my stuff together and then see my boss to get paid."

"I'm parked out back. I'll pull around and pick you up right at the front entrance in five."

He stepped closer and clenched his fist to keep from reaching out to stroke her hair.

"Everything is going to be okay, Amber. I know it doesn't feel like it right now, but I promise."

He hadn't known he was going to make that vow, but once he did, it settled into his bones like only the truth could. Even if Jax wasn't quite ready to see it, Amber had more than paid for her crimes already. He would protect her, or die trying. It was the right thing to do.

He turned and jogged out to the car, the cold air a welcome shock to his overheated skin. After he took her home, maybe he'd go for a long night-run. All the stress and tension was building inside him and if he didn't work some of it off, he'd be a powder keg ready to blow by tomorrow.

A couple minutes later, he pulled up to the front of the club and Amber stepped out. She was dressed in a puffy coat and a pair of crocheted boots, but it was the hat that did it. Knit with a big red ball on top and he couldn't help but stare.

One second she was this sexy, sultry performer, slinking around on stage with the confidence of a movie star, and the next she was bundled up with a poof-ball hat and freshly-scrubbed face.

And damn if she wasn't still just as sexy.

"Where are we going?" she asked as she climbed into the passenger's seat.

"Up to you. We can try to find a coffee shop-"

"No!" She shot him a grim look and shook her head. "I mean, I have some things to say and if anyone heard me say them…" Her voice trailed off, but he didn't need to hear the rest. If anyone heard her, they'd think she was insane.

Which meant she was still convinced that what she'd seen was real. He was going to have to do damage control and try to find out exactly how far she was willing to take things to get to the truth.

His conscience pricked at him hard, but he tamped it down. This wasn't just about his pack. If Amber kept kicking up dust, she was going to get herself killed. That thought was enough to put his guilt in check.

"I keep an apartment in the city for business," he said. "We can talk there if that's all right?"

She eyed him for a long moment and this time, he didn't stop himself from reaching out to tuck a golden lock of hair behind her ear.

"Do you know I would never do anything to hurt you?"

She let out a soft sigh and closed her eyes, leaning her head against the headrest with a weary sigh. "I know. I don't know how or why I do, but I do."

The words were a balm to his soul. More than the guilt, something about the thought of her being afraid of him made the bile in his belly burn.

As he glanced at the woman beside him, a sudden sense of foreboding washed over him. No matter how smoothly things went down, this couldn't possibly end well. In order to keep his promise and protect her, he had no choice but to betray her trust and lie to her.

And if she found out, she'd surely hate him for it.

But at least she'd be alive to hate him instead of lying in an unmarked grave somewhere after getting mauled by a pack of enraged wolves.

The decision made itself.

Chapter Three

"Coffee? Beer?" Billy stepped back into view from the kitchen, black T-shirt stretching tight over his massive shoulders as he shrugged. "Sorry, it's a bachelor pad and that's pretty much all I've got to offer you, unless four-day old pizza is your thing."

His smile melted just a little of the ice that had been wedged in her belly for nearly a month now. As terrified as she was about what she'd seen, she hadn't been lying when she'd said he didn't scare her. In fact, being around him made her feel oddly safe.

"I'll pass on the pizza and take a beer, thanks."

They'd talked some on the ride over to his place, but for the most part, they'd sat in silence as if they both knew the coming conversation was going to be a doozy and were content to have it wait just a little longer. Even now, her nerves were in tatters at the thought of speaking her suspicions out loud. As hard as the not knowing was, some part of her couldn't help but wonder if the knowing was going to be even harder to take.

Couldn't be helped, though. If she wanted to move on with her life, she had to get to the bottom of what had happened that night, and Billy was the key.

He came back into the living room with their drinks and flicked on the gas-burning fireplace before sitting across from her on a wide, leather ottoman. His closely-cropped, golden curls seemed to glow by the light of the flames, and the memory of him cradling her in his arms like an avenging angel flickered through her mind again. Whatever her fears, he'd protected her that night. If he'd wanted to hurt her, she would have known it by now.

"So talk to me," he said, his perceptive green eyes searching her face. "How have you really been holding up? I know it can't have been easy, after…"

She took a swallow from the bottle he handed her, needing a momentary reprieve. Every time she thought of that night she started to shake and had to remind herself that it was over. She was safe. And, more importantly, Chandra was safe. Everyone was all right.

With the likely exception of Tobias Wheeler.

There was no arrest report. No mention of the kidnapping in the paper. It was like he'd disappeared from the face of the earth. She hadn't heard of, or from, him since that night. And, judging by the fury on Billy and his friends' faces when they left her house that night, she would be surprised if she ever did.

A shiver ran through her as she locked gazes with Billy.

He might not be a threat to her, but there was no question, he was capable of violence.

She forced herself to speak, knowing it wasn't going to get any easier, no matter how long she stalled.

"I've been having nightmares. All the time. They never stop. At first they were about Tobias. His smile, that crazy look in his eyes. But then, lately..." She tucked a stray lock of hair behind her ear with a trembling hand and shrugged. "I've been remembering these dogs." She shook her head then, determined not to soft-sell it. "Not dogs. Wolves." She held his gaze, and tried to keep her voice steady. "What can you tell me about that, Billy?"

A strange expression flitted across his face and the hair on the back of her neck stood up.

He knew something.

Whatever he'd told her that night, there was some truth to what she was saying. She could see it in his face.

He crossed his legs at the ankles and leaned forward to set his bottle on the table between them. When he looked at her again, his handsome features were schooled into a blank mask and the tightness of his stubbled jaw had relaxed.

"Yeah, I remember you mentioned wolves that night, too. When you were delirious and we brought you back to the house."

"Right," she said, "and you told me I was hallucinating." She leaned forward until their faces were just a foot apart. "Now this time, try the truth."

The room was silent but for their breathing and the crackle of the fire. She could see the pulse in his neck leaping like mad and wondered if he was going to tell her more lies. Already, she felt like screaming at the thought.

His jaw flexed tight again, and he shook his head. "I don't think it was a hallucination anymore."

"Y-you don't?" Not at all what she expected to hear. She swallowed hard, mind racing with all the possibilities. Was this man about to tell her that there was really such a thing as werewolves?

Jesus, she'd thought she was prepared, but as the blood drained from her face she realized she was most definitely not. In fact, rather than proving her own sanity, having him validate her outrageous suspicions would only make her wonder if he was crazy too.

Maybe she shouldn't have come after all. She tamped down the desire to up and run. Leaving now would leave her right where she started. Confused, afraid and completely alone in this. It was the last part that made her stay. For the moment, she had an ally in Billy. A friend, when she needed one so desperately.

She forced herself to relax in her seat and wait for him to continue.

"Since that night, I've gone out and hiked a large section of the woods near your house a couple of times," Billy said in a low voice. "I didn't see any wolves myself, but the area was riddled with tracks in the snow. I called the local game warden and he confirmed that a pack was moving through the area at the time of Chandra's kidnapping."

The words took a while to penetrate through the nerves buzzing in her ears, but when they did, they gave her pause.

Could that possibly be right? Could what he was saying even remotely explain what she'd seen? She'd grown up in Montana her whole life. Wolves were a part of the culture, albeit in an abstract way for her. Some nights, when the moon was out, she'd hear them howling their mournful songs off in the distance, but she'd sure as shit never seen one in her backyard before.

"The warden believes that, due to the particularly harsh winter, they were pushed closer to residential areas to hunt," he said, answering her next question before she'd even asked it. He took a swig of his beer and then continued. "Since the temperatures have risen a little, and the lakes are starting the thaw, the wolves have headed back deeper into the forest. I don't think the public is in any danger, but you might want to keep an eye out until spring has sprung."

If that were all true, it still didn't explain why she'd seen it when Billy and his friends hadn't, even though they'd been far closer than she had.

And...

"I saw you-" she broke off, unable to make her mouth form the rest of the words.

I saw you turn into a wolf.

She would sound like a babbling idiot, the way she likely had that night. She let her mouth snap closed and turned her gaze toward the fireplace, tears of confusion stinging her eyes. How long was she going to feel this way? Like she was standing in a dark room by herself with no exit in sight.

"Why didn't you let me call the police that night?" she asked dully.

"We handled it ourselves, that's why. And the less you know about that, the safer you'll be. But I can promise you, Tobias won't be able to hurt anyone else ever again. And I can promise you whatever happened to him was well-deserved and necessary. I need you to trust me on that."

Billy blew out a sigh and stood.

"And I need you to trust me on this. Amber, after what you went through, I don't think it's any surprise that wires might have gotten crossed in your head in some form of PTSD. It's hard to get your head around everything that happened. But I believe you saw wolves."

He held out a hand and drew her to her feet, his beautiful emerald eyes solemn as he spoke.

"That's why I made the effort to go and check it out myself. Now you have to give yourself a break on the details. It was dark, you'd been tied up and traumatized, looking on from afar. No one is blaming you for questioning what was real and what was a trick of light and shadow. But you've got to let this go. Forgive yourself for the thing with Chandra and move on."

She wasn't sure if it was the genuine expression on his face, or the gentle way he spoke to her, cradling her hand in his, but something had her leaning in. Moving closer to soak in his warmth and breathe in the masculine scent of his skin. He seemed to hesitate for just a beat before closing the last of the distance between them.

"Amber…" His voice was half-whisper, half-groan, and it gave her the courage to roll up onto her tiptoes and press a soft kiss to his jaw.

"I want to let it go, Billy. Help me forget. Just for a little while." It was like being caught in a whirlpool. The closer she got, the less able she was to escape him. The pull was that strong. The desire to be close to him, that deep.

He slipped his arms around her shoulders, his eyes flashing with a raw need that had her head spinning. "This is a bad idea."

She didn't have a chance to argue with him on that score, because a second later, his mouth was on hers. If her goal was to forget, it was a rousing success. He was everywhere, his scent clouding her mind, his tongue addling her senses. She curled her arms around his neck and flattened herself, flush against him.

God, he was huge. His hard body was like a wall of muscle against her soft one, and she wished she could climb up and hold on for dear life. He'd either read her mind or shared her need to get closer, because he bent at the knees, gripped her hips in his hands and lifted her off the ground in one, smooth motion.

Instinctively, she wrapped her legs around his waist, lining up her pelvis with the thick ridge in his jeans. Her pulse skittered wildly as heat pooled between her thighs in a wet rush.

"Fuck," he growled against her mouth, fingers flexing to anchor her more tightly against him. "Jesus, you feel good."

She nipped his bottom lip in response and instantly flushed hot. What had gotten into her? It was like he had her under a spell. She put on her little persona on stage, but in her private life, she was a total introvert. She'd had exactly two lovers, and had never been the aggressor. Now, here she was practically throwing herself at this near stranger.

And *biting* him? Maybe she really had snapped that night.

She pulled away, "I'm so sorry, I didn't mean to hurt y-"

"Hurt me?" His low, pained laugh reverberated through his chest. "Shorty, you could hit me with a crowbar right now and it wouldn't hurt me."

It was like the devil took hold of her, because his words, followed by that pull low in her belly, had her arching her hips, grinding against his erection. She gasped as the sensation rocketed through her, spiking her nipples against his muscular chest.

"Oh, my," she whispered, letting her eyelids drift closed. "That does feel..." She didn't let herself think about it. She just did it again, crushing her pelvis against his.

"Amber."

Her name shot through the room like a whip-crack and her eyes flew open.

Billy's face was tight with need as his hot gaze locked with hers. "You've got to stop."

"But I don't want to stop," she murmured, clutching him tighter. Already, the icy tendrils of fear began to tease at her consciousness again. She needed this so badly. A break from reality, just for a little while.

"Please."

"It's not right." He shook his head slowly and released her hips, lifting his hands to tug her arms away from his neck. "You're still confused. And I want to help you, but I'm only a man." He disengaged her legs from his waist and set her gently back on her feet. "If we keep this up, we're going to find ourselves naked in a sweaty tangle, too far gone to remember our own names."

She stared up at him blankly. Was that supposed to be a deterrent? That was exactly what she wanted right now. She found herself leaning into him again and his low, sensual groan sent a shiver through her.

"You're not making this easy." He raked a hand through his hair and took a step back. "I'm not doing this for me. Hell, nothing would make me happier right now than to take you to bed and lick and touch you all night. Believe that." His eyes blazed with a heady mix of lust and sincerity. "But you would regret it. And you've been through enough without some asshole who thinks you're the sexiest woman he's ever seen taking advantage of you."

It was a sweet rejection, but a rejection just the same and all the anticipation and adrenaline buzzing inside her faded away as the stark reality hit her. He was going to send her home and she would be alone.

Again.

Sure, she'd see friends at work and at her yoga class, but none of them would understand what she'd been through. None of them would make her feel safe.

None of them would be Billy.

She refused to think about why that suddenly mattered so much.

Chapter Four

By the time Billy got back to the compound the next morning, he was even more confused than when he'd left. After he'd dropped Amber at her car along with his business card and instructions to call if she needed him, he'd gone back to his apartment in town to think.

Turned out to be a shit idea, because the whole place still smelled like her skin, and he'd wound up having dreams that would've made Satan himself blush.

Not conducive to clear thinking.

And then there was the guilt…

He squeezed his eyes closed and groaned inwardly. An image of Amber staring up at him with those big blue eyes pleading for the truth ran through his head. It had taken every last shred of his self-discipline not to spill his guts. If he'd been a lone wolf, he would have. But he had his packmates to consider, and it wasn't just his secret to tell. So he'd lied. Albeit more successfully than the last time. In fact, he suspected his story was just believable enough to get her to buy in. Now all he had to do was wait and see if she stopped her research and fell into line.

Either way, he'd know soon enough. He'd planted a bug in her purse when she'd gone to the bathroom before he'd taken her back to her car.

Another icy blast of guilt swept over him. God, he felt like a fucking heel.

With a growl, he stalked across the kitchen to the fridge and tugged it open. Once he ate, he'd go for another long run, clear his head some.

"How's things with you?"

He looked over his shoulder with a start to see Chandra standing behind him, a smile wreathing her pretty face.

"Good, you?" he asked, and then focused back on the contents of the refrigerator, opting for a carton of orange juice. More to buy time than anything, he popped open the carton, held it to his lips and started to drink. If Chandra got wind of his agitation, she'd press for details he didn't want to give.

"You're the grossest. Seriously," she said with a long-suffering sigh. "I won't miss living with this many boys when we move."

He turned to face her, frowning. "Move? What are you talking about?"

"Jax, Ryan, and I. We're going to build a new house on the grounds in the spring. Over by Spencer's place."

Her moss green eyes went dreamy as she talked, and she strolled toward him, tugging the carton from his grasp to take a slug from it. She wiped a hand over her mouth before putting it back in the fridge and closing the door.

"It's going to be awesome. We'll be close enough to see each other all the time, but we'll also be able to make some family time." That smile tugged at her lips again and he stared at her with dawning awareness.

"Holy shit. You're knocked up." It was a statement, not a question.

He didn't know how he'd missed it until now. Thinking back, she'd been acting super weird. Alternately weepy and then almost euphoric the past couple weeks. Getting up early to pack her stepson, Ryan, a lunch before he left for school, but then going back to bed. Rushing from the weekend brunch table as soon as the bacon platter made an appearance.

Most of all, though, he could smell it on her. She smelled almost exactly like Jax now, her own more delicate scent overpowered by her mate's essence and the baby—definitely male—that she was carrying.

Now, as he looked at her, happy tears filled her eyes. "Yep. Only a few weeks along, but we're so excited, we couldn't wait to tell everyone."

He'd been so preoccupied with the Amber situation, he hadn't been tuned in to his own pack enough to realize.

"Am I the last to know?"

"Everyone else guessed about a week ago. I figured you had a lot on your mind, but Jax and I wanted to talk to you about maybe being the godfather?"

A warmth spread over his chest and he nodded. "I'd love that. I'll be the best godfather around. I'll teach him to hunt and to fish and to pick up the ladies." He grinned as she winced and held up a hand.

"Take it easy there, Romeo, he's not even born yet. The ladies are going to have to wait."

They chatted for a few more minutes about possible names and what she and Jax had planned for the new house before she gestured to the kitchen table, her expression growing solemn.

"Can we sit for a second? I actually wanted to talk to you about something else, too."

His excitement over the big news faded as he strode over to the rectangular table and pulled out chairs for each of them to sit on.

"Shoot."

He had the distinct feeling he knew exactly what part two of their little heart-to-heart was going to be about, but after the tension with Jax the day before, he didn't want to rock the boat more than he already had.

"What's the deal with Amber?"

Annnd, bullseye in one.

He slung his arm over the back of the chair and tried to look casual. "There is no deal. I'm watching her. Taking care of things like I said I would."

"You care about her." With her intense gaze drilling into his, he couldn't bring himself to lie.

He tipped his head in a clipped nod and shifted his gaze to the big picture window. "I know it's dumb or whatever. I know she's human, and I know what she did to you and Jax. I'm sorry if it feels like a betrayal, but I swear, I won't do anything to jeopardize this pack. I have no intention of acting on my feelings."

It was the truth—at least, not any more than he already had—but he couldn't deny the stab of guilt he felt as he locked eyes with the mother of his godson in utero. His pack was his life. It would serve him well to remember that.

"My plan is to make sure she's all right, and then walk away." A renewed sense of determination settled over him. "The rest, I'll work through afterward."

"Don't."

"Don't what?"

"Don't work through your feelings or shove them aside." She leaned in closer, the intense expression on her face sending a stab of unease through him. "If you like her? If you feel like she's a person you could fall in love with? Don't throw that chance away because of me or Jax or anyone."

"Fall in love with her?" He drew back and barked out a laugh, ignoring the buzzing sensation in his head. "I hardly know her. I think she's a good person who fell into a bad situation, and I care what happens to her. That's nothing like what I feel for you guys. The pack is everything to me."

"We shouldn't be," she said softly. "We are your family and we always will be. But we're not supposed to be your everything. I learned that when I left the Big Sky Canyon pack. We all have to follow our hearts, Billy. We might live longer than most humans, but we're not like cats with eight more lives if we blow this one. Don't squander it."

"You're jumping the gun. I already told you, I don't know her that well and-"

"But some things just *are*, you know? Like with Jax." She settled against the back of her chair again and shrugged. "I knew, the second I saw him after Sara died, that he was my mate. Could I find someone else, live a life of contentment, and move on? Maybe. But he was the one for me. It was like my soul knew his before we even really spoke. If you even think that you could have a connection like that with Amber, you owe it to yourself it explore it."

There was no point in arguing with her. She saw what she saw, and nothing he could say was going to get her to believe any differently. Especially when he wasn't even sure what he was feeling himself. Better to focus on the facts.

"The rules are clear, Chan. Weres mating with humans is forbidden. It's not like it's my decision, even if I wanted it to be."

"We have free will. Everything is our own decision. Things have a way of working out if you want them badly enough. Look at Liam and Amalie. Their love was as forbidden as it gets, and they made it work because he was willing to fight for her. And we were willing to fight for him."

"A move which we all know has cost us allies, and nearly cost Amalie her life," he reminded her gently.

"But it didn't. Don't focus on the 'what if's'. Focus on what you know and what your gut is telling you. We'll get through it. This pack is too strong to let something like this get between us."

He wasn't so sure about that. "Jax hates her."

Her auburn brows wrinkled and she shook her head. "No. Jax hates what she did, and that wasn't even really her fault. He doesn't know the real Amber. But if you make her your own, he'll get to know her and he'll forgive her soon enough. I have." She took his hand and squeezed. "Times are changing, my brother. We can't stay stuck in the past forcing our people to live under rules that were created before streetlamps were invented. It's time to re-evaluate. That's what Liam is always saying. Be strong. Be brave. And know this. If the time comes, I will fight for you."

She let his hand go and pushed back her chair to stand. "Now, if you'll excuse me, I've got to see a man about a horse. I'm finding that the pup isn't a big fan of orange juice." She gave him a wan smile before covering her mouth and dashing from the room.

"Good talk," he called after her, "thanks."

Poor Chan. She had another few months of that to look forward to. Then, if she was anything like the other pregnancies in the pack, it would be smooth sailing.

He stared out the window and reflected on her words, wondering if she had any idea how much they'd meant to him. He still had no idea what to do with them. The magnitude of what she'd suggested—an echo of what his wolf heart told him from the start—was so staggering, he couldn't get his head around it fully yet. But the fact that she'd taken the time to let him know she had his back was everything. It meant he had at least one person in his corner.

And he was sure as shit going to need it, because it hadn't even been twelve hours and he was already trying to figure out how to spend more time with Amber Jansen.

***

"So, who was the guy last night?"

Amber spun around, hand held to her now-knocking heart. "Jesus, Mila, you scared the shit out of me."

Her friend and co-worker tossed her mane of black hair over her shoulder and smiled. "I clomped in here on these platform heels as loud as a Clydesdale. If you didn't hear me, it was because you're clearly preoccupied."

Amber had just finished her afternoon shift at the club and was sitting at the bar waiting to get paid when Mila had come up behind her. She couldn't argue, though. She *had* been deep in thought. Ever since Billy had dropped her back off at her car the night before, he'd been front and center in her mind.

That voice. That face. That body.

That kiss.

She barely suppressed a shiver and forced a smile for her friend.

"Sorry, I was just daydreaming."

Mila snorted. "I don't blame you. A hunk like that after you? I'd be daydreaming too. And night-dreaming, and dusk-dreaming, and—"

"Got it," Amber cut in. The heat was rising in her cheeks fast, and she spun her stool back around to face the bar again. Blushing like a schoolgirl with a crush wasn't going to get Mila to stop teasing her, that was for sure. "He's a nice guy and all, but he's not my type." And she'd probably never see him again, after she threw herself at him.

"Oh, sweetie, don't be silly." Mila slid her trim form into the chair next to Amber and reached out to pat her hand. "A guy like that is everyone's type."

A surge of irritation that felt an awful lot like jealousy raced through her, but she forced it aside. Mila was right. Billy was universally, undeniably gorgeous.

Sex on a Popsicle stick.

Which was exactly why she had to get him out of her head. Not only was he tied irrevocably to the worst day of her life, he was also far too tempting.

As strange as it was, being in his arms felt like home. Seeing him again would only make her crave more, and right now, the last thing she needed was a distraction like that. Not when there were still so many unanswered questions, not the least of which was whether or not she was clinically insane.

She shot a glance in Mila's direction. "Have you ever seen a wolf?"

"Like, in the zoo, or?" Mila stared back at her, clearly nonplussed.

"No, I mean in the woods. Or in your backyard or anything like that? Up close."

Mila shook her head, dark hair gleaming in the dim light. "No, I can't say that I have." Her black brows came together in a puzzled frown. "Why do you ask?"

Amber hesitated for a long moment. She and Mila had worked together for more than a year. Hell, they'd even shared some lunches and gone shopping together a few times. But as much as she needed someone to talk to, she couldn't seem to squeeze the words out.

A second later, though, her phone vibrated on the bar in front of her, saving her the trouble. She snatched it up and held it to her ear. "Hello?"

"Amber? It's Billy."

Like he had to tell her. She'd have recognized that silky baritone anywhere. Mila's gaze lasered into her, and she willed her face to stay neutral in spite of the fact that her pulse was beating like a kick-drum.

"Hi."

Her greeting might have been innocuous, but her brain was churning, double-time. He'd given her his number, telling her to call if she needed anything, but she'd never given him hers. Now, with internet magic, it probably wasn't too hard to find, but she was definitely surprised to hear from him. She'd gotten the distinct impression that he needed some distance from her and, after a long, restless night, she'd finally convinced herself that was probably for the best.

But now…

"I spent a lot of time thinking about you today and was wondering if you'd like to go out this evening. Grab a drink, maybe shoot a game of pool. Might help to get out and do something normal, you know?"

She snuck a peek at Mila who stared back with unabashed interest before plugging a fistful of bar-nuts into her mouth like she was snacking at the movie theater while she enjoyed the show.

Amber turned her attention back to the jewel-toned mosaic of bottles behind the bar and found her mouth working on autopilot.

"Okay. Yeah, that sounds good."

Probably, she should've thought about it for a second before saying yes. Maybe run through the pros and cons of spending more time with Billy MacKenzie again. Last she had checked, there were definitely more cons than pros. Not only did she have enough on her plate with this mystery of the magically appearing wolf. Even if Billy and his friends *weren't* thieves like Tobias Wheeler had claimed, something was still very strange about the way they all lived on a compound like some sort of eerily attractive and compelling cult. Being around a man shrouded in mystery who probably couldn't be trusted shouldn't feel so good.

But, god, it did. And, mysterious or not, she couldn't bring herself to back out and miss another chance to be near him. Who knew? Maybe she'd also luck into some answers she could cling to this time.

"Great. Pick you up at your house at seven, then."

He disconnected before she could respond and she set the phone back on the bar, still half in a daze.

"So can I assume by your five-alarm coloring and those dreamy eyes that it was Mr. Hardbody McSexmuffin on the line?"

Amber leaned forward and laid her head on the bar with a groan, relishing the feel of the chilled wood against her flaming cheek.

"Is it that obvious? Ug. How humiliating." She sat up and eyed her friend. "I don't really know him that well. Do you get a sense of…" She ran a hand through her hair with a sigh. "Something a little dangerous or strange about him? Not like he'd hurt me or anything, but just…different? Maybe I shouldn't go."

Mila shoved the bowl of nuts away and wiped her hands off on her jeans.

"He's like a golden-dipped sex god, for Christ's sake. Of course you should go." She leapt up and grabbed Amber by the wrist, dragging her to stand beside her. "And I know just how to get you in the mood. Let's go shopping for your date. It will be fun. We'll even pick out some sexy underwear, just in case you decide to do what I would do, and get naked with his fine ass as soon as possible."

Mila turned her attention to the bartender.

"Tell Max to put our money in envelopes, and we'll be back to get it around dinnertime. Me and my girl Amber are going shopping."

Chapter Five

Shopping.
  For sexy underwear.
  Billy yanked the headphones from his ears and tossed them onto the desk with a growl. He'd been monitoring Amber's listening device in real time since noon, but after all the chatter he'd been privy to over the past few hours, only the last thirty seconds of it stuck out in his mind.
  Sexy. Underwear.
  And Amber hadn't even put up an argument when her friend suggested it. That was baaad news.
  He shifted in his high-backed desk chair and squeezed his eyes closed in an effort to staunch the images flickering through his head.
  No dice.
  Like scenes from an old silent movie, they flipped by, one after another. Amber in a peach thong. Amber in a red thong. Amber in fishnet stockings, a pair of thigh-high, black boots and nothing else.
  Yeah, his imagination was in overdrive when he should be focused on one thing and one thing only.

Sexy underwear or no, Amber wasn't going to stop pushing.

Last night he'd thought—well, maybe not *thought*, but *hoped*—that she'd take the easy road and believe his little fairytale about wolves in her neighborhood. But just this morning she'd gone to the library on her way to work to get more books. And after work, she'd been asking Mila pointed questions about wolves in the area.

Clearly, he'd had no choice but to call and nip that convo in the bud. She wasn't just researching now. She was talking. And talking was very, very bad.

He had his order. Get close to her if he needed to and try to contain the situation. But there was no question, Chandra's words from earlier that day still played over in his mind, about love and life…

"Don't squander it."

She was so right. All the strife between the packs and the deaths and near-deaths. It made a body realize exactly how fleeting it could all be. Such a simple concept, but one that was reshaping his view of the future.

A sharp rap on the door interrupted his thoughts, and he straightened. "Yep, come on in."

His packmate, Maggie, strode into the room, her posture as no nonsense as her expression.

"You need a break? I can man the controls for a while." She jerked her chin toward the headphones on the desk and pinned him with her onyx gaze.

"Nope. No need." The lies flowed from his mouth, smooth as whipped cream. "I'm going to meet up with her tonight to double check, but I spoke to her last night and she believes the story about wolf sightings in the area. I'm confident she's going to drop the whole thing."

She eyed him hard and tossed her dark mane over her shoulder. "You sure? Because she didn't seem even close to okay that last time I tailed her."

"I've got it covered. Trust me."

The last bit tasted bitter in his mouth, but it was a necessary evil. And at least it wasn't a lie. She *could* trust him. He was going to make sure it all worked out in the end.

But Maggie was definitely going to disapprove of his method. Of everyone in the pack, she was the least trusting of humans, and hadn't even fully come to grips with the half-baked plan himself.

He was still running through all the possible pitfalls himself when he felt it. Maggie's consciousness reaching out to his, a gentle pressure in his mind as she attempted to link with him. He didn't fight it, because that would only make her more suspicious. Instead, he shut down all thoughts of Amber and focused on the computer screen in front of him.

A new building site. Missing permits. Numbers, numbers, numbers.

Jesus, not thinking of something when you were actively trying not to think of something was a bitch.

Right when he thought he might blow it, Maggie broke the mental connection and stepped back.

"Okay, you're obviously busy. As long as you say you're going to take care of it, I'll leave you to it. I've got loads of work to do at the office anyway." She turned on one, high-heeled boot, heading for the door, but paused before stepping through to shoot him a look over her shoulder. "But Billy?"

"Yeah?" He tried to look annoyed as he tore his gaze from the screen in front of him to meet her gaze.

"Don't let your little head do the thinking for your big one, all right? This human woman is a moment in time. The pack is forever."

With that, she strode into the hallway and closed the door behind her with a decisive *click*, leaving him staring at the wide, walnut panel.

Okay, so he apparently had the worst poker face in history if both of the packmates he'd seen since spending time with Amber last night were onto him. Both had different takes on how he should handle the situation.

Hell, even now, his head told him Maggie was right. Falling for Amber was a shit-show in the making. But his gut agreed with Chandra, one hundred percent. On a purely instinctive level, he wanted nothing more than to immerse himself in Amber and cross all the hurdles that would surely crop up in his path as they came.

The mind of a man versus the heart of a wolf.

There was no contest.

And, tonight, he was going to put his life on the line and risk his place within his pack to protect this woman.

He'd just have to hope his wolf had it right, and that she was worth the risk a thousand times over.

By the time he stepped onto the porch of her little Victorian house a few hours later, he was feeling irritable and out of sorts.

Now that he'd made his decision, he was restless, his wolf tensed and ready to claw its way out to get to her.

Before he even had a chance to knock, the door swung open, and Amber stood in the frame, a tentative smile on her lips.

"Hi. You're right on time."

She wouldn't meet his gaze and one hand fluttered to her chest to toy with the slim, gold chain around her neck. Apparently, whatever need had been driving her to kiss him the night before seemed to have been dominated by a bout of nerves tonight. That was good. They had a lot to talk about, and he had a chance of controlling his urges if they were his alone.

If he had to be strong enough for the two of them until he'd said his piece?

Yeah. Not happening.

"Um, did you want to come in and see the place or?" Her cheeks flushed and she rolled her eyes. "Wait. You saw the place before. How many times does somebody need to see a place, am I right? A house is a house. Seen one, seen 'em all."

Her laugh sounded tinny and he found himself torn between the urge to hug her and another, far darker one, to bend her over the nearest fussy little piece of furniture and slide so deep inside her, she could think of nothing but him.

Almost as if she could read his mind, she took the decision out of his hands by stepping out, yanking the door closed behind her and practically running down the pathway to his truck.

He followed, bemused by the start to the evening. She was obviously as conflicted about their relationship as he had been. Odd how, in spite of everything that was at stake, just being in her presence made the weight lodged in his chest feel a little lighter.

"You look great, by the way," he said when they settled into the seats of the truck. She was wrapped in a bulky, cream-colored wool coat, but he could make out her curvy form beneath it and he couldn't help but wonder what underwear she'd wound up with.

Not that he was going to see it.

"Thanks." She was wringing her hands together and staring out the windshield so intently, he wondered if he'd misread her nerves. Maybe something more serious was at play here—

"I can't sleep with you," she blurted.

His brain went into overdrive as he turned the key in the ignition and the truck's engine roared to life. He let the words sink in for a few seconds before finally responding.

"Okay."

She turned to face him, her breathing coming in white puffs of steam into the icy, night air. "I mean, I want to sleep with you. I've been thinking about it pretty much non-stop. But it would be a terrible idea for both of us. I'm not even sure if I'm sane or not, and, until I figure things out, I can't get involved. No matter how much I—" she broke off and swallowed hard. "I just wanted to be up front about it so you wouldn't think I was a tease or anything."

She'd been thinking about sleeping with him.

Pretty much non-stop.

That sent a hot rush of blood south, filling his cock with a pulsing need that had already been too close to the surface. But then the rest of her words sank in, reaffirming what he'd already known. She was digging her heels in even deeper now, doggedly determined to find out the truth.

A truth that could kill her.

The rightness of his choice settled over him like a blanket. This was his best chance to protect her, and that was the most important thing.

He backed out of her driveway and pulled onto the street, taking the time to choose his words carefully. "I don't think you're a tease, Amber. And I definitely don't think you're crazy."

Stubborn, yes. Like a dog with a bone, but that was a flaw he both shared and kind of admired.

"So why don't we do exactly what we agreed to do when I called? Just have a fun night and try to put the past behind us for a while. Kick back, relax. Enjoy each other's company." And hopefully, get a few drinks in her, so the shock of what he was going to tell her didn't kill her on the spot.

She let out a sigh and her posture went from stiff to relaxed in an instant.

"That sounds really good to me. I can definitely use a mental half-time. But I have to warn you." She twisted in her seat to face him. "I'm a fantastic pool player, so you'd better get your game face on, buddy."

He let out a chuckle as a little of the tension left him. So long as she was willing to spend time with him, that meant he still had a chance.

A chance to protect her.

A chance to prove to the others that she was worthy of their trust.

A chance to convince her that the beast she saw that night might have looked fierce, but it would never, ever hurt her.

It wouldn't be easy, though. Because, right now, he felt very much like The Big Bad Wolf from that old-time scary-tale, which made Amber his Red Riding Hood.

And he wanted nothing more than to eat her up.

***

"Nine-ball, corner pocket."

Amber leaned forward and lined up her shot, taking the time to suck in a steadying breath. She was two balls away from winning the game and she wasn't about to blow it just because Billy had brushed by her, leaving his masculine scent trailing behind him.

She pinched her eyes closed and willed herself to focus. God, what was it about the way he smelled? It literally made her whole body tingle with the need to get closer. Breathe him in. She couldn't pinpoint it…like exotic spices, and leather, and masculinity times ten.

Totally addictive.

And was it her imagination, or did he seem to touch her every time he passed by, just a little?

"Nine-ball, corner pocket," she repeated, more firmly this time, ignoring the pressure pooling low in her belly. She took two practice strokes before firing off the shot. The cue-ball met the yellow striped one with a soft *snick*, and Amber grimaced as she watched the trajectory, knowing it was a miss long before it bobbled in the pocket and hung there.

"Well, shit," she muttered under her breath before straightening. "Looks like you're going to get another chance." She met Billy's gaze and made a sweeping gesture toward the green, felted table. "Better make the most of it."

Weird, how disappointed she was. Sure, she liked winning, but shooting pool with a friend while they drank a few beers didn't typically bring out her competitive nature. Now, though, with Billy looking on, studying her every move, eyes filled with respect whenever she made a difficult shot, she wanted so badly to win.

Friend, my ass. You want so badly to impress him. *You couldn't care less about winning.*

She reached for her pint of beer and took a sip, watching from over the rim of the glass as her opponent prowled around the table, circling like a shark on the hunt. Odd to see a man so big and muscular who managed to move with such effortless grace.

It captivated her.

"Four in the side," he said, his low voice carrying in spite of the jukebox playing in the background.

She set down her beer and leaned on her pool cue, watching with bated breath. If he missed, they'd continue playing, but if he made it, the eight-ball was a sitting duck in the opposite side pocket. He was sure to win the game.

"What about a little wager?" she said suddenly.

Where had that come from? Maybe the beer talking. She'd had three already, and had been too nervous to do much more than pick at the buffalo wings they'd ordered when they first got there. Still, now that the idea of a wager had come to her, she couldn't shake it.

In for a penny...

"No way you make that shot."

Billy stood and eyed her, a smile tugging at his firm lips. "Is that so? All right, then. Put your money where your mouth is. What's the bet?"

She hadn't thought that far ahead and swallowed hard as dozens of inappropriate thoughts flooded her brain. After the stress and strain of the past month, she'd grabbed onto the one night respite he'd offered like a lifeline, but maybe it was time to pump the brakes a little.

"A drink?" she said finally.

Lame.

He shook his golden head slowly, a challenging light filling his eyes. "I can buy my own drinks. This shot is tough. If I make it, I want something good."

"L-like what?"

Out of nowhere, she was suddenly very aware of her new bra. The black lace confection had cost her more than she'd made that day at The Naughty Kitty, but once she'd seen it, she couldn't resist.

"A kiss," he said. The words came out in a guttural, half-growl. Like they'd been mined from between his lips with a pick-axe, against his will. A fact that shouldn't have set her body aflame, but sooo did.

She should say no, flat out, but she couldn't seem to make her lips form the word. Nothing good could come of saying yes. But, damn it, she'd get to feel that mouth on hers again.

Which will only make you crave it more, the irritating, persistent voice in her head reminded her.

Friends.

She'd decided sometime between her shopping trip and when his truck had pulled up to her house, they could only be friends. At least until she figured out what had happened the night of the kidnapping. Even if he wasn't hiding something from her and it was just her own paranoia or some form of PTSD, diving headfirst into a relationship—or whatever this was—with a near stranger was probably a bad idea.

"Billy, we can't—"

"Sleep together." He inclined his head in a curt nod. "So you said. And I agree with that part of it. Bad idea. But a kiss? Hell, we've already done that. What's one more going to hurt?"

She could almost hear the gears in her brain shifting, making way for the rationalization portion of the show. They *had* already kissed once. And who was she kidding? The second he'd mentioned it, she'd known she wouldn't refuse him. If she did, she'd have spent the rest of their time together thinking about it, and the rest of the week regretting that she hadn't done it. Plus, who was to say he'd even win the bet?

She took another long pull from her beer for liquid courage and then nodded. "All right, then. A kiss."

"And if I miss?"

Her already slightly tipsy mind went blank. If he didn't make the shot, then what did she want from him? A few silly things flitted through her head. To have him refer to her as "Champ" all night long. Maybe have him pen a limerick about her stunning victory. But as she stood there looking at him, words came tumbling from her lips, unbidden.

"I want you to tell me a secret."

He had one. She didn't know how she knew, but she did. Even now, although the heat in his eyes didn't cool even one degree, his gaze grew guarded, and she wished she could take it back. What was she thinking, taking his harmless flirtation and turning it into some deep conversation? They'd made a deal for the night and she'd broken it. Total fail on her part, and she hurried to backtrack.

"It doesn't have to be where the bodies are buried or anything like that."

God, kill her now. Why had she brought up bodies when she was pretty sure the crazy kidnapper and would-be murderer, Tobias Wheeler, was buried somewhere on the grounds of the compound where Billy and his friends lived? Yet another little tidbit that should probably alarm her far more than it did, but whatever they'd had to do in an effort to get Chandra back, she was on board with. He'd deserved it after what he'd done. But again, not a discussion for tonight.

"Forget the 'never told anyone else' part," she hastened to add. "Just any old thing is fine. Like the one movie you always cry at. Or even the name of your first pet."

Right when she was about to back out on the bet altogether and tell him it was okay if he just wanted to bring her home, he held up a hand to stop her babbling.

"I'm good with it. And you know why?" He strolled toward her, his swagger as confident as his expression. "Because I'm not going to miss." He stroked her cheek with his index finger in the softest of touches. "So you better get those lips puckered and ready, because it's about to go down."

Probably, she should've been worried. He sure said it like it was a threat. But damned if it didn't just send a rush of damp heat to her center.

She forced a chuckle and willed her heart to stop pounding hard enough for him to hear. "Talk is cheap. Let's see it happen."

This time, when Billy went to take his shot, the casual stance he'd taken the rest of the game was nowhere to be found. He was focused, every muscle drawn tight, eyes narrowed in concentration. It was a thing to behold.

As was the way those faded jeans clung to his fine ass when he bent lower.

"Like I said, four-ball, side pocket."

Blood rushed to her ears and her mouth went bone-dry as the ball landed in the pocket with a *thunk*. "Nice one," she managed to squeeze out.

"It was. Want to go again?" He hitched his hip to lean against the table and eyed her intently. "Another kiss if I make the eight-ball? And a secret for you if I miss."

It was a sucker's bet. The ball was a hair's breadth from the pocket. But if she was going to dig herself in deeper by kissing him once, doing it twice could hardly make things worse.

And, damn, did she want that secret.

"You're on."

He gave her one last hungry look before bending to position himself for the shot.

She watched, all thought suspended, as he cocked his arm and sent the cue ball careening toward the eight. The black ball fell neatly into the pocket, but before she could even process how to feel about it, the white cue ball fell behind it.

"Scratch! You lose," she murmured, a thrill coursing through her. She got to kiss Billy and she got her secret.

"Looks like it." He straightened, the expression on his face sending her pulse racing. "So what do you say we get out of here? I've been thinking of the secret I want to share, and I think it's better if I tell you in private. Then, if you're game, I'll collect my kiss. I'd prefer if we didn't have an audience, if it's all the same to you."

It wasn't all the same to her. In fact, the very thought had her jumping out of her skin. How was she going to stick to her guns and keep herself from acting on her impulses if they were alone and unsupervised?

But the lure of him…the promise of his secret, while terrifying, was also too strong to resist.

She drained the last of her beer and mustered up a smile and her courage.

"What are we waiting for?"

Chapter Six

It wasn't an easy task, but Amber tried to let the warm breath of the heater and the low drone of the truck's engine soothe her as they drove.

She wasn't sure where they were going, and oddly enough, she wasn't sure it mattered. She'd spent the past month floating in space, unanchored and alone. But she wasn't alone anymore, and she trusted him. He knew what she'd been through, had lived through the fear and terror with her, and just having him near again grounded her and made her feel safe.

"We're here," he said softly, the husky baritone pulling her from her reverie.

She opened her eyes and straightened, looking around. "We're where?"

They'd pulled off the bumpy, makeshift road he'd been on and into a tiny inlet. Tall, skeletal trees surrounded them on all sides, the sight only broken by the occasional lush jack pine or evergreen. The moon hung fat in the sky, like a milky wheel of cheese, and lit the tiny clearing in a warm light.

"I told you. Somewhere private."

He turned off the car, and let himself out before coming around to her side and opening her door. "Seriously? Weren't you just telling me about wolves venturing out of their territories?" She stared down at his big, outstretched hand and then glanced past him into the dark forest. "Your apartment is private. My house is private, and only like twenty minutes away. It's warm…and there are lights."

His firm lips twitched and he shook his head slowly. "That sounds great, but for now, this is where we need to be, all right?"

She took in a steadying breath and blew it out, wincing as it crystalized in the freezing air in a puff of white. "Do you at least have a blanket or something?"

His green eyes took on a curious light. "You won't need one."

She winced but nodded and reached out a hand to grab her purse.

"Won't need that either."

She opened her mouth to argue, but then let it close with a snap. He was it right now. The one person who had been willing to help her through this when the rest of his friends obviously still blamed her at least half as much as she blamed herself for all that had happened. If he wanted to share with her, she'd play by his rules. It was the least she could do.

She slipped her hand into his and murmured in pleasure as the heat of his skin warmed her.

He helped her out of the car onto the ice-crusted grass and led her toward the center of the clearing. There was a small fire pit there with wood already neatly stacked.

"Oh, that's excellent," she said, releasing his hand and bee-lining straight for it. "Please tell me you have matches?"

He brandished them with a half-smile and popped a squat next to the circle of rocks. "Like a Boy Scout, always prepared."

Less than a minute later, a crackling fire roared, and she groaned in appreciation as she leaned in to hold her hands over the flames.

"So much better."

"Have a seat." He gestured to a long, wide log in front of the fire and she sat obediently.

The suspense was killing her and she eyed him expectantly. "Okay. So let's hear it. What's your secret?"

What if he decided to kiss her first instead? She probably had beer breath. God, why hadn't she grabbed a mint on the way out of the bar?

"I think it's better if I just show you."

Any thought that he'd decided to take her up on her offer to share something silly with her about his favorite chick flick or his embarrassing middle name fled when she saw how serious he'd grown. So much so that her muzzy brain urged her to make a joke to ease the tension. Ask him if he'd brought her here as a ritual sacrifice for a raccoon worshipping cult or something. But his solemn expression sealed her lips and she waited, silent, heart galloping wildly in her chest.

He turned around and yanked his shirt off. Hysteria began to build inside her, and laughter bubbled from her mouth. Maybe he really was going to kill her after all. Or maybe he was a flasher and he was about to whip it out.

But even through the haze of the alcohol, a deeper part of her, the part that already knew—had always known—wasn't laughing at all. Visions from her nightmares battered her brain, images of monsters and men and teeth gnashing melded with the present. Shadows dappled Billy's skin as he moved, shucking off his boots, unbuckling his jeans and letting them drop to the ground, leaving him in only a pair of black boxer shorts.

He straightened and she almost told him to stop. Almost told him that she'd rather live in ignorance. She could still walk away right now. Go back to her little Victorian house and work her ass off to forget that she'd ever met Wheeler or Billy or any of his friends.

"Amber?" His low voice centered her and she met his intense gaze. He was offering it to her now. The chance to back out.

She took a steadying breath, suddenly as sober as a priest in church, and nodded. "I'm ready."

She wasn't sure what she'd been expecting, but it paled in comparison to what she got.

One second, Billy stood there, tall and strong and handsome, like a God from Greek Mythology. Thor without need of a hammer.

The next, he leapt into the air, head tipped back, body flexed, and exploded into something else entirely.

It happened so fast, the shock of it hit her like a bucket of ice to the face. The last thing she saw before she hit the ground was that tawny, green-eyed wolf of her dreams loping toward her.

***

"Amber?"

He was starting to get worried now. He'd done everything he could think of to wake her, and had followed all the protocol to stave off shock. For the past ten minutes, though, she lay in his now-clothed lap, knocked the hell out.

She didn't seem to be in any discomfort so he was loathe to move her, but it was getting to the point that he was considering bringing her back to the compound to have the pack doctor take a look at her. That wasn't the way he'd imagined breaking the news to the pack, but Amber's health was more important than covering his own ass, and if that was what needed doing-

"Billy?"

The chunk of ice wedged in his stomach melted at the sound of her soft voice.

"Hey there. You scared me there for a second."

She shook her head slowly and her body went stiff as she became more aware of her surroundings.

"I scared *you*?" She shoved at his chest and scrambled to her feet, fury blazing in her eyes, hotter than the fire that crackled between them. "You son of a bitch."

Her voice dripped icicles, and she nearly spat the words at him.

"I asked you. I begged you to tell me, and instead, you let me think I'd lost my mind."

He rose and stepped toward her, but she backed away.

He had to slow it down. She was still reeling and she had every right to be.

"I didn't want to lie to you. I need you to believe me when I tell you that I had no choice. Hell, even now, I'm breaking more pack laws than you could ever hope to imagine by telling you. Our kind doesn't do this sort of thing." He scrubbed a hand over his face and stared down at her. "Do you know how many humans I've shared the truth with, Amber?"

She glared at him before whipping around to face the fire, staring into its depths as if it held the answer to his question.

"None," he said softly. "You are the only person I've ever told about us. Because I hated lying to you and I thought you deserved the truth."

He'd known this wasn't going to be easy, but what if he'd gotten it wrong? What if she did the exact opposite of what he'd thought she would do, and betrayed him? Or, worse, betrayed his pack?

He steeled himself against the rush of emotions that swamped him and shoved it aside. They'd had a bad run with humans lately, what with Sara's death and Chandra's kidnapping, but Amalie was living proof that there were humans who deserved their respect. And Amber was one of them.

"So, just to state the obvious and make sure we're all on the right page, you're what? A werewolf?" she asked, her voice still tight with anger.

He mulled over that question, debating on arguing semantics, but opted to take the easy route to start. No point in overwhelming her this soon.

"Basically, yeah."

"All of you?"

"The people at the compound, you mean? Yes."

He'd originally considered only telling her about him, but had dismissed it out of hand. She wasn't stupid. Once the wheels were set in motion, the rest would fall into place whether he told her or not. No point in losing what little trust he'd earned by telling her another lie that wouldn't help the situation in any case.

She started pacing back and forth, muttering to herself, and he didn't interrupt her. Another five minutes went by before she slowed to look at him again. Some of the anger had faded and her eyes were clearer than he'd ever seen them, like she'd been lifted from a fog. The sight sent a shot of hope through him.

"And that's why Wheeler wanted Chandra so bad? He wanted to prove that you all existed, is that right? That was all the crazy nonsense he was rambling about."

He nodded, leaning back against a nearby tree. "And she wasn't his only victim. He murdered Jax's first mate, Sara."

She blanched and her already pale cheeks went chalk-white. "No wonder Jax hates me."

"You didn't know. You couldn't have known. You made a mistake." He pushed away from the tree, and this time, when he stepped forward, she didn't back away. "We made mistakes on our end too, and I'm trying to rectify that now. What do you say we start fresh? From today."

Her responding nod was tentative and slow to come. "We can try."

He would need more than that from her soon enough, but for tonight? He'd take it.

Her nod circled around, morphing into a dazed shake of her head. "I know I should be freaking out right now. Werewolves exist. Jesus, it's like a frigging bizarre dream. But all I feel is residual anger." She met his gaze, her brows knit in confusion.

"And relief. How crazy is that? Like, a frigging Mack truck ton has been lifted off my shoulders. Because I knew."

She bit her trembling bottom lip and the fire bathed her skin in a warm glow as she wrapped her arms around her waist and rocked slowly from side to side.

"I was so lost. I knew I'd seen something, but my brain just wouldn't accept it." Her throat worked as she swallowed hard enough that he could hear it. "Thank you for showing me. I know it must have been a difficult decision."

There was so much more to the story. So much more he needed to say before he could even imagine an outcome that didn't end in tragedy. But her words were a start. The kernel of hope he needed to push forward with his plan.

Tomorrow.

But tonight? He reached out and took her unresisting hand in his.

"There's something else I want you to see."

She hesitated but then nodded. He was humbled by her trust, which only made him more determined to make sure he proved himself worthy of it.

"I have so many questions," she said as he led her deeper into the forest. The wind had picked up to a howl and she was shivering again now that they'd left the warmth of the fire.

"Shoot."

"Well, first of all, is that how come your body feels so warm all the time?"

The fact that she had noticed and contemplated the heat of his skin sent a pulse of male satisfaction roaring through him.

"It is. We run a few degrees hotter than humans."

"And how did you...get that way? Are you like vampires where someone has to bite you or...?"

He slowed and pulled her to a stop, looking down into her curious face. "I can only speak for myself, and I was born to werewolf parents. There are some who are turned, but that's rare. We have rules and such."

Rules that would probably scare the shit out of her, so he opted not to share unless she asked.

"Are there others?"

"Others?"

"Other types of shifters. Like, lions? Or otters?"

Those wide blue eyes were killing him and he resisted the urge to wrap his arms around her. "Otters? No. Not that I know of, at least." Not a lie, exactly. Again, it just seemed like she had enough on her plate what with the whole wolf shifter bombshell. The fact that there were also bear shifters would blow her freaking mind.

And god help him if he mentioned the dragons.

"And the full moon thing?" she asked. "Because I don't remember it being full the night Chandra..." her voice trailed off and she turned her face away from him.

"The full moon is a lure, for sure. We like it. But a grown werewolf can control when he or she shifts, full moon or no." He reached out and laid a gentle hand on her shoulder, urging her to turn toward him again. "You have to stop beating yourself up about this. Tobias Wheeler is the one who kidnapped Chan. You are as much a victim as she was, okay? Chandra forgives you, you know. Now it's time for you to start doing the same."

She looked so forlorn, he didn't fight his instincts any longer. He pulled her into the circle of his arms and bent his head low to press a kiss to her forehead. So strange. He'd been attracted to hundreds…maybe thousands of women before, but never like this. Never in a way that made him want to protect them and hold them at least as much as he wanted to sleep with them.

She stiffened for a moment and then let out a sigh and burrowed closer, slipping her arms around his waist. It felt like validation. Acceptance, and it filled him with a relief so keen, his body quaked with it. She knew what he was, and hadn't run away screaming.

It was a start.

They stayed like that until she stopped shivering, and finally pulled away.

"Come on. You had something you wanted to show me." She tugged him by the hand back in the direction they'd been heading.

They walked in silence for a few minutes, and he was sure she was thinking of a dozen more questions to ask him. He only hoped when they reached their destination she would be too captivated to ask them. He had a lot of planning to do before he spilled the rest of it, no matter how much he wanted to waylay her fears.

A low hissing sound caught his attention, and Amber froze in her tracks.

"Do you hear that?" she whispered, squeezing his hand more tightly. "Is that a snake? Because I don't do snakes." She spun to stare up at him in horror. "Jesus, you're not going to tell me there are weresnakes, are you?"

He laughed, and the sound echoed through the forest. "No snakes, of the 'were' variety or otherwise. Promise." He started walking again and pulled her with him, a sense of anticipation building in his belly.

This, at least, he knew would be a welcome surprise.

They walked a little further until they reached a little break in the trees and he stepped to one side.

"Ladies first."

She hesitated for a split second. "Okay, but for the record, this shows a massive level of trust on my end. You did just show me you're a werewolf after all, and I am walking into a remote forest with you in the dark. Now you want me to walk in front of you through that tiny space between the trees. Seems like the script to a horror movie." She didn't wait for him to respond as she squared her shoulders and shimmied through the brush into the clearing.

"Oh my god," she gasped.

He stepped up to stand beside her and take in the view.

A huge, steaming, spring bubbled ten yards in front of them, the size of a small swimming pool. Even from where they stood, he could feel the heat pouring from it, warming the air around them. The steam seemed to emphasize the fresh forest smells—pine and sap and earth—to the point that even a human could detect them.

Clearly, she noticed, because she dragged in a deep breath through her nose and sighed with pleasure. "This is amazing."

She stepped closer to the frothy water, and waved a hand through the thick steam above it, scattering the particles.

"Seriously, the second most amazing thing I've seen tonight. Thank you for bringing me." She stood and stared at the scene for a long moment before wheeling around to face him.

"Is it…safe?"

The hopeful expression on her face made him second-guess his original plan. He'd wanted to show it to her to take her mind off the whole werewolf thing a little, but he hadn't planned on getting in.

Partly because they didn't have any towels and it was freezing out, but also because he didn't know if he could handle being in the water with her mostly naked without touching her. A concept which, at the moment, seemed about as naïve as sending a starving man to a buffet and expecting him not to eat.

It would be heavenly hell.

Exquisite torture.

He tipped his head in a curt nod. "Absolutely."

Twisted fuck.

But there was only one thing that seemed worse than getting in the water and not touching her, and that was the thought of not getting in the water with her at all.

"Totally safe. I've been here many times."

"Oh." Her face fell and she bit her lip.

It took him a second to figure it out, but when she averted her gaze, it came to him like a switch had been flipped.

"Alone. I've been here many times. Always alone. You're the first person I'm sharing this with." Her gaze warmed on his face, and she smiled.

"I'm glad," she said simply. Then, she gave him her back and started tugging off her clothes. The heavy fleece went first. Next her sweater, leaving her in only a thin, long-sleeved cotton shirt and her jeans. She paused and shot him a glance over her shoulder. "Did I mention that the last one in is a rotten egg?"

The words took a second to sink in, but when they did, he dropped to one knee and started unlacing his work-boots. Because fuck that. He wasn't about to be a rotten egg.

She barked out a laugh filled with such genuine joy, it made his blood sing, and then she began stripping off the rest of her clothes.

It wasn't until he stood a minute later, naked as the day he was born—only without the fur—that he saw her again. Only now, she was buck naked, standing in a moonbeam that had fought its way through the canopy of trees, seemingly just for her.

And she was gorgeous.

All ripe curves and smooth, creamy skin. Her golden hair hung wild around her shoulders, the ends trailing over her full breasts. She shivered beneath his gaze, her pink nipples peaking in the chilly night air.

"Amber…"

Her throat worked as she stared at him, letting her gaze trail over his chest, down his stomach and lower, where his cock pulsed and went rock hard.

"Rotten egg," she murmured in a husky voice. A second later, she whipped around and ran into the spring.

He followed her, saying a silent prayer.

There was still a world of unfinished business between them. More secrets to tell, more pitfalls ahead, before they would know whether or not they had a chance in hell of being together.

And something told him, once he got inside Amber Jansen, he'd never want to leave.

Chapter Seven

Lord, his body was like something out of a superhero movie.

She stepped deeper into the steaming pool until the water lapped at her nipples and covered her breasts. She shouldn't be ashamed. At least he'd had the same physical response to her nakedness as she'd had to his. And, man, had he responded.

Even now, she was trying not to look as he took a step into the pool, but there was no hiding it. His cock was thick and ready, stiff against his belly, and she ached to wrap her fingers around it and squeeze.

"Is it too hot for you?" His deep voice sent a thrill through her and she tried to keep it together and not throw herself at him like some sort of old-time Elvis groupie.

"It feels great. Like heaven."

It was true. The chill of the air outside tickled her heated cheeks but the rest of her felt like it was wrapped in a hug from Mother Nature. In fact, if it weren't for the hottest guy in the universe being in the spring right next to her, she was pretty sure she could've easily drifted onto her back and taken the most relaxing catnap ever.

As it stood, it was anything but relaxing.

It was energizing and life affirming. It felt like the first step into a whole new world.

She waded to the side to make more room for him, and he immersed himself. The pool covered her to her collarbone when she stood, but it barely reached his waist.

"Aren't you freezing?" she asked, bending her knees until she sank low enough that the hot bubbles tickled her chin.

"Nope." His whole body seemed tense and ready as he cocked his head in challenge. "Wanna check for yourself?"

Her throat went tight at the same time her nipples did, and she tried to find her voice. It was a new day. Everything had changed in the blink of an eye and there was no going back. She could tumble and flail the rest of the way down this rabbit hole, or she could tuck and roll, and enjoy the ride.

She ignored the nerves jangling around inside her and nodded. "I do."

She rose and closed the distance between them, lifting a tentative hand out of the water into the night air. She pressed her palm to his chest and someone—Her? Him?—let out a hiss.

He hadn't lied. His skin was hot to the touch and she wanted more of it. So much more.

"I'd like to collect," he muttered, his voice all grit.

"Collect?" She was sure she should know what he was talking about but she was so focused on the feel of him, she could barely think straight.

"My kiss. I won it fair and square."

"So you did," she said, tipping her head back so she could meet his molten gaze.

"I'm going to take care of you, Amber. No matter what, we're in this together," he said softly.

Before she could make sense of his words, he was swooping down, wrapping his arms around her and kissing her with a fierceness that would have overwhelmed her in another lifetime, but set her aflame in this one.

His tongue stroked hers in a dance that made her strain closer. When her breasts, already heavy with want, touched his chest, she cried out into his mouth.

This was happening. She'd woken from a nightmare only to fall into a dream.

He speared a hand into her hair and held her firm as he ravaged her mouth, sending wave after wave of need pulsing through her. She inched forward and gasped as his erection pushed insistently against her stomach. Instinctively, she rocked against him, reveling in the pressure.

He grunted and pressed her back against the edge of the pool. She gasped as he lifted her onto a small ledge. It left her top half exposed to the chilly night air and her sensitive nipples tightened even further.

He must have seen it too, because he groaned and swooped in low to capture one between his teeth. She threaded her fingers through his hair, tipped her head back and let her eyes drift close, blocking out the stars twinkling above to focus on the sensations coursing through her.

"That feels so good," she murmured, arching her back as the heat of his tongue swirled around her nipples.

He tightened his grip on her hips and she moaned, loving the feel of his bridled strength. It was there. The full measure of it, right under the surface, and suddenly, more than anything, she wanted to feel it. All of it.

"Don't hold back for me." It wasn't a request. It was a demand. "I won't break, Billy. Please."

He released her breast and lifted his head to meet her gaze. His eyes were like two glittering chips of emerald and his voice was guttural.

"Are you sure?"

Tuck and roll, straight down the rabbit hole.

"I'm sure."

And what had been a sensual dance…a sultry, winding path to ecstasy, became a battle. He jerked her upward, into his arms, using his immense power to hold her aloft, to make her wrap her legs around his waist for purchase. His cock pulsed and kicked against her pubic bone, and the increased pressure alone was almost enough to—

"I need to see you," he muttered through gritted teeth. "Fall back. I won't let you go under."

She didn't hesitate, letting her muscles relax, lowering herself into the water until she floated on her back, anchored by his steadying hands and her thighs around his hips.

The water sent her hair flowing and moving around her, brushing her shoulders and tangling over her breasts to catch on her nipples.

"You look like a fucking mermaid. Jesus, I will never forget the way you look right now."

A second later, her hips were free and he urged her to float completely, to let her legs spread wide as he helped her stay afloat by cupping both cheeks of her ass and then stepping between her thighs.

Slowly, he drifted her backward, to the opposite edge of the pool and she started in surprise as her back bumped against another underwater shelf.

When she peered up at him, she realized that his whole focus was on the apex of her thighs. He looked hungry…starving, and every nerve-ending in her body lit up in anticipation.

She wriggled until her back was supported by the smooth stone beneath her, and shivered as some of her skin was exposed to the cold. Her suffering was blessedly short, because a second later, he growled her name and was on her. All hot mouth and lashing tongue. It was no gentle exploration. He wanted to eat her alive, and she nearly died from the pleasure of it.

"Billy," she groaned as the undulating water worked in tandem with his mouth, like twin tongues caressing her needy center. He closed his lips tight over her clit and sucked, and it was all she could do not to scream as shudders wracked her now fevered body.

He murmured his pleasure at her reaction and dug his fingers deep into the cheeks of her ass, grinding her closer, pressing his face into her until the pleasure became so intense, the need to come so overwhelming, a scream began to build in her chest.

Billy tore his mouth away long enough to peer up at her with almost preternaturally green eyes and mutter, "You taste so fucking good," before diving back in, working that throbbing bundle of nerves with his tongue until she began to tug at his hair and thrust her hips restlessly.

She needed to stop him or slow down, before—

"I want to come with you inside me," she managed on a gasp, trying to ward off the impending climax that, even now, was threatening to drag her under. "Please Billy, I need—"

What did she need? To be connected with him. To look in his eyes and see his want, to know he was as far gone as she was.

He straightened, water sluicing over his thickly muscled shoulders, and met her gaze. "Yes."

"Protection?" she groaned, the rawness of her voice shocking her. She waited for the shame to come…but it never did.

"My kind is immune to disease like that and pregnancy is only an issue if we choose it to be."

"Oh, thank god," she whimpered.

She shook off his hands and scrambled to her feet, reaching between them to do what she'd been dying to do since the second he'd taken his pants off.

"Shit," he grunted, as she closed her fingers tightly around him and squeezed before working her hand upward in a firm stroke.

He was so hard, so ready, and her body responded to the call, clenching and fluttering in anticipation of his thick length inside her.

"Now," he bit out, shaking his head briskly, "it has to be now." He tugged her hand away and used it to turn her around, facing away from him.

She shivered at his words, and then again as he pressed her gently forward, dipping her breasts back into the steamy froth, the shock of the change in temperature adding another layer to the sensual onslaught.

When his big hands palmed her ass, she leaned forward until her cheek touched the water, and braced herself on the edge of the pool with her hands. Anything to make his path inside her as quick as possible.

He tucked one hand lower, teasing the crevice between her cheeks, drifting down until he reached her slick slit and then drove one thick finger inside.

"Mmm, oh my god," she groaned as the blood rushed to her head. Then he started to move, sliding in and out, then added a second until she cried out, slamming her hips backward in an effort to take him deeper still. Her legs shook as the need to come bore down on her like a coming train.

A moment later he was gone and she cried out for the loss, but he was back in an instant.

"Shh," he murmured.

She felt him then, the thick head of his cock probing between the petals of her center, sliding in, filling her, inch by inch. It was an almost painfully tight fit, but one that came with so much pleasure, she found herself murmuring incoherently just to keep sane for one moment more. She didn't want it to be over yet. She wanted it to go on and on, but her orgasm wouldn't be denied. She'd been on the razor's edge for too long, and what she wanted and what she needed were two very different things.

"Now, Billy, please, now," she cried.

He pulled back and plowed forward again in one, long, firm stroke, not stopping until he was seated to the hilt. For a second, she was suspended there, mouth open, body locked in ecstasy.

And then she exploded over his cock, twitching and squeezing and crying his name as stars burst behind her eyelids.

He held her through it, flexing deeper with each tremor, murmuring words of praise as he worked every last shudder from her.

When she was finally spent, he squeezed her ass in both hands and let out a groan. "So good."

She wanted to agree, but she still hadn't caught her breath. And by the time she had? He stole it from her again with another deep thrust.

The clawing need that had just been sated rose again with a speed that stunned her. Could she seriously come a second time?

He pulled back and drove home again, his hands sliding up and around to cup her breasts as he pressed his chest to her back.

Oh, she could definitely come again. It would be a first, and one she would have wanted with no one more than Billy. She hadn't wanted it to be over, and it wasn't. Already, she could feel the pull of it, shimmering in the distance. With every thrust.

He dropped a sucking kiss to her nape and she shivered.

"You sexy fucking woman, you."

His gruff praise sent her nerves into overdrive. The words had barely left his lips when his grip on her breasts tightened and he used the leverage to slide her further down on his cock. Then he was moving, and she was moving as he worked her over his swollen length. Every drag of his flesh against hers touching off another round of gasps.

He tweaked her stiff nipples until she bucked against him. He was like a machine now, hips moving like pistons as he worked them both toward the finish line.

"Oh, god!" The dam broke and her muscles strained as the orgasm crashed over her. A keening wail rose in her throat as he pounded into her, filling her to bursting.

She was still clenching, in the throes of it herself, when he stiffened behind her and growled. His hands dug into her hips as he leaned forward to sink his teeth into her shoulder, muffling his shout of completion as he pulsed inside her.

It was a long while before she felt capable of even opening her eyes. But when she did, everything seemed brighter. Clearer. She could feel his heart still pounding against her back, hear his harsh breath in her ears, and it felt like home.

"You're amazing," he murmured softly. He swept her hair to the side and pressed a kiss to the back of her neck. The simple show of affection sent her emotions tilting out of control. She'd never felt this way before and it left her reeling.

Because now she knew it for sure.

She was madly, inexplicably, crazy in love with a werewolf.

Chapter Eight

He'd just had the single most intense sexual experience of his life.

And it had been with a human woman.

Jesus, Mother Nature had a warped sense of humor. But he wasn't surprised. He'd known the second he'd seen Amber. Held her in his arms and comforted her after Chandra's attack, that she was special. His wolf had known from the very start what he was only now coming to terms with.

He didn't just want to help her. And he didn't just want to sleep with her.

He wanted her to be his mate.

There were still too many hurdles to cross to tell her yet. And it was too much, too fast, especially for a human to relate to. They could be so caught up in their heads sometimes, never staying quiet or still long enough to listen to the whispers from their true selves, so quick to dismiss what their instincts told them.

His instincts were telling him that Amber was as nuts about him as he was about her. The question was, would she be able to admit it to herself?

"Billy?"

Amber's soft voice pulled him back to her and he tightened his hold around her waist.

"Yeah?"

"Your pants are lighting up."

It was then that he focused, tuning in beyond the splash and hiss of the pool. His cell phone.

Shit.

He'd been so distracted, he hadn't even heard it. The pack had long ago selected a ringtone for calls from the emergency line at the compound in the event that someone needed to be reached but had put their thoughts in "private" mode.

That ringtone was pouring from the pocket of his discarded jeans.

A shot of adrenaline went coursing through him and he released Amber to make a lunge over the edge of the spring to grab for his phone.

"Yeah," he barked, with growing apprehension.

"What the fuck did you do?"

Maggie's voice sounded over the line like a whip-crack and he pinched his eyes closed before blowing out a sigh.

This wasn't part of the plan. Not yet.

"Look, I'm busy right now, and I'll be home as soon as I can—"

"No. You'll be home now, because—and I know this will come as a surprise—I didn't cover for your dumb ass. I told Liam what you were doing."

He paused, wracking his brain for how she'd known so quickly. He'd planned the date for a crowded bar, so the background noise would render the bug nearly useless in anyone had decided to monitor it. And when they'd gone out to the clearing, he'd had Amber leave her purse in the car, so how had Maggie—?

"I saw that googly-eyed, lovey look on your face when I went into your office and I knew you were going to do something stupid. So I placed a bug on *your* phone when you were in the shower." Her voice was thick with accusation. "I heard you tell her, Billy."

He felt guilty and angry all in the same go. She hadn't trusted him and had invaded his privacy, but she was justified on both counts. She had done it to protect the pack, and she was right not to trust him. However he chose to rationalize it, he had broken the rules, and disobeyed his alpha. He only hoped that Liam and the rest of his pack would stand by him once he had the chance to explain himself.

"Liam has called an emergency meeting. Don't add insult to injury by disrespecting our alpha at a time like this. If you care about the pack, you will stop what you're doing, get in your truck, and get back here, now," she said.

Without responding, he depressed the red button to disconnect and set the phone down next to his jeans.

"What?" Amber asked, laying a warm hand on his shoulder. "Is everything all right?"

He hadn't anticipated this. Not so fast, at any rate.

He kept his features calm and turned back to her, the ache in his gut worsening at the sight of her beautiful face. "No. We've got a situation to deal with. I'm so sorry to do this to you right now. I wanted to spend the next week talking. Explaining things, exploring our options. I know I've piled enough on your plate for the night, but there's no getting around it."

He tucked a wet strand of hair behind her ear.

"The timeline has changed. You have two choices now. I take you home to pack your most sentimental possessions and I put you on a plane to Budapest or Fiji or somewhere far, far away until I've assessed and eliminated the risks. Or you can come with me to the compound and face the pack. I've broken a lot of—" *Christ, so many,* "rules tonight, not to mention some direct orders, and I have to stand and face my brothers and sisters and explain why."

He hated this. Seeing her shining face grow solemn and scared again.

"Risks? I don't get it. I thought you said Tobias Wheeler was no longer a threat?"

How sad was that? The same night he told her about the existence of weres, he also had to tell her that they were often their own worst enemies. That, while they had dealt with Tobias, they had only traded one danger for another. One that could prove far more deadly.

"If you come with me," he continued, determined to get it all said quick, like ripping off a bandage, before he started answering questions. "You're going to be judged, and possibly mocked, and once the other packs know about you, you will be hated. Worse, you will be targeted." He took her hands in his and squeezed, making sure his gaze conveyed how committed he was. "But I will protect you. You have my word on that. So now you need to ask yourself if you're in, or you're out. Because once you're told the rest of it, and enter the compound, the wheels will be set in motion that can't be stopped. You won't have the luxury of just walking away, so you need to be sure. I won't blame you if you want to run."

Her furrowed brow and worried eyes seemed to take on a harder, more determined edge and she took a long breath.

"What are we waiting for?"

***

"Is this real life right now?" Maggie demanded, her voice shrill with disbelief as she looked at him, and then at Amber, and back again. "Liam tells you to come and you bring her with you? You realize, you have just confirmed to the Kotke and Big Sky Canyon packs that we are accepting another human into the Pray fold? The human they've been suspicious of for more than a month now?"

He stood his ground and squeezed Amber's trembling hand in his. He couldn't imagine how terrified she must be. On a good day, Maggie was intimidating. On a day like today, when she looked like she would just as soon slit both their throats and be done with it, she was chilling.

"I did what I thought was right. We wronged her, Maggie. All of us." He swept his gaze over the rest of his packmates scattered around the great room. "She thought she was losing her mind, and she'd started asking questions that would put her life in jeopardy. I wasn't about to stand by and watch an innocent woman die because a couple of backward old men don't like the fact that this pack has chosen to treat people as more than food, sport or some sort of nuisance to be exterminated. In this, I thought we were of the same mind, Liam." He let his gaze settle on the alpha and waited.

"And so we are, Billy. But there is a lot at stake. You've forced my hand by bringing her here, and I don't like it," Liam said, his tone matter of fact as he searched Billy's face for answers.

"I get that. And you know what your options are." Billy leaned closer to Amber. "I'm willing to accept whatever punishment you deem necessary."

Everyone in the room went silent as the ramifications of the men's exchange set in.

Amber flicked a glance from Liam to Billy and back again.

"Wh-what are you talking about?" She turned to face Chandra. "What punishments?"

Billy wanted to explain. To reassure her, but he was pretty sure nothing he could tell her was going to help. Because what everyone else in the room knew that she didn't was that Liam had the authority to handle this a number of ways.

He could stand by Billy and they could handle it together, as a pack.

He could turn his back on him and excommunicate him.

Or he could kill them both and be done with it.

By standing toe to toe with him now, Billy was letting his alpha know that he wanted to stay in the pack, but if that wasn't acceptable, he would leave with Amber. And if Liam chose option three? Well, then it was about to go down. He would fight to the death to protect Amber if he had to.

The idea of fighting his family sickened him and the idea of watching them kill his true mate sickened him even more, but no matter how many ways he'd examined this problem, once the other packs had become suspicious of Amber, she had been marked for death. He had opted to put his faith in himself and his pack to protect her and do what was right.

Now, all that remained to be seen was whether his faith had been misplaced.

"We need to prepare," Liam said, his face solemn as he rose from behind his desk. Amalie stood and took his hand, nodding in agreement, relief washing over her face. "You're right. The days of behaving like barbarians and killing humans on a whim is over. We'll stand for Amber now as we stood for Amalie then. And we'll fight."

His words were a balm to Billy's soul and he sucked in a steadying breath to thank him, when a short, harsh laugh had him turning his head.

"You can't be serious." Maggie's flat tone as her gaze flicked from him back to Liam again, was enough to have his hackles rising. "She nearly got Chandra killed." She wheeled around to skewer Jax and Chandra with her glare. "Are the two of you going to stand for this?"

Jax pursed his lips and stayed silent but Chandra patted his leg and lifted her chin. "We are. Amber was as much a victim in this as I was. I won't see her harmed."

"This is bullshit," Maggie spat.

That was the final straw. She was pissed. He got that. But enough was enough.

"Who the fuck are you?" Billy demanded, slipping an arm around Amber's shoulder. "This isn't your decision to make. And if you don't like it, you know where the door is."

"Have you all lost your minds?" Maggie spun in a circle to treat the entire pack to her glare. "Do you realize the Pandora's box you've opened? Our enemies are coming for us, and we're going to have no choice but to fight. There hasn't been a war of this size in a hundred years. And all this for what?" she demanded, her eyes wide with incredulity. "Because the boys in this pack can't keep their dicks in their pants?"

Amber flinched and white hot rage poured through him and he stepped toward Maggie, a low growl reverberating from his lips. "Watch yourself, woman. You have a lot to say about love considering it's a subject you know nothing of."

She flinched like he'd slapped her. "Screw you, Billy. This isn't about me or my love life. This is about family. Our pack. Every pain we've suffered in the past few years has been because of humans." Her voice broke and he saw something he'd only seen once in his whole life. Tears in Maggie's eyes. The only others he'd seen her shed were for Sara.

Shit.

"Mags—"

"Don't." She stepped back with both hands held up defensively like she was warding off an attack. "I don't know what's happening anymore. It used to be that we talked about things and how they would affect the family before we did them. Now all of a sudden it's a free for all."

Amber shrugged away from him with a shuddering breath and took a step forward. "I'm so sorry, Maggie. I didn't meant to-"

"Don't speak to me, woman," Maggie said, without even sparing Amber a glance as she spoke. "You're a very small pawn in a very big game. You wouldn't have the power you do if the men in this pack hadn't given it to you." She turned to Liam and swiped the tears from her face with the back of her hand. "You are to blame. You started this. I love Amalie, and I wouldn't change it, but your actions are what made everyone think they could do whatever they wanted no matter who it hurts. It has to end somewhere, and it's your job to see that it does."

Liam's jaw went tight and his eyes went flinty in a way that had them all shifting restlessly, except for Maggie, who was oblivious in her anger and hurt.

"Here's what's going to happen," Liam said, his voice deceptively soft. "I'm going to give you twenty-four hours to think about this all, and then we're going to meet again, just you and I. At that time, you will tell me whether or not you will stand with us."

She glared at him as she backed away. "Yeah, well, don't hold your breath. And don't say I didn't warn you." She stalked toward the front door and stormed out into the night.

They all watched her go, but no one made a move to follow.

"It's been a rough few weeks for her," Amalie said softly. "The kidnapping, and then we found out Chandra is pregnant and moving out, and now this. Things are changing so fast and she hates change. None of this is easy on her."

"I feel terrible that I'm adding to the burden. Is there anything I can do to fix it?" Amber asked, the miserable look on her face making Billy's gut clench.

"It's not on you, it's on her," he said, vowing to talk to Maggie again when she had time to cool off.

"As for the rest of you, if anyone would rather not fight, or has any other objections to add?" Liam asked to the rest of the room at large.

To Billy's everlasting relief, the room was silent for a long moment before Liam continued.

"All right. If the Kotke and the Big Sky Canyon packs already know she's here, we probably have only a few days to prepare for battle, maybe a week on the outside, while they work out a plan of attack. It's going to get ugly. Let's remember that we're not just doing this for Billy and Amber today. We're doing this to make a positive change among our people. For our generation but also for other weres who live under iron rule and can look to us as a beacon of hope for the future. If they want to come on our lands and try to stop us, they're going to have a hell of a fight on their hands."

Amber looked up at Billy and he gave her a reassuring smile. For the first time since the night of Chandra's kidnapping, he felt something close to whole again. He had the support of his pack—well, most of it—and he had Amber.

Now, all they had to do was what they did best.

Fight.

Chapter Nine

Amber snuggled closer to Billy's sleeping form, letting out a low sigh. She never could've imagined becoming so entwined with another person so quickly. After only five days at the compound—five nights in his bed—she already felt like he was her whole world. If he were to change his mind and send her away now, it would leave a giant hole in her life and in her heart.

And it seemed like he felt the same. He'd all but announced it to that pack that he loved her.

It was terrifying. But it was also liberating and healing. She'd taken the leap, wholeheartedly. Thrown herself into something at a time when she'd never been so afraid to trust her instincts. So far, so good. The rest of the pack seemed to be warming up to her, with the exception of Maggie, who hadn't been seen since her meeting with Liam. According to Billy, she would come around eventually. In the meantime, Amber had done her best to stay out of the way while the wolves prepared for the imminent battle.

She squeezed her eyes closed and forced herself not to think about it too hard. Billy had sworn up and down that, while they weren't immortal, werewolves were hard to kill. Typically, wars like this resulted in a lot of pretty gruesome injuries, but few casualties, as one pack typically conceded dominance or at least called a truce before too many lives were lost. If only she could be sure he wasn't just placating her.

A thought that always brought her back around to the same issue that had been keeping her awake nights. Wouldn't it just be better for everyone involved if she let him turn her? From what he had said, one bite would do it.

And it would leave her forever changed.

That, she'd already come to terms with. She would have done it already, except Liam and Billy had refused to allow it. There would be days of pain and fever, and then days more as they waited for a full moon to complete the process, and then weeks on top of that until she gained enough strength to be a help instead of a hindrance.

Once the fighting ended, if they were victorious, Billy would wait until the next full moon. And then? She would become one of them. The Kotke and Big Sky Canyon packs would do everything in their power to stop it, fighting tooth and nail to support their antiquated laws and outdated logic. Now that she knew about weres, they wanted her dead and no other solution would do. Once she was turned, though, she would have as much to lose as they did by exposing them to the general public. Both Billy and Liam felt there was a chance they'd let it be eventually, the way they had with Amalie.

But if she stayed a human in their midst, win or lose, they would never stop coming for her.

Not ever.

Even without that threat looming, she would have done it if it meant a lifetime with Billy.

She pressed her bottom against his groin, relishing the warmth pouring off his body. She was still sketchy on the details of some of the were stuff, but one thing was for sure, it definitely had its perks.

Her skin tingled when she thought of the night before. Her man was tireless and passionate and oh-so generous.

She slipped one hand behind her and realized that, while her lover wasn't awake yet, the bottom half of him sure was. In their short time together, he'd taught her that there was no such thing as too brazen. He'd encouraged her to take what she wanted sexually, to come at it with total abandon. With all the real life dangers around them and the strife of the past month and a half since the kidnapping, she became grimly aware of just how fragile life could be. There was no more leaving even an ounce of happiness on the table. She was going to grab every bit of it and hold on tight, just in case tomorrow never came.

And right now? What would make her happiest was Billy. On her lips. The taste of him on her tongue. The sight of his big, strong body, every muscle flexed and tense, teeth gritted as he worked his cock in and out of her mouth until he exploded.

Something about the uncertainty of the future added a sense of urgency that she didn't bother to try to control. Instead, she crawled beneath the covers, took him in hand, and suckled on the thick, smooth head of his cock. She started off slow, and she heard a sleepy hum overhead. Encouraged, she took him deeper, opening her throat to accommodate him, loving the feel of him pressing against the tender skin at the back of her throat.

His body stiffened and he rocked his hips toward her, groaning her name. A second later, a blast of cool air hit her face as the blankets were torn away and he peered down at her, his jaw tense with need, his eyes filled with naked heat.

"Jesus Christ, is this the way to wake up," he murmured, spearing his hands into her hair. "Look at you." Apparently, that was something he could no longer do himself, because he squeezed his eyes closed like he was in pain. "You must have read my mind. This is exactly what I'd been dreaming about. Seeing you, and those plump, sexy lips around my cock, sucking me off."

His words sent a blast of need through her that landed right between her thighs and she was already planning act two when his hips began to move faster.

"That's it, babe," he growled. "Deeper. Take it all."

The grit in his voice fanned the flames higher, and more than anything, she wanted to please him. Wanted to make him feel as wild and out of control as he made her feel. She swirled her tongue around the head of his cock, and brought a hand up to work his shaft.

"I'm going to come," he groaned, giving her a chance to pull back if she wanted to.

She didn't. Instead, she doubled her efforts, deep-throating him until she'd almost swallowed him whole. His fingers twitched in her hair as he let out a long, low growl.

"Fuck, yeah."

The hot stream of come jetted into her mouth and she swallowed hard, taking it all, eager for more as he bucked against her, his stomach muscles standing out in sharp relief as he came.

The breath was still sawing in and out of his lungs when she finally swallowed the last drop and pulled away to drop a kiss on his stomach, before climbing up to straddle him.

"I want you to ride my cock," he demanded, releasing her hair and reaching between them to press his still rock hard erection against her swollen clit.

"Ah, god, that feels good." Yet another perk of being a werewolf. Literally, no down time needed. Before she could even congratulate her good fortune, he was pushing inside her, sliding deep, sucking the very breath from her lungs.

"Come, take what you want, love. It's all for you."

She started off slow at first, but after only a few thrusts, her movements grew more fevered as the need built. She rode him faster and faster as the tension built, spreading from her pelvis to her belly. Her nipples tingled, and she didn't quell the urge to touch them. His resulting gasp as she tweaked them, pinching and tugging as she rode him, only made it hotter.

"I'm going to come," she groaned.

"Yeah, that's it," he urged, trapping her hips in his hands and working her over him.

"Oh, god, Billy!"

She came in a rush, chanting his name as shockwaves took over, shimmering through her like a thousand points of light.

He was right behind her, calling out on a groan as his cock spurted inside her in a rush of hot liquid.

They stayed like that until their bodies grew cool and her leg started to cramp, but even then, she didn't want to get up.

"I've got to take a shower and get ready for our watch," she murmured, leaning forward to nip his chin before rolling off him. The pack had someone manning the cameras and the compound security twenty-four/seven since they were on high alert. Tonight, Billy had the midnight shift and she had convinced him to let her keep him company.

His sexy mouth curved into a wicked smile. "You want me to scrub your back?"

She shimmied off the bed with a laugh. "No way. Last time we used up all the hot water and we missed breakfast." She bent to gather up her yoga pants, along with her purse and a change of underwear.

Regardless of the fact that she'd had to refuse him on his offer of a round three, the fact that he'd wanted one put a pep in her step as she headed into the bathroom. She closed the door and peered at herself in the mirror with a groan.

What a cliché. Grinning like a fool, cheeks pink and glowing, she looked like the poster child for love. He might not have said to directly yet, but surely…

"You've got to get a grip, girl."

She set down her stuff on the corner of the sink and made to turn on the shower, gasping in surprise at the thud behind her. The clicking sound of plastic on the ceramic sent her whipping around with a groan. Her purse had fallen, sending its contents spilling to the floor all over the bathroom. She dropped to a crouch and started picking up. All in all, it could've been worse. Her favorite eye-shadow had survived, but her peach blush along with the attached mirror had shattered into tiny pieces.

"Seven years bad luck," she murmured under her breath. Even that didn't dampen her mood. She hummed softly under her breath as she cleaned up the last of the mess, tossing what was broken into the tiny trash can in the corner of the room, and the rest back in her purse. She was just about to tug off her shirt and climb into the shower when she saw it.

A tiny, metal disc that had skittered halfway beneath the cabinet. She reached down to pick it up and stared at it for a long moment.

She'd seen something like this before on Scandal. A bug. Someone had planted a listening device in her purse so they could spy on her. How long had it been there? And, more importantly, who had put it there?

Her heart pounding in her chest as she yanked the door open and stepped back into the bedroom, trembling hand extended. "Have something you want to tell me?"

Until that very moment, she'd held out the tiniest hope that it wasn't Billy. That he would look at the bug and shake his head in utter confusion. Then, whatever happened from there they could deal with together. But as she looked at the sick guilt on his face, that last little nugget of hope died.

She fisted her hands at her side to stop them from shaking. "When did you do it?"

"The night you came back to my apartment." He rose to his feet and took a step toward her, but she backed away as she tried to keep it together. "That's how we knew you'd been researching werewolves and asking questions."

"And that's why you got involved with me. To shut me up."

"No."

She had to believe at least that much, or she would drive herself insane.

"I have other people I need to think about. People who count on me. As much as I wanted to trust you, I didn't have the right to make that decision for my pack until I knew you could be trusted. But then, once we spent some time together, I knew."

He was right to be cautious. Especially when she had almost cost Chandra her life. But he'd told her a dozen times that she needed to forgive herself for that. It hurt something fierce realizing now that maybe she wasn't the only one who hadn't forgiven her yet…

"So why is it still there?" she asked, her throat aching with unshed tears.

Billy raked a hand through his hair and began to pace back and forth. "It's part of the condition for your staying. The night I brought you, Liam spoke with me privately, and told me that we had to leave the bug in place to monitor your calls. It was a precaution to ensure that you weren't sharing the information you had about us with anyone else, nothing more."

His face was earnest, his emerald eyes clear, but one fact remained.

"But if you trusted me, you could've told me it was there."

He held her gaze and inclined his head. "I can see how it would seem that way, but when you're part of a pack, you'll see yourself. It's not that simple. You aren't just one person anymore."

She nodded slowly, her insides hurting just looking at him. "I've seen you all together enough now to believe that."

And still, her heart felt battered and bruised. She'd quit her job a few days before, without even the courtesy of doing it in person because they'd asked her to stay at the compound. She'd packed up her clothes and her life and moved in, few questions asked. She accepted him immediately when he'd revealed that he was, in fact, something straight out of legend. A creature that many would fear. She knew for a fact that he and his friends were responsible for a man's death, yet, from the moment she'd moved to the compound, she never once feared that they would hurt her.

Because she trusted them.

She trusted *him*.

With her life.

Suddenly, the weight of it all threatened to crush her and she was desperate to get out, far from the place she'd felt so safe in just moments before.

"I…need a little time alone." She bent and began to tug on her yoga pants when his low voice stopped her cold.

"You can't leave the compound, Amber. I know you want to, and I understand that. But it's not safe."

She strode toward the door, spurred on by the threat of tears she refused to let him see. Because that mirror she'd broken wasn't the only thing shattered.

Chapter Ten

Billy stood, staring at the door, frozen with indecision as his world crumbled around him. In her mental and emotional state, she could very well head straight for the door. It was one thing to tell a person they were in mortal danger. It was another for them to truly understand it. If she left their borders, she would be murdered in cold blood before she made it a mile. Thing was? Even if he stayed put, one of his packmates would stop her before she even got down the walkway.

And then you won't have to be the one forcing her to stay against her will. She wasn't going to like that one bit and, added to the crimes he'd already committed against her, would likely never forgive him.

He weighed his options and realized that it was a no brainer. As her mate, it was his job to care for her, even when she didn't want him to. He would deal with the fallout when it came.

Filled with a grim sense of determination, he yanked on a shirt and gym pants and then stalked down the stairs after her, catching up with her at the front door and scooping her up into a fireman's hold.

"Put me down," she demanded, her voice breaking as she wriggled and squirmed. "Put me down, god damn it."

He tried to block out her words and focus only on the job at hand. Getting her somewhere safe until she was calm enough to realize she had to stay.

He was managing okay until her yells turned to sobs.

"I just need some air, damn it. I won't leave the grounds. P-please, Billy."

His heart gave a squeeze, and he wanted nothing more than to set her onto her feet, pull her into his arms and beg her to forgive him, but he knew she was in no shape to hear him. Until he was sure she was calm and rational enough not to do something foolhardy, he had to assume the worst.

They'd built in the east wing when Sara was pregnant with Ryan to ensure her protection should they come under attack, and he was halfway there when he heard it. The first of the trip wires had been activated sending a low but insistent droning sound through the house. Adrenalin coursed through his body as he bit out a string of curses.

"They're here," Jax's whispered voice called up the stairs from a few yards behind him.

Amber stopped struggling and squeezed his arm.

"Put me down." She sounded far calmer than she had, and he held his breath as he set her on her feet.

"This is not a drill, Amber," he said solemnly, fear for her safety making his stomach roil. She swiped at her tear-streaked face and nodded.

"Got it. What do you need me to do?"

His relief was so great, his head spun with it for a second. She was hurt, but she was nobody's fool. They would deal with the enemy at hand, and work through their issues later.

He took her elbow and led her into the great room where his packmates had all converged with the exception of the two pack elders and the children, who had left town at Liam's insistence until the fighting had ended.

"Who's at the cameras? Do we know how many?" Billy asked.

"Maggie. She says fifteen," Liam said.

"Maggie?" Billy turned to pin him with a questioning look.

"Yeah. She came back this morning. She's in."

It was the last piece of the puzzle. He didn't even realize it was missing until it clicked into place with an almost audible snap. It was right now. The way it should be. They were all together now and the feeling filled him with renewed determination.

They would fight their enemies as a family. And they would win. He'd never felt more sure of anything in his life, except his feelings for Amber.

"You guys feeling strong?" Chandra asked, a stoic expression on her face.

"Always," Jax said. "We're not going to have to tie you up, are we?" He tried to keep his tone light, but there was no question he meant it.

"I would never risk our baby like that. You have my word. Protecting our son is my top priority." A fierce light filled her eyes as she covered her non-existent belly with both hands.

"Now you guys go make sure I don't have to raise him alone, all right? Amber and I can take care of each other."

"If the interior of the house gets breached, you head straight for the panic room, understood?" Jax tugged her into his arms and kissed her firmly on the mouth before letting her go and turned to face the rest of the pack. "Let's get these motherfuckers."

Billy turned to Amber and found her staring up at him. "Please be careful," she murmured, pressing a hand to his chest and then clutching a handful of his T-shirt. "And promise me you'll come back. I didn't even have a chance to yell at you properly yet."

"I'll be back before you know it," he promised. He dropped a kiss to her forehead before Chandra came and led her away, murmuring soft instructions as they made their way toward the table where a host of weapons were laid. Chandra was a deadly weapon as it was, but Amber needed a little help in the event that all their security measures failed. In the past few days, she'd learned to become a proficient shot, and they had enough tranquilizer darts to fell a wooly mammoth.

He dragged his gaze from her and focused on Liam, who was giving direction.

"Billy, you and Amalie take the back of the house, Jax, you come with me to the front. The rest of the pack is going to patrol the surrounding woods."

He wasn't sure which of the packs would have the balls to attack them on their own grounds, but the second Liam opened the door, the scent was unmistakable.

Kotke.

Which explained why Liam had sent him to the back of the house with Amalie. She'd had her own run in with this pack when she was still human and one of their members, Mikhail, had nearly killed her. No doubt, Liam hoped for a chance at revenge and thought that keeping Amalie in the back of the house with Billy at her side would offer her some measure of protection. Given what his alpha was risking to help Amber, Billy vowed to make certain he didn't let him down.

"Ready?" At their collective affirmatives, Liam whispered, "Go, go, go."

They moved as if they were one, leaping off the porch in tandem. He and Amalie stayed in human form to start, as was the plan. They needed to access the most strategic parts of their minds until the fighting started. Because once it did, their wolves would take over, and it would be pure instinct until the last of the blood was spilt.

The smell grew suddenly thicker, and they both stiffened, on high alert.

His keen eyes picked them out a second later. Two men, walking toward them. He recognized one of them instantly.

Mikhail.

He let out a cold bark of laughter, his Rasputin-like, maniacal eyes glinting in the moonlight. "Perfect. It's about time I got a second chance at you, bitch."

Amalie grinned, and the sight was chilling enough to make the hair on Billy's arms stand up. His alpha had chosen his mate almost as well as Billy had. She was bad ass.

"Been a while since I was the defenseless woman in the woods, Mikhail. You think you can still take me?"

Mikhail's laugh turned to a growl as he shifted in mid-step. He wasted no time, breaking into a loping stride to close the twenty-yard distance between he and Amalie.

Billy didn't have to think about the change. The second he saw his alpha's mate under attack, his wolf burst into being, his muscles lengthening and shifting with a snap.

Before he'd even taken a step toward her, Amalie's mind tapped at his and he opened to her.

He's mine.

Liam wouldn't approve, but he understood Amalie's need to exorcise this particular demon, so he hung back for the time being, ready to step in the second she needed him.

The other man shifted then, turning into a small silver wolf. He was fast, and streaked by so quickly, it was a blur. He was headed straight into the fray, snarling as it descended upon Amalie from behind.

Billy sprang from his spot to land on the smaller wolf, pinning it to the ground and sinking his teeth into the animal's thick shoulder muscle.

The silver wolf howled in pain, but Billy didn't let go. Not until he heard the crack of bone. The animal whimpered and scrambled to its feet, its speed no less impressive as it ran off into the night.

Billy considered following, but he couldn't leave Amalie here until Mikhail was defeated. In any case, that wolf was incapacitated for the rest of the evening at the very least. One down.

Mikhail and Amalie continued to fight as a giant, tawny wolf came barreling from the woods, lunging toward Billy, all teeth and blood red gums. He might have been a threat, except he was as slow as he was big, and with one slash of teeth to his throat, he was on the ground in a heap.

Mikhail let out a howl that was cut short as Amalie closed her teeth over his jugular. Elation soared through Billy in a rush.

They were winning. So far, none of the wolves had even gotten close to entering the house, and they were dropping like flies.

Amalie sent him a mental warning and he wheeled around just in time to see another rounding the corner.

Even at first glance, this one was pathetic. In fact, aside from Mikhail, none of the wolves were as strong as he'd have expected. Why would the Kotke send these weak-ass, mangy animals to take point on this attack? Surely their alpha would know that any one of the Pray wolves would be able to dispatch this riffraff with little trouble.

He was in the midst of doing just that with his most recent attacker when another came, equally as scrawny. And then it hit him, sending his heart dropping to his stomach like a stone.

This wasn't the attack at all, these poorly trained, subpar wolves coming one at a time. This was the diversion. They'd sent the B team to fight this battle because the A-team was busy trying to win the war.

And the war was Amber.

***

When the glass of the French doors shattered, she barely flinched. Something had told her it would come to this. Instinct, or a premonition of some sort. Whatever it was, she'd known she wouldn't be just a pawn in this fight.

She would be a soldier.

She leapt up from the chair she'd been sitting in, pistol in hand, right as Chandra reached for her.

"Panic room, now," Chandra shouted, moss green eyes lit with urgency.

The woman yanked her down the hallway toward the room as the glass continued to shatter in the great room followed by the thump of paws and scrabble of nails on hardwood. By the time they reached the massive steel door, Amber's heart felt like it was going to explode.

Did the breach mean the rest of the Pray pack had fallen? Dear god, what if Billy was dead? What if he was injured and needed her help?

"Are they okay? Can you hear their thoughts?" she asked, heart in her throat.

"They shut me out the second they left. They didn't want me to hear something that scared me, knowing I'd come running. Now come on," Chandra shouted, releasing Amber's arm to shove the door open.

The decision was made on a dime, but, just like her choice to stay with Billy, she felt the rightness of it all the way down to her bones.

She blocked out the noise behind her and leveled the pistol at Chandra.

"Get in."

Chandra's eyes narrowed and she took a step toward her. "What the hell are you doing?" Chandra hissed. "We have no time to—"

"Exactly. So every second you argue with me is another wasted. I need to go. That's non-negotiable. If you come with me, and something happens to you…" she trailed off, overwhelmed with emotion. "You almost died because of me once. I won't let that happen again. So my choices are limited. I can shoot you with this tranquilizer gun and shut you in there. Or you can agree to shut yourself in and protect your unborn baby, while I try to help the pack."

The sounds were growing closer, and Amber said a silent prayer. She didn't know if she had it in her to shoot Chandra, even if it was for her own good. One last try at convincing her.

"If you make me tranq you, I'm pretty sure Jax will kill me anyway." She lowered the gun and pleaded with her eyes as well as her words. "Please, Chandra. Let me try to help the pack. I owe you both that much."

She could almost hear the gears grinding in Chandra's head when a wolf came skittering around the corner, snarling. This time, she didn't hesitate. Pulse banging, she turned toward it, leveled the tranquilizer gun and fired.

The animal dropped to the floor with a yelp, twitched once, and went still.

She turned back to face Chandra, who had slipped a protective hand lower to cover her belly. She met Amber's gaze and nodded slowly.

"Go, then. Find our mates. Help protect the pack. You're one of us now, Amber, in every way that counts." Chandra stepped back and yanked the door closed. The locks tumbled and she pressed a hand to the tiny glass window.

Relief coursed through Amber and she sucked in a steadying breath. Chandra was safe. If Amber met her maker tonight, she would go knowing she'd done at least one thing right.

She hefted the gun higher and headed back down the hallway, skirting past the felled wolf as she went. If Billy was alive, he needed her now. And if he wasn't?

She shoved the thought aside and made her way to the closest exit, a side door that led to the grounds through the garage. The second she stepped outside, she could hear the sounds of fighting. Snarls and yips, howls and growls. They were coming from every direction and she closed her eyes to focus.

Which way should she go?

A protracted yowl sounded in the far side yard and she moved in that direction. It was only when she heard the crunch of leaves behind her about ten yards in that she realized her mistake. There was a wolf behind her.

The hairs on the back of her neck stood up and the world spun as a dump of adrenaline coursed through her in a rush. Fight? Or flight?

She couldn't die out here. In the cold. Away from Billy. Now when she didn't know if he was alive or dead, and she'd never even gotten the chance to tell him how much she loved him.

The crunch of leaves and brush as the animal padded closer seemed to reverberate through the icy night air.

Make a decision.

If she ran, there was a one hundred percent chance the wolf would catch her. Fight was the least worst option. And if she was going down, she was going down fighting.

She turned to face the massive creature loping toward her. It moved slowly at first, but then more quickly. Amber's skin broke out in a cold sweat as the animal sped up to a flat-out sprint. She raised the gun and closed one eye. She had six darts in a holster at her side, but only one fit in the chamber at a time. She had to wait until she had the perfect shot, and that meant close.

Its fangs seemed larger than life as it came leaping at her, jaws snapping. She couldn't wait any longer and squeezed the trigger. The dart went whizzing by the wolf's head and she screamed as the animal landed on top of her, sending her sprawling back into a pile of branches. A jarring pain shot up her side as the creature's rank, hot breath washed over her face.

All she could think in that moment was that Billy was willing to fight for her. Hell, maybe even die for her and she'd spent the last few minutes they'd ever have alone together being angry at him.

I'm so sorry.

Instinctively, she covered her face, waiting for the tear of teeth, but it never came. A second later, the weight of the creature was gone and it lay by her side, bloodied and still.

What the hell had happened?

"Run back toward the house," a low, male voice called from what seemed like overhead. "There are two there waiting, but there are four more coming down the pathway behind you. I will stall them if I can."

She looked around wildly, trying to discern where the voice was coming from in the inky darkness of the thick tree line, but came up empty. Was that the best course of action, or just a trap?

"Run," he urged in a low, gritty voice.

She stood, still frozen with indecision as another wolf came trotting toward her. She was scrambling for a sharp branch when it shifted right before her eyes.

Maggie.

"You humans are so fucking stupid sometimes," she growled. "You heard the man. Run, god damn it!" A naked Maggie shot a glance over her shoulder and then took Amber by the arm, half-dragging her down the path, back toward the house.

She could see the house, lights glowing in the distance, only twenty or thirty yards away now, just through the next row of trees. If they could get there, maybe they'd be all right.

And just maybe she'd have a chance to tell Billy how much she loved him.

By the time they got back to the front entrance of the compound, her lungs burned and there was a searing pain in her side. She winced, and pressed a tentative hand to it.

"Were you bit?" Maggie demanded, slowing her stride for the first time to glare down at her.

"I don't think so, no. The branches cut me."

Her savior blew out a long sigh. "Thank god for small favors. Come on then, we're almost there. Once we're inside, stay the fuck put," she grumbled.

Amber had to resist the urge to hug the woman. Because whatever she had to say about it now, the fact remained, when push had come to shove, she had treated Amber like one of theirs. Whether that was for her sake or Billy's, she couldn't say, but whatever the reason, it gave her hope. Hope that, if they all got through this alive tonight, and she was allowed to stay, maybe they could be friends.

"Have you had any contact with the rest of the pack?"

Maggie shook her head. "I've reached out and gotten bits and pieces, but in a fight, it's chaos. Better to let them focus on what they're doing than distract them."

Amber shoved back her disappointment and resisted the urge to press. Maggie knew better and she wasn't about to make herself an even bigger burden.

They'd made it down the winding pathway and were heading to the porch when Maggie stopped dead in her tracks. She lowered Amber slowly to the ground. "Get behind me," she whispered.

The words had barely registered when she heard it. Movement behind the shrubs in front of the house. Two wolves, one brown, one white, converged on the porch. Both had their gazes locked on Maggie, and the fur on the ruffs of their necks stood up.

Amber swallowed hard, willing herself not to throw up. This looked bad. Two, large, male wolves against one smaller wolf and a wounded, pathetic bag of meat and bones that half their kind considered part of the food chain.

Still, Maggie had proven time and time again tonight, that she was a real, bad ass bitch. Surely that meant they had a chance.

"If I get them both occupied, do not waste a second. You run. Get around to the side of the house, and into the panic room." The wolves were moving toward them now, in slow, deliberate steps, their bared teeth and trembling lips like something out of a nightmare. "Do not stop for any reason," her words were clipped and coming faster, the urgency more and more apparent. "And whatever you do, don't look back."

Amber nodded, but inside, she was screaming. There was no way in hell she was leaving Billy's packmate and friend at the mercy of two murderous wolves. Not even if it meant that she would die right along with her. She couldn't live with that.

"Got it." She lied without remorse, already searching the ground for some sort of makeshift weapon.

Luckily, Maggie had turned her attention to their attackers. She laid a hand on one hip, seemingly unconcerned about her nakedness... almost flaunting it, even. "I sure hope you assholes have a couple friends hiding in those azaleas, because if not, this is going to be a real snooze-fest," Maggie drawled. Gone was urgency in her voice. It was replaced by sheer confidence. Balls-out bravado, and, for a second, Amber forgot her fear under the sheer weight of her awe for the woman's inner fortitude. Whatever faults she had, she was a warrior and damn if Amber didn't want to be her when she grew up.

The two approaching wolves exchanged glances, and for a second, it seemed like they were confused, but it was fleeting. Almost as if by tacit agreement, the moved faster, loping toward Maggie and gaining speed with each step.

The animals' incandescent eyes glittered in the light of the moon and Amber shivered with fear and revulsion. They wanted to kill her and Maggie both. To rip them apart like they were rag dolls. She'd never felt like prey before today and she found herself wishing she could turn like Maggie, if only so she never had to experience the sensation again.

Maggie was apparently not a fan either, because she was done playing the victim. Rather than letting them come to her, she began to run toward them, her pearly white skin gleaming in the moonlight, long, lean legs eating up the distance before, an instant later, she shifted into wolf form.

The fight was fast and furious and, by the light of the moon, it was hard to see who was winning. At one point, it seemed as if Maggie might do it. She had one wolf by the haunch while the other lay at her side, bloodied and still. Right when Amber's hopes were highest, the motionless wolf let out a snarl and leapt up, lunging for Maggie's shoulder. She released the haunch of the larger wolf to focus on this latest attack, and then it was done.

The wolves worked as a team until she was well and truly pinned to the ground, blood running heavily from a wound on her hip.

She was out of time and out of options. Praying for strength, Amber made a dive for a rock she'd spotted on the ground a few yards away. She ran forward, and Maggie met her gaze. She could almost hear the woman's voice in her head, demanding she go. But she blocked it out and focused all her energy on staying silent as she moved toward the thrall.

She raised her arms high, and swung with all her might, smashing the rock into the skull of the smaller of the two wolves. It yelped and instantly released the hold it had on Maggie's leg, and she shot to her feet, back in the game one on one. Amber eyed her quickly recovering target and swung again, grimacing as the rock hit its mark again, this time right over the animal's eye.

It rolled to its side, and rapidly began to change. Dark fur became tanned skin and a second later, a man lay at her feet, bleeding and swearing profusely as he pressed a hand to his bloodied eye. Before she could get off another shot, he rolled onto his feet and took a menacing step toward her.

"You stupid cu-"

It happened so fast, it was a blur. One second he was standing. The next, he was flying through the air, as a huge, tawny wolf—*her* wolf—mauled at him.

Billy had come to save her. And right on time, too, she realized as her vision blurred. Her muscles shook with fatigue and shock, and even if she had managed to hit her target one more time, she wasn't sure she could stay upright beyond that.

A soft chuffing sound caught her attention and she turned to see Maggie's wolf struggling to all fours before falling back to the ground in a heap on top of her felled opponent.

"Don't get up," Amber called, squeezing her eyes closed to stave off the dizziness. She needed to be strong now. Strong the way Maggie had been. "I'll help you." She stepped closer, yanking off her sweatshirt as she went. When she reached the sable wolf's side, she scanned her for injuries. The one on her hip seemed to be the worst of it, and she leaned in to examine it.

The jagged laceration was deep enough that she could see bone, and she winced. "I'm going to apply pressure to stem the bleeding all right?"

Maggie growled low in her throat, but she didn't pull away. A moment later, Billy's wolf was there, sniffing at his fallen comrade before stepping back and shifting to human form.

"Are you okay, Mags?"

She inclined her square, sable head and he patted her gently. "Good."

A long, wavering howl sounded, and Billy turned to lock eyes with Amber.

"Jesus, thank god," Billy muttered, bending to carefully scoop his injured comrade up in his arms. "That's the Kotke's surrender. They're calling back what's left of their pack and admitting defeat. We need to get inside and hope that they are the only ones who suffered losses."

They crossed the yard together and headed into the house, tension still high. As relieved as she was that Billy was okay, she knew the condition was fleeting if something had happened to one of the pack. They stepped through the door to find Chandra standing there wrapped in Jax's arms, sobbing.

Amber's heart stuttered as she took in the scene. "Is everything okay? Is the baby…"

"The baby is fine," Jax said with a nod. "Thank you for what you did, Amber. It means everything to me."

Her cheeks warmed and she shrugged. "I didn't really do anything."

"You did." Chandra turned her red face toward Amber, her moss green eyes filled with gratitude. "And thank you for it. I'm so glad you're all right." She turned to Billy who set Maggie on the couch. "How is Maggie?"

"A bone. It hurts right now but she'll be fine," he replied.

"Glad to hear it," Chandra said, the rest of the tension seeming to leave her in a rush. "That's everyone. Amalie, Liam and the rest are in the kitchen. Everyone is accounted for and okay." She paused and called his name softly. "And Billy?"

He turned and met her gaze.

"Your woman has already proven her worth."

Relief and joy filled Amber's heart and she swallowed the lump in her throat. They thought she was worthy.

Worthy of them.

Worthy of Billy.

Worthy of all their sacrifices.

If they thought that, just maybe it was true.

Chapter Eleven

Once they cleaned up and dressed, they all met back in the great room. They drank coffee and brandy, and shared war stories while the uninjured members of the pack swept up glass and boarded the windows. It had been a harrowing night, and the Pray pack was shaken but intact.

And his mate was all right. It was the best of days.

"The man by the path, he told us to run. I think he even stalled the rest of the wolves…who was that?" Amber asked softly, tugging the blanket more tightly around her shoulders. "I need to thank him."

Maggie frowned, now back in human form, her hip already on the mend. She ran a hand through her dark hair before shooting a glance at Liam. "She said there was a man, but he'd shifted by the time I got there. On the overlook. He told us how many wolves would be waiting by the house and ran interference for the ones coming behind us." She shook her head slowly, clearly baffled. "The weird part is, he smelled like he was Big Sky Canyon."

Liam's golden eyes flashed and his expression went thoughtful. "Impossible. They hate us as much as the Kotke. Why help the enemy? What color was he?"

"Black. Big. I'd say he was your size, Liam."

Billy cocked his head as he listened to Maggie talk. When she finished giving a more detailed description, he shook his head slowly. It didn't make any sense, but there was only one wolf he could think of who matched that description in the area. "I could be wrong. Hell, maybe they added a new rogue to the pack over there, but I gotta tell you, it sounds an awful lot like Greyson West." He shrugged. "Doesn't make any sense, but there it is."

The room went eerily quiet until Amber finally broke the silence. "Who's Greyson West?"

Chandra's face went a little pale and she snuggled closer to Jax. "Before I came to Pray, I was part of the Big Sky Canyon pack. I left because their alpha is more like a dictator and he thinks much like the Kotke do. Grey is his son, and next in line for the job."

"Exactly," Liam said, his black brows furrowed in a thunderous frown. "So why the hell would he be doing anything to help us right now? They hate us. We need to get to the bottom of this."

"Grey wasn't like his father when I knew him. He'd been a voice of reason in the past, but then he left for a year or so to work on setting up some businesses internationally. Things got really bad when he was gone. I didn't realize he was back," Chandra said. "Who knows? Maybe he really was trying to help."

"Or maybe he's fallen into line with his father's way of thinking and there is a bigger plot at play here," Maggie added from her spot on the couch.

Billy stretched his torso as another broken rib shifted beneath his skin, knitting itself slowly and painfully back together. No question that their healing power was a gift, but sometimes it hurt like a motherfucker.

"A definite mystery," he agreed, pushing himself heavily to his feet. "But one for another day. For right now, I'm going to thank him tonight in my prayers, lay with Amber, and marvel that she's still alive for me to hold."

He reached a hand out for Amber's, and she laced her fingers with his. He lifted his gaze to meet that of his alpha and dipped his head low.

"I will forever be in your debt, Liam. All of you," he added, scanning the room to make eye contact with each of his packmates. Only Maggie turned her head, but it didn't faze him. She would come around. She might not realize it, but she already had. She saved Amber's life. They had rallied around him and his human and protected them both.

That was the meaning of family.

"I know I don't need to say it, but if ever any of you need anything. Anything. Come to me. You have my undying and everlasting loyalty."

He pulled Amber close and headed for the stairs. They both winced as their injuries collided, but he didn't pull away and she only nuzzled closer, looping an arm around his waist.

They still had some talking to do, there was no question of that. But for the moment, he was as content as could be. She was alive. She was in his arms. And that was everything.

The second his bedroom door closed behind him, he turned to face her. Tomorrow was promised to no one, and he wasn't willing to wait another second to say what he'd known the moment he laid eyes on her.

"I love you, Amber. From the moment I saw your face. The second I touched your skin. The instant I breathed in your scent, my wolf knew. You are my one true mate. Forgive me for the secrets I kept, and know, if you have me, there will never be another between us."

Her eyes went glassy with tears and she rolled up onto her tiptoes, and kissed his jaw lightly. "I don't have a wolf inside me to guide me yet, but I knew it too. I dreamt of you. I felt you everywhere, Billy. And I can't imagine a life without you. I'd be honored to be your mate. I never imagined I would ever find something like this. At best, I wanted safe. Average. Content."

With a twinge of regret, he shook his head slowly. "You will never have the latter with me. It will always be wild and chaotic, and exciting. But Amber, you need to understand that it will never be the former either."

He speared a hand into her hair and forced himself to continue.

"Pack life is dangerous, even during peace times. This is a new era and this battle was just the first of many until we win this war. I will protect you as best I can, but from the day you saw me shift, you've been in danger. Once you become like us, it will be better, but the threat will never be totally gone, and that's not going to change unless you run and hide. Because I love you, I want you to know that I will still help you do that if it's your choice."

In that moment, he knew more fear than he had in any battle. But she didn't hesitate, and cupped his face in her soft hands.

"You're my choice, Billy. And a life without you isn't one I want to live."

He bent low and kissed her, his heart feeling fuller than it ever had. There would be dark days ahead, but for now, he had it all.

His woman.

His pack.

His land.

And it was enough.

Opposition

Montana Wolves Book Three

Chloe Cole

Introduction

Times are changing for the Montana wolves, and they're changing far too quickly for Maggie Porter's liking. After a bloody battle with one rival pack and another on the horizon, she wishes things could just go back to the way they used to be. But not until she gets to the bottom of this latest mystery. Who is Greyson West, really, and why did he help her escape the enemy?

Greyson West can't wait to bring his all too traditional pack into the future. Stuck under his father's tyrannical rule that still supports arranged marriages and allows the murder of humans for sport, he knows the time to step in and take over as alpha is now. But his mission is derailed when he meets a stubborn female who he can't get out of his head.

Sleeping with the enemy could cost him his chance at becoming alpha, but he's never been much on following the rules...

Chapter One

The tension was like aging blood on Greyson West's tongue, bitter and metallic. The entire pack was sitting at a round table; all gazes focused on his father, though none would meet the man's eyes. Instead, they focused on a spot somewhere around his chin as they listened intently, like they hadn't already heard the very same speech many times before.

But they had. His ranting was the same as it had been almost daily since the Kotke had made a run on the Pray wolves and lost a few days before. The Kotke, his father claimed, weren't as strong as they, the Big Sky Canyon pack, were. Someone needed to teach the Pray wolves a lesson and if the Kotke couldn't manage, it was up to them to take the mantle. Liam, the Pray alpha, was too headstrong and committed to his new wave thinking.

He would be the ruination of all of them, and he must be stopped.

Grey tuned out, focusing instead on mentally disproving his father's flawed reasoning, which wasn't hard to do. Not that the nonsense he fed the pack was the heart of the matter at all.

OPPOSITION

The fact was that the tyrannical alpha Grey called sire had been searching for a motive to crush the Pray pack for years, as soon as he realized that the younger generation of wolves were much more open to Liam's more liberal way of thinking than to his own. They'd already had one wolf defect, and there were surely more to come if his father didn't give up his role as alpha soon.

It was just by luck that scandal had so recently fallen upon his father's enemies, leaving them vulnerable and out of favor with several of the more traditional packs that had him digging in his heels. One more coup de grace against the upstarts to make sure future generations would think twice before rebelling.

Grey shifted in his chair, focusing again on his father as the old man finally started winding down.

"Brothers and sisters, we have to fight for our way of life. For our divine right to eat and hunt and live as we wish. These Pray wolves who dare to call themselves a pack are nothing but posers. Abominations who would eat and speak and *sleep* with humans."

His father paused in his speech, looking around the room and Grey followed suit, irritated by the genuine scowls of the older pack members, and equally so by the feigned repugnance of the younger ones.

They knew better than to defy him by now. The last member to speak out for human rights had been beaten within an inch of her life. The person before that had had his throat torn out. Better to feign disgust than to be burned at the stake for tolerance.

Grey, on the other hand, was willing to roll the dice on that front. God only knew it wouldn't be the first time he'd done so. His father would take up no action against him, no matter how infuriated the man became. So, rather than joining the exaggerated sneers of his fellows, he sat back in his seat and waited for the speech to end so he could finally step in and try to bring some semblance of reason to his people.

"We tried to bring an end to this pack's disgusting ways." Grey's father sneered at him pointedly, and Grey scowled back. During the fight with the Kotke, Grey had been dispatched to watch and ensure the human housed by the Pray wolves met her end.

At least, that had been his father's plan.

Grey had no such intention—and when he spotted the woman in a battle for her life, he'd known that it was not his to take, no matter what anyone had to say about it.

Not to mention that her savior—a gorgeous, sable-colored wolf who fought like a lion—had touched something inside him he still hadn't been able to put a finger on.

God, she'd been amazing. Even at the end, as he'd watched from afar, she was nearly overcome by two wolves. Just when he'd been about to step in—a move that would be looked on by the Kotke as an act of war against them—she and her little human friend had prevailed.

He hadn't stopped thinking about her since.

The alpha's droning broke through Grey's thoughts, and he focused again in hopes of getting a word in edgewise.

"This reckless pup who dares to call himself an alpha has taken a human into his pack yet again, like some sort of pet. I ask you, when will the madness cease? The Kotke may not have been able to kill this human female, but that does not mean it cannot be done."

Blah, blah, blah. Next he'd mention something about loyalty and—

"I call upon you all, now, to prepare for battle. We will find this female and finish her."

What?

Grey nearly jumped to his feet, then stopped short when his father growled low in his throat and signaled the rest of the pack to howl back in agreement. The response was low at first, tentative, but the power of the alpha was strong, and it grew louder as his will pressed in on them all. Even Grey could feel it, the desire to obey…to please him.

Didn't his father feel the vibrations of the pack? The fear and anxiety? The turmoil?

If he did, he certainly didn't care, but that didn't mean that Grey could idly stand by while his people fell to the knee for a cause they didn't believe in. They had already suffered enough at his father's hand. As next in line to lead the pack, it was his duty to stand in disagreement.

Pushing himself from his seat, he rose and faced his father. Grey already towered over him by a good six inches, and the man glared up at him.

"I have not dismissed you," Joseph growled.

"I am not asking to leave. I'm asking you to listen. I don't—"

"This is a summit, not a discussion. I am telling you that this is what we will do. You will not fail me again. When we march on the Pray wolves, you and Willa will lead the pack in front, I will hold the line in the rear."

Grey glanced at Willa as his father gestured toward her. Her light brown eyes widened slightly, but she stiffened her jaw and gave a firm nod until her sandy hair fell over her cheek. Grey tried to penetrate her thoughts, to will her to stand beside him and take a stand, but she only pursed her lips and pretended not to notice.

Leave it to Willa not to listen at a time like this.

"But you—" Grey started.

"I believe I made it clear this was not a time for questions," his father barked. "Now, all of you should spend these next few days training. These pups may be misguided, but if the Kotke have taught us anything, it's that these Pray dissenters are strong. We must be stronger."

Without another word, his father stepped from the room and slammed the large, oak door behind him. Even after he'd gone, the rest of the pack did not move. They grumbled and sighed, but none of them so much as scooted their chairs back. All except Willa, that was, who was already practically leaping over the table to talk to Grey.

Or, more accurately, to screech at him.

"What the hell was that?" she asked. "Are you trying to get us both killed?"

"I'm not going to let him keep walking around here like he's not losing his damn mind. You know what happened to the Kotke. Six dead and even more maimed. I can't let that happen to our people."

"I'm fine if you want to play hero, but save it for when you're the alpha. A time that will come much sooner if you keep your head down and play nice. Arguing now is only going to get someone slaughtered and make your father feel like he needs to stay in his position longer. We need to wait. Bide our time."

"Waiting is going to get all of us killed." He stalked toward the door, and then walked through the kitchen and the foyer until he was finally in the crisp night air. A clear evening, perfect for a long run.

Exactly what he needed.

He unfastened his belt, preparing to shift into wolf form, but before he was able to yank off his pants, the door swung open again behind him.

"It's not up to you," Willa said, following him out. "You aren't the alpha."

He took a deep breath before turning to face her.

"And you're not either," he shot back. Seriously, when would the woman give up trying to boss him around? She should know better.

Willa's features softened. "I'm not going to ask where you're going so I don't have to lie if asked, and I know better than to think I can stop you, but will you at least try to be safe?" She crossed her arms over her chest. "I would hate it if Joseph killed you. It would be such a hassle to find a new partner in crime around here."

He laughed softly but wasn't about to let her convince him that easily. As much as her friendship meant, the pack still came first. And right now, the only way to save them was to stop the fighting before it started. If his father wouldn't listen, maybe the Pray wolves would.

"We'll talk about this tomorrow." He edged toward the vast expanse of forest that separated the Big Sky Canyon lands from the Pray territory and began pulling off his clothing.

"If you're still alive," she called after him as he transformed, but he didn't let it stop him. Instead, he began his sprint, letting the wind rush through his fur as he took in the smells of the earth and the early spring breeze with every step. Already the voices of the pack were growing fainter, but as he loped toward enemy lands, he felt Willa's mind touch his.

Please be careful. If your father doesn't kill you, the Pray wolves just might.

***

Maggie placed the last of the dinner dishes into the sink and then leaned back against the counter with a sigh. Lately, she needed every second of alone time she could get, even if it meant dish duty, and today was no exception. Since their run-in with the Kotke the week before, life in the pack had been a lot more stressful than usual. The constant threat of a second attack was bad enough. But she could hardly breathe with the constant togetherness.

She was all about the pack life. Hell, she was the one who had the hardest time when members mated and left the big house to move into one of the smaller cottages on the compound. Having the noise and bustle around, and the constant camaraderie made her feel…safe. A part of something bigger than herself.

This, though? This was a little much, even for her. It was like every move any of them made required a frigging quorum over it. And she wasn't the only one who was feeling that way.

The wolves were all getting testy. Not ideal when things were already sketchy between her and most of the rest of the pack because of her issues with having another human in the house. Amber had hardly come down from her bedroom since the skirmish and it seemed like every two hours, the rest of them were gathering around to discuss the state of the union, plans to turn Amber into a werewolf come the full moon and everything in between.

Never a dull moment.

It should have thrilled her. Should have heated her blood and gotten her adrenaline going in preparation for combat. Battle was what she'd always lived for. The thrill of the hunt. The togetherness of the pack.

But ever since the Kotke, things had been off with more than just the pack.

Things had been off with her.

She let out another sigh and opened the dishwasher. Loading each of the dishes in with a practiced rhythm, she played out the battle over and over again in her mind.

She'd done well. In fact, it had been one of her better fights, and as a pack, they had prevailed without sustaining a single casualty. It was a near-perfect scenario, if there was one in war.

That didn't change the fact that she had almost died, though.

She'd had Amber with her, and was about to run straight into the woods and find a safe hiding place for the foolish human so she could go back into the fray again without worrying about her. It was only that low, rough voice that had stopped her.

"*Run.*"

He'd warned her. Had told them where to go. In real terms, he'd very probably saved both her and Amber's lives.

And he was out there somewhere.

That alone would've been enough to capture her imagination. The fact that he was also probably her enemy? Well, that was driving her bananas.

Why had he let her live when he could have ended the whole miserable thing right then and there? He wouldn't have even had to do the deed himself. He could've just…let them pass by and not said a word. The half dozen Kotke wolves less than a quarter mile away would've done the job for him. Amber would be dead and all would be right in the werewolf world again. At least, according to his brethren.

Just like this whole sudden change of the rules with the pack and Amber, none of it made any damn sense.

She muttered a string of curses under her breath and closed the dishwasher, setting it to start. After running her hands over a dishtowel, she squared her shoulders and tried to pull herself out of the fog she'd been lost in. Maybe a late night run would help.

The pack hadn't gone out to hunt since the battle. Liam, their alpha, wanted to keep everyone close in the event of a second Kotke attack. He hadn't specifically mentioned running in the more protected area right outside the compound, though, and she was about to take advantage of his oversight. Besides, without Amber at her side, she was hardly a target, and she'd stay close enough that she could run back to the house quickly if she needed to.

And who knew? Maybe if she got outside in the open air, and ran fast enough she would feel like her old, kick-ass self again.

If not, at least she'd get to see something other than these stupid walls for a while.

She crossed the gleaming hardwood floors and stepped out onto the back porch, peering out into the moonlit darkness. It was just after midnight and the rest of the pack had long since gone to bed, but it never hurt to check before stripping down to her birthday suit. Once she was sure the coast was clear, she pulled her t-shirt overhead and shimmied out of her pants.

She set them on the porch stairs and began to jog. Then, there was nothing but the wind. She didn't even focus on shifting. The wolf form would come on its own, but the exhilaration was something she was going to have to work toward tonight. Without so much as noticing the change, she found her feet had become paws, pounding hard against the damp earth, kicking twigs and pebbles into her fur.

She didn't care. She wanted to roll in mud, to bound around trees like they were part of an obstacle course, to chase her tail until she was dizzy with the effort.

Alone in her wolf form, all the troubles of the pack were behind her. The harder she ran, the further they seemed. It wasn't until her lungs burned that she reluctantly slowed her steps.

If only she could run forever—

Her ears pricked up and she stilled, sniffing the cool night air. There was a strange scent on the air. One that didn't belong, but, at the same time, was not unfamiliar. No, this was definitely something she'd encountered before. Like the lake over on the Big Sky Canyon lands and something else... fresh cinnamon?

The smell was growing stronger, edging toward her. And the more pronounced it became, the more certain she was that this was no coincidence or wayward woodland creature moving from one territory to another. This was the smell of the enemy.

A Big Sky Canyon wolf on her land.

Maybe that was why she'd been so on edge. Her intuition had sensed the predator even before she had.

Briefly, she considered making her way back to the house, but she dismissed the thought out of hand. It was a single wolf and there was no point in waking up the whole house over something she could handle with one paw behind her back. If by some miracle she was bested and he continued onto the grounds of the compound, the sensors would catch him and alert the pack of his presence. She was only risking her own neck here, and that was fine by her.

Besides...what if it was *him*? Her savior?

No, that smell she would remember. The scent of jack pines and earth. This was different. She dismissed the thought before it dug its hooks in deep.

Instead, she focused instead on readying herself. She poised for attack, angling her back legs for the pounce while she searched through the leaves for a sign of motion and listened carefully for the crackle of leaves. Anything that might give her adversary away. All she had to do was lay in wait, hold back the growl already building in the back of her throat and—

A snap of twigs. There he was. Practically in front of her, blending into the night with his thick, dark coat. If the moonlight hadn't shown her his shadow, she might not have seen him at all. But as it was?

She had him, dead to rights.

She sprang into action, landing on him with fierce determination and clawing at him. The scuffle was so fast that she could hardly tell which part of him she had, so she snapped her jaws wildly, trying for his throat or something soft so she could do some damage.

When she finally caught flesh, she let out a fierce, guttural snarl.

How dare this interloper cross into Pray lands unannounced?

She didn't have long to think on it, because one second she was on top, and the next they were rolling across the damp earth, over and over again as they battled for supremacy. Razor-sharp teeth nipped her shoulder, and she yelped, bucking hard against him and lunging forward, narrowly missing a shot at his ear.

Even in the midst of her anger, she had to admit, he was an excellent fighter. Far more crafty than the rabble the Kotke had sent the week before, and twice as strong than their strongest.

He was like a professional boxer, deftly avoiding all her attacks and trying to tire her until he could land the knock out.

Well, if that was how he was going to play, then he was in for a rude awakening. She had stamina for days, and when it came to their territory, there was nothing she wouldn't do to protect them.

No sooner had the thought crossed her mind than he disengaged and stepped back to circle her slowly. She felt a weird tickle in her brain, a sort of vibration, almost like he was trying to communicate with her. She shook her head to clear it and reassess. That was ludicrous. He wasn't of her pack. Either she was addled from the fight or she was imagining things so, even if she'd wanted to hear what this wolf had to say, she couldn't have.

She growled low in her throat, leaning back on her hind legs as if to pounce again. Before she'd gotten her chance, though, he was already trotting behind her, continuing his circles.

She kept her gaze locked on him, appraising his every move. Waiting. Anticipating the next strike.

He was bigger than she'd thought, and had landed a good many blows himself. She was fatigued, and nearly every joint in her body ached with the effort of her battle. Still, even if he was twice her size, there was no doubt in her mind. This was a fight she was going to win.

He paused for just one second and, heart racing, she pounced.

Apparently, it was exactly what he'd thought she'd do, because he was ready for her. She watched in mid-air as he sidestepped her, allowing her front paws to connect hard with the ground as he pinned her down from behind. She tried to roll again, but this time he was having none of it. Each of his paws was the size of an oven mitt, and he kept her there, every inch of his muscular frame tensed, holding her in place.

She flexed and wriggled beneath him in an effort to slither from his hold. If she didn't get out of this, she was done for. She couldn't allow it. Wouldn't let herself go out like this.

But even as she flailed, she sensed a change in him. The weight of him seemed to lessen, the tension seemed to uncoil, the pressure holding her in place became infinitely more concentrated.

She strained to move her head, and with one eye she spotted it in the dim light. There was no longer a paw on hers, but rather a big, masculine hand.

"Shhh. Stop fighting," he said, moving to grip her wrists when she ignored him.

Maybe her luck hadn't completely run out after all.

If she transformed now, his hold on her would slip as he adjusted to the change in her size. Sure, it was a long shot, but she had to take the chance.

After all, it was the only one she had.

Closing her eyes, she focused all her attention on her human form, willing her body to react. Not so easy in this situation when her blood was running hot and her adrenaline was high. When it did, she didn't hesitate. She bucked hard, yanking her arms outright to her sides at the same time. His grip was strong, but her speed was legend, and she flipped him off her and made for the path.

Okay, so maybe she couldn't beat this guy, but she could get back to the house. She could warn her pack. She could—

Fwap. Something hard and warm snagged her ankle, and then she was flailing toward the ground, hands outstretched to break her fall.

So this would be the end. Not in the midst of an epic battle between warring packs. Not after logging her tenth kill. No, Maggie Porter, badass extraordinaire was going to go out like a punk, buck naked in the woods.

Leave it to Fate to keep her humble.

Chapter Two

"Oh for crying out loud, will you calm the fuck down," Grey said, tightening his hold on her legs.

He was trying to go easy on her, but she wasn't making it easy.

He felt her scrabbling for something with her hands and then promptly regretted not stopping her as a rock hit him in the forehead, dead center.

Not bad. He resisted the urge to rub at the offended spot. She had pretty good aim. He had to give her credit for that much. What he didn't have to give her credit for was, well, anything else, because she was a real pain in the ass so far.

He'd been standing with her ankles in his clutches for a solid minute and she still hadn't said a single word.

"You do realize that if I'd wanted to kill you, I could have done it about a hundred times over by now."

He tugged on her silky ankle and pulled her toward him, and though she tried to use the move to wriggle for escape again, she did nothing more than reinforce his hold on her and give him a stellar view of her pert little ass.

She growled low in her throat.

"How about you throw more rocks at me? I'll make a target in the dirt, and you can make a sort of game out of it. Like a poor man's game of horseshoes." He chuckled at his own attempt at humor, but she was clearly unimpressed.

"How about I make a chair of your bones?" she asked, her voice modulated to sound falsely pleasant.

And what a voice it was. Like hot, buttered rum, smooth and silky. Melodic and just husky enough to make him wonder what she sounded like during sex.

"She speaks," he observed lightly, making sure to keep his reaction to her from his own voice. Goodwill visit or not, he still shouldn't be thinking about sleeping with the enemy.

Not even one with a fine ass like that.

He shoved the thought aside and considered his options before finally settling on a compromise.

"Look, I'm willing to let you up, but you have to promise not to run." Her head was already bobbing in the moonlight and she was opening her mouth to agree when he cut her off. "And you have to promise not to hit me. Or throw rocks. Or bite me. In fact, let's just go with a sweeping 'no violence' rule. Give me five minutes to talk to you and I won't hurt you if you don't hurt me. Deal?"

She fell silent again. Was this how he was going to spend his night? Staring at the backside of a naked woman who wouldn't listen? Not that he hadn't had worse nights, but this definitely was not what he'd had in mind when he'd decided to make the trip over here.

Before he was able to come up with another solution, she nodded her gleaming, dark head. "Fine. Five minutes."

He released her ankles and rolled to his feet, tensed to break into a sprint and chase her down if he had to. But she surprised him by rolling onto her side and shifting to her feet to stand before him.

He had a speech all planned out on the way over. Something about war. And peace. Except every thought drained from his head along with the blood and went straight to his cock. It was dark out but the stars and the moon gave off enough light, even through the thick canopy of trees, that he could see her fairly well.

And what he could see? Was spectacular. Long, thick black hair hung past her shoulders, the waves brushing the tips of her pert breasts. Her stomach was lean, her hips full, and those legs went on forever.

"What are you, like five ten?" he heard himself ask.

She snorted and crossed her arms over her chest, not out of modesty, but out of amusement. "Is that what you came all the way her to ask me? Yeah, I'm five ten."

He cleared his throat and forced himself to think about the issue at hand. He'd been in a pack his whole life and had never been so distracted by nudity before. It would behoove him not to start now.

"I have something to tell you and your people."

"Why would I believe anything you have to say? You're from the Big Sky Canyon pack, right? I've heard enough from Chandra to know better than that."

A low blow. Chandra had left his pack and joined the Pray clan months before. For his father, it had been a tipping point.

The sharpening of the arrow's head that was now directed squarely at the Pray wolves.

Grey hadn't said it out loud, but he hadn't blamed the woman for leaving. In truth, he wondered why more wolves hadn't followed her. If anything, the fact that so many pack members remained was a tribute to just how much fear his father could inspire in his people. Grey himself had left, only to come back when he got word of how bad things had gotten. Which was why it was imperative to keep war at bay as best he could until he convinced his father to let him take his place.

"Again, I refer you to the previous comment. The one about how you're still alive. Surely that earns me a kernel of trust." He returned her hard gaze, and she narrowed her pretty, dark eyes. "Listen, maybe we started off on the wrong foot—"

"*You* started off on the wrong land," she cut in.

"None of that matters," he snapped, at his wit's end with her now. "You're not going to *have* any land if you don't listen to me. Your pack is in danger. The human—"

"Amber," she corrected, her eyes now little more than slits.

"Amber, then, has caused a rift in the community."

"We settled this with the Kotke when they came a-knocking, and we'll settle it with you too, if we have to. We will not kill her. She belongs to the pack now."

"She belongs to the pack, but she's still a human?" This time he tried to make his words sound calmer, but the result was much the same as it had been before.

"We're not prepared to let her turn right yet."

"Well you don't have much of a choice in the matter. It needs to happen, and fast."

"Who do you think you are to come in here and tell us how to run our pack? Don't you have some children to eat or something? Last time I checked, that was the Big Sky Canyon M. O."

The words burned like acid but only because they were true.

His father's cruelty had not been restricted to tormenting the pack. The last time Grey had left Joseph unchecked, he had gone for a hunt and stumbled upon a family in the mountains. When Grey had returned home, it was to find what was left of their carcasses waiting for him. The older wolves had been proud, had celebrated the alpha and toasted to him.

The rest of the pack?

They looked to Grey, waiting for him to step in. Waiting for him to confirm the one thing he'd suspected since his return.

His father was losing his mind.

He'd always been strict and old-fashioned. Since Grey could remember, he'd had a blatant disregard for human life. But now? He was a bloodthirsty monster, and disregard had turned to zealous hatred. Age had brought on a dementia-fueled paranoia that was eating away at what was left of his compassion. And this encounter with the Pray wolves was about to be the tipping point. If they followed him into war, win or lose, the aftermath would lead the pack from reluctant obedience to total chaos in the form of mutiny and civil war.

If he could put an end to all of it—if he could stop the battle before it began, then he had a chance of saving dozens of lives.

All he had to do was convince the woman in front of him that, if he had a little time to work, the future could be altered.

Though, it seemed that was going to be far easier said than done.

"Stick with your pre-conceived notions of me if you want to, but I defy you to find a single wolf who would say I would kill a human for sport," he said wearily.

She cocked her head in confusion but rebounded quickly, pursing her lips and pinning him with a challenging gaze. "But you sit by and allow it from your packmates, though?"

"Not everything is so cut and dry, woman," he tried again, though frustration was already burning to the surface inside of him, ready to erupt. "From what I hear, even your pack was divided on the topic of your human, so spare me the soapbox. I'm not here to argue with you,"

"You're here to attack me—"

"God dammit, woman. I'm here to save your sorry ass. Big Sky is bigger than the Kotke. We're smarter, faster, stronger. Do you honestly think you can defeat us so handily? Even if you prevail, there will be heavy losses on both sides. You have to tell your pack. Get them to turn the human at the very least. That will buy me some time. It won't stop my father, but it will make it much less palatable for the rest of the pack to get behind him, and that's all I need right now."

She shifted restlessly from foot to foot and stepped into a moonbeam that lit her from head to toe. God, she was beautiful.

Color flooded her chest, snaking along her neck until her cheeks were a bright, rosy red. "What's your endgame?"

"Sorry?" he asked, trying to get him back in the game.

"You obviously don't care about 'the human'." Her fingers curled into air-quotes around the word. "So why are you here?

Do you care about my pack or werewolf relations? Or is this just politics, and you're trying to stage a coup?"

Anger bubbled in the pit of his stomach, and he clenched his fists. His patience for this had worn so thin it was threadbare. She didn't want to tell her people about the battle? That was fine. But he wasn't about to let her stand in judgment of his ethics.

"I care about my people," he growled.

"Enough to give us a warning so that me and mine are prepared and at the ready now that we know you're coming for sure?" She let out a laugh. "Sounds like love to me. Good luck in your bid for becoming alpha, buddy. You're going to need it."

He was so done with the conversation, he didn't bother with a response.

He wheeled around and plowed into the foliage, back in the direction he'd come.

Screw her.

If she wanted to watch her people die, let that be on her conscience. At least he'd tried, and it wouldn't be on his.

What did she know about caring for a group of people? She wasn't trying to alpha from the second-in-command spot in secret. She didn't have nearly two dozen wolves coming to her for guidance behind her alpha's back. She wasn't the one responsible for her pack's future.

Which was why, tomorrow, he would cross the boundary again and this time, he wouldn't stop until he found Liam, like he should've from the start. Maybe the Pray alpha would be more willing to listen.

And if not? If he, too, was mistrustful of some nefarious Trojan horse plot?

Then they were all going to find themselves in a little town called Fucked.

***

Maggie banged her head against the bark of the tree and let out a deep sigh.

Damned Amber.

Maggie had said from the beginning that they shouldn't have let her in. Just like they shouldn't have let Amalie in the first time around. Exceptions like that only led to confusion and chaos.

She should have listened to her instincts. Shouldn't have been such a weakling and backed down when the rest of the pack pressed to bring her into the fold.

Shouldn't have grown to like her.

Sure, it was begrudgingly, but Maggie couldn't lie to herself anymore. "The human" was growing on her, in exactly the way Amalie had. That was the only explanation for her anger when this interloper refused to call her by name.

Now, she a choice before her, and one of her options was quickly slipping away through the trees. She'd witnessed how fast he was firsthand. Once he was gone, she'd never be able to catch up with him once he found his stride. Even with his now-familiar scent to track him by, he'd be in Big Sky territory before she even got close.

It was now or never.

She rolled her eyes and shifted, charging through the foliage for a few minutes until she spotted his tanned skin through the branches. He hadn't shifted and, even in her wolf form, her mouth watered at the sight of his firm backside and chiseled obliques. The man had muscles to spare, and combined with that shaggy black hair and those piercing eyes? Well, she was sure the ladies were lining the block to get a piece of him.

Not that any of that mattered. He was still the enemy.

Probably.

And she had to stay on her game. Right now that meant getting ready to pounce again.

He stepped into a little clearing and she made her move, leaping through the air and knocking him to the ground. All paw, no claw this time, in deference to the fact that she was starting to second-guess herself on his motives.

"You know, the first time I was willing to let you slide, but now I have to tell you. There are other ways of greeting people." He ground the words out before rolling over and shoving her onto the dirt as she became human again.

"There are a few more things I need to know."

"So now you want to talk?" He lifted an eyebrow, rolling to his feet with a sigh. She started to say her piece, but even though the words had been crystal clear in her head a moment before, they were all but lost to her now.

He'd been cloaked in shadow before, so she only saw him in short bursts, when the moon hit him right. Now, he was in full view and it was clear that her nakedness had had a profound effect on him, and even if he didn't bring her attention to the fact, it was hard to ignore. Her mouth still open, she tried to pull her gaze away from the thick erection jutting between his muscular thighs.

Yep, definitely alpha material.

"Impressed, sweetie?" A cocky smirk was spreading across his handsome face.

Stupid. Stupid. He's the enemy, not a plaything.

What was it about men and their dick hubris?

"Not really," she snapped back, willing him to believe the lie in spite of the heat flooding her cheeks. "And my name is Maggie."

"Maggie, huh? I gotta admit, that's a little less rough and tumble than I expected," he said.

"Then maybe it will be easy to forget."

"I don't think so." His eyes roved over her naked body and her nipples pebbled under the heat of his gaze.

God damn it, hold it together, woman.

To the pack, she was like a sister. Aside from their teen years, they were immune to one another's nakedness. But it wasn't like she'd never had a man look at her this way before. Still, his gaze felt different. Hotter. More intense.

"Was that all you needed?" he asked. "To stare at my twig and berries and then introduce yourself so that when I tell the story of this harpy I met in the woods, I could give her a name?"

Okay, she probably deserved that.

"Not quite." She stood and moved until she was partly shielded behind a bush, suddenly feeling very exposed. Brushing her hair over her shoulders to cover her breasts as nonchalantly as possible, she said, "It's been a rough few months and I may have been hasty, but I did hear what you were saying."

"Apparently that's half the battle."

She ignored the quip and said, "But I'm still not sure about your motives."

He paused a beat, his gaze trailing from her eyes to her hair and lower still. "I think you are."

"If I was, I wouldn't be here asking."

She didn't have time for this. She wasn't in the market for enigmatic answers or lingering glances. She needed him to get to the point so she could run home and put some clothes on.

"You want me to say it? Fine." He approached slowly, every step seeming carefully measured. When he'd crossed half of the distance between them, he said, "I was trying to be a gentleman about it and not rub it in your face, but this isn't the first time I've saved your ass, Maggie." He tilted his head to the side, apparently waiting for his words to sink in.

If that were the case, then he needn't have waited too long. Since the first time she'd seen him, she thought there was a familiarity there.

But his scent...

Blood rushed to her ears, and her head felt light. "Don't lie to me. My nose is legendary and—"

"I masked my scent that night to get past the Kotke. If they knew I was there and not helping in the fight, who knows what could've happened. So I bathed in tomato juice and then pine-scented oils to evade detection."

She took a step closer and closed her eyes, taking a deep breath in. And there it was. It had been just a hint that night, buried under all the other smells and mixed with the scent of blood and battle in the air, but it was there.

"It was you," she breathed. "You're Greyson West."

He gave a single nod.

Which meant he didn't need to angle for politics. He was next in line for the alpha spot regardless. Shaking her head, she said again, "I still don't understand. The Big Sky Canyon pack doesn't care about humans. Or the pack of Pray, for that matter. What is this all about?"

"Doing the right thing. They wanted to kill her."

The answer was simple, and heartfelt. She respected the hell out of that. Even if she still couldn't get her head around it.

In fact, she couldn't get her head around any of this. The man before her was Greyson West. And he had surely saved her life and the life of her charge.

The last of the anger that had been sustaining her drained away and she swayed on her feet, suddenly tired…so tired. All the strife, all the worry, all the discord, it had been weighing on her so heavily that no run in the world was going to make her burden feel lighter.

But here and now, it did. Because alpha or no, she could feel it. Greyson was a leader and a man of integrity. It oozed from every pore in his body and she found herself inexplicably drawn to it and him.

He must have sensed the change in her because, then, he was moving toward her again.

She should have backed away. She already had the answers she needed to tell Liam and the others about the Big Sky… And yet, she was locked in place. Entirely unable to move as her heart thrummed louder in her ears with every step he took toward her.

Before long, that smell barraged her again. All cool air and cinnamon…and man.

Then he was right in front of her, his full lips slightly parted.

He'd already betrayed his alpha this much, what would it be to him to close this inch? She ran her tongue over her mouth, trying desperately to pull in air that wouldn't come.

"Your father seems unhinged. What makes you think they won't kill you when they find out you spoke to me?" She whispered the words, and the air steamed in front of them, forming a wall in what little space there was between them.

He offered her a half-smile, then said, "I guess I'll just have to depend on you to see it doesn't come to that."

Then his lips were on hers, crushing into her with all the warmth and passion she could handle. Without thinking it through, she responded, parting her lips further to take his tongue into her mouth. Sucking lightly, then swirling. At odds with each other and, at the same time, totally in sync.

But just as quickly, it ended.

"Take the information I've given you back to your alpha. Tell him he has less than a week to turn her before an attack. I'll be in touch if I can."

Without so much as a goodbye, he turned and started running, his body morphing into a massive, black wolf as he bolted between the trees and disappeared.

For a moment, she stood and watched, focused on the place where she'd seen him go. She wouldn't chase him. No, whatever he did now was Big Sky Canyon business, not her own. Still, he'd left her with more than one dilemma.

How was she going to explain what had just happened to the pack?

…And when was she going to see him again?

Chapter Three

What the hell had gotten into him?

He took all the energy roiling inside him and channeled in outward, tearing ass through the woods and crashing through bushes like they'd insulted his mama.

As hard as he ran, though, he couldn't get her out of his head.

It had been stupid to kiss her, though.

He should have known as much, but he'd let his pride get in the way of his reason. He'd started off thinking of it as a way to get her attention. Maybe with the added bonus of catching off guard enough that she's top arguing for a second.

But then, what was it they said about the best-laid plans of wolves and men?

He shook his head and bounded over a fallen tree before landing directly in an icy cold puddle. The water blasted him in the face and as he continued to sprint toward home, the droplets on his fur flying as he went.

What were the odds of running into her out there? Like it was fate. But it seemed to him that fate could've gone a lot easier on him if it had sent another wolf in her stead.

She was something, though.

Gorgeous. Sexy. And as good a fighter as any male wolf he'd ever tangled with…

His blood ran hot at the thought of her lying on top of him, grappling and biting as ferociously as she could. The way her eyes had glinted before she snapped at him. That same intensity that had been in her kiss…

When he reached the edge of the trees, he shifted back and stood for a long moment, hoping that the evening's chill would take his mind from her.

It was a bad time to be thinking with his dick. Right now, he had more important things to worry about. If he didn't nip this in the bud, there was no telling how many lives might be lost in a battle that didn't have to happen at all.

He padded the rest of the way to his little cabin, and slipped in through the back door, sighing as he closed it behind him. At least he'd made it back without anyone noticing he'd been gone. Her scent still clung to him and would be hard to explain, to say the least.

He sucked in a breath through his nose, letting that scent fill his senses.

So fucking good.

He made his way into his bedroom and tugged on a pair of boxers before climbing into bed. The best thing he could do for himself right now was to put her out of his head.

If only his cock agreed. Even now, it ached, so hard, the head poked out from the waistband of his underwear.

Shit.

He closed his eyes, helpless to stop the memory of her naked body from taking center stage. The swell of her breasts in the moonlight. The perfect figure-eight of her curves. The second he'd seen her, he wanted to take each of those perky pink nipples between his teeth and suck until she begged him to stop.

Or screamed for him to keep going. With an attitude like that, she was probably a screamer.

A smile tugged at his mouth. She was probably a hellion in bed. Just like that kiss of hers. Hot and fierce.

His cock throbbed again, and he reached down to grip it hard through the thin cotton, trying to control the near-dizzying effect of his erection. Jesus, one kiss and this woman had him completely sprung. He could only imagine what the sex would be like.

Not that he'd ever let it get that far.

That would be reckless. And careless.

And hot as fuck.

He squeezed again, stroking the shaft once, biting back a hiss as he thought of Maggie straddling his lap, lowing herself slowly onto his waiting cock. Teasing him while those dark eyes of her glinted. Then, when she worked him harder, he'd watch as her tits bounced with every thrust. He'd coil his fingers in those dark locks of hers and pull her closer.

Close enough that he could kiss that defiant scowl from her lips. Then even closer still, so he could push himself as deep inside of her as he could possibly go.

His balls tightened as his hips pumped, and he shoved his boxers down. For a second, he considered pulling away. Taking this little fantasy to the end would only make it harder to stay away from her.

But then a image of those full lips flashed through his mind. Those lips wrapped around his cock, sucking pulling....maybe this was a good thing.

Maybe, if he could just imagine himself fucking her, he could wipe her focus on what was really important.

That was all the permission the beast inside him needed, and then it was on. Memory collided with fantasy as it played in his mind like a double-x film.

Maggie, on all fours in his bed, that sweet, round ass high as he plowed into her from behind.

Maggie, on her knees, sucking his aching cock so hard, his eyes crossed.

Maggie, on her back while he licked her swollen clit with his tongue until she clenched his face with her thighs and cried his name.

He gritted his teeth as every muscle tensed, all his nerve-endings firing at once. The orgasm came barreling at him like a runaway train and he let out a low growl as hot liquid spurted from his cock onto his belly.

It was a full minute before he could work up the strength to open his eyes, and another still before the breath stopped sawing in and out of his lungs like he'd run a double marathon.

Not good. His pack was a total shit-show right now. His father was losing screws left and right. Grey had to figure out a way to get back on track.

Because fantasy Maggie was hot as hell. And something told him that real life Maggie?

She would consume him.

OPPOSITION

***

She'd thought about it three ways to Sunday, but it couldn't wait until morning. The pack needed to know what was going on sooner than later.

By the time she'd gotten back to the compound and dressed, she'd already woken Liam with a mental tap on the shoulder. He was waiting for her in his office, and she filled him in quickly.

"So what do you think?" she asked softly as she finished her tale—omitting the kissing part.

Liam was deep in thought, his dark brows caved in a frown as he looked off into space. "Is he trustworthy?"

"I don't know him," she hedged. The words tasted bitter in her mouth, like she was betraying him, but facts were facts. She might be letting her attraction to him and that tiny bit of hero worship she felt cloud her judgment. She couldn't pose her feelings like they were facts.

"What does your gut say?"

"Yes," she answered flatly and without hesitation. "I believe we can trust him."

"Then we have some decisions to make."

At his command, the rest of the pack was assembled, including Amber and the members in the carriage houses. By daybreak, every seat in the great room was full.

Liam took his place in front of the fire, exuding power and confidence despite the fact that his face was lined with concern and his dark hair was still mussed from sleep.

"Maggie, will you tell us all what you shared with me?" Liam asked.

He motioned for her to stand beside him and she picked through the dozen or so people blocking her way. Harder was describing everything Grey had said with so many onlookers. They seemed as confused by the warning as she was, and just as concerned. The memory of the last battle was so fresh. She was loath to tell them they might have to face it again so soon.

Once she'd finished, the room fell silent.

Then there was a polite cough and a shaky, breathy voice sounded from the corner. Amber had one of Billy's arms slung around her shoulders, but she sat up tall, even though her gaze was downcast.

"I think maybe he's right. If it will forestall another attack, even for a while to give us a chance to work out some sort of compromise with Greyson behind his father's back, I will turn now." She faltered on the last word, and Maggie's heart twisted for her. It must be hard to be a human. To be weak and fragile. To be full of emotion all the time and have no reliable instincts to guide her.

Billy's jaw tensed like he was gearing up for a fight, but Liam held up a hand.

"No, Amber. The pack has already chosen. The time will come for you to be turned, but that time isn't now. The warning of an impending attack from this stronger pack only cements it more clearly in my mind. Turning will leave you weak and ill for days. Even then, it will be more than a week until the next full moon where you can truly become a wolf. You'll be more vulnerable than ever if we turn you now."

Amber opened her mouth as if to argue, but Billy gave a brief shake of his head and she pursed her lips.

"I agree with waiting, but I think we've got to take him seriously about the attack," Chandra piped up from beside Liam's mate, Amalie. "I was a member of the Big Sky Canyon before I came here. Grey is one of the good ones. We all knew he wasn't on the same page as his father, and was biding his time to take the mantle. Seems like he realizes that the time is now."

Maggie let those words sit for a moment. So she and Chandra agreed that Grey's motives were pure, but was that enough to risk the whole pack on?

She glanced at Amber, who had been looking paler by the second, and came to a decision.

Let me handle Grey.

She sent the message to Liam and Liam only, and waited for his response as the rest of the pack chattered around them. They would only argue with her and try to make it a pack activity, but the fact was, Grey was acting alone in this. Calling attention to his actions by bringing in the cavalry would only put him in danger. If Liam would allow her to act as emissary, surely she and Grey could come up with a plan together.

Are you certain you can handle him? Liam finally responded. His feelings were right there on the surface and she could feel the turmoil. He was torn. He hated the idea of her taking a risk if her instincts were wrong, but as always, he had to think of the pack as a whole.

She found herself reiterating what Grey had said to her.

If he wanted to hurt me, he could've done it a hundred times by now. Let me do this.

He surveyed her for a moment and then tipped his head in a clipped nod.

A shiver of anticipation at the thought of seeing him again mixed with a cold wash of apprehension. This was a big responsibility and she hoped luck was on her side. Because might talk a big game, but she'd lied to her alpha about one thing for sure.

She had no idea if she could handle a man like Greyson West.

Chapter Four

Three hard knocks on his bedroom door were followed by the door slamming open into the wall with a crack and the sound of crumbling sheetrock hitting the floor.

If Willa was going to storm into his cabin first thing in the morning, she could at least show the common decency not to break his stuff. Again.

He growled and burrowed deeper beneath his comforter. Maybe if he pretended he was still sleeping, she'd go away. Stranger things had happened, right?

There was a blinding light followed by a rush of cold air, and then he was being accosted by something white and papery. An envelope? Whatever it was, apparently Willa had decided it was the perfect murder weapon.

"What are you hoping to do? Paper cut me to death? Calm your shit, woman." He rubbed his eyes and, when the barrage finally subsided, sat up against his headboard.

He glanced toward his clock. She'd woken him up at eight AM? And without coffee, no less.

"What the hell is wrong with you?" she hissed, then sat at the edge of his bed and tucked one ankle under her thigh.

"Have you seen the time?" He smothered a yawn, and then continued; "I think the real question here is, what the hell is the matter with *you* showing up at people's houses this early?"

"You're lucky it was me and not one of the others. Do you know what this is?" she spat. Pulling her other leg beneath her, she settled onto the mattress until she was sitting crisscrossed in front of him.

"How would I—"

"Exactly. And maybe if you did, you would be a little more freaking grateful that your father didn't stop by your cabin for a visit before I did." She raised her eyebrows and tossed the envelope in her hand onto the space between them on the mattress.

"Honestly, sometimes I think you *try* to screw with me. Like, you just leave the house and think 'hmm, what can I do to make Willa's life more difficult today? I know! I'll hit up a rival pack and make sure they tell everyone what I did and—'"

"What?" He snatched up the letter. Was this about his warning? Or worse, was this about Maggie and their incident in the forest? Not that a kiss would mean much of anything, but his father would see fraternizing with a Pray wolf as tantamount to treason.

Whatever the case, Grey wasn't about to wait to find out but when he examined the seal, he found the edges wavy. Like the letter had already been steamed open once and then put back together very carefully.

He read his name scrawled on the front and raised his brow at her.

She shrugged and tried to look innocent, but he knew better.

She already knew what was inside. That was good news. If it was truly dire, he'd know it by now.

He dragged his thumb beneath the seal. It sprung open easily enough and he unfolded the letter, scanning it once, then twice.

"I don't see what you're freaking out about. A meeting at the intersection of our lands? It's a chance for peaceful negotiation."

"Yeah, I think that's definitely how your father would see it if he found the letter. He wouldn't wonder at all about, I don't know, how they found out about his plans or why they reached out to you specifically or—"

"Okay, okay, I get your meaning." He hit his head back against the headboard and took a deep breath.

If he could meet with Maggie and just get her to agree to change the human—*Amber*—then he was sure he could convince the pack to stand up to his father. None of them were comfortable having a human in their midst who could expose their existence to the world, but they would be much less inclined to kill her if she was just another wolf...

He pictured the mulish look on Maggie's face and her stubborn refusal and groaned.

He'd already made as many compromises as he could with her. Even if he promised peace, there was no accounting for his father. Hell, even if his father agreed to peace, that didn't mean he'd keep his word.

He had to think of another compromise, and fast.

"Who delivered this?" Willa poked at the letter with an outstretched foot.

That was a great question, and one that sent a shaft of dread straight through him. Had she seriously snuck onto their lands when he'd told her they were gunning for her pack? That seemed beyond reckless and his stomach knotted at the thought. Only the fact that he would've heard if something had happened if she'd been caught settled him some.

"Maggie, it says," Willa read over his shoulder. "She's not their alpha. I wonder why she contacted you?"

He glanced at Maggie's signature at the bottom of the letter, then back at Willa. Christ, when it rained, it fucking hail stormed. Though, truly, he had no reason to share more than necessary about Maggie.

There wasn't much to tell.

She was just a pack member. What would any of that mean to Willa? Alternately, he could lie. How hard would it be to say he didn't know?

But even the thought of lying to his best friend's face made his stomach uneasy.

"Another complication," he said. Simple enough and most certainly the truth.

"Well, whatever it is, see that you handle it." Willa's mouth was a solid line. "I'm serious, Grey. You've gotten this far because you're your father's son, but it won't get you much further. You're putting yourself in front of two firing ranges at once."

He scooted toward her and flung an arm around her petite shoulders. "Everything's going to be fine."

He hoped it was true. If one side or the other *did* kill him, Willa might come around and kill his ghost for lying to her.

"I've got to get ready to go. You stay here and hold down the fort. Tell the others I went on a hunt if they ask."

She nodded and eased herself away from him before finally rolling to her feet.

He had a few hours to think and prepare. The only problem was that whenever he tried to focus on what he'd say, his thoughts would wander back to *her*. The black hair, the slamming body, hell, even the bad attitude. Something about her drove him nuts in the best and worst way. Already he could feel his blood going hot at the thought of seeing her again.

"What if she doesn't come alone? What if it's a trap and there are others with her?" Willa tried again, but he was already pushing past her, heading for the door.

"It's really just the one that worries me," he muttered beneath his breath.

He padded down the stairs, brain whirring as he tried to fashion a plan even as his wolf prowled restlessly inside him, hungry for another taste of her, and making plans of its own…

***

Maggie ran her nails along the broken-down table in front of her. He was already fifteen minutes late. Hardly a good way to start off a two-man war council.

And maybe he isn't coming at all.

The thought sent her stomach sinking in a way that irritated the crap out of her. He wasn't her boyfriend, after all. He was the next alpha of what was still, at this point, an enemy pack. Walking around with her head in the clouds was a sure recipe for heartache.

Exactly the reason she'd avoided getting involved with men to this point. They were nothing but trouble.

She padded across the room and pressed her cheek to the door, breathing in deep.

There it was.

The smell was faint at first, but unmistakable. Sweet like the trees that lined the way to the Big Sky Canyon lands, but strangely spicy and clean. Like the stream that ran high onto the fragrant grasses by the rickety little shack she was standing in.

Greyson.

Steeling herself, she ignored her suddenly dry throat and swung the door open to find him standing there, looking handsome as ever in jeans and a crew neck, navy sweater.

His mouth was twisted into a grim line and she cursed her heart for thudding even louder at the sight of him.

"Hello again, Maggie."

He was already sidestepping her and heading into the wooden shelter before she got her voice back to invite him in.

He settled onto a metal folding chair opposite the one she'd occupied earlier. As she returned to her seat, he folded his arms over his muscular chest, sending his biceps bulging against the fabric of his sweater.

"You really shouldn't have risked coming onto our land," he said softly.

She shook her head to clear it, still enthralled in his scent. Jesus, how hadn't she noticed it that first night? Had it been this tantalizing then? This masculine and tempting? Or had the kiss just brought it all to the forefront for her. She shook her head, trying to focus on the here and now. "Yeah, well, I didn't have much choice."

"Next time, I'll give you my cell number." He shook his head slowly in disapproval. "That was foolhardy, Maggie. You could've been killed on the spot. And what if someone else had gotten to your letter first? You could've been a sitting duck here just ripe for an ambush."

She squared her shoulders but didn't bother to reply.

His frown turned to an outright scowl as he set his feet back onto the ground. "Funny, I don't remember you being this close-mouthed the last time we met."

She got up, ready to scramble over the table and thrash him. Just as quickly, though, she sat back down. That was what he wanted. He was trying to get under her skin, although why, she couldn't say.

"I'm way stealthier than you are. The chance of me getting caught if I didn't want to be were slim to none," she said finally, not comfortable with the idea of him thinking she was a reckless fool but not willing to delve too deep into the why's of that discomfort. "Besides, just because I've decided to trust you doesn't mean I'm willing to risk my pack on it. My neck is one thing. The whole pack? That's another entirely."

The anger in his eyes seemed to cool a little, replaced with what looked something like a grudging respect. "Well, we're here now, so let's talk. Did you speak to Liam? Have you reconsidered about the h—" he broke off before correcting himself, "Amber?"

"We did discuss it, and it's just not going to happen right now. The risks are too high."

His jaw went tight and he scrubbed at the dark stubble shadowing his cheek. "Then I'm not sure what I can do to stop my father. Unless I have the support of the rest of the pack, I—"

"You're just not trying hard enough." The words came out louder and angrier than she'd wanted, but she wouldn't apologize for them. She was here, for Christ's sake. She was trying. How could there be no other solution?

"You were the one with the job. You were supposed to convince your wolves to turn her. If I'm not trying hard enough, then neither are you." His speech stung like a slap in the face and she blinked at him, not sure what to say. It was a cold truth that neither one of them was in charge, and it was a helpless feeling that they could both relate to.

After a long, silent moment, he continued, "If you won't stop this, then the least you can do is run. Leave Montana. Before you get yourself killed."

"Are you calling me weak?" She couldn't stop herself from leaping from her chair this time, towering over him before he got the chance to stand again.

"I'm calling you foolish. There's evidence enough of that by the fact that you came out here alone after coming onto enemy territory and dropping a note under my door. So either you're foolish or you're crazy."

"It was a strategy."

"It was a death wish." He stood and she was forced to crane her neck in order to stare up into his silvery eyes.

He was close to her, his chest practically pressed against her own, his body heat radiating off of him until she had no idea what the temperature was in the air. All she knew was the rage in her belly, the muskiness of his scent, and the warmth of his skin. It was like his presence consumed her, and the more he spoke, the more she wanted to kiss him and punch him in the gut at the same time.

"That's not true," she finally said, but the words came out far more strained than she would have liked.

He tucked a finger under her chin. "Maybe not an intentional one."

She wanted to step away. To stumble back until she was as far from him as the little space would allow, but every signal in her brain misfired. She couldn't move, couldn't speak. Her breath caught and she met his heated stare, daring him to risk kissing her again.

She wanted that so badly, she could taste it. The desire to escape faded as she let her instincts override her reason. Rather than stepping back, she stepped forward and pressed herself against him, the need clawing at her guiding the way. "Say what you will, but it sure seems like you're glad to see me."

The truth of her words was evident as the thickness of his arousal pressed against her belly.

He let his quicksilver gaze trail past her mouth, down her throat to her breasts, where her nipples pebbled beneath her cotton shirt. "You seem pretty happy to see me, too."

He shot her a slow, crooked grin and she opened her mouth to argue, but before she got the chance his lips were on hers, crowding her against the wall with his body.

God, he was warm. His muscles were so hard against her, and even if she'd wanted to fight him, she didn't think she could have. Still, she couldn't let him believe that he'd won. She struggled weakly against him as each of his hands encircled her wrists and pressed them against the wall. The lean plane of his stomach pushed against her chest and her nipples strained at the rough feel of his skin.

She caught his bottom lip between her teeth and nipped him, half playfully and half daring, but he only grinned.

"What's so funny?" she hissed when he came up for breath.

"You're still putting on a show." He released her wrists to slide up the contour of her stomach, resting just below the curve of her breasts. "But there's no fight left in you."

The devil in her couldn't resist. She tackled him to the ground, straddled him, and pinned each of his wrists in her hands before he'd realized what she'd done. "I could always change my mind," she growled.

She'd no sooner spoken the words than she was tumbling onto her back, held in place by the sheer power of his weight on top of her.

"You won't." He moved to hold both of her hand above her head with one hand and then slanted his mouth over hers again. His breath was sweet and spicy, his lips more tender than she'd expected. With him, she thought it would be nothing but hard edges, but even in all his intensity, there was a tenderness.

And even more surprisingly, she wasn't sure which she liked more.

She dipped her tongue into his mouth, meeting his in yet another battle for supremacy. They twisted and swirled, plunging deeper, then pulling back.

His free hand found her breasts at last, and as he cupped her overly sensitized flesh, she found herself arching into him against her will. She simply couldn't help it. Worse, a low moan escaped her throat and he smiled against her mouth.

"It doesn't mean anything," she breathed between kisses, but the huskiness of her voice only made his smile broaden. Dammit.

"Whatever you want to tell yourself is fine with me," he said and tweaked her nipple between thumb and forefinger. "I don't mind giving the lady what she wants."

"I—"

He cut her off with another searing kiss, but by that point her head was swimming too much to resurface again. She'd always been the good soldier. The one who spent her whole life living for her pack, to the detriment of everything else in life.

She'd never taken those cooking lessons she'd wanted to take.

She'd never gone to Greece, or Paris, or even New York City.

And she'd never allowed herself to feel the way she did right now about a man.

Yeah, if she was going let herself get lost—even just this one—she wanted it to be with Greyson West.

Chapter Five

He wasn't sure which he liked better, her bark or her bite.

The fight in her was hot as hell, but the way she kissed…

That was pure sex. Wild and carnal. Even better was the way her body responded to him, almost like they'd mated before. Like her body knew his and was desperate for what only he could give her.

He reached behind her with a muffled growl and unclasped her bra, a move that sent her pert breasts spilling forward to press against the thin cotton of her shirt.

He cupped her then, pinching her straining nipples, and she spread her legs a little wider beneath him, arching herself against him so that he could feel every curve of her gorgeous body.

God dammit.

He broke their kiss, lifting her shirt and dipping his head, lowering his lips to her nipple. He'd expected her to argue again, to try and pin him down or fight, but she ran her fingers through his hair instead, spreading her legs wider as his tongue swirled around her peak and his thumb flicked the other sensitive bud.

"At least we know you can do one thing right," she murmured, half on a gasp. He glanced up at her to see a teasing smile tugging at her mouth.

Her cheeks were a rosy, sexy pink, her lips full and red...

"It's a shame you don't put your mouth to better use," he shot back and she quirked a brow.

"All right," she said, her eyes going soft as she wriggled from beneath him. He knew he should've have, but he couldn't bring himself to stop her as she pressed him onto his back and slithered lower.

He ignored the resulting throb of his cock and held her still, cursing himself. If he let her do that, he was in deep trouble.

"There'll be time for that. But first I need to look at you." He moved to unbutton her jeans, but before he even got the chance to touch her, her nimble fingers were at his fly.

"Now you think you're calling all the shots?" She yanked his pants down along with his boxers, and his pulse kicked into overdrive as she stilled, her face only inches from his swollen head.

He caught sight of her sweet, pink tongue as she inched closer...

God, what he wouldn't give to feel her there. To have her warm mouth close around him and suck until he—

One swipe of her tongue, and his vision went hazy.

He growled, halting her with a hand in her hair. "I don't think I'm calling the shots. I *am* calling them." He rolled her off him and this time, he wasn't letting her up until he made her scream. He undid her pants then tugged them down her legs. "And this time, I go first."

She opened her mouth to argue, but before she got the chance, he slid her panties down her thighs and past her ankles before tossing them aside. For a long moment, he just stared down at her, his throat going tight with need.

The narrow swatch of dark hair, those silky thighs, suddenly he was desperate to see the rest. To know if she was as pretty there as she was everywhere else.

He spread her thighs wide and, even in his fantasies, he'd never imagined that she'd be so pink, so wet, so ready as she was right now.

"I can't wait to taste you," he muttered.

He bowed his head between her thighs and lapped at her slit with one, long swipe of his tongue. She rocked into him with a muffled groan, thighs tensing around his shoulders, and he pressed his tongue deeper, committing the taste of her to memory.

He let his fingers trail between her legs, tracing a pattern over her soft skin until she shook beneath his touch. Again, she made a sound from above that was nothing more than a squeak.

He ignored every instinct urging him to keep going. To lick and suck and consume until she came so hard, she felt it down to her very soul.

Instead, he pulled back and looked up at her tense face. "You're biting your lip so hard, it's bleeding," he said softly.

Her eyes snapped open and the look of concentration faded as her already flushed cheeks went a fiery shade of red.

"I was trying to be quiet."

"Why would you do that?"

"That's just...what I do." Already he could feel her pulling away from him, her thighs straining to close, her expressive face shutting down.

"Why?"

"I don't know," she snapped, a little of her sass coming back now, but it was fleeting. She took a deep breath and met his gaze. "I guess it makes me feel..."

"Vulnerable?"

Her nod was slow to come, but when it did, he felt a rush of tenderness that he couldn't ever remember feeling before.

"Don't." He'd kept his voice soft, but there was no question it was a demand.

"Don't what?"

"Don't pull away. Don't hold back. Not with me."

***

She swallowed past the dryness in her throat and stared at Grey sitting back on his haunches, glancing from her face to the apex of her thighs and back again, as if he couldn't help himself. God, he was sexy.

But did he have any idea what he was asking of her? Why couldn't he just make this easy?

"It's okay to let me in Maggie. I would never do anything to hurt you."

The moment was so emotionally charged, she briefly considered making a run for it, and even glanced at the door.

And then what, stupid?

And then she'd get to spend the rest of her life wondering what it would have been like...

"I don't know if I can," she whispered, meeting his gaze.

"Only one way to find out."

There was no gentle re-introduction. He just dove back in, consuming her, licking and sucking until she arched helplessly against him. A low moan built in her throat, and she fought the urge to swallow it, letting it break from her lips like a plea.

For a moment, it felt like weakness.

And then? It felt like freedom, because Grey was there, murmuring his encouragement against her, his strong hands flexing over her hips and pinning her as he took her higher.

She swallowed hard and closed her eyes, scraping her nails against the wood for support as his tongue pulsed inside her, sending delicious shivers through her, from head to toe.

The pressure was building steadily, like a river after a heavy rain, and her body shook with the effort of trying to control it. Manage it in some way that wouldn't leave her wrecked when it was over.

Then he caught her clit gently between his teeth and rubbed his tongue against the aching knot just as he skimmed a hand over her stomach and tweaked her pebbled, pink nipple.

"Oh god," she cried, surprising even herself, as he worked her to a fever pitch. He growled in response, and that only stoked the flames. She strained toward him...toward it. The orgasm that waited like a ripe peach, right there for the picking.

Then he dipped a finger inside of her and her body froze, another cry escaping her lips without her consent.

"So tight," he groaned against her, his voice all grit and need, his heated breath fanning against her skin. He pulsed a finger inside of her until her entire body shook.

The thrusts were gentle at first, but once he'd set the tempo, that beautiful rhythm, all thoughts of staying quiet fled and his name became a low chant, growing louder by the second.

So close, so close...

She couldn't take it anymore. She needed him. Needed to come, needed to feel that thick cock deep inside her.

"Please," she gasped. "Please, Grey. Now."

***

He pushed onto his knees and nipped his way up her stomach, taking a second to draw one, taut nipple into his mouth and suck. Her body was like a fucking carnival and he didn't want to miss even one ride.

He pulled back to look down at her and his cock jerked with the need that had been building since she'd pounced on him in the woods. He was going to make her come so hard that she wouldn't be able to think straight for days to come, and the only way to do that was by driving her insane now.

Even if that meant he would be driving himself crazy in the process.

"Not yet," he ground out. She was close enough to feel. Her heat was only inches from his cock. One subtle move, one thrust and he'd be inside of her, warm and wet and perfect.

He nipped her throat, working his way to her earlobe and teasing her.

A soft moan escaped her lips and her hips arched up, pressing her slick folds to his hard length.

"God damn it," he groaned, the blood pulsing so loudly in his ears, he could barely think straight.

"Please, Grey."

His strong, mouthy, bossy Maggie was asking him so nicely, and she was so ready for him—

"Fuck it," he snarled. He took his swollen cock in hand, and positioned himself, muscles quaking as he dipped the head inside her molten heat.

They both gasped as he slowly sank in, inch by throbbing inch, until he filled her.

"Jesus," he ground out. She was the best kind of tight, the most perfect kind of warm. He was torn between the urge to lay into her nice and slow, and feel the liquid drag of her flesh against his until they both lost their minds, or to pull back and plunge deep, and fast, riding her hard until they both exploded.

All he knew for sure was that he never wanted to leave.

But the wolf was rising fast inside him, and the clawing, driving need made rational thought impossible. He was moving without thinking, working himself in and out of her, hard and deep.

She took in a sharp breath as her hips rocked against him and she circled her arms around his back, digging her nails into his skin, urging him on.

He pulled back so he could watch her, mesmerized by her breasts bouncing with every move, and then moved close again to feel her nipples branding his chest with every thrust.

Jesus Christ.

"I'm going to come," she groaned.

Her pussy pulsed around him and he closed his eyes, feeling every quake and movement of her shuddering muscles. What he wouldn't give to bottle this feeling. To feel her coming around his aching cock. To hear her sweet cries in his ears. To bathe in her scent until there was nothing but her.

"Ah, Grey!"

She gasped again, her channel clutching at him like an unseen fist, and it was all over.

The world went black before his eyes and he was lost. His balls went tight, locked and loaded for takeoff and then it was over. Every muscle in his body seemed to expand and contract all at once as he came, cock spurting and twitching inside her, filling her with hot liquid as he called her name.

Maggie.

His one true mate.

And the woman he could never have.

Chapter Six

When their bodies cooled and he finally rolled away from her, she was unsure whether the low hum in her mind was from sheer exhaustion or from the adrenaline that was still snapping in the air between them.

She glanced at him, focusing too long on the way his chest moved with every deep breath. A soft smile curved his lips and he flopped an arm out beside him, inviting her in. To her surprise, she felt a pull toward him and the humming in her head grew louder.

This had been a mistake. A moment of weakness.

It was hard to remember that, staring at him now, but she would sure as hell be reminded of it soon enough. He might not be like his father, but he was still a member of an enemy pack. That could change in the future, but right now? She had to deal in facts.

The Big Sky Canyon wolves were murderers. Not even out of necessity. Sometimes just for fun. And against it or no, Grey hadn't defected, or overthrown his father to put a stop to it yet.

When she looked at him, that's what she should think about. Not how good he looked in the moonlight or the way his stubble had felt against her thighs. A shudder of pleasure traveled through her at the thought, and she scrambled to her feet, looking around for her scattered clothes.

Until or unless something changed, she couldn't trust herself to be this close to him. Couldn't let her emotions blind her again.

"This was a mistake," she said. "I'm sorry."

He looked up at her, still unmoving, his silver eyes cooling to pewter. "If that was a mistake, imagine what we could do on purpose." His tone was light, but there was no missing the underlying tightness.

She tried to ignore the way her heart wrenched when she looked down at him. "We can't do that again."

She passed by him on the way to collect her top and his fingers closed around her ankle.

"I'm afraid I have to disagree with you again. In fact, I think if there's one thing we should do again, it's definitely that." He rose his eyebrows in challenge. "Or variations on a theme."

"Grey." She moved her ankle away, but could still feel the warmth of his hands on her skin.

"Maggie." He rolled to his feet and crossed his arms over his chest, not bothering to hide the fact that he was watching her dress.

Her stomach sank. He wasn't going to make this easy, which sucked because it was already the hardest thing she'd ever had to do. It was exactly this she'd spent her life dodging and the one thing she hated about being a wolf. The way their instincts chose a mate. The way they fell head over heels for someone out of nowhere. So completely, that everything else ceased to matter or exist.

Like Liam had with Amalie.

Like Billy had with Amber.

And, for all her judgment, she was on the verge of joining their ranks. Grey might not be human, but he was no less off limits to her. Loving him was a weakness she couldn't afford that would come at a price she would never ask her pack to pay.

"You know this is wrong. At least my alpha knows I'm here. What are your people going to do when you go back smelling of Pray?"

Something flashed in his eyes but it was gone before she could put her finger on it. He yanked his sweater over his head and tugged his jeans on before leaning against the knotty pine kitchen table. "I'm a big boy. I'll handle it. I'm more worried about you."

"Me?"

"If you were smart, you'd leave Pray. If your pack isn't going to turn the woman, then it's going to be a bloodbath. If your alpha can't see that then he doesn't deserve your loyalty. But I imagine that isn't what you're asking me, is it?"

She wouldn't leave her pack. They were all she had, the only people she could count on. One night of amazing sex didn't change any of that, even if it was with Grey.

She hardened her heart and clenched her trembling hands into fists. "And your alpha deserves your loyalty? Why haven't *you* left?"

"I did. And I came back not for my father, but for the rest of my pack. And, when the time is right, I will take over. It's coming soon. All I'm asking is for you to try to stay alive until it does so I can make things right."

His words did dangerous things to her insides, igniting a tiny flame of hope in her heart that she dashed without prejudice.

There were no guarantees in their brutal world. He could stage his coup only to find that his entire pack had turned on him. He'd be ripped to shreds. And then she would be left with nothing but an obliterated heart and bitter regret.

Her pack was the backbone of her life. The one constant that held her together, and she couldn't—wouldn't—give it up.

"You already know what I have to do," she said.

He gave a curt nod. "Yeah, I guess I do."

Silence stretched between them, thick as molasses, until he finally spoke again.

"Five days." His throat worked as he stared at a point just over her shoulder. "You have five days. My father made the announcement early this morning."

Her stomach pitched and she swallowed hard. "How?" she asked.

"Not like the Kotke. It will be one, massive push, through the trees to the west and then a bum rush through the gate."

She nodded. She knew that would be the go-to. There were too many carriage houses to hold a unified front except from the main gate. She'd been over the plans with Liam more times than she could count. If someone were going to strike, that would be the smart way to do it, especially since they were still repairing the security equipment that had been destroyed in the Kotke attack.

"Will you be there?" She kept her eyes downcast because it was too hard to look at him.

"Yes."

She flinched and blinked away the hot tears rushing to her eyes.

"But only because I can try to control things that way," he continued, reaching out and lifting her chin so that she would look at him again. "Which is why I told you the plan. Because I trust that you'll try to do the same. Let your alpha know that my pack is only doing what they've spent a lifetime hearing was right. Most of them aren't evil, they're just afraid. The best we can hope for now is that neither side sustains losses. The full moon and Amber's turning is around the corner, and if we can all get through this, there is a good chance things will settle after. If you can, try to convince your pack to injure instead of kill and I will do the same. Can you do that for me?"

She nodded and then finally stared up at him again.

"I'll try."

In another life, he could have been her perfect mate. Smart, levelheaded, strong enough to go toe-to-toe with her and argue. She squared her shoulders and pulled away from him, allowing herself a moment to mourn for the life she could have had. They could have had.

"I'll see you on the battlefield when you and your family come and try to kill me." She sounded so much tougher than she felt. "I guess this is goodbye."

He shook his head. "It doesn't have to be."

He skewered her with his soul-searching gaze and she resisted the urge to lean into him.

God, this man.

"Let's meet back here every night before the siege. We're living on borrowed time, but…" His fingers circled her wrists and her breath caught in her throat. "If something were to happen, I want to know I got to spend every second with you that I possibly could."

Before she could process what was happening, his mouth slanted over hers, filling her to the brink with warmth and that woodsy musk that was indefinably his. She swam in the sensation, closing her eyes as she rolled her tongue over his.

It was wrong. This moment, this night. She was only sinking deeper into a pit of quicksand that would swallow her up into misery.

But what if this was it? What if something were to happen, how would she feel knowing that her own pride and sense of honor was the thing that had kept her from feeling this, one last time? That her last days could have been filled with Grey, and instead she'd opted out?

He broke away from her and stared down into her face.

"What do you say?" he asked, his voice a husky plea.

"It would also give us a chance to find a solution," she started slowly. "Maybe if we keep talking, we can find a way to stop this. Maybe."

"Maybe."

His face betrayed his skepticism, but she didn't care. She yanked her t-shirt over her head and let it drop to the floor with a soft rustle.

"I'm in."

Chapter Seven

Four days had never moved so quickly.

When Grey stepped into the shack the night before the battle, it was with all the sadness of a former soldier visiting the tomb of a fallen comrade.

He knew she would already be there, waiting for him as she had been every night that week. Hoping for good news, and though she always tried to look indifferent, the lines of worry and purple smudges under her weary eyes grew more pronounced with each passing day.

The boards creaked beneath his feet and she turned her face up to stare at him. Sometimes—his favorite times—she was already naked when he arrived, still pink in the cheeks and breathless from a run. Today, she was in black leggings and a hoody, her arms curled around her knees so that her entire body fit onto the small space of a rickety chair.

"Any news?" She asked the question, though he could tell she already knew the answer. They both did.

At least he had one good bit of news. "The Kotke confirmed that they don't have enough healthy wolves to join the fray."

She nodded solemnly, stretching her legs out in front of her as she leaned back in the chair. "That's a positive, at least."

There was no need for him to add that the Big Sky attack would go on as planned. He'd tried his best to test the waters with the other high-level pack members, but with the human still unturned, they wouldn't even contemplate calling it off.

"How is Amber? This must be tough on her." It was the first time he'd asked about her, and Maggie blinked up at him for a long moment before answering.

"She's as well as I could expect her to be. Scared. Unprepared, I think. The last battle did a number on her mentally, and that was nothing compared to what this will be like. She's terrified for the pack." Her gaze penetrated him, and finally she added, "Apparently, she and I have more in common than I'd thought."

Grey crossed the room and took the seat opposite Maggie. "You haven't been running today."

She glanced down at her clothes. "No. I'm better in battle if I've pent up my energy. It makes me more ferocious."

"I have trouble imagining you more ferocious." He offered her a smile and, to his relief, she returned it.

For the past week, she had been the only bright spot in his life. Even Willa had grown tired of his constant attempts to stay the attack and was starting to get suspicious of his absences. He'd been careful, showering in a hunting cabin the pack kept on the outskirts of Big Sky territory before going back home, but if Willa was suspicious, that meant some of the others wouldn't be too far behind. As much as he hated what tomorrow would bring, he would be glad to bring an end to the deceit.

"You're dressed too." She nodded toward his jeans and T-shirt.

"I didn't want to expend any energy unnecessarily running over her. Somehow, I thought I might find better use for it elsewhere."

"Cocky as always," she chuckled, but like his own levity, it felt forced. Tense.

He stood from his seat and moved to drop a light kiss on her mouth. She accepted it easily, parting her lips against him so that he could once again taste the minty sweetness of her breath. Smell the lavender that filled the air around her.

"No fight in you today," he murmured against her lips.

"I need it all to destroy you tomorrow," she whispered, melting into him.

The bitter sweetness of the moment settled over him like a blanket, comforting and smothering all at once.

"Don't talk to me about tomorrow."

He weaved his fingers through her hair and tugged gently, pulling her more deeply into the kiss as his tongue swept out to meet with hers. Where their kisses had once been battles, this was a dance. When he moved, she joined him, swirling around him gracefully with just enough pressure to tease him in for more.

***

Every night, she'd met him here and every night she'd given in to her basest instincts. Still, tonight it felt like so much more. Like every time his tongue flicked against her mouth, he was trying to bottle the memory of her taste just in case it was lost to him forever.

Or maybe she just felt that way because that's what she was doing with every lingering kiss.

He pressed her back against the wide oak table, but she shook her head.

"No," she said, "Tonight I want to have all of you." She made short work of his clothes and kicked them aside before sinking to her knees to take him full in her mouth, licking long and hard until he growled with pleasure. He laced his fingers through her hair and she closed her eyes, losing herself in the sensation as he massaged her scalp and sent tingles skittering over her sensitized skin.

She sucked him in deeper as she swirled her tongue around his smooth, blunt head, memorizing his scent. Committing his taste to memory.

She pulled away and licked the base, working him up and down with her hand until a bead of pre-come leaked from the slit at the tip of his cock. She stared up at him, and when his heated gaze met hers, she dipped her head to catch the droplet with the tip of her tongue.

He gripped her hair harder and pulled her up, gently enough not to hurt her but just forceful enough to send a bolt of need through her. With a tug, he pulled her shirt over her head and groaned when he saw she wasn't wearing a bra.

"Beautiful," he whispered, bending low to capture one nipple between his teeth. She gasped as he pressed her back against the wide, wooden table, and tugged her leggings to the floor. When she was naked, he straightened to spread her knees wide, staring with longing at the juncture of her legs.

"You have the most gorgeous pussy on the planet," he ground out at last, and then reached to stroke it with one hand. With the other, he circled her waist and pulled her closer until her breasts were flush against his wide, warm chest. God, the heat of him alone was enough to drive her crazy, but the smell of him could have sent her to heaven on the spot.

His hard, long shaft was pressed against her belly. So close. If she moved just right, he would have the perfect angle to—

His hands gripped her hips firmly and she realized she'd been grinding against his cock, begging him to fill her.

"Take it slow," he said in a gruff whisper. "If tonight is all we have, then I'm going to take my time with you."

He didn't wait for her to respond. Instead, he dropped a kiss on the hollow of her throat and licked from her collarbone to her shoulder and back again, kneading her breasts as he went.

It was so unlike all of their other hot and hard encounters and she shivered with every new touch, every extra kiss.

If he were truly mine, I would never leave his room. We'd spend every day exactly like this.

He reached her earlobe and nibbled at her gently until electricity sparked throughout her body. She closed her eyes, taking in the sensation and trying to hold herself together. Because he wasn't hers. They were enemies. Sworn to—

His lips met her nipple and he swirled his tongue around the stiff peak until she lost the capacity for thought.

"Now, Grey, please now."

He must have sensed her desperation, because he didn't argue. He slid his thick cock between her folds and drove deep.

As she stretched to accommodate him, she lifted her legs, wrapping them around his lean waist, pulling him in as deep as he could possibly go. He began to move and she matched him, keeping time, arching with his hips, breathing with his breath, beating with his heart.

The smell of him, the feel of him, and the taste of him was everywhere, and she clamped her teeth around the cord in his neck to keep from saying the words that were trying to fight their way out.

I love you.

He reared back and pressed her flat against the table, his eyes glinting in the moonlight as he stared at the space where his cock drove in and out of her.

His motions grew wild and desperate, and he squeezed her hips, using his hands to work her over his cock faster and faster. She gripped the sides of the table, thinking it was the only thing that could keep her body from coming apart at the seams, but even as she edged closer to release, another part of her wanted to slow down. To stop.

That maybe, just maybe, if they didn't finish they could stay here forever and they'd never have to fight. Never have to part.

She slammed her eyes closed and pushed into him, rocking harder. She wouldn't get to keep Grey, but she got to keep this. This moment was hers, and she'd be damned if she were going to ruin it.

A second later, the world went a hazy red as the climax crashed over her, wave after wave of ecstasy dragging her down, pulling her under. She was on fire and cried out his name as her body milked his in greedy clutches. A second later, he let out a protracted growl and joined her, bucking against her, his fingertips digging into her hips.

For a long while, there was no sound but their labored breath. No feeling other than his warm, tanned skin against hers. She was wrecked, totally and completely.

When he finally slid away, it felt as though he was taking the entire world with him.

"You should go home and get some sleep," he said softly.

She nodded but couldn't make her mouth work.

"I don't want you to. If you asked me to, I'd say screw it right now. We'd throw some blankets on the floor and sleep here for all I give a shit. And then we'd move to Bora Bora. What do you say?"

Tears clogged her throat and she shook her head.

"You know we can't do that."

He nodded slowly and picked up her discarded hoody. "Yeah, I know." He gestured for her to lift her arms up and she did, letting him dress her like a child, the tenderness of it almost more than she could bear.

This was it. Time to say goodbye before she couldn't do it at all.

"You should go."

He opened his mouth, closed it again, and then finally said, "Stay alive, okay?"

"Me? I'm a survivor."

But when he stepped out the door, shifting into his black wolf before slipping away between the trees, she felt like anything but.

Chapter Eight

They were all in the great room, each stationed by a window and waiting. The last rays of sunlight had long since disappeared behind the tree line and the three-quarters moon hung fat in the sky. There was no escaping the tension and restlessness coating the air.

Chandra sat beside her, stationed next to Liam at command. Normally, Jax would have been planted there, but he was in the security room, watching each of the monitors on the fence and waiting for the tripwires to signal the arrival of the enemy.

None would come.

Grey had told her as much. They were going to attach some new-fangled surge inducer to the wire which would also render the cameras obsolete after a few minutes, but at least when everything stopped working, they would know the enemy had arrived.

"I see something," Chandra whispered and they all leaned in as they followed her gaze to the security camera they'd wired into the television set.

Her heart kicked against her ribs as Grey came into view in his human form. Tall, heavily-muscled and menacing, she should probably feel afraid, but all she felt was the overwhelming urge to run out and throw her arms around him.

"That's Greyson West," Chandra said. "Oh, and look, another." She pointed to the moving bushes beside Grey and sure enough a woman appeared beside him in the darkness. Rather than staring at the enclosure the way Grey did, though, the female kept her gaze on Grey, as if waiting for direction.

The thought brought on a stab of jealousy, but she shoved it away. So what. She deferred to Grey the same way Maggie would to Liam. It made sense, since, with any luck, he was soon to be alpha. It certainly didn't mean anything.

Still, she found herself asking, "Who is she?"

"Hard to see with the weird light of the night-vision camera, but I'm pretty sure it's Willa Stone. Which makes sense since…" Chandra glanced at Maggie and back at the screen again. "Oh, and another!" She pointed through a thrush of trees to a menacing-looking brute who'd come crashing in before shifting into a massive, grey, timber wolf mid-stride.

"Ew, that was the guy they tried to arrange for me to marry when I was still in the pack."

Amalie let out a low whistle. "He looks—"

"Savage," Chandra finished for her. "And he is."

Maggie only barely heard the words, though.

"What were you going to say before that, though. It makes sense that Willa would be there since what?"

Vaguely, she was aware of Liam giving instructions as one enemy after another showed themselves in the clearing, but all she could focus on was Chandra, whose brows were knitted in concern.

"Willa is Grey's intended. I thought you knew…"

Her packmate trailed off, as she must have realized by Maggie's stricken face, she hadn't known.

That son of a bitch.

Suddenly, everything happened at once. There was shouting, and shifting, and cries for battle, but Maggie barely heard as her gaze locked on the image in front of her. Grey turned to face his future wife and stroked her hair gently, sending the knife between Maggie's ribs deep enough to pierce her heart.

She'd loved him.

She'd given everything to him.

Jesus, she'd contemplated leaving for him.

And she'd been played. How strange that she'd always wondered, in the back of her mind, if she would be. But never like this.

A battle cry sounded again and this time she joined the fray.

"Are you ready?" Liam called.

She was more than ready, and she only had one target.

His name was Greyson West.

***

Be careful.

Willa had shot the words at him and Grey turned to find her staring at him.

You too. He transmitted the thought back to her and she gave a nod.

It was then that's Joseph's thoughts superseded his own.

It is time, my brothers and sisters. We must fight for what we know is right. Obliterate the dissenters. Find the human. And kill her.

He could feel the will of the alpha pressing down on him, as it was on all of them. It was a difficult thing, to fight off that instinct, but it only took the thought of Maggie to give him the burst of strength he needed to break the mental chains.

He only hoped he could help his pack do the same.

From the corner of his eye, he saw his father flank him to the far left and he swallowed hard, staring intently at the door. He would wait until Maggie came bursting forward to make sure she was near before he tried to run interference between the other wolves. But as soon as those doors opened?

It was as if the air itself had exploded.

Like total pandemonium as wolves toppled on top of each other, grappling and growling until the air smelled of iron and sweat and salty tears.

There was no sign of Maggie's sable fur anywhere.

Maybe she was doing as he asked and trying to stay as clear of the fray as possible…

Even as the thought ran through his head, he knew it couldn't be true. She would never leave her pack to fight without her. She was here somewhere.

And hopefully unharmed.

He froze in his tracks as a familiar howl rent the air nearby. He spun to find Willa pinned beneath an enormous gray beast. Fury blasted through him as he leapt at her attacker, closing his teeth over its haunches, tearing at the ligaments just hard enough to immobilize but not maim.

Willa rose to all fours, snarling as he released the yowling animal.

Remember. Fight, but no killing, he reminded her before moving along with single-minded determination, not wanting to waste one precious second.

Got it, boss.

Grey barely heard her response as his father's voice sounded in his mind.

Fight on! Never give up, my people. Not until every last one of them is dead.

This time, the pull of the alpha was far less compelling. Almost like a fly buzzing around in his head instead of a deep and resonating voice as strong as a wolf's own consciousness.

Strange. Grey paused in his tracks, and looked around the battlefield. He was still searching the warring wolves for a sign of his father's silvery fur when a movement in the woods captured his attention.

In the distance, a flash of movement…a creature, skulking away from the battle into the heart of the forest.

Willa had started heading back into the fray, but he called out to stop her.

Have you seen my father?

She shook her sandy head and he nodded toward the animal's still retreating form. It passed through a small clearing and a moonbeam struck its fur.

Silver.

Willa's mental gasp reverberated through him.

Search the battle, he commanded grimly. She met his gaze for a long moment before loping off. A rush of anger warred with the wash of anticipation. If that son of a bitch had led his pack into battle and then abandoned them in secret to protect his own ass, he deserved the gravest of punishments. It would explain why his will had seemed so weak when he'd tried to command. Because, instinctively, Grey's wolf had already known that Joseph was no longer alpha.

That meant this could be it.

The end for Joseph West.

He paced the edges of the forest, sending out mental feelers to connect with his father to no avail.

Maybe it was a mistake. A trick of the light, or a Pray wolf who resembled his father from afar. But the fact of the matter was that he knew what Willa would say before her voice sounded in his head again.

He's not here. I looked everywhere.

He breathed deep and then let out a low, wavering call to his packmates that remained.

Big Sky wolves, I ask that you take a look around. Where is your leader?

The battle raged on, but the difference was notable. Between jumps and lunges, every wolf was turning left and right, checking every inch of the field for something they could not—and would not—find.

He has abandoned you to bleed for him. Is this the life you've signed on for? Is this your idea of an alpha?

More low growls joined his own.

As you fight, wonder why you're fighting, and consider ending this. We can start anew. No longer do you have to live in fear. Let me bring this pack into the future.

He closed his speech with a snarl, and then shook his head.

Part of him expected to feel some sadness. His father was even more of a bastard than he'd thought. It was one thing to be a crazed monster, stuck in the days of old. It was another to be a coward and a hypocrite.

The only good news was that at least the pack would finally see just how bad it was. Even now, some of them were backing away, disengaging, probably feeling what he himself had felt. The hold was loosening. And clearly Maggie had done her part in convincing her pack to be merciful, because the Pray wolves were allowing them to retreat.

It was the best outcome he could imagine.

But right now, the only thing that mattered was getting Maggie in his line of sight and making sure she was okay.

He'd barely completed the thought when white-hot claws dug into his back, breaking his skin as he tumbled back into the tree line, scrambling for a foothold. Damn it, he couldn't afford this kind of distraction right now when—

Wait.

A familiar scent flooded his senses and he froze.

Maggie.

He rolled on top of her and she clawed, so he pushed in return, grappling back until she was on the defensive while he forced her step by painstaking step back into the thick woods.

She tore at his shoulder, but he didn't care. He just had to pin her down and get her to talk. Rearing back on his haunches, he rushed hard against her, pinning her to a tree. If she'd been human, the move might have broken her spine, but as it stood she only growled at him and lunged to bite his face.

He shifted to his human form, holding her in place.

"God damn it, stop. Talk to me."

She fought him even harder then, but he didn't relent. She slowed and finally stopped. Then she was there, naked against him, her face twisted into a mask of fury.

"What the hell is going on?" he demanded. "We had an agreement. The last thing I want to do is hurt you, Maggie."

"Ha! That's rich, considering," she spat, bucking against him until he released her.

"Last I checked, I was warding off an attack from you."

"You should be glad that's the worst I've done to you. I haven't gotten a clear shot at your balls, or you wouldn't have any by now."

"What? You know I couldn't have stopped this. I did my best and—"

"This isn't about the attack, or your backward people. This is about you," she screamed, her hot breath washing over his face. "And your *wife*, Willa."

He stiffened, his gut clenching hard as the ramifications of her words crashed over him.

"Maggie, I—"

"So what was it, Grey? I can't imagine you needed me to get laid. So what, then? Just bored? Or something far more nefarious?"

"She's not my wife," he began, wondering how he could possibly explain the situation to her in the state she was in.

"May as well be. I should have known better." Her words were like tiny blades, each one gouging deeper. "This is just one more reason I never should have—"

"Don't say that. Listen to me, I was going to tell you."

"When? The tenth time we fucked? The eleventh? You know, there were points when I wondered if you would betray me, but I never thought it would be like this. Especially not when I was falling—" She stopped short and shook her head briskly. "I don't have time for this nonsense right now. My pack needs me."

She turned, but then paused, leveling him with an icy stare over her shoulder.

"And Grey? If you come near me again, make no mistake. I will go for the jugular."

A second later, she burst into her wolf form and sprinted through the trees.

He rushed after her, trying to catch a paw or a tail, anything to keep her from leaving it like this.

She broke through the tree line and he trailed behind just close enough to see her get tee-boned by one of his packmates. The wily bastard had gone for her throat, and she'd been so intent on escaping Grey, she took the attack full on.

She yowled and snapped fiercely in the air in an effort to free herself, but to no avail. Blood ran, steaming and red, onto the ground as Grey shifted, leaping through the air, only one thought in his head.

Kill.

He'd knocked the other wolf off Maggie with a viscous swipe of his paw and was going in for a lethal bite when his packmate scrabbled wildly and sprinted away.

He was an older wolf, and a supporter of his father. One who Grey would deal with the second he became alpha.

He sucked in a shuddering breath, shoving his fury aside to focus on Maggie.

She lay in a heap at his feet, motionless, and he nuzzled her gently, panic lapping at him. Vaguely aware of the last vestiges of the half-hearted battle around him, he grasped the scruff of her neck gently in his teeth and dragged her prone form toward the house. Luckily, the rest of the wolves were far too busy to bother with them as they reached the doorway.

That was, until Willa leapt in front of the door. She shifted to her human form and pinned him with a probing stare.

Her mouth was a hard line. "So it's like that, then?"

He tried to touch her mind, to let his heart explain what his mouth couldn't right now, but she blocked him, opting to say her piece.

"All our lives, it was you and me. Our parents were monsters. The pack was falling apart. We were coerced into becoming betrothed for politics instead of for love. Everything else sucked, but at least I had a friend in you and I knew, some day, I would be by your side to command the pack and bring honor to Big Sky Canyon. And now what, Grey? Now what do I have?"

She didn't wait for his answer. Instead, she turned on her heel and disappeared through the trees. The second woman desperate to escape him on this night.

He would grieve the loss of that friendship later. But for now, nothing else could stand in the way of tending to the woman he loved.

Chapter Nine

"You have to go back at some point." Chandra stood in the doorframe, a bowl of soup in her outstretched hand.

It was the same thing all of the Pray wolves had said to him when they'd come to check up on Maggie, but he still wasn't in the mood to listen. The battle had ended eight hours before, and still Maggie had barely moved. How the hell was he supposed to leave knowing she might need him?

He lifted the gauze that covered her rapidly healing wound and let out a sigh of relief. It had been deep. So deep, he wasn't sure if she would survive it. But if she was healing, why wasn't she waking up?

He took the bowl from Chandra with a nod of thanks, but didn't deign to respond to her questions. Right or wrong, he was staying right here, next to Maggie's bed until he knew she was okay.

"They'll be needing you," Chandra insisted.

She was more stubborn than the other Pray wolves who'd come through every hour on the hour with the same advice. Maybe she thought they were on a different level because they'd been pack members once. Whatever the case, he turned to her and spoke, though his voice was hoarse from all the howling and barking the night before.

"They're licking their wounds. They will need me, but not now. Willa has things under control."

"Not your father?" Chandra quirked a brow.

"No." Grey frowned. He hadn't allowed himself to dwell on that part of the aftermath yet. He was determined to take things one step at a time, and the first step was making sure Maggie was safe again.

"How did you get Willa to do anything for you? I mean, after—" she broke off and eyed him questioningly.

"She's a reasonable woman."

Apparently Chandra was determined to make him face every remnant of the battle's wreckage.

He was okay with the fact that the Big Sky pack had conceded defeat. Once his father bailed, none of his packmates hearts were in it, and his never had been.

He was even okay that his father was locked away in a cell for treason back on Big Sky lands, probably foaming at the mouth with rage.

He just hated that Willa had been hurt. Not in the battle. She was one of the few who had escaped unscathed. But when she'd learned the truth about his feelings for Maggie, and again, afterward when he'd stayed behind to care for her overnight rather than returning to the pack.

He and Willa had been promised to one another for longer than he could remember, and she was absolutely right. They'd been each other's support system when the world went crazy. She'd stood by him when he left for that year. She'd covered for him when he'd snuck out. And he'd repaid her by not trusting her enough to be honest.

He stared down at Maggie's pale face and stroked her cheek gently. Looked like he was two for two on that front.

What a fuck-up.

As if waking up just in time to concur with that sentiment, Maggie stirred and he stared from Chandra to the patient. "Can you give us a minute?" he asked.

She quietly exited the room, and he listened as her footfalls grew faint and vanished.

He'd had a lot of time to think things through while Maggie had slept and healed, and, with any luck, this would be his chance to share those thoughts with her now. And with a whole lot of luck, she might listen without mauling him again.

His chest tightened, and she blinked once, twice, and three times until her eyes narrowed and she swallowed a yawn.

"Hey there," he said. "How are you feeling?"

She glanced from him to the heavy gauze that covered her shoulder and neck, and then back at him again. "Sore. And tired."

"That was a nasty bite."

"I've had worse from better." She shrugged and then winced at the movement. She might be groggy, but he could still see the outline of hurt etched across her face, and wondered when she would strike.

"Does your mate know you're here?" she asked, looking bored, her voice ice-cold now.

And there it was. The other shoe landed with a *thunk*.

"I hope so. I'm looking right at her."

She tried to keep her face expressionless, but he could see the color rising in her cheeks.

"Grey—"

"It was an old family agreement. Maggie. Before I left Montana last year, I told her I couldn't marry her. She assumed when I came back that things would progress the way our families had planned when I became alpha. I was wrong for not telling her otherwise. But I do care about her." Maggie stiffened and he touched her arm gently. "Because she's a good person and an even better friend. I didn't want to hurt her standing in the pack under my father's rule, and hoped she'd find someone before it became an issue. Then, when I became alpha, I would free her from her obligation. We never loved one another. Hell, we never even slept together. I do need to find a way to make things right with her, but we were never going to be together, whether I met you or not. I'm sorry I didn't tell you from the start."

Confusion filled her eyes now and he pressed on, hoping the fact that she didn't stop him cold was a positive sign.

"It's going to be a shit storm when I get back—the Big Sky old guard believes very strongly in arranged marriages—but I'm hoping to change all that." He took a deep breath, gearing up for what he was sure would be their biggest fight yet. "My father is under lock and key for his actions last night in battle and, according to some correspondence that was sent here early this morning, I'm to be named the new alpha. I want you to come with me."

***

"I—" She choked on the words. Her heart thrummed in her throat, but she swallowed hard, staring at him. Now that she knew the truth and that his relationship with Willa wasn't one of love, she could see her way to forgiveness, but her giving up her pack?

"Grey, you know I can't do that."

"You can. The Pray pack is thriving with Liam, but we need you in Big Sky. *I* need you."

She tried to keep it together, forcing herself to remain calm. Surely, this could never work...

"This is my home."

He stroked her cheek and she closed her eyes, savoring the warmth of his knuckles as they brushed her skin.

"Your home is with me, and mine with you. The pack needs us to lead them into the future. To teach them the right way to live. You have all that knowledge from your time here, Maggie. Bring that with you as my mate. Stand by my side and help me rule so we can become worthy allies of the Pray pack. I love you."

She stared up into his eyes, taking in everything he'd said. He'd spent this whole time by her bedside. He'd left the woman his pack had chosen for him because he loved her. And he'd saved her life again.

In more ways than one.

When she looked at him she felt at peace.

Like she was home.

"I love you too, but..."

There was no way to make a rational decision with the way she felt when he touched her. She reached out to her pack with her mind, hoping for some guidance, but found only a distant buzzing. Maybe they'd gone on a hunt? Strange, the day after a battle. So now, all she had were her own thoughts, and feelings, and she closed her eyes and focused on them intently.

What did her gut say?

She let her lashes flutter open and met Grey's silvery gaze. Then, she reached for him, cupped her hand around his neck, and pulled him toward her, kissing him with all of her might until his scent enveloped her.

"You should rest," he said, still so close to her lips. Close enough that if she reached up again, she could feel his full mouth on hers…

"I think I've rested long enough," she whispered, then pulled him down to her again, parting her lips so that she could take in his minty sweetness.

As the kiss deepened, she pulled him toward her again, ignoring the dull ache of her nearly healed wound. Right now, all that mattered was her gratitude for him. And something else that burned low in her stomach and spread through her chest.

"I don't think you're well enough," Grey whispered against her lips, but she nipped his bottom lip.

"I'll be the judge of that." She slid from the bed and pulled off her clothes with ease. Then, when she stood there naked before him, she tilted her head to the side and smiled.

"Want me to do jumping jacks to prove I can handle it?" she teased.

"I'll take your word for it," he said, tugging his pants off hastily and pulling her close.

The current of his kiss, of his touch, was like a lightning bolt, traveling down her throat, coiling around her spine, and coursing between her thighs. She pulled in his warm bottom lip, flicking her tongue over the tender flesh there before deepening the kiss to taste him.

Before she knew it, she was falling back, his hands guiding her onto the plush sheets as they continued to nip and tease and play. And then he was on top of her, his full weight pressed against her. His hard length pressing into her belly.

She wanted to close her eyes, to focus on the push and pull of their bodies, but she couldn't. His face—the way he looked down at her, eyes full of hunger and need and love—it warmed her to her toes.

The blood rushed to her ears as he slid deep inside her, and the distant buzzing in her head grew louder. She tried to ignore it, but it was insistent. It thrummed through her with every thrust, joining the tingles of Grey's thrusts.

He nuzzled her neck and she breathed deep, taking in the feel of his soft hair against her neck. She let out a tiny moan, and when his lips met hers again, the buzzing finally faded into crystal silence, right before—

I love you.

The voice reverberated in her brain and she gasped.

"I can hear you," she murmured and he stared down at her in wonder.

I love you too.

He crushed his mouth to hers, pleasure, and need, and a thousand emotions, his and hers, blasting her at once. Only one question rang out above all the rest.

Is that a yes?

Could she do it? Would they be all right without her? Would they still be family?

After all she'd been through in Pray, she knew they would. Always.

The last of her doubts disappeared as she pulled back to stare into her mates quicksilver eyes.

Yes. It's a yes.

The End

Want more steamy shifter stories? Here come the dragons in Willa and Drake's story, *Coercion*, out now!

When Willa Stone is cast aside by the alpha-wolf she's been promised to since birth, she's humiliated and angry...but also secretly relieved. Now, maybe she'll have the chance to mate for love. If her power-crazed parents will just give her a little time, she's sure to find the man of her dreams...

Dragon-shifter, Drake Blackbourne, has an itch to scratch and precious few options for an outlet. When the Stone family offers up their daughter's hand in exchange for protection and political favors, he agrees to wed her, sight unseen. Drastic times call for drastic measures and, so long as she does her part and keeps out of his way the rest of the time, surely he can manage to bed her, no matter how plain she might be.

What he doesn't expect is that captivating, defiant Willa will ignite a fire in him that will burn everything in its path, and turn both of their worlds upside down...

Printed in Great Britain
by Amazon.co.uk, Ltd.,
Marston Gate.